THE SMILE
OF THE LAMB

David Grossman was born in 1954 in Jerusalem, where he now lives with his family. He has won several awards including the 1985 Israel Publishers Association's Prize for the best novel in Hebrew. *The Yellow Wind*, a non-fiction work which describes the symptoms of the Israeli occupation of the West Bank, and his novel *See Under: Love* are both published by Picador.

DAVID GROSSMAN

The Smile of the Lamb

TRANSLATED FROM THE HEBREW
BY BETSY ROSENBERG

PICADOR
Published by Pan Books
in association with Jonathan Cape

First published 1991 by Jonathan Cape Ltd
This Picador edition first published 1992 by Pan Books Ltd,
Cavaye Place, London SW10 9PG
in association with Jonathan Cape Ltd
The Smile of the Lamb was first published in 1983
in Hebrew under the title *Hiyukh ha-gedi*
1 3 5 7 9 8 6 4 2
© David Grossman 1983
© translation Betsy Rosenberg 1990
ISBN 0 330 32296 6

David Grossman has asserted his right under the
Copyright, Designs, and Patents Act 1988 to be identified as the
author of this work.

Printed and bound in Great Britain by
Clays Ltd, St Ives plc

THE SMILE
OF THE LAMB

1

No, no, believe me, Khilmi, I made them up, all of them. Shosh, the woman I loved, the woman I left three days ago, and Katzman in Italy, and that boy who died of love, whose name I never knew. And even you, Khilmi. You'll be better off as a figment of my imagination, you'll see. With me you can be sure everything is what it seems. No surprises. I'm not telling you to join this dangerous life I lead, where nothing is what it seems, but as a story, Khilmi, as *kan-ya-ma-kan*?

Let's start now before I get to your village with the news I dread bringing you. Why don't we hide away instead and pull the covers up around us? And so, Khilmi, *kan-ya-ma-kan*, there was or

3

there was not, as all your tales begin, or as we say, once upon a time . . .

I used to think this sort of thing could happen only in the shade of your lemon tree, Khilmi, in the darkness of your cave, with the little gears and cranes and cobwebby curtains, and the earthen jars that will be filled someday with rarest air so you can fly again. That's what I used to think, but I guess I was wrong: I guess there must be a Tel Aviv version of *kan-ya-ma-kan*, too, in the harsh sun, under glaring neon lights, in those immaculate rooms, gleaming white, where they record and transcribe your every word.

And so—*kan-ya-ma-kan*. I say it as you would, Khilmi, leaning back against the lemon tree with my eyes shut tight, groaning as if I had to pull a long string out of my belly, and here it comes, *kan-ya-ma-kan*; once upon a time there was a little girl with a bright and open face, a small, straight nose, blond hair she wore tied in the back, and round-rimmed glasses, and the little girl's name was Shosh.

Once upon a time, a kindly maiden set off to visit herself in the woods, but losing her way, she left a trail of love seeds and had to tunnel home through stonyhearted people, crawling in what she called a gyre, *kan-ya-ma-kan*.

Enough. It's all an act. I don't have the strength to tell the story. I don't have the strength to bring Khilmi the news. I should have made a U-turn and headed back for Tel Aviv, back to Shosh's story. Because I'm afraid she won't make it, and Katzman agrees. Help her, Uri, he begged me. You're the only one who can.

Not me. I need my strength to demolish what we had together, the things we said, the dreams we dreamed. But it won't be easy. I can see that now, after three days of scoffing at our little secrets, at the vows we made, kicking the furniture I built for us, obliterating

4

the wonderfully simple words, as she called them, but it isn't working, strange to say; lies and illusions are much hardier than I supposed, and don't topple over just because you notice them. And when I try to pull them out of me, I feel a tugging at my roots. And I know that one or two of my lies have been disguised as private pain, words that have to be rendered physically. What will be left of me when all the destruction is over?

Kan-ya-ma-kan, once upon a time, and nowadays, too, roadside villages wakened from their slumbers, and princesses of yore clad in richly embroidered gowns walked out before dawn to collect dung for their *tabuni* ovens, and the smoke curls, and the fields are gray, but soon, when the sun rises, they'll burst into flame.

Like the villages in Italy. Maybe that's what draws me here. Maybe that's why I'm filled with longing. Santa Anarella, after a night of earthquakes; here, too, the olive trees stretch out in the morning, yawning through their knotholes, their leaves a bluish gray. But in Santa Anarella, the catastrophe was sudden and soon over. Here it has stretched out over five years. Time—says Abner—seeped through the perforations of injustice, like a poison that paralyzes the body and corrodes the mind, Abner said.

Here's a donkey. Hi, little fellow. He's just a foal. Didn't anyone teach you to be afraid of cars? To pull over when you see a car coming? Okay, I'll wait for you. Ah, I see. You've been fettered. I'm beginning to interest you, aren't I? No? Well, why are you staring at me? Your little mane is damp with dew. Go home to Mama, she'll lick it dry. I've got to run now. No, wait, how can you move with your legs tied? I'll have to pass you carefully. Nice of you to happen along to grace my story. Whoa, boy, I just saw your dead brother rotting in the lane over in the el Sa'adia neighborhood, and don't think it's easy for me to stand here making faces when I can see right through you. I'm very sorry to say, I can see everything you have inside. I guess I must be warped or something. I didn't always know how to see behind appearances.

Where am I going? Khilmi is no more than a *kan-ya-ma-kan*, a fictional inventor of fictions. How can I believe that nonsense? Those stories about Darius, his patron and redeemer, or the hunter who drew lions in the sand, or even his dead son, Yazdi. The ravings of a madman. I mean, I don't understand any of it.

Shosh said once that what we think we understand, the bits of information we draw on, are like the least fit members of some imaginary herd. "Darwin's law of consciousness," she called it: that's what the herd uses against the deadly effects of human intelligence, leaving us with the poorest meat, and not much pleasure in the hunt.

It was during our trip abroad that she started honing her concepts this way, and I didn't understand what she was talking about. Why was she interested in hunting all of a sudden, when we were farmers, she and I, or so we vowed to each other, shoulder to shoulder, rustic as potato soup and the embroidered lining of our double quilt? Why were we hunters now, and what were we supposed to hunt?

Kan-ya-ma-kan, death is so near. Khilmi's Yazdi is dead, and the donkey down in the lane, and Shosh's boy. Burned matches all, but together they strike a flame by the light of which I will know who I am. Three days ago I switched on the tape recorder in Shosh's room and heard her tell the boy: Mordy, you don't know who you are and what you have inside, and the only way you can find out is by letting it out, she said. And I'm afraid of what I'm about to let out.

Enough. I've obliterated enough of her already. I don't belong to her anymore. This is where I belong, on this narrow, winding road, with the brown hens scurrying under the tires as I drive through the soft fog that blows itself over the hills, to the olive trees and mud-brick walls, the dirty sheep, and the paths drawn in the dust, like Santa Anarella waking after a night of disaster so sudden, recovery will be just as swift, and they will smile again like the urchin Katzman took for a gallop on his back around the feeding station, around the big white tents marked with red crosses, and the gaping earth, and the open fields sighing through the night; that's where I long to be, though I spent only two weeks of my life there, because that was where I learned to love, to love myself, that was where I let it come out of me—and I knew.

But stop. Go back. No one asked you to drive out here to tell Khilmi his son is dead. Disaster drew you to Andal, as it always does, the undispatched courier of bad news. Go back, Uri, you loon, this is no job for the likes of you.

Last night was endless. It's been rough for several nights because of the thoughts I was having and because of hunger. I seem to have declared a hunger strike as I did once at my agricultural boarding school, haKfar haYarok. This time my reasons are just as good: all the things that Shosh has done to me, all she did to the boy, only that's not why I'm fasting. I'm fasting because I've been tied up in knots ever since she crossed her legs and announced it was time we had a frank and open talk. Her fingers began to tremble and I haven't been able to eat since then.

Last night was the roughest so far, though, after the skirmish in Juni, and before dawn the soldiers returned to the government building, and I could smell the coffee brewing, and I heard the big stove bellow in the kitchen and the quiet chatter of the men, so quiet it scared me, because I'd heard a helicopter taking off a little earlier, and helicopters are bad news. I lay there in the jail room they fixed up for me, staring at the window screen. I could still smell the donkey carcass. I must have imagined it, because the military government building is nowhere near the lane, but I still kept smelling

7

that smell, so I thought I must be going crazy from hunger and all the thoughts running around my head.

Then I heard Katzman coming down the stairs, and I heaved a sigh of relief. There was no mistaking those footsteps. I remember the first time I saw him in Santa Anarella, staggering up the street like a sick animal, bumping into everything in sight, though there wasn't much left standing to bump into. Only this time he was carrying a submachine gun. It's all gone now, I guess, everything we shared.

He walked up to the door, fiddled with the keys, and opened it. Then he came over to my cot and said to me calmly, "Stop acting like a ninny and open your eyes. I know you're not asleep." I opened my eyes and looked at him. So thin, his inert upper lip drooping sadly. I asked if there had been any casualties.

Three on their side, he said.

And the helicopter?

The general's. He stayed with us all night. What a mess, Uri.

He sat down on my bed, his head in his hands. His thinning hair was filthy and wild and stank of sweat. I felt kind of sorry for him because now he was going to have to get rid of me; I mean, after everything I'd done to him, he couldn't let me hang around in Juni anymore.

Want some coffee, Uri?

There, that's when I should have said, In case you're interested, Katzman, I haven't touched food or drink in three days, almost sixty hours, to be precise, and I'm not eating anything until you remove that donkey carcass; but the donkey wasn't my real reason for refusing to eat, so I said, Gee, I thought prisoners are only entitled to lukewarm tea in the morning, to which he answered coolly, "Fuck you, Uri. You know exactly why you're here." And he was right.

Then it went like this:

Uri?

What?

One of the three we killed last night—

Yeah?

He was the son of your friend.

Which one?

The old man. The one from Andal.

I was stunned. I could hear Khilmi say as plainly as if he'd been in the room with us: "He's an idiot child, that Yazdi"; and then I saw Khilmi the way he was last time we were together in his cave, smiling eerily as he told me that if I wished, I too could be a wonderful idiot; and I also remembered Shosh just then, and the harsh expression on her face, the blue veins standing out on her neck when she said, You'd be surprised how fast a lie develops layers of life around it.

And then I whispered to Katzman: Yazdi was an idiot, he was retarded. El Fatah exploited him. Khilmi took his mother in for money before he was born, in exchange for a handful of limp notes, as he puts it. Her father brought her to Khilmi's cave when she was no more than a frightened girl. Katzman rubbed his eyes, looking paler and a little more miserable than usual, and when I gazed up despairingly, I saw his key in the door.

Someone got her pregnant, you hear, Katzman, someone from a neighboring village; that kind of thing is more common than you might think, but they don't always kill the girls who disgrace their families. Sometimes they try to hush it up. And this girl's father came to see Khilmi and asked him to marry her. My mind was in a turmoil because I had calculated that one swift leap would take me to the door, so I just kept talking to Katzman, my lips saying one thing, my heart another (I had learned something in the past few days after all). Yazdi's mother was so skinny she looked like a string knotted in the middle; that's what they did if a girl got in trouble, they married her off to Khilmi, and people laughed at him behind his back, but he let them think they'd tricked him because his quarrel was not with them. I mean, you have to know the guy, Katzman, and then I leaped up from the bed like the wolf in Little Red Riding Hood, remembering to snatch my army shirt from the chair on the way, and I was out of there, with only my shorts on, and I locked the door behind me and ran, free as the breeze.

Speeding down the corridor, I put on my army shirt, but got the buttons wrong (Shosh used to fix my collar), and holding back a laugh, I opened the door on the second floor, groped in the dark for a pair of anonymous trousers and an army sweater, and beat it out of there. I tried on the trousers—too big. Never mind. Running cautiously past the officers' mess, I overheard Sheffer talking about the skirmish. A great bear, that Sheffer. Yesterday he practically tore me apart. There's a field radio outside the toilet. Somebody's in there, taking a piss, whistling to himself. Well, somebody's field radio has just been swiped. Hey, man, be more careful next time. Out the back door to the parking lot. Hot steam rises from the vehicles. I choose Katzman's Carmel sedan, because I know it best. The keys are in the ignition. The guard gives me a nervous glance. No sweat, I honk him out of my way.

Then everything opens up.

But first, before heading out to the open spaces, to the painted villages, and Khilmi, I return briefly to the donkey. I tear through the back streets of the bazaar, past the roller shades of the closed shops, whispering good morning to the canaries and finches asleep in their cages inside, and then, bypassing the circular platform of Abu Marwan, Juni's spit-and-polish policeman, I graze the old water well, splash mud from the permanent puddle outside the mosque, and skid to a halt in the middle of the lane.

Here in the clear light of dawn, the stench seems to freeze. Perched atop the swollen carcass are a couple of birds I'm sure would never have dared show up in broad daylight. And there are also two mean-looking little dogs eyeing me suspiciously over the donkey's back. A brief pause before getting back to work. Sounds reverberate in the stillness. The dogs of Santa Anarella used to drive us crazy, dragging bodies out of the ruins and common graves at night and gnawing on them, and we were too exhausted to drive them away. And now, here—the sounds of gnawing and slurping, tooth and bone. I take a closer look: the birds strut over the exposed rib cage, within range of the dogs. Playing it cool. Neither side wants trouble. Who needs this? Why did I come here? I'm glad I came. I came to say goodbye to the donkey. To watch him decomposing in the dust, consumed by the dogs and the birds. Now I'm beginning to understand.

Slowly I start off, back up, pass a three-wheeled motorcycle loaded with grape cartons, and the houses that are emptying out the chamber pots of night, as I rehearse the main points, the most important words. Oh, my weary head. Why does Khilmi tell himself stories in order to remember when I tell them in order to forget, to break them up into fragments and throw away all that has been stifling me for the past year and a half, Shosh's growing success at the institute, the juvenile delinquents she cracked the way you crack a nut, and the crazy loop I ran between the government building and the lane in Juni, between the townspeople and their weary, whiny protests against arrest and seizure and humiliating treatment, and Katzman and Sheffer grabbing my arms and carrying me off, kicking and screaming, to the jail room. So much has to be thrown away, like big Zussia, with his perfume smell and his top-secret designs for a kite, and Abner, too, and those wonderful nights we spent together on civil-guard duty, walking through the quiet streets, talking and talking, and Leah, Shosh's mother, her strong, open face and her wise way of bending Abner to her will.

I try to throw them away, but they keep bouncing back. So I try again. They'll give up eventually. I mustn't become so emotionally involved. My time with Shosh has softened me. Left me vulnerable. Before her, this would never have happened. What I found with her and her parents, Abner and Leah, was so addictive I was in a great hurry to forget everything I had been before. They had given me a home, a place where I could nestle with their wonderfully simple love, and I wasn't careful enough.

I'd better not think about them now. I'd better just drive back to the army, to the despair that drained me day by day, back to those months after the breakup with Ruthy, the girl I ached for though we never met, and even further back, to my agricultural boarding school, to the radishes and strawberries I toiled over, back to the laughter of my classmates: You always want to be the scorekeeper, Uri, you're always on the sidelines. Back to my poor dead pigeons, and Zinder, the teacher who said I had a flair for writing and that I ought to keep at it, but how could I keep at it when all that mattered was surviving from one minute to the next. And now I clear a path through sticky clumps of memory, good and bad; there's Khilmi's village on the horizon, and right before it, my grandfather, muttering incantations, and so on through the morning mist, to a back yard far in the distance, where I picture a big kennel with a round hatch, and waiting for me there, as always, the red-eyed bitch with the floppy ears, a smooth warm body and sores on her back, and so much love for me.

During the War of Independence, when I was four years old, my grandfather Amram crawled under the bed with some dry biscuits and a prayer book. He was, as they say, in the prime of life, but he taught me never to open the door to strangers and to whistle penitential hymns when "the brass" came near. His two sons—my father, David, and my uncle Moshe—had been POWs in Jordan, but only my father returned. He called Grandfather a stinking coward and a deserter, and swore he would never eat at the same table with him again. My father had gone a little crazy in prison. He composed a prayer for the quick and agonizing death of Arabs everywhere, and made us recite it in the morning, after the "I offer thanks." But he wasn't content with that, and started spending all his money on printing a special book of his own collected prayers and numerologies against the Arabs, and he used to accost people in the street and rave about it. He banished Grandfather to the shed in our back yard, and within a few days, hours, really, Grandfather began to age. I've never seen anything like it: he started speaking his childhood Arabic again, and thought he was back in Iraq. His skin hung down in folds—it almost crinkled when he moved, which wasn't too often. And he told the future by the red ants that crawled in through the cracks between the tiles. He kept getting skinnier and skinnier, lying there on his bed in the dark, mumbling in his sleep, calling me strange names and stuffing notes into his mattress, revealing things I didn't know because it wasn't me they happened to.

And child that I was, I grasped the crazy key to his hallucinations: *kan-ya-ma-kan*, once upon a time, in the glorious days of the War of Independence, there was a man of Israel who suckled at the teat of fear. And once upon a time there was a boy who hated his parents, who hated school, who hated "Here comes Laniado, 'Sin of Samaria the Second.' " And this boy used to play hooky and hide in a certain back yard in the Bet Yisrael neighborhood, not far from his house, in a kennel that smelled of crushed straw, where he lay all morning beside the big, warm dog, with the books he had borrowed from the Histadrut library, straining his eyes in the dim light, and emerging as Michel Strogoff, David Copperfield, or Ben Hur, so happy he

13

forgot to be careful when the other children came home from school and threw their school bags down.

But drive on. Lies, all lies. The menfolk's square you're passing now, for instance, with its skeleton of a car that probably dates back to the Ottoman Empire, this square, too, is a lie, and so is everything that is supposed to have happened here, such as Khilmi flying overhead like a quiet old bird; I mean, that's preposterous, and so are the other things, like Katzman's father imprinting his own fading memories in Katzman's mind, or Shosh lecturing me so eloquently on the morphology of lies; and Zussia isn't the only abstruse sort of hero, as Abner calls him, who mustn't be pushed too far. We're all *kan-ya-ma-kan* around here, and the only real thing about us is the pain we bring.

The sight of the car, or maybe the sight of my face, catches Aish mid-yawn in front of his tin-built café, but I don't have time for him. I park in the middle of the road, at the foot of Khilmi's hill, run up the gravel path, fall down, and pick myself up again, scared now, chilled with fear, mustn't think about what I have to tell him, blurt out the terrible words. The bend in the path so soon, and the grape bower, and the mouth of the cave, and nearby, inscribed on the chalky hillside, the incongruous pistachio-colored Arabic script that screams at me *khayen*, "traitor," and here he is, here's Khilmi, sitting on his stool, leaning back against the lemon tree, the transistor radio around his neck singing to him softly, and now he sees me.

And we fly at each other, with the violent force of physical knowledge. And Khilmi asks me, beseeches in terror, Yazdi? Yes, I nod, because I can't talk. His one seeing eye nearly pops out, and a thick blue vein winds up his other eyelid. Gasping for breath he says, He was here yesterday morning and I told him not to go. And in bewilderment he adds, Why did he disobey me?

He stumbles back till he bumps into the stool, and drops limply

14

down upon it. Wearing his robe of Cyprus silk, with his hard little hump, his black beret pushed down over his forehead, and his furrowed yellow face, he looks like some huge colorful insect drying in the sun.

And he groans. Ripping me right down the middle. No, that's no groan, that's a blind drill press. A frantic search for a vent to let out the pain.

2

Katzman's fury was short-lived. It dissolved into grateful relief almost as soon as the key turned in the lock. Quickly he tore his thoughts away from Uri and what he'd done. He made no effort even to sort out his own embarrassing predicament, but lay on the bed curled up on his side, abandoning himself to a vague feeling of euphoria.

He was more in tune with himself now than he had been in quite a while. For many months he had managed to elude himself almost completely, and yet here, where he was trapped, inside not outside, he no longer felt threatened. As a matter of fact, he had been yearning for this, to plunge into his remotest depths, hidden from pursuers. He pulled the prickly blanket over his head and dozed off. Then he awakened with a jolt. He listened.

No one had noticed he was missing yet. He tapped the steel bed frame with his forefinger, surprised to discover a new kind of loneliness within the loneliness he knew so well. It pleased him for a moment or two, and then he became restless. The blanket was dusty. As he lay on the bed, the heat of Uri's body was almost palpable. Katzman thought about Shosh. The new loneliness was breached. The moment of grace had flown.

He stretched out, guiding the pleasant tingling sensation from the soles of his feet to the back of his neck. He was exhausted after the previous night and the two nights before that. There were dark blue crescents under his eyes. Now he had to think.

At thirty-nine, Katzman's appearance was deceptive. His ageless face and hollow cheeks, and his gangling body, scrawny rather than boyish, made him look frail. But Shosh, who always sought the child in men she couldn't fathom—an instinctive trick of hers—tried in vain to imagine Katzman as a little boy. His narrow visage left no room for even a glimmer of childish innocence.

He knew it, too. He had sensed his disturbing effect on people even as a boy, an orphan, dragged off from Europe after the great war to a little kibbutz in Israel, to be transformed there as quickly as possible from an obstinate Polish-speaking enigma who fought with the fierceness of a wounded animal against any invasion of territory—into a Sabra boy, assimilating sunshine into muscle.

When people talked to him, their eyes would trace hasty diagonals from his protruding ears to the hollows of his cheeks; from his bloodless lips—the upper one paralyzed—to his eyes, sensitive, sensual even then, fringed with thick dark lashes, and oddly set, even more widely, or so it seemed, than his face. From his sharp, arrogant nose, red at the tip, they would look down at the disappointing chin receding toward his narrow chest and shoulders.

With the bravado of an outcast, Katzman prided himself on baffling the people of the kibbutz, but their frank dismay came through to him in cold bursts of truth and depression. He began to develop a hard core of muscle-bound self-sufficiency, with a wild and bitter fortitude verging on self-hatred, and a fine, detached perceptiveness.

Now, in the narrow jail room, Katzman began to assess his situation. He knew where Uri would go. He could imagine Uri in Andal now, throwing his arms around the old man, drowning in his grief. Maybe he would even forget his own pain. With some amusement Katzman recalled his visit there a few months before. That was when the trouble began. Uri, who had taken up his new position with disconcerting zeal, came upon the town during one of his enterprising patrols of the area and asked Katzman to accompany him there. He was hoping the military government would provide fantastic sums of money for local development, and all the way to Andal, he talked Katzman's ear off about the flower beds he was going to plant in the dusty soil. He might have been driving down a newly paved road, to hear him speak, or smelling the roses in the garden already. On his face there was a foolish smile, the smile of the lamb, as Shosh had called it once in irritation.

It was the smile he had worn to greet the reception party in Andal, his mouth aquiver and his hands twitching with excitement. All the villagers had assembled there together with the five sheikhs and the mukhtar. Uri delivered a short, impassioned address in his amazing Arabic. The villagers nodded assent. The young mukhtar, sleek and sweaty, responded ceremoniously. Katzman followed his evasive reply with indifference. During his six months of service in Juni he had picked up not only the rudiments of the language but the vagaries of local thought as well. The meaning behind the words. This made it easier for him to communicate with the inhabitants than it was for Uri, despite Uri's fluency in Arabic. The mukhtar asked for money. That was the gist of his reply. A lot of money, and yes, the right to use it as the village council saw fit. Katzman was familiar enough with this line from countless meetings in his office with the mukhtars of other villages. Uri was taken aback. He hadn't expected this. He threw Katzman a bewildered glance, a plea for help. Katzman's face was sealed. With secret glee he observed Uri's growing discomfiture; the tortuous trail of words he was obliged to follow. As Uri spoke, the five sheikhs wound their *kaffiyehs* over their mouths. The mukhtar, who sweated profusely though it was still early in the day, wiped his face with a discolored handkerchief. He was about to answer Uri, and Katzman was already peering at his watch, when another old man came running over, shrieking and waving his arms, hurling curses at Uri and Katzman and the sheikhs, and aiming them at the mukhtar as well.

Katzman recalled the tension in the air. The crazy old hunchback had touched off an enmity that hovered over them all like a torch testing the wind. For a moment it seemed as if invisible circles were closing in around Katzman and Uri, but at a signal from the mukhtar several youths pushed the old man away. Katzman thought the incident was over and turned back to the mukhtar, but Uri, with the pained expression of a child chasing a butterfly, approached the shrieking fellow and touched his hand in wonder.

Katzman was suddenly angry. He got up and walked over to the screened window. There was already a trace of dawn in the sky. The new day revealed his pale, stubbly face. He looked like a man who had spent a lifetime in darkness. A sudden breeze dispersed the morning mist outside the building. Katzman saw the people there: prisoners' families lining up for their weekly visit to the government building. They were huddled together quietly, chafing their palms and blowing on them to keep warm. Drowsy children nestled between the heavily laden food baskets. From where he was in the basement, the scene above appeared to be taking place upon a stage. Katzman watched with curiosity. The mist gathered again. He caught a glimpse of a woman's colorful dress, a man's black cap, and then the lovely, animated face of a young girl. These vanished, and Katzman turned away from the window. Again he winced at the intimate memory of Uri touching the old man's hand in front of everyone. The old man had seemed suddenly chastened, as if Uri had absorbed all the bitterness inside him. Katzman rattled the door handle. Then he decided to wait a little longer, to take advantage of his temporary absence, though he wasn't enjoying it much anymore. Distant visions, poignant memories were beginning to erupt. Nervously he paced the narrow room, retracing the exact route engraved upon his memory. His restless movements here were like his father's there. From the "library" to the blanket where Mother lay dying. He even revived the old about-face. He remembered the way Father's white mane would undulate each time he turned on his heel. His graceful good looks, Katzman guessed, made him irresistible to women, and he was sorry when Father began to lose his hair. The three of them—Father, Mother, and he—had spent the war hidden together in an underground pit somewhere in Poland. By the war's end, Mother was no longer with them, and Father was too demented to understand that their lives had been saved. The pit remained with Katzman evermore. Having learned to conjecture the world above on the flimsiest of evidence—a gust of wind, a brash cascade of light, a spasm of fear across Father's cheek—he was always alert. For him, infinitesimal realities loomed large as the forces of nature. Katzman had boasted once to Shosh that he knew all about the human condition. Shosh noted his fondness for saying "the human condition," though in time she realized that what he really meant by this was human dissolution, the erosion of everything human, in all its manifestations. In this he was truly an authority.

The memory of the pit was no longer just a vague apprehension in the back of his mind. Katzman forced himself to sit on the edge of the bed and concentrate. In Santa Anarella, while telling Uri about his years in the pit, he had been dismayed to realize that, though he was a man now and the pit was in the distant past, he still kept his ears to the ground for the sound of possible survivors deep in the earth or in his thoughts. He would always belong to them. They were not really people as such but vague torments, thwarted desires, secrets only he could shade from the deadly light of the sun. Having said this aloud—while speaking to Uri—he experienced the agony of perpetual exile. Suddenly, in the darkest recess of his mind, he saw a picture of two Katzmans juxtaposed like the figures on a playing card.

He looked at his watch. A quarter past six. Then he remembered—and flung himself on the bed dramatically. On top of everything, last night's tribulations and those in store for him now, today was Katzman's birthday. Solemnly he offered his right hand to his left and gave it a congratulatory shake. Yes, a birthday is a milestone, and a milestone is a sign of continuity, of an exacting symmetry at the root of things.

Katzman was an avid seeker of this symmetry perhaps because it frightened him. He could not define it. He could only explain it vaguely as he had to Shosh as a kind of final reckoning. But that wasn't good enough. To understand the magic symmetry you had to have a sixth sense, a kind of fine inner tuning. Katzman imagined it as very peaceful, but it was also a token of the cruel punishments in store. He couldn't resolve the discrepancy. He looked for symmetry everywhere, conducting endless experiments in the hope of encountering it. But he never succeeded. If indeed there was some hidden logic at work, Katzman had yet to discover it. All he had discovered so far was that he was hurting the people he cared for most. Daily life itself was the great, unmitigated threat.

He knew he had some more collecting to do before he would be able to find the elusive thread of logic, to touch it for a minute, and—perhaps—achieve a kind of salvation. Maybe this was why he needed his few close acquaintances so desperately, almost violently. They were his clues. The guideposts to his thoughts. But he needed more: he needed every detail, every piece of the puzzle; to take in every animate being with a single glance and shed some light on the symmetry of at least one person's life. He was smart enough to give up the hope of recognizing himself in that glance. Sometimes he thought Uri might be the right person, he was so earnest and predictable. But Uri, too, had proved baffling just when he thought he understood him.

When Katzman first encountered him in Santa Anarella, Uri had seemed like one of those holy fools, the playthings of a complacent world. He was quickly disabused. He began to listen. He realized that Uri, without intending to, was teaching him something. Uri was rash enough to let the world filter through to him, and Katzman wondered how anyone so vulnerable would be able to survive in this disaster area.

Katzman was less affected by it than Uri. He had witnessed too many horrors in his life. For him, a disaster was just a normal process speeded up as by a film projector gone berserk. In themselves, the ingredients of disaster were unremarkable. The earth was always quaking beneath Katzman's feet, and people were always killing each other, only it all happened so slowly and subtly that hardly anyone noticed the way he did.

That was why it had been Uri rather than the earthquake that really alarmed him. Once, at the big refugee camp in Nablus, Katzman had felt the same sweetness Uri experienced in Italy, only he couldn't feel it anymore, much as he longed to. He vaguely sensed that he had brought Uri there to mediate for him, and Uri had been mediating for him ever since.

A simple psychophysical law inhered between the two of them: energy from the more pressurized container flowed into the less pressurized one. Katzman was a contracted muscle, Uri was open to the world. The current that flowed from one to the other was like a work of art, like harmony, though they were singing in different keys of reality. Katzman's anguish throbbed within him till it trickled out to be distilled in Uri. He had once tossed Uri a disjointed clue, that all he could really believe in was the painful instinct for survival at any cost, by any means, an instinct made manifest only in the midst of grave danger.

Katzman felt better for having said this aloud, and so went on to confess his deepest secrets, to tell Uri about the various women he had involved himself with at his peril, about his short-lived marriage, and about his unwillingness to have a child. Night after night, by the dying embers of a bonfire around which sleepers crowded together in the open field, he unburdened himself to Uri with a spontaneity he scarcely recognized, describing his childhood years, telling about his father's lectures on Ariosto's epic, expressing his fear of open spaces—oceans, plains, deserts—anything expansive, whether a person's character or in nature. He even confided to Uri, out of a compulsion to tell all, that the only time he felt at home, for a few minutes at least, was when he was with a woman.

And Uri listened intently, licking his chipped front tooth, with eyes wide open. Katzman could almost feel his words coming to life. Like children, his and Uri's. He and Uri were inextricably joined now, if only because of their duty to the newborn.

The noise of the gate sliding open startled Katzman. There was a loud commotion outside. Visiting day was about to begin. Prisoners' families passed between the stiff pipes in the prison yard. Katzman hurried to the window. Stooping down, he could make out the eastern watchpost on the roof. The guard was sipping from a cup that gave off steam. Katzman remembered that he, too, was a prisoner now. Yet here he had discovered scattered islets of repose.

There was of course a certain symmetry about what Uri had done yesterday. A crude sort of symmetry: two local women, mother and daughter, had walked into Uri's office to complain about the soldiers who searched their house. They had been eating lunch with their family when the soldiers walked in, violently overturned the table, and stamped on the food. Uri used the interoffice phone to ask Katzman who had been in charge of the search party. Katzman could tell from his tone of voice that there would be trouble, but he was unable to get away.

Uri escorted the two women to the officers' mess. Sheffer was eating lunch just then, and later he reported to Katzman what took place: Uri had walked up to him, and "coldbloodedly" (in the words of the staggered Sheffer; Katzman could just picture Uri with his big ears drawn back, his wispy beard bristling with a fury so terrible it inscribed circles on his thick-lensed glasses) "He turned the table over on me! Boiling soup, salad, coffee, everything!" Then Uri had muttered something Sheffer didn't quite catch, a threat, or something, and then with complete indifference he had stomped off past the two frightened women and out of the dining room, till Sheffer caught up with him and dragged him by the collar into Katzman's office.

But this was not the kind of symmetry Katzman was looking for. Katzman's symmetry took form slowly in the dark. If he caused pain, he knew enough to expect his share of pain in return. Certain places he passed on his way from Tel Aviv to Juni gave him pleasure, and these were the very places he knew disaster would strike someday. And when anything desirable came his way, he knew he had lost something else, something more valuable perhaps. When he allowed himself to feel friendship and trust for Uri, he lost his tough, inviolable loneliness. Sometimes he wondered whether he would ever get it back again. He continued to pace nervously around his cell, treading down the rearing heads of unresolved questions. He was very tired, but he knew he wouldn't be able to sleep until Uri was found. Ever since his conversation with Shosh three days ago, Uri had been utterly impossible. He would become maudlin and make a scene, then grow nasty and aggressive and, just as suddenly, soft and dependent. He refused to tell Katzman what Shosh had actually said, what had actually occurred between them. The day before, Uri had given him the keys to their apartment and asked him to bring back some books and clothes for him. He had no intention of living with Shosh anymore, he announced. Not in the near future, at any rate. And from now on, he would put everything he had into the job Katzman had brought him to Juni for, whether Katzman liked it or not. Later, feeling a little calmer, he told Katzman that he'd found out she'd been lying to him for a long time. Katzman sat up in his chair. Something to do with the Hillman Institute, explained Uri. Katzman studied his fingertips. He was angry with Shosh and he pitied her, too. He'd thought she was made of sterner stuff; he hadn't expected her to break down and tell the truth before it was strictly necessary.

Still out of temper, and with growing apprehension, Katzman unthinkingly released the safety catch on his gun, faced the wall, and fired at the bottom of the lock. The shot made a deafening noise in the little room, and the door opened slowly. Katzman stepped out.

3

The light is soft. Drafts of hot air and cold entwine like snakes that couple and recoil. It is the hour of dawn, the hour of grace before the world despises us.

Down in the village everyone is still asleep. The red cock's comb, a giant Coca-Cola sign, looms up from the roof of Aish's café. But the brown houses all around have not yet rallied to the crimson call of the American rooster, and the mud walls leaning against each other exhale a morning mist like the breath of sleeping horses.

But I am not asleep. I have not slept a wink these many years. My granddaughter Najach, the silent child, does not believe me when I tell her this and breaks into her thread of a smile, but as heaven is my witness, heaven and the moon, it is so.

I may doze off from time to time. This wise old gourd nods drowsily on its spindly neck before the jinn begin to frolic in the empty socket of my eye, the eye that rolled inward once when I was like a bird flying over the village, over the menfolk's square below, and they, the jinn, with lightning feet, kicked up the glittering dust to confound my memory. No, that is not so, they croon, this and that are figments of your mind, this and that happened not to you but to Shukri Ibn Labib, who went off to the city, from his lips you heard of it, and this burden of care is not your own, it was purchased from Nuri el Nawar, the gypsy peddler, together with your robe of Cyprus silk, the ostrich plumes, and the English sun helmet.

And then I shudder with fear and press the socket of my alabaster eye to wipe away the tracks of the jinn, and I meekly twist the raveled ropes again—the pockmarked face of my brother Nimer glowering as he brought my food out to the courtyard; my father, Shafik, who took his byname Abu Sha'aban from someone else's firstborn son, and the way he would wander wretchedly from room to room, steering his great paunch through the doorway and swinging his elephant arm like a rubber hose; the boiled beans my patron and redeemer Darius would slip between my toes to treat the blisters, and the little bald pate on the top of his head.

And yesterday Yazdi came to me. The youngest of my bastards, the only one I did not kill with folly when he grew to be a youth. Him, too, I faithfully revived, and cherished his living spark as the scald of truth, yet he returned to me yesterday, strange and stiff as the slough of love. He arrived before dawn, rigid of limb, and death lurked in the boyish face with the newly sprouted mustache. He came to me like the sudden reflection of my thoughts. A year I had not seen him, a year since he went away with the strolling players, the guild of reciters. And for the first three months I knew not whether he was alive or dead. Like an exploding oven was my body then. And I wept as I wandered, gnashing my teeth, beating my brow and breast like a blind lamenter, sleeping in the fields or beneath the terebinth tree in the wadi, his name upon my lips, Yazdi Yazdi.

And three months later, the letters began. Messages from him and wishes inscribed by the wind in a cleft of the terebinth tree, where Darius, my patron and redeemer, found me, and where I brought Yazdi to teach him the language we would speak together. And how the wind found its way to the cleft I do not know, for there were no tracks around the tree. I dragged my dusty feet down the wadi, reached into the cleft, and groped around the secret hiding place, where I usually found no more than a handful of straw or a nest of black bugs, though sometimes I could feel a letter in my hand, and my heart would burst.

They were not paper letters. He was unschooled, and I never learned the *alif-bā*. But he knew the language of plants, because I had taught him, and he would send me, by invisible courier, crushed leaves or twisted stalks, or perhaps a broken thistle, and I, with trembling fingers, spread out the contents of the dewy parcel, sorted out the piles of tidings and grievances, and read: This is the dried *qarsawa* fruit to purge the heart of longing, and these are the crushed yellow flowers of the *gaisum*, bitterest of plants, and I set the flower upon my tongue, and I drooled and cried in the voice of my son, Parting is more bitter than the *gaisum*, and sometimes I would find the serried leaf of the *khashishat-el-nakhl*, for curing sadness.

And I could hardly wait to read the vegetal words of my son telling of his love and care and longing, and I was proud that he remembered so far from home the lore of plants which I had taught him, though my pride was not unmixed as I crushed the green message in my hand, because Yazdi had done wrong to follow them, to allow them to come inside us and between us, would that he had boiled the *khashishat-el-nakhl* and moistened his forehead and rubbed his temples with the essence before sending it to me, because the plant cures more than sadness, it cures folly, too.

Yazdi did not hear my thoughts and did not return. I began to find other plants in the cleft, and my finger froze at their touch. I did not wish to bring them out into the light of day. I recognized the brittle leaves of the *azak* tree, which weeps its resinous tears when wounded. Parables he sent me, my son. But at other times he spoke more plainly, saying, Here are leaves of the *shakik-el-Na'aman*, the wounds of el-Na'aman, who rises from the dead, and these I came upon in springtime. It was Yazdi whispering to my fingertips about a new uprising. A war against the tyranny around us. Indignity shed in a tear.

And then one day I found a piece of paper in the cleft of the terebinth tree, and I knew I had lost him. It was covered with a crude, thick scrawl, and I imagined his tongue pointing out with effort while he wrote, his curious eyebrows twitching over the pencil. Would that he had not written.

So I had no choice but to go to the cave of Shukri Ibn Labib, and to wait outside till he had finished the Koran lesson he was teaching the village children, while his yellow bees swarmed around me hoping to suck nectar from the painted flowers on my silken robe, and I smote them with my hat, screaming and cursing, and the welter of their buzzing resounded in my ears with the singsong of Shukri's pupils reciting verses from the Koran, and Yazdi's crude scrawl crinkled in the palm of my hand, burning like firesticks.

Then the children put on their shoes, removed the red *lafa* from their heads, and kissed the hand of their teacher, winking at each other and emerging into the light, where they began to throw stones in all directions, and did not miss their mark with me.

In the cool of the cave Shukri washed his hands in a tin basin, unhurriedly arranged the three books of the Koran on a small wooden shelf, and turned to me, as he always did, his lips pursed tightly, with his hand outstretched. And he unrolled the paper and looked it over, shook his huge horse's head, and said, These lines are dead, Khilmi, spilled ink, and once mated, they beget more death.

Shukri is the only friend I have in the village—and the only one who surpasses me in years. I can still remember him on his way to the *kutab*, the school of Sheikh Faher, together with the other laughing boys who crossed the courtyard where I was tethered to a tree, and Shukri stirred up mischief, tying my leg to a donkey and sticking a burning cigarette into its behind, or stuffing my mouth with live grasshoppers, or forcing me to drink a bottle of dog urine. But he has long since set aside such mischief, and has forsworn even smiling since his visit to the *zawiya* of Sheikh Salakh Khamis, the illustrious dervish of the holy city of Jerusalem, who learned the Koran from an old *Shikhiyat*, and there, in the *zawiya*, in the corner of the mosque, young Shukri Ibn Labib made a pointless vow of penance and self-mortification, renouncing laughter and even smiles, though in truth he came away possessed of great wisdom and is the only man in Andal whose counsel I am not ashamed to seek.

Harsh words Shukri's lips made of the ugly scrawl. Blood and holy war and a popular uprising. Yazdi's words were so hot he did not see whose blood had been spilled in the ink, and Shukri continued to gouge the words out, an organized revolt, terrorism and destruction, the need to unbend our broken backs and redeem our pride. And I shuddered with surprise, with agony. The world had struck me a blow. It had deceived me, had stolen my only son from me, the sweet idiot I saved for love.

And once a picture arrived. A cracked and crumpled photograph of Yazdi, my dear son, his large head bald as ever, dressed like a *karakoz*, in a mottled army uniform, holding a paper rifle, with a snakelike mustache crawling over his lip.

Yazdi was alone in the picture, for the photograph was cut out to keep me from seeing the friends on either side of him, but a severed hand still rested on his shoulder in comradely fashion. And seeing him thus, with the dark glasses that covered half his face, and his childish chin jutting out, and running my finger down the cut-out sides of his body, I felt in him the infinite loneliness of one who has been bereft of life, whose body is but an empty hull stuffed full of the cotton-woolly words of strangers, and just then he resembled one of the animal trophies hanging by the tail in the tent of Sha'aban Ibn Sha'aban, the mirthless hunter.

He was so proud and so foolish when he tore himself out of my thoughts and away from the hillside and stood before me, a full-grown man in his own eyes. *Ya ba*, he said to me in a voice as thin as a boy's. *Ya ba*, I am here, and he approached to kiss my hand, but I pulled it away from his mouth, because I did not bring him up to lick a man's hand, and Yazdi stood up in shame and tucked his head between his narrow shoulders and said, You are unchanged, *Ya ba*, and I answered, A man of fourscore years and ten does not seek learning in the *kutab*, and you know me well enough, I think.

He said, You are still angry with me, *Ya ba*.

I answered, Angry, yes, but let us not speak of that. It would be vain to speak of it, like a muezzin calling in Malta, where there are no faithful Muslims.

He said, And did you receive my letters?

I said, Yes, I received them. And who taught you how to write so handsomely?

He said, They teach us everything. And I have comrades there, too.

And then I suddenly remembered the severed hand resting on his shoulder, and I looked at him and saw he had truly been cut out, for the morning light was very jagged around him, and the blue sky quailed. And when he saw my face, he said with the stutter that beset him whenever he was vexed, What should I have done, *Ya ba*, stayed to rot in Andal?

Then I led him by the hand into the cave and bade him sit on the mat. I poured some coffee beans out of the box Nuri el Nawar gave me and began to grind them, my eyes never leaving the boy. It was Shukri Ibn Labib who revealed to me that just as the characters of script are dead, lacking a life of their own, begetting neither joy nor sorrow until they meet and touch, so it is with people, or with dogs or the books of the Koran, or grapes upon the vine or the bees that live in broken jars, and so it is with the soldiers and the mukhtar, the terebinth tree, the gypsy and the hunter, and so it is with Darius, and so I say—with my granddaughter Najach and the errant Israeli soldier who touched my hand and came to live with me for five days, turning my heart to love, and so it is with the medicine plants and the poison plants and the wedding songs and the lamentations for the dead and the crows and the vultures and the shadowplay of fingers upon the chalky rocks, what are these but dead markings, the writing of an invisible hand? So it is, Shukri instructed me, the white hairs on his craggy nose fluttering in the breeze like a horse's mane, they are only dead markings, and the pain and joy we beget upon each other passes understanding. Perhaps, he explained, shutting his eyes as in dark meditation, only a madman can understand these children born of travail. Perhaps only a mute can suffer them, rejoice in them, perceive them like glass needles inside: perhaps only a blind man can read them in the seven shades of white inside his eye.

But I could not say this to the youth who sat before me, twirling his wispy mustache and smiling faintly. And because I was silent, he began to speak. He told me of his friends. Of the city of Beirut, where he lived. Of training camps and dolls made of paper that he shot with a gun. And of his stalwart commanders. And I listened in wonder. Whence came all the words to him? He who was almost mute until the age of twelve and who could speak with me only in our infant tongue.

In supplication I addressed him, not with words, but with my empty eye. I took him back to trifling things. To the moment just after his birth, when I snatched him away from the women and salted his flesh and would not allow the *daya*, the midwife, to look at him or mutter her timeworn charms, for he was to be different from the other children. After that, with my own crooked hands I embroidered the *tob* and the *takiya* spangled with the amulets given to me by Shukri Ibn Labib and the gemstones Nuri el Nawar purchased from a merchant of Aqaba, and I rubbed him all over with basil juice, for he was to be different from the other children.

And I told him further how I nursed him from a goatskin bag and rocked him in his cradle under the tree so long I might have been churning butter, and I told him how I carried him on my back like a horse, with the help of an old yellow corset Nuri brought from the holy city of Jerusalem, and how I ran around the yard with him, whispering in his ear. For he was to be different from the other children.

And I spoke further, not with words, but with the flickering of my eye and the fluttering of my heart, about the village we labored hard to build in the brief years of our love, and how we filled it painstakingly with everything we could find, men and women, plows and saddles, jackals and tobacco, whips and crying babes, the flow of milk in the teat, and the kilns where they burn lime, and the thick *karami* used for fuel, and everything had a name or a grunt, and it was a wonder to us that we understood each other's heart so well that I could tell the meaning of his every utterance, and he could knit my words together in his hoopoe-egg brain, and to the village of our delight we added the sweet strains of the *rababa* and the millers' songs, and the chatter of the men at the *maq'ad*, the twinkling of the women's amulets and the gleam of the barber's razor letting blood, and all the written characters. It was like a game to us. One of many; our own invisible village. Like Andal, because we knew no other, only it was ours alone. And we breathed life into it as we lay on our backs in a field of nettles or down in the wadi, sunning ourselves like lizards, and wordlessly we spoke of old Naffi, a man so stingy that if names had a price he would have called his son a niggardly name like "Dung" or "Mud." Or of Sa'adi el Az, slippery worm turned mukhtar, or of Dahaisheh the crone, who told fortunes by the moons on fingernails, and Shukri Ibn Labib wandering the streets with pins in his lips and hands to keep from laughing, and many others, old men and young girls, everyone we knew in Andal, only with us they were milder, fainter, like pale smoke seen through a tear, never laughing loud or baring their teeth.

He was a child then, Yazdi. A hairless boy, his smooth skull pointed and gleaming, staring at my lips and drooling out of the corner of his mouth. I fled to the fields with him, away from the taunts of the villagers. Down to the wadi and the jackals' caves. There we carved the air and hewed the wind. Grunting our deepest words to each other and sobbing like human cubs, as I had in my youth, before the world congealed inside me into written characters and people, while it still careened like a colorful wave of splintered glass.

We scarcely spoke. I could not have told him more than three stories in the years of our love. Four at most. And no more than a hundred words passed between us. But such lovely, welcome words they were, filled with the sway of life. And now—there are so many words, yet we say nothing.

Father, he says, you dream. We have important things to do. We have to fight.

They are very powerful, I answer, and cannot be beaten by force.

By what, then? By silence? By dreams in a barrel?

How he spoke. How ugly the word "barrel" sounded coming from his lips.

No, not by silence; but by being softer than a feather. More fragile than an egg.

It won't do any good, *Ya ba*. They understand only the language of power.

This will be a different kind of war. Long and arduous. And for weapons we will use stubborn patience and infinite weakness. They will not be able to bear it.

He shook his head. His strange, thick brows twitched like furry, fear-struck creatures. He knows my thoughts and despises them. I will not see him again. I know this already. So many youths go to their graves these days, while an old man like me is doomed to live. Would that I had kept him an idiot.

And how are things here, *Ya ba*, how is the village?

I am silent. What can I tell him? That since he went away there is no one to talk to except Najach, who is mute? That I have not been to the village in two weeks now, and that when the governor came with the young soldier I broke down and played the fool?

36

What can I tell this stranger? That in times of pain I drag my old bones back to the wadi, to the days of my childhood, to Khilmi-the-Accursed-Mal'un-Alla, and Khilmi-Go-Away-Rukh-Min-Hun, and Take-Him-Drown-Him-in-the-Well, or Give-Him-Back-to-the-Cuckoo-Bird. What can I tell this stranger?

So I am silent. He will surely hear worse from his mother, who lives in the village, if he goes down to visit her. It was she who came here one morning to drag Najach away by the hair, and when I raised my head out of the barrel and asked why she was so angry, she let go of Najach's hair and stared at me in horror, saying, Ha, he can talk, and then she ran away.

This was a sign for me, what the foolish woman said, that I was returning to infancy for the fourth or fifth time in my life, in the same amazing way, shrinking into my hump, into the pain that flares in the darkness, bathing in twilight all that I have beheld with my blind eye, the weeping, fallen, and forsaken people, and even my father, Shafik Abu Sha'aban, who one evening came down to the terebinth tree in the wadi, wailing bitterly, and, finding me tethered there, cried out in amazement, Why, you can talk, ya Khilmi, you can talk.

I can no longer speak to Yazdi of these things. I have lived in the world too long, and watched the wheel revolve too many times. The faces of the old reappear in the faces of the newborn, and the newborn are also old. None escapes the mockery of flesh. I gazed at the infant faces with the fondness of a woman. My courtyard teemed with the children of others; the children of the unhappy women who were led up the hill to me in the dark of night to be sold for a roll of damp notes plucked out of a secret pouch. And I played the fool, pretended to be blind to their swelling bellies, deaf to the scoffing names I was called by the villagers—Khilmi Abu

37

Ziad and Khilmi Abu Sa'ad and Khilmi Abu Khamdan, after the latest arrival in my courtyard, just as they had called my father Abu Sha'aban after the son my mother bore the hunter.

But oh, I loved their infant faces, and I would sidle up to the women while they suckled their babes and peer from behind at the greedy little faces, observing cheek and brow. But always the women pushed me away with an angry curse, or called upon their sons, my older bastards, to drive me out of the courtyard with a brandishing of boughs, or to pelt me with sharp stones, as boys have always done to me as far back as I remember.

But the magic lasted only a few months, and then life congealed in the infant faces and was rendered into a deathly script, into ashen letters posted by a hasty hand. None was spared, and the living idea I had beheld in them, the living idea by which they were begotten, faded as soon as they learned their first words.

And Yazdi, *kan-ya-ma-kan*, bastard of my old age, the sweetest grape at the tip of the cluster, blessed my life when I despaired.

For he was a scraggly child who never lost his light, even at the age of five, or ten. He was a laughing child, drooling and beaming at me over his mother's arms, and I mustered my courage and stole him away from her, away from all the womenfolk, hiding him at my breast, and I bared my teeth and cursed them, swearing I would make known their shame if ever they dared to take him from me, and I slept with a dagger up my sleeve, but they gathered around me like furious geese, calling me Um Yazdi, mother of Yazdi, and pelting us with rotten eggs, till at length they tired of us both and left us alone.

And I carried off the tiny babe-in-arms, bawling at me with his eyes shut tight. And I dipped him in a tub of salt water, and rubbed his skin with olive oil, and wrapped him in swaddling clothes, and every seven days, as customary, I peeled the strips of cloth away and kneaded his ruddy limbs with fresh oil, till he was forty days old.

Happy I was then and shamefast. Counting his breaths and tracing misty dreams upon his lids. He rode my hump in the yellow corset when I took him around to my secret places and whispered in his ear what came to pass, what might have come to pass, and many a time when I dandled him just to behold the splendor of his luminous face, the abiding truth, he would smile at me, his two wormlike eyebrows aquiver with emotion.

How glad I was, *ya rab*, how gladness surged within me, when I saw that he was not like other children. He was different from the rest. He was the perfect idiot with a brain no bigger than a hoopoe's egg. There was not a hair upon his skull, and his eyes stared fixedly in wonder; he was all arms and legs, and his voice was thin as a finch's.

And he smiled, running his tiny hand over my face, breathlessly touching the empty socket of my eye with its maze of red blood vessels, releasing the slumbering images inside, lifting them out from the depths of my life and sweeping them up in his hand, like nails longing for a magnet in the shop of Nuri el Nawar.

Kan-ya-ma-kan. He was the only one of my bastards I did not kill with folly, did not scratch from my heart after he was weaned of mother's milk, and I spoke to him in the infant tongue I had not forgotten, because I spoke no other human tongue until the age of fifteen, and the world within me was a colorful wave of splintered glass, a great, undefinable pleasure, and Yazdi and I—ah, I will tell this a thousand times over—we lay together on the grass among the nettles, and when butterflies glanced off our hands, we read the pollen tracks they left that told of the sadness of passing beauty, and we learned from them about another realm of time, the realm of slow-ripening pain, time consumed between the leaves of the *awarwad* when touched by a burning cigarette, the anguish that suddenly overcomes the plant, its loss of heart, and the death of its fallen leaves. But nothing of this was I able to recount when he returned at dawn, in the uniform of the *karakoz*, reciting what the strolling players had put into his mouth, and *tuta tuta khelset elkhaduta.**

---

* Tuta tuta, so ends the tale.

40

4

It's four o'clock in the afternoon. Padded doors slam shut along the corridor. Young men and women joke quietly among themselves as they lock up once, twice, and then disperse. Now somebody walks by, whistling a flute concerto. It's the same thing every day when he or she goes home, that lilting sound, and the silly game I play till it dies down the corridor.

But today the whistling is forced, almost frantic, as though all the music were being squeezed into a single breath, like the wail of a siren.

Four o'clock and here I am, still in my office. About ten minutes ago Ovadia, the attendant, took the new boy away. I handled that initial interview about as expertly as a raw recruit. It reminds me of my early days at the institute, not too long ago, when I used to get more nervous than my patients and wound up bungling any chance for intimacy with my compulsive chatter.

It's very quiet. I hear the hush of heavy carpets in the corridor as I prepare myself a little anxiously for the silence that will soon prevail. Meanwhile, I'll just sit here in my streamlined leather armchair, which doesn't even squeak when you wheel it around—nothing but the best for Professor Hillman's staff—anticipating the first flurry of memories. In a way, it's lucky that I botched today's interview, lucky for the patient that he was spared my expertise. But will he be spared tomorrow? And when I look down at the glass-top table I see reflected a pale young woman with a pointed chin, her hair so tight that her temples hurt. Nor is there any relief in the gleam of her gold-framed glasses. Her competence, her suitability for the job are obvious as she folds her hands in a spasm of determination, her shoulders raised in the too perfect posture of little girls' ballet, and her knees demurely pressed together under a tartan skirt.

Who would raise an eyebrow to see her piling papers on the glass-top table and depositing them in a stiff cardboard folder with the star-shaped emblem of the Hillman Institute for Juvenile Delinquents shining over the name MORDY, *File #3*. She sets it down at her right sleeve. Good. The table is now divided into squares and spheres; the cardboard folder is tangent to the heavy round ashtray; the black cassette recorder is tangent to the dish of sour balls; the flower bowl reposes beside the stack of cassettes. Only one thing spoils the symmetry: a diamond-shaped reflection falling across the table whenever the sun strikes Viktor Frankl's portrait on the wall. It seems to burst in its passage, plumbing its own depths and flickering behind the scenes. Soon. The woman before you will pull herself together. She will compose herself forthwith into a graceful sonnet, fourteen lines rhyming as prescribed and breathing the chill of death. And meanwhile—the attendants on the morning shift are going off duty now, hanging up their checkered gray uniforms, exchanging information and kidding around with the night shift. Locker doors slam shut in the cloakrooms. The attendants adjust each other's silverplated name tag: Shabtai. Daniel. Micky. Like delegates at a convention, only they all carry little cylinders in their pockets with a minute but nasty quantity of "compulsory" tear gas, as our beloved director, adviser, etc., Professor Heinrich Hillman, once jested in properly apologetic tones. Soon they'll flock together at the front gate, nurses, criminologists, smiling macho attendants; they'll greet old Yankl, the watchman, grope in their pockets, jingle their keys, start their cars in unison, and then there will be silence.

I know the whole sequence. I never noticed it before when I would leave with the others, I never realized we were all swaying to the same soft music, but in the past three days I have trained myself to anticipate the sounds outside, the way a child fills in the words of a favorite bedtime story before the nightmare of darkness sets in; before taking the plunge into the mysterious and the fragmentary—interview files, tape recordings, typed reports and evaluations, and the cryptic parcel wrapped in brown paper behind two books on the shelf. And even before going over these hundreds of pages in my own handwriting, in the familiar, cultured-pearl-like strands of script, I know I will not discover anything new here. A inevitably leads to B, B to C, and so forth, just as surely on to Mordy's death, though tonight I guess, I know for certain, that I will fail once more to bridge the limpid gap between myself and this conclusion.

And here Abner would have said, Think of it as a story, Shosh. You have your characters, you have dreams and emotions generating warmth and tension, now all you need is an intelligent narrator to weave us all together and bring our many virtues to light.

Abner wants an intelligent narrator, but even he knows that's asking too much. The edges will remain rough and bony, and longings will forever fill the empty spaces, so let me avail myself of a simpleminded narrator this evening, and instead of reading over my spurious summaries and unlocking familiar doors with timeworn keys, I will open the cunning door of the black Sony, insert a single cassette from the stack on my right, and press Record.

Please, Shosh, don't clam up now, and don't start giggling. Everything's on the record. It's like being in the spotlight suddenly, an intrusive spotlight that won't relent until you've finished what you set out to do when you locked yourself in here a few days ago after the police sergeant called you into Professor Hillman's room to hear the results of his inquiry, and you went straight home to Uri and said things that made him cringe, so go on, say something, something like, This Opus cassette promises: "Sixty minutes of the highest quality": and since I have all this high-quality time at my disposal, in addition to an infinitely tolerant narrator-listener who will never lose his temper with me, as all he registers is the magnetic residue of what I say, and since now—at last you're speaking audibly—I am alone in my office in the deserted purple ward, and through the tall windows before me I glimpse a group of green-ward patients playing basketball on court number 3, and—to complete the picture—I see Samuel, our philosophical gardener, in the distance, and Sigmund, too, that wicked goose, safe from even the biggest bullies of the blue ward, I had better start talking to myself at once, tossing words into the ingenious trap I set on the table, in the hope that beyond the little glass door things are going to be tied by the roots somehow into a meaning that will bring me consolation, because I can't go on.

I can't. I just can't. I used to be alive. That was years ago. Once upon a time I was Shosh Avidan, the daughter of Abner and Leah

Avidan, blooming triggerlike and pushing her way up through clods of soil. "You can tell right away she's an Avidan," and "Ho ho, the apple fell right into the cleft of the tree," and "You know that article she wrote in eighth grade for the party paper, something about youth's fervent search for values," and they whisper that Avidan is bringing up his own successor, he says so himself, that she will outshine him, she has the brains and the determination, his greatest achievement, raising this child in his own image, though we have all heard about educators of his stature who failed in their own homes; and the tiny shoot grew into the child with glasses and braces in all the photographs, towing the tired, hulking Zussia along, and then, she's the nine-year-old on fragile stems who refused to take off her heavy knapsack on the school trip or drop out of the raucous singing, even when she ran out of breath—Your daughter, Mrs. Avidan, is as tough as any of the boys—Don't I know it, she's just like me, that's how I used to be on school trips; and thanks to the slow, thick stream of days, the heart-to-heart talks with friends who never quite understood, and the rare minutes of knowing exactly who she was, which were definitely not her moments of triumph, and thanks to the searing verses of a certain poet, she grows, like soft clay under the potter's hand, into an earnest girl of fifteen, disconcerting to her peers and the adults who court her with silly chatter and wither at a glance, and all the while she squeezes herself inwardly to bring forth new secrets, and an ancient pain which none of the boys who wriggle over her body can ever assuage.

Always observing. That's Shosh in the reflection. Abner's eyes and Leah's eyes and Uri's eyes, and the clods of soil that hem you in, the puzzling sense of suffocation when they're only doing it for your own good, they love you so much, don't be an ingrate, and ignore the scream of fear mounting inside you, use its dammed-up power to eject yourself onward, upward in a gyre, and your little

45

face is clearer now, with a wonderful symmetry and a doll-like brightness coating it like melted wax; yet the puzzling whispers continue, something is amiss, and though the pieces fall into a familiar picture, a different picture is forming on the other side, only you are too busy to notice, there's never enough time . . .

You're jumping the gun, or worse—sidestepping. It's been three months since Mordy died, and you still haven't allowed yourself to think about what happened. And before that you never even took the time to wonder. And for three days now you have been locking yourself up in this glass cage from four o'clock till midnight, only to discover that even here you can't drop out of the race, out of the sly reversals and the false tracks you scatter with your every move, with your every thought, no matter how ordinary.

Calm down. You're so tense. Tension seems to be the one thing that reverberates through every cell of your body. But today you're just going to have to break it down and pry out the remains of other feelings, living ones that serve as food. Then you can begin again. This is war, Shosh, and the invader lies in wait. Do not tarry.

So let's begin. This is Shosh. Yes, my name is Shosh. Shosh means rose. Too common a name for me. Uri said, Shosh is the haughty rose in *The Little Prince*, and Katzman said, In that case, Uri himself could be the Little Prince, with all his questioning. And in the book Abner gave me he inscribed: "For Shosh, the rose on our family tree, our flower of wisdom."

I was Mrs. Laniado to the insolent young police sergeant who interrogated me till he was replaced at my request by the tired old inspector who called me Mrs. Avidan-Laniado, and summed up the inquiry three days ago with the simple words: "No apparent link between the psychotherapeutic treatment received by the deceased and his suicide." And old Hillman, when he clasped my hands and urged me to return to work, called me Madame Shoshi.

Yes, I know, this rhythmic whirring will drive me insane. Impartially, painlessly, the magnetic ribbon collects itself. Many terrible things can be said on tape, words like "betrayal" or "suicide"; "Uri and Katzman" go in with a single breath, or even, "No signs of violence," and the tape will merely collect them, like a stoic gardener sweeping up the leaves. Listen to me, what's done is done, Hillman explained more authoritatively than usual: And now, Madame Shoshi, you will please shake this off and come back to your senses, and make use of this tragic incident, that's what he called it, in the interests of our profession. Let the memory of it serve as a moral beacon against the damnable arrogance of some of us; the death of Mordy is a puzzle, and it had best be left as such, so stop tormenting yourself.

Easy now. Calm down. You're so tense. Remember, you are the patient here, and you are entitled to every sort of buffer, from the wall-to-wall carpeting to the book-lined shelves. In this office you are the victim, you are the center of interest and concern. Others have significance only insofar as they are of significance to you, and even if justice is on their side, never fear, we will not punish you, so relax your thumbs, see how white the moons of your nails are, how difficult it is to heal, to close your eyes and let things happen; there, press your thumbs against your eyes the way Zussia used to do when you were a little girl, when he took you to the Boxer Club on Saturday mornings for a frothy beer from the barrel, but you had to keep it a secret from Mama and Papa, fold it into a tiny wrinkle of your memory, that's what a secret is, feel the damp warmth spreading there, maybe that's what they mean by longing. You see? A stream of memories. It feels almost good. Katzman tells you that man is a puzzle with more than one solution, and you answer, Yes, but he's usually too lazy to try more than one key to his identity, until he happens to unlock a forbidden door, at which point Katzman

47

lost his temper and said one thing, and you said another, and Uri made peace between you with a joke, and while you were all teasing and bickering and joking together, Mordy walked into the kitchen of the ward, closed the windows and turned on the gas, and died without a sign of violence.

And of course, Madame Shoshi, the institute will give you every possible support, support is our business, after all. I cannot urge you strongly enough to carry on your research in the name of the friendship and esteem that exist between us; the police have cleared you, haven't they, and all they ever had against you was the blame you took on yourself, and don't forget that poor young Mordy was a very peculiar boy, and death was always lurking around him, as you should know, you're more familiar with the case than I am, yes, the way he courted danger, the way he challenged death, so never mind what certain people said at the staff meeting, Madame Shoshi, and never mind that horrid graffiti in the blue-ward bathroom, it stems from ignorance, I only ask you to be strong, because we all want what's best for you.

I don't understand. It may be obvious, but I still don't understand. Step by step he led me into himself. Painstakingly I built him up again, or at least tried to, and just when he was nearing his life, when it would have cost him next to nothing to make the change, he went and killed himself. That is not how it happened, but the truth is of no consequence in our private investigation. We are searching for poetic justice, which is rarer and more to be desired than other kinds of justice. A moment's compassion and forgiveness, who could ask for more? To know, if only for one moment, that somewhere inside me I am innocent, not by dint of a shady deal, and not for lack of evidence; and maybe this was the difficult goal of my three days' journey, but if only I knew how to free myself, if only I could slip away for a moment from our Shosh, she who will never write poems and will lead a sane and sensible life, maybe I would tumble sweetly down the rabbit hole and learn my other name at last, the name that was branded inside me.

Stop. Now rewind and listen.

You hear? Just listen to those clichés: "poetic justice," "the name that was branded inside me"; aren't you glamorizing the situation, Shosh darling, when you know you're back on your feet again, nursing your agony? I have to hand it to you, that was a lovely choice of words, our daughter of the Hebrew language, remember when Leah said once that even in the worst of times one mustn't be an animal, but scream one must, scream out the fraud that produces people like you, decent folks trained to send a double-agent dupli-cate of themselves out into the world, unnoticed by others, because others do the same, and so, Shosh, tonight I want you to let go and be an animal; yes, it may help you to find a solution, it may be your only chance to prove yourself worthy of the cynical term "poetic justice," which, for the present, is only a rather startling form of the aesthetic blackmail you practice on yourself, so please, press Record again and start talking.

Was that a smile, Professor Viktor Frankl on the wall? Did I see a light sweat breaking out under your glasses? I thought you liked me. After all, I am your most devoted pupil. No one has more loving insight into the nature of her fellow man. Nothing to say? How cautious you are. Man, you say, is in search of meaning. My father, Abner, on the other hand, says man is in search of words. Words for a footrest. Words, like stones in a flowing brook.

He's lying, you know. He, too, is deceiving himself. You can tell by his impassioned way of pronouncing "meaning" when he ad-dresses his Scout troops; This is not a time for words, he declaims to the leadership committee meeting at our house. This is a time for action that cuts through rhetoric; and he packs a hollow meaning into threadbare clichés. Like some mad bloodhound he burrows into the "ground of our national myth," ferreting out more and more symbols and historical parallels, and the example of famous men who tamed the beast "meaning" and harnessed it to their lives.

And this rustling sound. The imperturbable tape rewinding itself around my wounds like a fresh bandage. The setting sun hits me right between the eyes, but it doesn't hurt because of the dark glass in the windows, and because it has spent itself painting the clouds a cruel, flowing red, and I am excited now and scared; maybe I should get up and leave, and switch off the black machine which is forcing these torrents out of me, maybe I should send off Mordy's three files and the brown package behind the books on the shelf to the incinerator, repeating to myself that it's possible to suffer without turning into an animal by enlisting all the heroic obtuseness Abner aspires to, but what's this, what's happening to old Samuel, the philosophical gardener Hillman brought us from the London branch of the institute? Why does he gambol across the lawn like a lunatic, arching his back and hunching his shoulders? Is there something going on that I should get on tape? Is it a disaster or some rare sort of discovery that I should document in the name of science? And so, the scarecrow legs in knickerbockers, blue with cold, knees pounce maniacally high, and now he grabs something—I can't see what from here—aha! His black sweater! He picks it up from one of the bushes and runs for his life, when suddenly the picture is blurred by a short, wicked blow—no, it's blocked by the tall, decorous windows—and big drops of water run down the pane, and Samuel, blurred in the distance, stands panting and amused, surveying his army of sprinklers like a general, yes, they're all in working order, spurting water with the full pressure of their destructive powers.

They're all in working order, yes. Water silently spurts up at me.

Moist whiplashes crisscrossing each other. We're in a submarine and I'm looking out the porthole at the waves, where I occasionally find a piece of the puzzle: the foul purple sky and Samuel, putting his sweater on, reaching down to pull up his socks and fold the cuffs over thick gray rubber bands and he turns to go, tall and tough, and there in the lower-right-hand corner of the picture, following him slyly yet respectfully, it's Sigmund the goose.

Whoops! With a whir and a snap, our sixty minutes of quality time from Opus have come to an end. Fine. Now we'll rearrange our papers, clear our throat. Another fruitless session, Mrs. Avidan-Laniado-Shoshi. Once again you have reverted to clever diversionary tactics and feigned devotion. But we will not judge you, and there is no rush. You may sit here until midnight to avoid going home to your anxious mother-father, who would never say anything, or even mention Uri's name, and of course they have no intention of interfering in your personal life, out of respect for your silence, your pain; no one will ever try to coerce you, Shosh, because you have willed yourself off on a sidetrack of time, a track no longer in use, where you can move forward or backward, and have fun in the station house where clock time has no set value like high-quality Opus magnetic tape, because a different time exists there, and Mordy's death is woven out of the love you implanted, which is something police investigators could never understand, and Uri and Katzman will find their rightful place amid the various strands of you.

And suddenly—the rustling noise. A meek light flashes on the blue telephone. Anichka, the dietitian from the blue ward, is calling me, as she does every evening. No, Anichka, I am not hungry. The sandwich you sent for lunch will tide me over. It was delicious, Anichka. No, I won't come to supper in the dining room. I have a lot of work to do. Backlog, yes. But really, there's no need—oh well, all right. How can anyone refuse you, Anichka. The white cheese, then, that will be enough. No, don't insist. I've been a vegetarian for three months now, as you know. I can't bear even to look at meat. Sure I'll be in my office, I'm not going anywhere. See you later.

Let's take a break. Out comes one cassette, in goes another, shut the glass cage. Now wait for Anichka. Everyone's so good to me here.

5

There. Now he knows. The world has cracked his eggshell; but why am I so angry with him all of a sudden? Is it because he refused to accept the pain I brought him? Or because I know that as he sits here rigidly, with his face half hidden under a crumpled beret, he's telling himself a different version of the story, and the strong enzymes of *kan-ya-ma-kan* are even now dissolving his dead son into splashes of color and points of memory which will recombine without the pain, because Yazdi is not dead, there is no death, there is only a sudden flagging of one fiction out of many.

And again Khilmi says, "He was here yesterday, he came to say hello." And in the long silence that follows he almost nods off, then shakes himself awake and says, staring blindly at me, "I told him about you, Uri. I told him you lived with me here for a few days. That I cannot hate you anymore. And he knows how to read, he read the inscription, that was when I realized I had lost him." Khilmi wearily nods at the word KHAYEN smeared above the cave. We had awakened one morning to find it painted on the hillside in dripping red letters. Khilmi asked me to read it to him and I did: *Khayen.* Traitor. He said nothing. That evening, as I climbed the path after surveying the fields and meeting the villagers, I saw that the writing had turned to green. Khilmi was sitting under the lemon tree as usual, his hands stained, trying to look nonchalant. I asked him why instead of crossing out the word he had gone over it in green. He stared at me, crestfallen. Since he couldn't read in any case, he had decided to paint over the hatred and brutality of the color red, and now the inscription looked almost beautiful, like a bright festoon. Was I too blind to see?

But Yazdi had seen the word and read it, too. Khilmi is distressed about this. I ask him cautiously what Yazdi said when he heard about me. He is silent. He thinks about it and, searching for the words, says, "He was ashamed. He was pained. At first I thought he was angry because you are an enemy. But then he inquired over and over about what I had told you. If I had told you about Darius, and about Sha'aban's feasts, and about the invisible village, and about himself. And when I said I had told you some of these things, his face turned red and his eyebrows quivered with rage. For a moment he forgot the words forced into him by the guild of reciters and began to whimper in our infant tongue, but we were both so frightened, he soon fell silent. And then I understood: he was jealous of you, Uri."

When Khilmi speaks to me like this, in the squeaky voice of an ancient baby, I stop feeling angry. What right have I to be angry with him anyway? He handles his problems the only way he knows. I wish I could handle mine better. What a mess, I say. I wanted to make Andal a better place to live. I had big plans. More water for your lands—remember? Here, under this very tree, you traced the tobacco fields and the little wellspring with a stick—and I wanted to build a health clinic, and pave the roads, and send the village girls to be trained as midwives so that filthy old Dahaisheh will be prevented from killing off more babies; but what I wanted most of all was to win your trust and overcome your determination to shut us out. We had some really great arguments, you and I. Remember how we used to scream and shout through the night?

He hunches over. It's a terrible strain. He looks like a turtle. The folds in his neck almost crinkle. But he spreads his pink palms in perplexity, as though he can't remember how to pull them back into the shell. "But tell me how my son died."

I told him what Katzman had told me. The only thing I didn't tell him was that Katzman had taken part in the raid, because I couldn't tell him a thing like that.

Khilmi met Katzman the first time he and I came out to Andal together. He couldn't have seen Katzman for more than half an hour, but that was enough for Khilmi. And during one of our incoherent talks at night, when I told him that Katzman was my only friend, Khilmi said Katzman needed me more than I needed him. It frightened me to hear him say that. Shosh had said the same thing once, and when I told her she was wrong, she insisted that he needed me like a lightning rod—those were her words—to ground his fear and cruelty.

It was morning. At least eight-thirty by now. Khilmi was silent. We both were. There wasn't much to say. I suddenly had a crazy anxiety. Paragraph 119 of the defense protocol, the emergency regulations from Mandate times, states that the IDF has the authority to blow up a terrorist's house: what if the Engineering Corps was on its way up the path this very moment?

Hey, what could they do—I was too weak to manage a smile—blow up Khilmi's cave? Or the cleft in the terebinth tree in the wadi where he lived while Yazdi was in Lebanon? Or what about the water barrel, the divine pool in which he immerses himself every morning to think his thoughts? Where is home anyway? Abner would say that home is the empty space between the tip of his pen and the paper. And Katzman would answer that he has no home, or if I pushed him, he'd admit that women provide him with a kind of temporary dwelling. And me, what would I say? Grandfather Amram's shack? Or the little apartment where Shosh and I lived, or maybe her parents' home? Which of them could I blow up without severely injuring myself? Hey, wait a minute, why am I getting so carried away? Stop this nonsense, let's be practical.

But Khilmi says, You're tired, *ya* Uri, try to get a little sleep.

I haven't had any sleep for three nights in a row. It's incredible. I mean me, the guy who usually falls asleep like a bird, a talent Shosh considered positively insulting. Khilmi raises himself with difficulty and takes my hand. He forgets he's not allowed to touch me. How small he is standing at my side, so wrinkled and yellow. He's starting to smell bad. Soon he'll pick lemon leaves from the tree and rub them slowly all over. The doctor at the regional clinic said Khilmi was probably suffering from some gerontological disorder of the glands when I described the smell to him, but Khilmi claims he smelled so bad when he was born, the midwife dropped him.

He leads me into the cool damp of the cave. He guides me to the straw mat. Sleep, he says gently, sleep now. And I collapse on the fragrant straw that reminds me of Grandfather Amram's mattress, the one he used to stuff his notes into, with a conspiratorial gleam in his eye. Then when he died they burned his things, including the mattress with the notes, and I never found out what he'd written.

It's quiet in here. I open one eye. Khilmi is still beside me. I see his skinny feet poking through his torn sneakers. He starts to leave. With difficulty I make out the pale stone walls and the tripod from which a goatskin bag of milk is hanging. The junk Khilmi has collected all his life must be a little farther in, his boards and bellows and burners, and his pulleys and chains and gears, and the jugs and jars and earthen pots he plans to fill with steam. Now I feel perfectly calm. I have no qualms about what I did this morning. About deceiving Katzman, and about all the exclamation points that are about to move in on me from various official reports. I just don't care.

Because I remember the smell of crushed straw in the kennel of the red-eyed bitch, where my eyes watered with the strain of reading in the dark. The bitch had no name, I never named her. She would rub against me, and when I pulled her long, silky ears up to the narrow streaks of light, I could see the veins running through them like the veins on a leaf. She must have thought I was some kind of strange, overgrown puppy. One day a neighbor caught me crawling into the kennel and called my father. My father considered me a perfect idiot, too, but he wasn't exactly overjoyed about it. He banished me to an agricultural boarding school and let me home three times a year: on Rosh Hashanah, Yom Kippur, and Independence Day. He thought everyone should learn to be self-reliant. He sent my three brothers away, too, and was killed shortly after in a car crash. I didn't love him, because of what he did to my grandfather.

I can't sleep. When I try to sit up or lean against the wall, my head spins. When I lie down, the thoughts start coming back and I feel terrible. For three days I went out of my way to be utterly obnoxious, but no one was willing to cooperate. Even Sheffer refrained from punching me before he brought me in to Katzman. I think maybe Katzman had warned them to leave me alone. Poor Katzman—the things I did to him. I barged into his room in the middle of a meeting, yelled at him and called him names, and I drove back and forth along the crazy loop between the administration building and the el Sa'adia neighborhood, bringing him detailed reports three times a day on the state of the donkey's putrefaction, and addressing him with a hatefulness and contempt that were probably intended for someone else. But he just listened to me, suggested that I take a leave of absence, told me to get more exercise. He was gentle all of a sudden. He said he couldn't understand why I was leaving Shosh at a time like this. She needs you now, Uri. Nobody else can reach her. Go home.

And his words rang in my ear as I raced along the crazy loop between el Sa'adia and the administration building, just missing the frantic chickens and the nuns in black and the boys with trays of coffee on their heads, splashing puddle water at Abu Marwan in his shiny uniform, and arriving in the narrow lane like a burned-out firecracker.

The local people were used to me by now and simply ignored me, except for the children, who still liked to giggle as they crowded around my jeep. Only this time I didn't mind their giggling. I felt only pity for them. As Khilmi says, my quarrel wasn't with them. So I rested my chin on the wheel and breathed in the stench, watching my glasses reflected in the exposed ribs of the carcass in the windshield, and suddenly, just like that, I took off, and the children scattered with shouts of laughter as I raced along the winding route and burst into the administration building, roaring, "Where is Katzman, where are you, you fucking liar, you brought me out here to stop you from doing things like this, who gave you the right to—"

Everything's ruined, Shosh. I'm lying here in the cave above a village so tiny it barely has a name. And you, what about you? Still sort of living in our apartment, and sort of working at the institute. Sort of everything. And only I know how lost you are. But I don't pity you. You took too much away from me.

Try to explain it, Shosh. You know I'm slow. But quietly, patiently, tell me where our lies converged. How did burned matches strike such a flame? And we looked into the light, you and I, and we said We.

Without rancor and without resentment, Shosh. I'm trying, too. Speak softly to me, as if I were one of your patients. I'll use my memory, the memory of your voice and the words you spoke while tutoring me for the night-school final in mathematics; step by step, you said. Some people skip part of the process. But we can take our time, Uri. We're not competing with anyone. A leads to B, and B to C. And that way there's no mystery, no blank spaces in between to swallow things, or worse—transform them.

That's why I'm taking it slow. In dribs and drabs, as they say, with no blank spaces in between. You and I. Love. Marriage. See how many blanks there are, in a single word. And if I go on thinking, I might not ever want to speak again.

Take love, for instance. What exactly does it mean? My timid love for you when I was a poor slob of a soldier in the reserves with thousands of identical twins during an army maneuver in the Sinai? Or the volatile love that made you single me out; or your love for the dead boy, Shosh, the short, deadly spurt you used to destroy him?

See? Mystery lurks between the letters of the simplest words. And it takes a keen eye to discern when the intentions go wrong and the whispers slip in between the letters. In fact, I am willing to conduct an experiment with you now, because when you came home to tell me the truth, when you ripped off the bandages all at once, I couldn't answer; you know how long it takes me to put things into words, but now I'm ready.

Love, we were saying. L-O-V-E.

Let's look at it like this: four little tiles, like the wooden Scrabble tiles at home. Not a bad example. It's Friday night at Abner and Leah's and the three of you sit around the Scrabble board, humming and joking, with the smell of Abner's pipe and Leah's peppermints in the air, and Zussia sound asleep, with his mouth open, in front of the television.

I feel so good when I'm with you. I feel so good when I look up and see your steam-pressed face. Smiling at me. How easy it is to love you now in Leah's confident features.

Fine, we have "love." And there are plenty of other wonderfully simple words to go around it. To this we add: sudden smiles, and our parallel lines of development, there, see how the phrases flow, and we train ourselves not to reach too high, to live a meaningful life, to know what we have and play the tiles on our racks. That's what we said, right? Right. So now, Shosh, I very carefully set down the word "peace" at right angles to "love" on the board inside my foggy brain, together with our quiet confidence and modest resolutions not to accept money from your parents, and to build our own furniture, even if it takes ten years, and to read every book on our bookshelves.

In Italy, when I told Katzman about us, about me and you, he said, I bet God finds it pretty boring to direct that shtick. I was furious. I wanted to make some scathing reply, but couldn't think of anything appropriate. A few days later he gave me one himself when he said that every human being is unique, a responsibility most of us can't handle. He said it was heartless of "somebody up there" to have burdened us with such a heavy responsibility. But by then it was too late to remind him about what he'd said and use it in argument. And by now I've learned such a lot from the three of you—you, Abner, and Katzman—that I could go on arguing with myself for the rest of my life. Maybe you don't even know what I'm talking about. Do you see, all those arguments you planted in me, all the conflicts and mistakes and your terrible misunderstandings, have made me both very happy and very miserable, and utterly transformed me.

But we're getting off the track, Shosh, because it's you and me I wanted to talk about. About your enthusiasm; about the two oval blushes on your cheeks, one for me and one for you. With you beside me I can make it; with you everything is possible. Together, you and I. During those army maneuvers in Kseima you used to walk right past me as though you'd never laid eyes on me before. Neat and petite even there with all that sand and dirt. You may have been a mere unit commander's secretary, but you ran that HQ trailer singlehandedly, orchestrating the maneuver, scolding us over the communications network for using foul language or holding up the drills, and we obeyed you, dog-tired reservists that we were, smirking at your earnestness, and knowing just how we looked to you in your little round glasses.

It scared me that you pretended not to know me. Maybe it was all my imagination this time, too, like it was the first time I fell in love. I didn't want to believe that was happening again, that I had only imagined you, when, the night before, in your field bed, for the first time in my life I—

You spoke. We're so similar, you said. People like us, you said. And: How smart I was to have found you. And you told me about your parents, and about Zussia, and about school, and about your friends, till I was hypnotized and felt like part of your life and part of the family.

You spoke. I burned in silence. Because I couldn't answer; I was afraid I'd spoil everything. How could this be happening to someone like me? She must have made a mistake. Mixed me up with somebody else. How does she know so much about me when I've hardly spoken a word? And even if some of the things she said were not entirely true, I would try to become what she wanted. To see her enthusiasm in the perfect oval blushes on her cheeks. So I am silent. But tomorrow night you'll get my letter telling all, and you'll trace the words with your finger and look up at me with the first shock of pain in your eyes, and it will shock me, too.

What comes next? After this simple chain of events, from A to B and C, comes a dead end, and Katzman, who betrayed me. And I will slowly trace my steps back to you, because I have to find out how this happened to us, and build myself a new life. I don't know all the details yet. It's only three days since Monday afternoon, when you came home from the institute after your meeting with the police sergeant and called me into your room and crossed your legs and blurted out the story.

Well, not the whole story. But in our private language, the blanks you slipped in are charged with meaning now. And someday, when I'm out of here, when I'm strong enough to face what I did in Juni, when I'm strong enough to tell Katzman what I have to tell him, maybe I'll be able to read the blanks you opened up, the cryptic passages in the story behind the story.

6

Slowly, my toes curling around the wooden hoops, I turn on my pivot in the barrel, under a watery weft. The last vine tendrils hang down from the bower and touch the water. And the *za'akuk*, the stinging gadflies, hover over me, golden green; it is their morning dance, before they leave for the fields to bite the bulls and drive them mad.

And I am in the barrel. With a slow, winding motion, like a big spider spreading its legs, I delight in my doughy, wrinkled flesh, washed clean of foulness. The eyes of morning are wide open now, but Uri is still asleep. I am in no hurry to wake him. He looked so weary and defeated when he arrived here, let him dine on rice with the angels.

I love Uri, he is a son to me. Like the son I had. My heart went out to him the moment I saw him with the military governor. For he was the living youth with the light in his eyes who came to the cave of my secret thoughts, and when the mukhtar, Sa'adi el Az, dripping oil into his ear, declared that Jews-and-Arabs-will-surely-profit-from-each-other, I screamed out, Lies! Lies! There is nothing for you in our villages, go away, go back to your own country, shut the door behind you, roll over and lick your crimes.

Then Sa'adi blushed more crimson than if a donkey had thrown him in front of his wives, and he rumbled "Huzz!" but I had nothing left to fear, since my Yazdi had disappeared with the guild of reciters, and I boldly shouted at Uri and the governor that they would never find their place among us, and that we want neither their kiss nor their bite, and I spat the words like watermelon seeds, yet he held me spellbound with his searching eyes and crooked smile, and I woke up just as Sa'adi's lackeys grabbed my arms and tried to carry me off, muttering, *Eib 'ya ghid!* For shame, grandfather!

But Uri, my champion, approached us swiftly and removed their hands from me and, peering curiously into my face, spoke to me softly in Arabic: "Speak, *ya sheikh*, I am listening." And he smiled till I was struck dumb, like the cracked jars where Shukri Ibn Labib keeps his vicious bees, and I shivered when he reached a trembling hand to me. And in his gentleness I felt the answering touch of other hands, the venerable hands of Darius, my patron and redeemer, who taught me that evil has a thousand faces and as many veils of sight and scent, but there is no mistaking the touch of goodness.

Slowly, curling my toes with a winding motion. Soon I will have to strike a blow. There is no way out this time. All my life I have hoped to escape this moment. To be like the others in the village.

I fled, but the moment caught up with me. Deep in the maze of clefts where I lay hidden, the clammy hand reached out and touched me. I have been touched without mercy. Now I am an outcast.

I learned of this yesterday. When Yazdi came back to me after a year; when he laid down his weapons and the belt of ammunition, and I saw death lashed in his face. And I saw the gun and the hand grenades and the chains of bullets in a pile before him, like a mound of manure from an iron horse, but before he left I slipped away with one of his icy pistols and hid it in the cave, and I have known since then what the end would be.

But not yet. I will wind around the hoops a little longer, here in the barrel where I spend my summer days, especially the *arbainat ashub*, the forty days of heat unfit for the works of man.

And soon Najach, child of my accursed daughter Zoheir, will climb the hill. She will come on cat's paws, reflected in the colored stripes inside my pool, and I will raise a finger and touch her liquid brow, there, and gently burst the likeness into splashes of color, and rise in joy to greet her: Ah, Najach, my golden chalice, sweeter even than fig cakes.

And she, with the thousand hues of her smile, with her sinuous arms, will wait for me to leave the barrel, her eyes averted as I put on my handsome robe, biting her lips. Then we will sit together, she and I, and eat the breakfast she has brought me from the village. Goat's milk and a boiled egg and porridge in a cup, over which I will sprinkle a spoonful of soil from my courtyard, and say to her, as I do each day, When I finish eating the soil I shall die in peace, and she will laugh her gentle laugh, twining her arms around her legs, a tangle of tawny strings, never uttering a word, for she is mute.

And then Najach will reach up to the broken branch of the lemon tree and take down the graybeard's friend, my lavaliere, the radio on a rope, and she will adjust the rope so it will not rub against my skin, and in the cool of a new morning, my belly swelling as we sit facing each other, we will wait to hear which of our faraway friends will call on us this morning: Farid el Atrash, wishing—*Ya retni tir latir khawalek*—that he were a bird, or perhaps Mother Um Kultum will climb the hill to sing for me and my grandchild about *shams elasil*, or perhaps we will be lucky enough this morning to hear our dearest Abd el Wahab on Cairo radio, lamenting, "*Fi elbachr lam futukum, Fi elbar futuni, Biltibri ma baatukum, Bitbni baatuni.*" And I cup my ear and moan, my eyes filling with tears because his voice is sweeter than honey when he sings that he would not sell you even for gold, while you—for straw—have sold him. And Najach, sitting before me like a painted dervish, like tawny rings of smoke, sways with her eyes shut, humming voicelessly to herself and smiling her waking secrets to the sun.

I love Najach, who is like me; I, too, was a secret child, sprawling behind tree or rock, cast out of the bustle of life, out of memory, waiting for an older brother to take-Khilmi-el-Kazza-the-dwarf-from-my-sight, someone-take-him-to-Dahaisheh-the-soothsayer-to-wind-a-*khajab*-around-his-finger-and-cure-him-of-his-idiocy, 'Y'alla-y'alla-Wednesday's-child-take-him-away, take-him-to-Sandorf-Jacobson-of-the-golden-hair-and-ask-him-to-find-Khilmi-a-place-in-his-convents-in-Jericho, *y'alla!*

And so I was Khilmi-Forsaken-by-the-Village, living in the silences and blessed darkness of a blinking eye; and I was Khilmi searching through the dustheaps for a kernel of love, for the soiled poultices of the wounded soul, for the magic herbs that wilt beneath the pillows of childless wives, and in fear and trembling I sniffed the laundry hanging out to dry, and raked through mounds of ordure, and listened to the intimate speech of babes in their cradles, or lurked behind walls like a lizard listening to the groans of pain and pleasure and the secrets spurting out, and throughout this time I knew not how things were called, the throbbing of life had not yet hardened into words, but churned in my belly like needles of colored glass.

And for hours on end I lay under the hot white sun, dreaming of darker realms, until my mother, the beauteous one whose body was her trial, remembered me.

Where-is-he-my-worm-my-Khilmi-for-two-days-he-has-not-been-here-to-vex-my-eyes; and she would send my brother Nimer to look for me in the fields tied to the *silsila*, or down in the wadi, tethered to the terebinth tree, and he would leave me the clay *sherba* with scraps of food or a piece of rotten fruit, or traces of *labni* cheese good for fortune-telling but little else, and I suffered my hunger and would not come near until Nimer had gone away with a scowl on his pockmarked face, and only then would I draw the plate closer with my teeth and eat from it like a dog.

Kan-ya-ma-kan, fi kadim elzaman, usalef elaasar walawan; once upon a time, in days of yore, in ages of bittersweet recall, *kan-ya-ma-kan*, my father, Shafik Abu Sha'aban, made his way to the wadi in the twilight hour, trudging and tripping, his soft features glowing pink in the sunset, his arm swollen and slippery as an elephant's trunk.

He was a moon-faced man who always seemed to be fighting back his tears, of whom it was said that, because he failed to satisfy my mother's lust, other sticks went into her blazing furnace, and from secret reflections in the well I learned that Mother had left my father nine months before my birth to live with Sha'aban Ibn Sha'aban.

Sha'aban lived in the biggest tent for miles around, a tent made of buckskin fastened with hyena teeth and carpeted with the striped furs of desert tigers. For he was the doughtiest hunter in Palestine, and hunters and explorers from all over the infidel world found their way to his tent wherever he pitched it and begged him to lead them into the thickets of the Jordan in pursuit of the fleet-footed panther, or through the wilderness of Kerak after the furious ostrich, and I myself remember how here in this village of sheep, red-necked Germans would sit at the café belonging to Aish's father, Abu Aish, together with rosy Englishmen or wizened Mongols, day after day and week after week, drinking beer and roasting in the sun, as they waited for Sha'aban Ibn Sha'aban's return.

He was a massive man, with a slow, mirthless laugh, who distributed gold and silver coins among the people of Andal, coins they could not use for buying, and who took what he pleased from the village shops and ensnared our beauteous women with a glance no one reproached him for, because in times of drought or when worms spoiled the tobacco crop, he fed the village from his bountiful cupboard, and twice a year, at Id-el-adkha and Id-el-fitr, he prepared munificent feasts, sumptuous beyond belief, with tables extending all the way from my hilltop to the menfolk's square below, and he brought us bands of dervishes with colorful banners and children from the school for the blind in the holy city of Jerusalem, and paper lanterns from Bethlehem, and from Nablus, wax candles carved by wanton hands, and the tables bowed under platters of pinecone nuts and roast rabbit and basins of saffron rice the color of amber and trays of *samane* with garlic and tender goslings, their bellies stuffed with walnuts.

And when Sha'aban Ibn Sha'aban gave the signal, the orchestras began to play their different songs, and burning candles and flaming torches gleamed in the dark glasses of the blind children, and the dogs of Andal went mad with the wailing of the violins, and Sha'aban Ibn Sha'aban, who drank wine like an infidel, slowly waved his heavy hand to a beat that no one else could hear.

And then with a scowl and a wordless curse he would silence the orchestras, and nod to us to approach the tables. And we would follow the first brave soul to emerge out of the shadows, floating on clouds of succulent smells, but also on the thunderhead of the hunter's scowl.

It was my mother, that wiry woman, who was the first to draw nigh to Sha'aban with everyone watching, though I kept an eye on my father as he swung his elephant arm entreatingly. Everyone knew that the children of this miserable man, my father, were not his own, and that some of them boasted the heavy jowls of the hunter himself, and harbored his secret name in their hearts.

One by one, the people of Andal emerged from the shadows, dragging their feet and darting looks at the head of table, the mountainous man with the terrifying laugh, and they swallowed expectantly as he dipped the fingers of his right hand in the *ibrik* of water, solemnly crossed his legs *tarbieh*-wise, then slipped the first gobbet of meat into a hot pita, and began to eat.

This done, a cheer went up and the guests swarmed over the food, loading their plates from the basins of rice, glutting themselves and pelting each other with sweetmeats, *melabas*, and *khilwa* and *ka'aban*, for the sin of dissipation had sent them into a frenzy.

And I beheld Sha'aban sitting cross-legged in the darkness that overspread his scowling countenance. He did not eat, but slowly ground their shame between his teeth, and fixed his red bull's eyes upon them, moving his lips in silence.

I tell the tale, though it has never been told to me, nor did I witness these happenings myself. Three months before my birth, Sha'aban the hunter died of an illness of the liver, and the hyenas finished most of him before the stench reached Andal. Whenever I ask Shukri Ibn Labib about Sha'aban, about his feasts and the sad-eyed dog he used for a gaming table, he tells me that the *rulla*, the she-monster, must have devoured what was left of my brain, for he never heard of any man called Sha'aban Ibn Sha'aban, and no one in our village ever feasted on roast rabbit and pinecone nuts.

And still the tale blows in the autumn winds and leaps out of the reflections in the well, and I know Sha'aban as though I were his woe and his crossbow, as though I were his son, for what hope have we, I answer the scoffing Shukri, save in yearning for him, save in believing such a man existed here, that in the rocky soil of Andal, in the heart of a village made of dust, there once flowed such a fountain of grief and gloom.

For he was the mighty huntsman, ravaged by his own ferocity, who took no pleasure in killing animals but dreamed of one prey only, the lion with the shaggy mane he saw in the picture books of infidel hunters and explorers, the beast he heard roaring in their reverent whispers.

And slowly the lion entered his life, till he could not throw it off. He began to dream of lions at night, to twist his bread into lions, and something of the noble stealth of the maned one showed in his gait.

And it lurked for him deep in the desert clefts and the caves of Saffi, and in the streams that flowed to the Dead Sea. He would blink at wolves and partridges, jackals and leopards, never cocking his rifle, for his war was not with them. But he fired at the lion's head when he saw it flash between the burning rocks or, with blood-shot eyes, sent his knife at shadows bounding through the sand.

No one, I say—I whisper tenderly to him from my shelter in the shadows of time—no one alive then could have told you what even Nuri el Nawar the gypsy knows, that there are no lions in this region of the world, and that the knife will cool upon your thigh, never to skin the striped golden hide, for you are doomed to live out your days, *kan-ya-ma-kan*, hunting the fox and the marten and putting the ostrich to flight, but as for the lion, you will only draw its wild mane in the sand and watch the wind carry it away.

Kan-ya-ma-kan. He who weaves a dream becomes a slave. He who is tempted by hope loses all. Only with the greatest diligence can freedom be found. Only with the eye that turns inward. But Sha'aban was beyond advice. He watched as the villagers grappled over a hunk of rabbit, green with gluttony and vomiting in their plates. Grief lay heavy on his breast and his arms filled with hot blood. A moment more and the rumbling of his stomach might have toppled them down like playing cards. And I saw him, *rabenah yasahal*, leap up on all fours with a bristling mane, drawing a mighty roar out of the depths of their misery, and flailing them with his tail.

And he ran the serpentine of tables from the top of my hill to the menfolk's square, trampling the meat with his filthy boots, spilling bowls of boiling beans with his flinty face, butting into trays of pine nuts with his horns, until he was suddenly caught, struck by the wise, cool breeze of the desert night.

And for a moment he awoke. He let his shoulders drop and his eyes grew round. He turned his shaggy head to us with the exhaustion of a trapped animal, and saw us creeping in the shadows, retching up the dregs of our short-lived happiness. Then he jumped down from the table and staggered off into the darkness, to the tent that was never pitched in the village.

This is how I always told the story. This is how Yazdi heard it from my lips, and Uri too, my butter and honey. But it is not enough anymore. Over and over I rub my skin against the sharpened words. I find no peace. My Yazdi is dead. I have failed. I have failed. When Yazdi was an idiot, I protected him. I gave him life. But then the world touched him and branded his flesh. The world had mightier stories to tell. The wandering guilds wove him into their dream. Tempted him with their hopes. My stories were no longer enough for him. They were no longer enough for me. Never more will I tell the tale of Sha'aban Ibn Sha'aban. For a day I have been weaving the cool strands of death into a dream, and I know what will befall me but cannot save myself.

Never again will I tell my stories. I will enter the maze of clefts one last time today, and one last time I will immerse myself in my heavenly pool. For I know, and Uri is waiting for an answer. In his eyes I read the question. But now, while he dines on rice with the angels in the darkness of my cave, I will perform a final kindness for my faraway friend, Sha'aban the hunter, and I close his eyes in his tent, not with a grinding of hyena teeth, but the way he wanted . . .

For *kan-ya-ma-kan*, there was or was not a fearless hunter who could wrestle leopards with his bare hands, and brave the lair of the *debah*, the hyena, for he knew there was no respite from his pain and that it was himself and not the *debah* he must fear, and in his tent he hung the likeness of the lion he tore from a book of the German hunters, and he bellowed and babbled to himself, and with the last of his coins bought a lion skin and lion heads which hunters had brought from faraway lands, and he lay on his bed sniffing the fur and running his fingers around the heavy skulls, for perhaps they held the secret of its winding route into the hills.

Kan-ya-ma-kan, foaming like a madman he appeared one day at Abu Aish's café and made known to the six rosy Englishmen sitting there that he had finally tracked down the king of beasts and would lead them to its den this very night. And without delay, they picked up their rifles and water jugs and sun helmets and hastened after Sha'aban. One helmet was left behind in the haste of their departure and found its way to Nuri el Nawar, who sold it to me.

For three days they girdled the hills and doubled back again till they began to suspect he was leading them in circles, that he was avenging himself somehow. Sha'aban had not touched food for three days and nights, and the Englishmen dared not speak to him when they saw the terrible glint in his eye, the phantom tail that lashed the rocks, and the jagged marks of his own hooklike claws on his back and shoulders.

And on the third night he led them into the thickets of the Jordan and told them to eat their fill and to wipe the dust from their rifles and load them with bullets. And then he led them down a narrow path to the river, and stood them in a row, and paced off the distance between them, informing them that as soon as the moon disappeared behind the blackened clouds, the lion would come down from the hills to slake its thirst, as he had observed it do for seven nights before the hunt.

And they huddled together in the darkness, wrapped in their jackets and scarves, chafing their hands and cursing themselves for following a madman to this godforsaken place, into the rustling thickets where angry snakes crawled underfoot and birds swooped down at their eyes. And feathery clouds blew in from the east, followed by fleecy clouds, and then raven clouds that swallowed the nib of the moon.

And in the dim light, beyond the silvery water, the six hunters heard the glorious padding of the king of beasts slinking through the thickets as only a lion can. Six rifle shots reverberated with the wretch's roar of death and exultation, the ecstasy of one who has at last destroyed the dream, wrapped in store-bought furs and riddled with the bullets that inscribed his victory.

Kan-ya-ma-kan. Three months before I was born it happened. Nine months before I was brought into the world, into the arms of Dahaisheh, the midwife, my mother was driven by lust to the hunter's tent to become his golden lioness in the mistaken womanly belief that she alone could make him see the truth. But after only a few weeks in his majestic tent, he tired of her and drove her off like a ewe, and I read her life with him in the play of light and shadow in her eyes and in her rueful groans and bare-toothed hatred; I envision her as she was then, a young wolf-woman nestling barefoot on the carpets, dressed in softest fawn skins taken from the gravid does he trapped; I see her padding over bullet-riddled tiger skins; I imagine the amusements he devised for her, like painting an ostrich egg with seven colors, smashing it on the ground, and letting her paste the pieces back together; or teaching her to set a hidden spring between the heavy jaws of a hyena skull, so that the lightest tap on its nose made the hyena laugh in hideous silence. This I beheld.

And the tale was inscribed in every hair of her head, from red tip to silver root, and her withered chin bore the unmistakable signature of the nights she slept on a pallet of panther skins, moaning with love under the yellow eyes of a stuffed karakul that hung by its tail from the tent flap; or playing a game of cards together, using a sad-eyed sheep dog Sha'aban Ibn Sha'aban had been given by a red-necked hunter, for their gaming table, and the tent was lighted by wanton candle figurines from a certain shop in Nablus. *Tuta tuta khelset elkhaduta.*

7

At eight o'clock on the morning of his thirty-ninth birthday, Katzman drove the army jeep from Juni to Tel Aviv. He was tired and angry. Sheffer, the first to reach the jail room when the gun went off, was plainly furious that Uri had managed to get away. It was Katzman's second blunder in twenty-four hours. He would most likely have been killed during the skirmish the night before had Sheffer not been faster than the kid aiming the gun behind the curtain. Katzman ignored Sheffer's silent reproach. He told Sheffer he would be back in three hours and put him in command. Sheffer expressed amazement that Katzman was leaving at a time like this, after the events of the night before. Katzman repeated his orders woodenly. "I'll be back in three hours, Sheffer." "Sir," answered Sheffer, bridling the way he did whenever he despaired of understanding Katzman.

It didn't make sense for Katzman to be leaving Juni just now. There was ferment in the streets. He had an appointment with the mayor at noon that day, and other important meetings would follow, no doubt, in the wake of the skirmish. The general's comment the day before that the town was becoming more and more insurgent sounded to Katzman like an admonition. But how was he supposed to stop the cycle of violence, which, if anything, had escalated since his transfer here? Clamp down on regulations and restraints? There was no point. A bold new strategy was called for, only Katzman didn't quite feel up to it, maybe because of his unspoken war with Uri.

Katzman tore across Samaria in the balky jeep that wasn't his. He hit a traffic jam on the coastal road, inched along the fast lane, past orange groves and apartment blocks and drivers exuding public-spiritedness with every flick of their newspapers as they waited at the crossroads, past narrow lettuce fields toiled over by Arabs toward whom he felt a startling affinity now, having lived among them for so long, these men and women in their colorful rags and limp straw hats.

Shosh and Uri's flat was in the suburb of Ramat Aviv. As he walked to the door, Katzman smiled glumly at Uri's handmade copper nameplate: SHOSH AND URI, it said, like two characters in a children's book. Katzman remembered Shosh's habit of pressing down on the loose screws that held the plate up whenever she left the house—she was afraid it would fall—and now he, too, pressed down on them, like a vicarious observer of the rite.

He hesitated before opening the door: Uri had given him a key a few days earlier, asking Katzman to bring him some clothes and books from home. But Katzman had another key, the one Shosh had given him, about which Uri knew nothing. Katzman wondered why each of these identical keys had a different way of unlocking the same door. Perhaps the key he selected would determine what he found inside. He used Uri's key, pausing on the threshold with theatrical tact so that the stagehands inside could carry out a quick scene change.

Yes, it was definitely Uri's house this time, and in this kitchen he and Uri had cooked their little suppers, talking together and arguing, opening up to each other and then withdrawing till Shosh came home to dispel the oppressive intimacy. Katzman coughed. The windows were shut and the house was stuffy. Shosh had apparently slept elsewhere the night before. He looked around for a clue as to what might have occurred when Shosh told Uri the long-stifled truth.

He wasn't sure what she had told him. Uri had been in a terrible state Monday evening when he burst into Katzman's office. Not that Uri's logic was ever easy to follow. He always drew wildly emotional conclusions. Katzman listened raptly to Uri's ranting. Shosh had deceived him, he said in astonishment. He couldn't tell Katzman everything just yet. He had to let it sink in first. But he now knew that he had been living in a sort of bubble for the past few months. She had betrayed him. No, no. It was too difficult to talk about. And you, Katzman—no. He had to think first. Don't press me, Katzman, not you, because she told me the truth this time, and I don't know what the truth is anymore.

But there were no clues anywhere. No signs of wreck or ruin. One truth had simply been replaced by another, like a defective part of an appliance. Like a cataclysm that vanishes without a trace. Katzman walked into the bedroom, scrutinizing himself closely. The wide wooden bedstead Uri had built no longer gave him the quiver of excitement he remembered, like a hint of Shosh's perfume in the air.

He tore his eyes away from the bed and stared at his image in the mirror. Now he understood why he had been in such a hurry to leave Juni. He had felt an urgent need to come here ever since Uri told him about his talk with Shosh. Alone on the scene, he thought, he would be able to find a connection among the insane events of recent months. He would be able to consider his actions. Without putting it in so many words, he had been hoping to find reality in the interplay of people and emotions that were becoming so detached and so terrifyingly free.

But as soon as he set foot in the house he knew: he would find no comfort here. Here his anguish would harden into words. Shosh had committed an unpardonable sin: she had told the truth in vain. Uri had tricked him and fled to Andal, where his own distress and the old man's grief welled up into a menacing wave. Uri and Shosh had escaped the consequences of their actions, abandoning him to this latest revelation.

So be it. Uri had escaped, and now it was Katzman's duty to bring him in. To protect him, though it was from Katzman himself that Uri needed protection. Because Katzman was his nemesis. "What a mess," he sighed, repeating the words like a curse. He had always felt an irrepressible urge to make a hopeless mess of things so that he could fling it angrily in someone's face, the one responsible for life being as it is, and say, You take it. You figure it out. You explain it.

Only he had discovered the futility of this quite early. The web secreted by the human organism seemed to get inextricably tangled in the world. He couldn't really expect to find a comforting explanation. It was true that in the tortuous course of things there were occasional shocks and leaden descents, or moments of fleeting brightness and fortuitous gropings at truth. The trouble was that they never came at the right time. He was never punished for what he considered to be his transgressions; on the contrary, retribution seemed to come when he least deserved it; and even the good things in his life, like Uri's appearance on the scene, were a bit too arbitrary. At the age of thirty-nine he was as far from understanding his symmetry as he was at birth.

Katzman found Uri's green knapsack on the top shelf of the closet. There was still a string dangling from it, with an orange card bearing the Red Cross insignia and the Fiumicino airport stamp. Uri was intensely proud and sentimental about his days in southern Italy. He had once shown Katzman his collection of mementos: a laissez-passer from the Italian Army to the disaster area; a medal given him by an old woman he found dying in a ruined cathedral; a couple of anti-malaria tablets. Katzman broke the string, crumpled up the orange card, and stuffed it in his pocket. He tossed some underwear and a couple of shirts into the knapsack. Uri's sneakers were on the bottom shelf. The room was becoming unbearably stuffy. Katzman stood up, with an abject glance at the bed. Every way he turned, strings broke. Objects trembled. Screaming out to him. Pining for his eyes and memory.

Uri had asked for books. Katzman threw the knapsack on the bed and went into Shosh's study. On her desk he saw the bulky tape recorder and her notes. For a moment he felt as if he had been led into a trap. His head reeled. The clues laid out for him had been shuffled around. Reluctantly he reached out and pushed Play and heard the sound of Shosh's voice: "Mordy, you don't know who you are and what you have inside, and the only way you can find out is by letting it out. Do you understand me?" Katzman was startled. He quickly pressed Stop and interrupted the revolving spool. It was amazing. He had said the very same thing to Uri in Santa Anarella, and later on to Shosh in an entirely different context. He had used the same key to unlock two seemingly identical doors and had made a very frightening discovery.

Katzman leafed through Shosh's notes. Scribbled phrases met his eye. Shosh, when he first knew her, had been riding the crest of success and perfect happiness. This in itself put Katzman off. She was full of goodwill, exuding what he called "positive energy." At the time, one year ago, she had been engrossed in the treatment of two delinquents with learning disabilities, using an experimental method she and her professor had devised. Katzman was perplexed by what he saw as her conflicting tendencies. The pieces didn't always fit. Her obstinacy, her professional affability, her self-imposed asceticism, her determination to crack the nucleus of love in her juvenile delinquents. They had once argued about this. Katzman had told her he approved of her cynicism. Shosh, appalled, answered coolly that there was nothing cynical about her methods or any other department of her life; that the corrosive nihilism underlying any form of cynicism was utterly abhorrent to her. She didn't give Katzman a chance to explain what he meant. Whenever she got worked up like that, the words would come spilling out of her like long quotations. Katzman didn't deny that her patients showed signs of improvement and a desire for rehabilitation. They were obviously less hostile and antisocial now. But trying to pique her, Katzman asked what she would do if she found somebody whose experience of "primal love" was inaccessible to her, and Shosh— quoting Uri, who must have been referring to something else— answered dourly that we all have a nucleus of love inside us, it was just a question of knowing how to find it.

A war of innuendoes raged between them, which they both feared would go too far, and which Shosh refused to acknowledge even to herself. Katzman said that his own nucleus of love was inaccessible because he had never really loved. This, however, was untrue. He had certainly loved his father, he had loved his adopted father on the kibbutz, he had loved various women for brief periods of time, and he loved Uri. But Shosh was furious. She didn't like his mordant wit or his air of faint contempt for all she deemed important. And yet, the fact that she wasn't willing to give up the underlying challenge between them seemed a good indication that she considered Katzman worth saving from himself. He kept trying to provoke her, against his will, trying to strain her Jesuitical patience to the breaking point.

But she would not oblige him, deftly paraphrasing him instead, revising and forgiving the things he said. They were both concerned about his relationship with Uri, and carried it gingerly between them like a sleeping baby. They dreaded reaching a point of no return. Those evenings when he arrived from Juni and had to be alone with Shosh until Uri came home from night school became irksome. And he resented his loss of independence. One night he blurted out that he felt Shosh was doing her damnedest to contain him, that she forgave him only because she didn't quite have the guts to believe him, and that he couldn't quite believe in her unflagging cheer.

He spoke with vehemence, watching her grow more and more rigid. Her eyes bulged. A mild tremor of fear passed through him, but he kept talking. She couldn't go on deceiving herself, he said. Something inside her was trying to break through. She trembled. Her pale lips cut her face like a string. Cruelly he said—guessing, really—that she couldn't contain him for long, or the image of him that she carried within. He thought he heard her snap inside, and hated himself for not shutting up. He mourned his friendship with

Uri, his banishment from this home he loved so much in spite of everything. And Shosh stammered, "Oh, you miserable man, I want you so badly," her hand fluttering over her mouth.

The telephone rang, shattering time into fragments that whirled around his brain. A cold tide surged through him. Someone was calling Shosh. If only he had the strength to pick up the receiver and shout something into it. Unexpectedly a splintered image caught in the tender flesh of his memory: the Arabs toiling in the lettuce fields by the roadside this morning. He reconstructed the scene: there was no violence. They were all wearing straw hats and resembled cotton pickers in American films about the Old South. For a moment he almost suspected them of dressing that way out of a subtle sense of irony. The telephone tore relentlessly at the air. The final ring faded away, vibrating harshly against invisible grains of dust. Katzman was neither disappointed nor relieved. He had no expectations.

Shosh had known what she was getting into by allowing him to resonate inside her. By inviting him to, in fact. With her, he descended bleakly and wearily into the subterranean maze that was so odiously familiar to him. He would emerge safe and sound again, he knew, full of self-contempt but in the clear. And he hated himself more for his vigorous defenses and for the way he always landed on his feet.

Now, as he sat at Shosh's desk, he didn't want to make any decisions. He just wanted to remain in the state of indifference he had fallen into the moment he saw she had cracked. He tried not to pity her or to feel remorse. He had always made it clear that she must not expect his love. Nor did he need hers. So what was it, then? Why had he done this to Uri; why had he persuaded Uri to come to Juni with him? Why couldn't he have been stopped in time from wreaking havoc?

He ran his eyes over the shelf. There were books there which he had given to Uri and Shosh. Katzman was enthusiastically eclectic in his reading. Shosh had been shocked on occasion by his taste, but he could also delight her with his sensitivity, his empathy and willingness to suffer with literary characters.

Katzman ran his fingers over the books. In his present vulnerable condition, their wonderfully simple titles resounded like savage screams: *The Stranger, The Fox, The Slave*, and finally *The Plague*, the book he loved the best. He leafed through it, recollecting passages that had affected him deeply just a few years before. He felt a pang of sympathy for Tarrou fighting the plague and read: "It is tiresome to be infected, but even more tiresome not to want to be so. That is why they all show signs of fatigue." He chuckled quietly and replaced the book. *The Stranger* was less dangerous. Katzman turned to the flyleaf and read: "To my dearest stranger, and closest friend." And Shosh's initials.

Suddenly he felt dejected. He sat hunched over, listening to the slow drip of gall inside him. Shosh was just another string binding him to Uri. This perhaps explained the sense of loss he was experiencing, with regard not to Shosh but to Uri.

Katzman stirred himself and hurried to the kitchen. He gulped down two glasses of cold water and pressed the glass to his forehead. Could all this really be happening? The girl and boy on the memo pad were smiling at him. Memos were a family tradition handed down from Abner and Leah, who liked to read the witty messages they wrote each other aloud at their annual Purim party. Katzman lifted the cover of the pad and read familiarly:

Man is a riddling riddle,
The bard doth us remind.

And when you fathom the dishes in the sink—
A reward in the fridge you will find.

But the fridge was empty. Katzman glanced at his watch with alarm. He hurried to the bedroom and slipped the slender book into the knapsack. He wondered why for all his vagueness of sentiment he could still feel the flickering of a raw attraction to Shosh's body and her smell. He fought it; he sealed himself off from the small articles on the bedside table; he did not construe the whispering of the small round mirror on her bureau. There was a sickle-shaped crack in the ceiling which they liked to trace on each other's body, and a climbing plant whose leaves she had twisted childishly in the shape of a heart. Katzman was surprised to discover these islands of intimacy and tenderness in their strange, unsentimental relationship.

He hurried on, pushing aside the traces of her angular movements in the air. He bent down and buckled the knapsack. Allow me, I'll zip you up. Katzman felt disgusted, but he forgave himself, walked out of the house, pressed down on the two loose screws the way she always did, and locked the door with her key. The old symmetry.

8

Sixty minutes of quality time. Anichka came in with a trayful of sandwiches, a hard-boiled egg wrapped in cellophane, and a cup of warm tea. As she was leaving she said, with a sympathy I hardly deserve, "You don't look so good, Shoshi my girl. You mustn't overwork, it isn't healthy." And I saw she was biting back a question.

Alone again. This used to be Mordy's hour. A special time for special treatment. The attendant would bring him to me and close the door. Sit down, Mordy, I say wistfully, my fear beginning to mount, as it does every day when I remember what I'm doing to him, and what Katzman said about me—that I would fight to Mordy's last drop of blood, and then I plunge into the files, inspiring myself with hope, because I mustn't lose courage, the courage that frightens Uri so, and I quickly run through file number 3, and with a sigh of relief that all is in order, I envision Mordy stretching out in his shell, groping after the rays of light I send him, placing fresh trust in my words, slowly breaking out of the horny armor that covers him up to his eyes, softly pronouncing my name. "Shosh?" he probes. "Shosh?"

Wonder of wonders, he wants me to teach him to read and write, and asks one day, "What's a museum?" Then he shoves a pencil in my hand. "Draw me a bird." What for, Mordy? "It's a surprise." But I guess: he wants to hammer out the picture for me, as a present. Good guess, Shosh! How eloquently you summarized the following hour. Hillman, who went through the file later, noted with a hint of disapproval: "Sheer poetry!" But he, too, was wonder-struck by the clumsy bird Mordy hammered out on a smooth sheet of copper (gazing off uneasily as you guided his hand).

And this is how Mordy used to sit here, with a sidelong glance at the chocolate bar I set with cunning foresight on the table before him, not that he would ask for it, his tongue crashing against the jagged rocks of his teeth and his brown hair falling over his eyes; and in the glass-top table I see a strange reflection—the dazzling red playing-card queen tears away from me and walks joylessly around the table to put her paper hands on his slender shoulders. There is no explanation for this. The road from truth to falsehood is the same dirt path you tread each day, where every pebble has a name and even the thorns smile in greeting. You could walk it blindfolded. But if you come from the opposite direction, you may discover that there never was a path.

Locked behind a little glass door, I have waited so long for life to break through to me. I close my eyes and press down with Zussia's thumbs, and against the darkened sky I see glittering dust.

Silence. The words are always spoken, but they are not always warm with truth. They are like faceless sentries barring my way. So now I will tell the truth I never dared to say out loud—I need love. How painfully obvious it is: the high priestess of love, who turned her deficiency into a lethal profession; but how did I fool myself so long, me, the great authority on love? I was born in the house of love, to my loving parents, and our loving, compassionate Zussia, surrounded by love, if only I had believed it, the love of my best girl friends and the hot-blooded boys, my first tentative lovers, and the lust of the officers in the army, whew, what an inventory, and Uri, who loved me with a kind of infantile joy that always brought remorse, and Katzman, who scorched me like a laser beam, and Mordy, my patient. Still, there's something missing.

There always is. A wall of glass separates me from my loving lips. A glass partition cuts me in two, turns me into a laboratory, with a culture of passionate bacteria devouring itself on a thin glass slide. An immovable, transparent screen keeps me isolated from the burning hands that knead me, the hands of those who brand me with long, hasty lines, or ring me round with pale, uninspired loops, or try to squeeze a few mysterious drops out of the tight, defiant fruit, saying in their infinite wisdom, "Listen, little girl, you're not letting yourself feel anything, stop fighting it"; or the pained and painful insults they hurtle at me, like "You're a real slut, soldier girl. I've had a lot of women in my life, but I never met a ballbreaker like you before. You make me feel disgusted with myself. Who the hell do you think you are, Sergeant, with your processed ardor and spitefulness? Let's just say goodbye and forget about it, okay?"

A glass partition separates these men from the knot whispering in the darkness, rotting away in the thick juices of anticipation.

Who will come, who will burrow through to touch what lies in wait and ignite the vital force inside it?

None of the men I knew. Neither the hot-blooded boys in my class, nor the officers who lusted after me, nor Uri, who delighted in my body, nor Katzman with his scorching laser beam; a most unexpected solution was found to the knotty riddle, and the splinters of the shattered glass partition flew deep into my every cell. That is why I dare not move.

Drink your tea; it's getting cold. Tell me what you wrote about Mordy.

No. Not yet. You're not ready for that yet. Just describe the thrill you felt, like a giddy astronaut, your pen skipping over the paper. Uri and Katzman were talking animatedly in the other room while you deceived them, all three of you, by digging your own secret tunnel which you feel in every fiber of your nerves when the springy wire starts to unwind and empowers you to write the simplest words in a wild, new language that invents itself, drawing you out and writing you, though Leah would never approve: Darling, you can say the same thing more intelligibly, this isn't your style, it sounds more like a travesty of Steinbeck or Tennessee Williams, your old favorites; you don't fool me, darling, I know you too well; and even Hillman raised a bushy brow when he went through the files with the police officer, saying he never realized our Madame Shoshi had such flair, so how about using some of it on our Hillman newsletter, ho ho; I tell you, Shosh, I beg you, give yourself over to the old impetuousness, and allow the darkness of this quiet night to pierce through to you in a gyre and plummet you down to a place where truth and falsehood are only different names for the same thing.

Is this what you wanted? It was easier working with your boys, wasn't it? Sit comfortably. Move a little closer to the tape recorder so the microphone will pick up your silences. Your anxieties. The chills running up and down your spine. Fine. Now listen. So much is going on in the silence. Empty your mind of all the knots and wait patiently for them to float up in the slow eddy of your thoughts, till they revolve like sad-eyed horses on a carousel: Katzman, with his drooping head, and Abner, with human fingers sticking out under his hooves, and Uri, addicted to the ride. And galloping up behind them now, like a clumsy centaur, Zussia. Members of the jury, I beg to start with him. Now, about Zussia . . .

Zussia is a hefty, green-eyed man with a rugged face, deeply tanned and hardly wrinkled at all despite his age, and his hair under a black fur cap is a thick mass of silver curls. Zussia—so Abner says—fought with the Jewish brigade of the Lithuanian division against the Germans in the Ariol ("Oriol," Zussia corrects him apologetically), and because he studied chemistry at the university, the partisans made him an instructor in chemical warfare. Abner used to tell the story over and over during Zussia's first years with us. He doesn't tell it anymore, and no one asks. I was three years old when Abner brought him home, and for me, Zussia was like a fairy-tale giant come to life. I could never hear enough of Abner's tales about his wars and adventures. And Abner was only too happy to oblige, always introducing new characters who hadn't been there the night before, describing Zussia's life among the partisans, and beautiful Suzy, the signal woman, or young Ignaz, who blew himself up on the railroad tracks, and Zussia would listen in wonder, nodding his head as though hearing it all for the first time. Who knows, maybe he really was hearing it for the first time, maybe Abner got a secret charge out of making up stories and weaving Zussia into them, but it doesn't matter anyway; the thing is, Zussia's eyes relaxed and lost the glint of fear.

When the war ended, Zussia wandered around Europe till he fell into a titan's stupor on the banks of a blue fjord in some Norwegian village, where he worked for a time unloading fish from Arctic ships and learned to drink like a Norwegian sailor, and his soul, so Abner tells me in secret, sank through the swirling seaweed inside him.

He wound up in Israel. Without a dream. Like a sealed bottle swept over the ocean, he was packed into a ship carrying hundreds of Jews, and then dropped off on our shores, where they dressed him in an ill-fitting army uniform, equipped him with weapons he didn't know how to use, patted him on the shoulder, registered, numbered, and forgot him, hoisted him onto a truck, and sent him to be killed on a battlefield somewhere near a fire-spitting Arab police station.

He died there. Abner states this matter-of-factly, with infuriating nonchalance. How can you kill a man like that, even for the sake of a surprise ending? My father was the frightened young commander of Zussia's division, and in the two hours before this famous battle of the War of Independence, they crouched together in a trench, conversing in Russian. The only information we ever got about our beloved Zussia was the information they exchanged in those two hours.

I don't really know what happened there. There was a terrible battle and lots of people were killed. Nearly all of them, in fact. Abner, even when he drinks too much and turns talkative, never gives the secret away. Anyway, Zussia died, and Abner came out of the war unscathed. And two years later, when Abner was already the assistant editor of the party paper, Zussia turned up. They've been inseparable ever since.

Stop. Say it again: "They've been inseparable ever since." There's so much behind those wonderfully simple words. Abner could have found Zussia another place to live, with a foster family, maybe. But he brought him home to us instead, and insisted that Zussia stay, in complete defiance of Leah, who thought Abner must be out of his mind to bring "that" into a house with a young child. "That" being all but mute at the time, able only to utter his own name, over and over, Zussia, Zussia, like the message in a bottle set adrift on the waves.

"They've been inseparable ever since." I don't really know why Abner brought him home to us, or why he's so protective of him.

But the cautious decoder would surmise that it was to Zussia and his ilk Abner was referring when he wrote about the secret promises he made to hoodwink himself so he could get through life without recognizing the truth, and Zussia, I believe, is that "shadow streaking stealthily/Into a great shaft of light," because Abner is always saying that reality can't withstand the test of reality, Shosh, any more than logic can withstand the test of logic. How many times have I heard him say that in his jocular way, never realizing that it was just a catch phrase; that like an old winebibber, he used it to lure me down to the cellar, where the special vintages are kept. How was I supposed to know that, Abner? How was I supposed to distinguish the false trails from your talon tracks of fear?

What's this, then? There's a ringing in the room. The blue telephone is calling me. Wonder of wonders: it's Zussia. Bellowing words of congratulation. Leah's been manipulating him, I bet. "What is it, Zussia?" She must have said to him, "Shosh wonders why you never call her anymore. Yesterday she asked if I thought she hurt your feelings or something." And teary-eyed, trembling all over, he leafs through the address book Abner gave him, in which there are only three or four numbers. Then he dials me in supplication.

But now that he's reached me, what will he say? That he misses me, or the little girl I used to be? That he misses Uri and wants an immediate explanation for his disappearance? Or maybe he will demand to know what Uri and I were fighting about, and order me to stop torturing everyone with my silence.

No, he calls me Maliutka and starts to giggle helplessly. We miss you bad, he explains at last, Leah is so frightened for you; he gives her away in his guilelessness. Here it comes, the order, fast, cool, and incandescent, thoroughly confusing him. I can just imagine her whispering it to him from a certain distance, say, from just inside the kitchen door, not too close, because she doesn't mean to intrude on his private conversations, and she leans against the refrigerator, a luckless kitchen towel twisted around her strong hands, and the angry dark blush winding up her furrowed neck; and Zussia, who peers at her fearfully, ready to drop the receiver and flee to his room, now clears his throat, coughs heartily, and is relieved to remember his reason for phoning me in the first place. Today at long last he received his book in the mail, the expensive volume Abner ordered from Holland, full of photographs ("Lots of pictures") of the kites that are used in modern meteorology, and now Zussia is on familiar ground; sixteen-meter kites, just imagine, their frames are made of a special kind of nickel, and tomorrow we'll go to a factory where they use the same kind of nickel to make furniture, and we'll get a couple of sticks and build a small model, yes, that's what I wanted to tell you, that's why I called, goodbye now. What? Wait! Oh yes, I wanted to know if you're coming home for dinner. Yes. I wanted to know that very much. Because you were so late last night. Well?

How can I resist teasing her? No, Zussia, I won't be home until Great Birnam wood to high Dunsinane hill shall come. Yes. Yes. You heard right. Now repeat after me: Until Great-Birnam-wood— Enough. She gets it, clever woman. The long-suffering towel is slapped against the chair. Now her thumbs slide down in a gesture of mastery over her thighs, as though ironing the housecoat that falls austerely from her shoulder to her ankle—where are my cigarettes?—and her pride wounded, she leaves the stage of our little fantasy, head held high, with quick, small steps, like an Egyptian figurine.

Bye-bye, Zussia my sweet, don't you worry about me, I'll be late again tonight. And he hangs up hesitantly, his perfumed hand lingering on the receiver, turning around bewilderedly for a rebuke from Leah, who is no longer there, who is in her room by now, slapping the ironed clothes down on the shelves.

Hold it. You're upset. It's Leah's fault you're so worked up, though your easy acquiescence makes me suspect that she's merely an excuse. One of those timeworn keys to a familiar door. So let her be, why don't you, and let's get back to Zussia now, and please, try to remember whether you loved him or not.

The word "love" is inappropriate here. I'm certainly very fond of him. We have shared many secrets, and have had many intimate talks in our own private language. He used to let me ride on the back of his bicycle and he took me to the Boxer Club; in short, he was a kind of faithful pet you didn't have to think about too much. No. The word "love" is inappropriate, and in any case, I think I was too wary as a child to be able to love anyone. That's easy to see in the photographs. The skinny little girl in the ugly dress, Shoshi-takes-after-me-she-hates-dressing-up with the braces on her teeth, and the tension that makes her seem aloof, please-don't-give-me-that-ironic-look! Until the pediatrician explained that there are no ironic children, irony is a grown-up disease, there are only nearsighted children, and then everything fell into place; that is, from then on, the shy, uncharming girl in the photographs wore glasses.

But back to Zussia; he came to live with us twenty-two years ago. Gradually he adapted to us, made himself useful in his way, learned to cook, to do the laundry and other jobs around the house. I remember his bouts of apathetic staring, his heavy movements, his hesitation, the way he hummed to himself. We cleared out a roomful of books for him, and Abner took him out to buy new clothes. Gradually the glint in his eyes faded, and he would sometimes mutter complete sentences in Russian. He met a friend from the Old Country in the street one day and asked permission to invite him home for a drink. He called me Maliutka, "dolly." He could make wonderful things out of paper, and whistle through his palms. When I was learning how to read, he learned to speak Hebrew. He asked Abner to sign him up at the Russian lending library. One morning he said to Leah shyly, Today is my birthday.

He just happened to us out of the blue. Leah was furious at first; her benevolent disposition was severely tested. She considered leaving but feared that this time Abner would not relent. Gradually she softened. She began to speak to Zussia, to teach him this and that. Suddenly seeing him as a kind of challenge, she swamped him with affection. I don't actually recall those days—I can only conjecture them, based on old quarrels. Eventually she relented. She warmed to the convenience Zussia provided. She even gave him driving lessons as a present, and he's been our chauffeur ever since. There's a kind of tacit agreement between us that Zussia is simply a good friend paying back a favor, and everyone is happy.

But he will not lend himself to being deciphered. The friendship between him and Abner is cautious, tactful. They drink together in a thick, stubborn silence. Abner is fonder of Zussia than he is of most people, or so I think. And for over twenty years now they have walked together in resignation, sharing an invisible burden. I never ask what it is.

Then, seven years ago, Abner found Zussia a job; he remembered that our Zussia was a chemist in his youth and got him a position at a cosmetics factory, where he now works, though not as a chemist, and his salary—so he decided—goes to Leah, who gives him a modest allowance according to his needs, and our home smells of perfume, though Leah has never used even a drop, and her opinion on the subject is no secret. Zussia with his silences and swollen hands gives off a delicate fragrance that softens the rugged impression of his face.

I was fond of him. He used to carry me piggyback around the house, and gently fix my broken dolls and tell me stories in Russian, and sing me marching songs in a deep warm voice, and in the photographs the two of us are always together: a baby leading an elephant by the nose ring of love. On Saturday mornings he would take me to the Boxer Club, which was a kind of neighborhood pub that opened its doors to a few select members; some of my earliest memories are of heavy men drinking frothy beer in the darkness and singing hoarsely, the air smoky and thick with hiccups and the syrupy sadness that trickled into me, and I also remember the taste of onion sausage and the whispering followed by raucous laughter, and a man with a bare pink stump of a leg on the chair.

When we left, Zussia would lean down and smooth my dress and my knee socks, and comb my hair with spit-moistened fingertips—Isn't she a lovely child—and then he would press my eyeballs with his thumbs till I saw the glittering—just a little pressure. Maybe it was a Russian superstition. Or maybe he wanted to wipe away the sights I had seen. And we would hurry home in silence, hand in hand. And I never said a word to anyone.

That's my Zussia. A big man, quick to crumble; real to me only when I see him, but out of sight, a thick monotonous essence, waxing and waning according to the emotional tides at home, mortifying us on occasion with tiny electric storms of infantile joy or penitent rage. And in all those years I felt a great responsibility for him, because of which, with some relief, I turned him over to Uri when he arrived on the scene.

I should point out that Zussia was utterly indifferent to the boys who came around. He would withdraw to his room or become engrossed in his little chores, "his servant role" (Leah), until the day I brought Uri home, when Zussia's face practically dropped with relief, and he pressed Uri's hands in an embarrassing display of emotion. Maybe that was how Uri became one of the family. "If Zussia approves," laughed Abner, "what more is there to say?" Uri and Zussia took to each other immediately. They threw our lives into a whirl of improvements and renovations: they turned the overgrown back yard into a magnificent garden with a vegetable patch: then—according to Leah's plan—they broke down a wall in the living room and made it into a depressing football field, and then they disappeared mysteriously to the basement, where, within a few weeks, they built a magnificent desk with various contrivances for Abner.

Wait a minute. Stop the tape. Open the little glass door. Look in. Is there enough quality time left to tell about Zussia's kites? But what's the point of wasting precious time, quality time, on stories about Zussia, who isn't important in any case and has no logical explanation to offer me for what I did, for the way I lived with Uri while longing for Katzman, longing passionately not for his body but for his need of mine; and what has corrupted me so that I can lie to anyone, or worse, that I can lie so naturally, so expertly; what went wrong, I ask my anonymous listener, what dissolved my good intentions together with the slogans I was taught, and enabled me to go on living without too many pangs even after I killed Mordy?

No no. Don't use that word! No direct link or evidence, etc., etc. What we want is a reasonable cause, not childish guilt. And certain words are better left unsaid. Words that change the chemistry of the air, infecting all the innocent words. Why don't you tell us something else, yes, tell us about the kites, for instance. Drink your tea. It's probably cold by now.

Ah yes, the kites. Zussia's fascination with kites seems easier to grasp now than almost anything else. Even his enthusiasm for long-tailed paper bats, colorful rhomboids with crosses of nickel and bamboo; and the way he spends his modest allowance at the store and orders books that touch on his obsession, and the way he leafs through the shiny giants in a foreign tongue, running his fingers reverently over the chrome pictures and the complicated diagrams, rolling his eyes, carried away on the wind.

I remember the time the kites first spoke to him: I was ten years old, and we all went out to fly kites with Abner's Scout troop. On the banks of the Yarkon River, that cloudy autumn Saturday, one of the boys put a stick with a ball of string wound around it in my hand, and a colorful kite tossed on the ground till a gust of wind picked it up, almost tearing my hand off, and set it reeling joyfully in the gray sky; and then, all at once, discordant cries of joy and alarm rang through the air around me, and the wind raised the woolly collar of my coat against my chin. Zussia came running, shrieking words that flew up in the wind, pleading for something with his hands, the kite, Maliutka, "*bumazhnyi zmei.*" Take it, then, Zussia, take the string from me, watch out! Good now, run, run. He tries to take off, his neck working, his eyes raised as he grabs the cord with both hands, hopping clumsily like the overweight baggage of a dirigible, till a molehill puts a hasty end to his euphoria, and we all rush over and find him laughing wildly as he has never laughed before.

That was how it started. He would build strange kites and then improve on them, working for days at a time, filling his room with the special semitransparent paper that rustled with longing for the wind to breathe life into its folds, and there were paper tails fastened to his hangers, and his fingers were crusty with the fragrant white glue he allowed me to peel, and in his face I found the secret he so stubbornly concealed.

Then we heard about a kite club in Haifa. Abner helped Zussia make contact, and once a month Zussia would drive out and gallop over the slopes of the Carmel mountains in a fierce wind with a crowd of elderly German Jews in knickerbockers and gaiters, and once, five or six years ago, we all drove to Haifa with him to hear him deliver a lecture—God, he was nervous, and proud—about the role kites played in the battle of Hastings, or some such thing.

He doesn't go to Haifa anymore, and there's no glue on his fingers or tiny brass tacks between his teeth when I come into the room nowadays. But the secret is still there. He asks Abner to buy him a physics book in Russian, and in a startling gesture of courage and urgency even initiates a meeting with a new immigrant, a professor of aerodynamics from the Soviet Union, and we don't know what he's dreaming about, we would never dare question him about it, because everyone is entitled to privacy, to his own *mishegas*, as Abner says, adding that so long as Zussia doesn't tie our house to a jet-propelled kite, he couldn't care less what he's planning.

But I cared. Because Zussia was becoming distant, hovering over a network of dreams that took him back to the days of his muteness. Now I am trained to identify those furtive glances; his tense spring-like mouth that locks all the way up to his nose. And he drinks a lot.

He drinks with Abner. There, I've said it. I've divulged a state secret, and the cassette will self-destruct in ten seconds: in the early morning, before Zussia leaves for work, they down a whole bottle together, and in the evening they raise their glasses again. Night after night we hear their whispers, and the clinking of glasses in Zussia's room, and then Abner staggers out for a square of cheese or a bowl of olives from the kitchen, with utterly heroic obtuseness as he passes the ambush of daggers in Leah's eyes and returns to his lair.

No one talks about this. Naturally. It's not so bad really, and Abner doesn't actually get drunk, he only drinks till his eyes shine and his wits are sharpened. And he drinks with friends, he drinks with people who come to discuss burning issues like the need to educate the next generation, and breathe new life into Zionism, and so on and so forth, all the while casually emptying one glass after another, till Leah screws her mouth up disapprovingly and bites her lip, and tries to sneak the bottle off the table, Nu, she smiles sweetly, and Abner takes her hand, smiling fondly in return; they never yell at each other, those two. What's the matter, Leahleh, he pretends to be amused, what else does a man my age have left, how else can he appease his demons, and there are white finger marks on her wrist.

The more he drinks, the more lucid he becomes, the sharper his wit. His pen lets loose the most dazzling phrases, the most penetrating essays, like a sword cutting through illusion and pretense. But poetry, Shosh, I can only write poetry when I'm sober, how would you explain that; over brandy, he writes his complex reflections on the tension between dream and reality, about the importance of symbols in daily life, reflections that are precise and cruel, packed with a visceral kind of truth that speaks even to cynics.

Only I can't believe him or the pain behind his words anymore. Because now I know that the human inclination to deceive will use anything, even love, as a lethal weapon, and a passion for one person can be translated into the body language of another, nothing is ever in and of itself. Which is why Abner, who has not believed anything in four years, can persuade people to believe everything and use the windy gusts of his despair to fan the embers of dormant hope in others, leading them onward like a zealous robot, and those who see his decisive gestures fail to see his crooked face, but I, into whose room he burst four years ago, trembling and haunted with the elegy he'd written for Chagai, I know that his feverish words and frenetic activity are the last threads with which he can sew up his tattered world.

9

I don't want to get up. There's a long, long way to go. A lot of things to do. I have to do them slowly. I have to sever the connections, the circuits of memory, and neutralize the detonators of explosive words. I'm not getting up. Not budging. I'll just take a peek. From where I am I can hear the soothing sound of water splashing against the barrel. Khilmi is taking his bath and thinking things over, singing me a watery lullaby.

I have to get up and make a decision. Maybe I can still avert the severe decree, as they say. Find some plausible excuse for what I did in Juni, back down, erase it all. Or maybe I really should have gone to see Shosh in Tel Aviv. You'll decide how you're going to handle this, she said. You can either punish me or you can help me. But I ran away, like a child. What could I do when she started saying those things? A week ago I might still have been able to help her. I still believed her then. I had resolved to make her my ever-happy wife. It was my life's mission. How hard could it be to make one person happy, I thought. But now that I know what really happened, I see my life's mission wasn't so easy after all.

Which is why I'm not moving. I feel good here in the cave, with the smell of straw around me; this is where I belong. This is how it's always been. A transparent old man and a grape bower. A place to be quiet. In Juni there are words and people waiting for me, rage and recrimination.

You know, Shosh, maybe this is it, the moment you've been waiting for. You were always resentful of what you called my "malignant optimism." I guess you were afraid I was fooling when I promised you that things would work out for us. When I told you not to worry about the passing clouds, that you and I would always be together, because how could it be otherwise.

Damn me. I've tried so hard to believe, to convince myself. It's only a passing crisis, I thought. Nobody says a couple has to develop along parallel lines. I won't pressure you. The truth of the matter is, we were made for each other. But you had misgivings. Sometimes you overwhelmed me with your love, and sometimes you gave up on me and said, "It's not going to work, Uri. We're too different."

Still, we spent three years together. You made the rules. But how wonderful it was when you let me break them and forgot about your "responsibility to both of us" as the "director behind the scenes." Go on, bullshit all you want. You're just like Abner, always quibbling, always brooding. That's what I thought anyway. That's how I could go on loving you so patiently. I'd never known a woman like you. So damn smart, so scrupulous and confident . . .

Maybe I watched you too closely. I wanted to learn your every move. To be worthy of you. I forgot that everyone needs some shade, a few dark corners, and I was too eager, too carried away in my efforts to skip brainlessly over the middle stages of our relationship, wanting us to be all wrapped up in each other, and to say all the important things.

And then suddenly you bristle and tell me it's amazing how much latent aggression there is in mild-mannered people like me. Or you sting me if I intrude on your silences, and then with a smile—always with a smile—you lay down the "law of indemnity for dreams and fantasies," or turn on me for no apparent reason and say I scorch you with my breath.

Here, Shosh. Accept this moment as a gift from me. I'll keep my distance. There comes a time, you gloated, when our traits and experience combine with a temporary laxness and the residue of fatigue in the veins to lead us into some stinking alley where even you, Uri, might attack yourself viciously and turn into a stranger.

I guess that time has come. Here I am, still spitting fire, but the fire is cooling off. Deep inside there are scraps of old arguments and the debris of obsolete sensations. Are you pleased with me? I've always been amazed by the contradiction in you: you live your life so rationally and prudently, yet you're convinced that it's all going to blow up in your face someday. And I couldn't help feeling sometimes that—how shall I put it—you were actually looking forward to the big explosion so that you'd finally be able to believe in what there was before. Hey, I think I'm beginning to understand you.

The wheel has turned. You used to say I was locking you into my smiling dream. Now it seems that I was only playing a role in yours. It was a kind of game, Shosh, but I had no idea I was playing. Bluff tag, you could call it, and the rules are very simple, child's play: if someone tags you with a lie, you're it, and you have to pass it on. And then there are concentric circles of lies that fade into mistakes and misunderstandings, into alienation and unspoken despair. There are so many ways to evade the truth, and one way, Shosh, is to feign love for a boy you never loved, and to let him die when you tire of your little game; another is to pretend we're living on a map in Khilmi's dream, which is unfurled to the four corners of the earth. Or we could let the donkey carcass asphyxiate the innocent people in the lane, or just stop smelling the stench.

Now I have the words, Shosh. I see myself more clearly since I came to Andal. The breath you said was scorching you has cooled off in the cave and condensed into bright little words. And, Shosh, I didn't come here just to tell Khilmi about Yazdi's death. I came to learn wisdom, to learn his art of lying to the lie. In all honesty.

You see, it isn't his cave, it isn't the lemon tree or the grape bower. It's the lies. It's the blue tunnel into his right eye where words flow like fiction. *Kan-ya-ma-kan.* The people of Andal say Khilmi is an idiot. Maybe he is, and maybe I am, too, for arguing with him. There's no point to these arguments. They're just like my arguments with Katzman. Like two worms devouring each other on a falling stone. And whenever I argue with Katzman about the occupied territories, I answer him through Khilmi, using Khilmi's arguments against him. That way I can slip out between the two kinds of justice.

I ran away to Khilmi. You don't know Khilmi, because by the time I met him, you and I had drifted apart. But maybe I don't know him either; all I know is what he's told me about himself, and the little I heard about him in the village. I mean, did he actually marry all those women and was he really a mute till his brother Nimer found him under a tree in the wadi the night of their sister Naima's betrothal? And was his mother really the most beautiful woman who ever lived in Andal, and did she really have one child after another by that hunter whose name I keep forgetting, or was she just a hag, a *rulla*, which is what they say about her?

Is it true? Is it true? What does it matter? Why favor one truth over another? I mean, let's live by the laws of the underworld. Let people stop pretending that they're telling the truth, and then we won't have to pretend we understand each other, and that way it'll be a lot easier to be honest.

And yet, in all the confusion, there is one thing I can't get over. Your parents, Shosh. Abner and Leah. Your parents are the ones I think of whenever I think of parents, not my own parents. And I don't even feel wrong about it.

Because they took me in as if I had been their own child born to them in their fifties. The only reason I didn't call them Mom and Dad was that you objected.

You can't understand it, can you? You're their daughter, after all, but I find it amazing: parents you can talk to about anything at all, even sex. A father you call by his first name, like a friend, and a strong and cultured mother. And the quiet atmosphere: being able to solve problems by talking them over instead of yelling and swearing at each other. Reasonably, with mutual respect. There aren't many couples around like them, Shosh. Their total honesty; their unswerving morality—how did Abner put it when we were talking one night on civil guard duty—a unity achieved not by mutual submission but through creative struggle and suffering, Abner said.

You probably think I'm blinding myself to what I don't want to see. But it isn't as if I don't perceive what's going on between them. I know that Abner suffers and that he isn't always easy to live with. I've been around them long enough to know when they're hitting each other below the belt, in that decent, elegant way of theirs. I also see Zussia wandering around the house like a zombie, and I'm aware of what Leah thinks of him. But I still believe they've built something strong enough to weather just about anything, even Zussia. Even Abner's drinking.

You may say, you did say, that I'm exaggerating as usual. That it may be easy to idealize them, but that they can be damned difficult to live with. You may say, you did say, that their "decency" is stifling, like the unconditional support they offer the little circle of friends from their days in the Palmach, and that there's something subtly smug and provincial in the way they talk about "the good old days" in Israel. My parents, you say, have been dead since 1948.

But maybe it's your fault, too. Maybe you should have fought back more openly. Three days ago you suddenly blew up and attacked them with a boundless hatred. You said that everything they taught you to believe was an illusion. You said they'd brought you up to live in a greenhouse.

I don't want to gloat, Shosh, but I must admit I have noticed a certain phoniness about you. Nothing specific, just a feeling. It's persistent, though. Like that time in Rome, for instance; remember the fight we had that sent me literally flying to Santa Anarella? The busker at the train station?

Let me remind you. We have all the time in the world now. I went to the men's room at the station and you waited outside for me. A young guy with a beard was playing his guitar and singing. As we were walking away, you suddenly turned around. Like a mechanical doll, that's how you seemed to me then. You told me to wait and you went back and tossed him a coin. And then you tossed him another coin. As you walked back to me I saw that priggish sneer on your face, and I laughed and asked you what was going on.

It's silly to dwell on this now, but there are some incidents that irritate like a pebble in your shoe. I often think back on that fight.

You explained that you felt obligated to pay him because his playing gave you a few moments of enjoyment. Fine, I said with a smile, but why were you so angry with him? "Because he forced the enjoyment on me." So don't pay him and forget about it, that's his professional risk. "You're getting on my nerves, Uri," you said, walking faster. "But just so you'll understand, if there had been anyone else around, I wouldn't have felt obliged. Since there wasn't, however, I had no choice, and I don't wish to discuss it anymore. Why do I owe you an explanation for everything I do? If it's the money you're worried about, let me remind you that I'm the one who's paying for this trip, and if it's the principle that matters, then try to understand that I consider it important to do the right thing. According to my criteria, not other people's, okay?"

And this was where I made my second mistake. I muttered to myself what Abner always says after Leah tells him the story about you and the lost mathematics exam—"I think we'd better get in touch with De Amicis right away, maybe he can use it in his next episode of *The Heart*." And then I added that, luckily, since we were in Italy, it wouldn't be a long-distance call; and then you started screaming at me, saying it was a damn good thing we *were* in Italy, where nobody pays attention when people make scenes in the street.

Yes, maybe it's your fault, too. You've been seething inside for months now. I didn't really want to see it at first, though it was obvious enough. I would look at you without noticing that your face had changed. You always looked like Leah with your straight little nose, your hair, your smooth forehead. I used to love to watch the two of you sitting together. I would suddenly want to love you the way you'd be when you were older, when your wars with yourself were over.

I found you in your mother's face, but in your own face I lost you. How can I explain it: the same features created a completely different impression. Something hard had gotten into you, and I was too dumb to know what to do about it, or where I'd gone wrong. I didn't know who the enemy was. And I turned away so I wouldn't see. I searched for you where you no longer were—in your mother's face.

And I'll tell you something else, Shosh. Another point I wanted to make in the feverish letter I never wrote: I have never felt uncomfortable in your Polish-Russian home. You know that. You know how sensitive I am about being Sephardic. But with Abner and Leah it wasn't a problem, despite their occasionally overwhelming candor.

I believe them, Shosh. I believe your father when he says he's sorry he wasn't born Sephardic; when he hammers the point home, to me and to others, in articles and lectures about the perils of the ethnic problem; phrases like that come through to me over super-sensitive loudspeakers. The slightest tremor of falsity gets registered. I believe your father. Not you. Your voice sounded so mean when you said he was just uttering platitudes. That he never really tried to cultivate the Sephardic Jews in the party. That it was very convenient for him to have me around to flaunt like a medal. And as for some of the other things you said, I simply don't believe them.

Because there's a lot I've had to let go of over the past few days, but I will not give up your parents. I used to think that even if I stopped loving you, I could never betray you with another woman. How would I be able to look Abner and Leah in the eye? Childish yet true. And now I can't look them in the eye because of what you did. It's almost as if I were the guilty party. As if they were the guilty ones. I mean, how could you? We were so proud of you, we trusted you so.

I want to keep them. Not for too long, though. Maybe by the time I get out of here I'll be strong enough to let go of them, too. But not yet, because I'm going through what you might call a reverse conversion right now. I'm learning not to believe. And I'll cling to them the way a pagan clings to his idols even as the missionary baptizes him.

What's this? My ears must be playing tricks on me. A kind of mental reflex. It's Khilmi, outside in his divine pool, crying shamelessly, mercilessly, and I don't think I can stand it.

Time to get up. To go out and touch him. Because he has the answer. I know he has. If only he would take me with him. Bring me into his embroidery. He who knows nothing about my life outside this little village, he who lives in the shadows of *kan-ya-ma-kan*, he will show me the way. I'm not one for murky explanations, as you know. I can only believe in the visible and the tangible. Yet lately, Shosh, there doesn't seem to be much point in the visible and the tangible. On the contrary.

So be it. I, an Israeli soldier, am being held captive in the imagination of a crazy old Arab who will explain what I have to do in order to outwit the lie, and even now, as he rises out of the barrel and shakes himself off like a wet dog, and approaches me wrapped in that hideous robe of his, with the transistor radio dangling from a rope around his neck, I guess what the answer is flickering in his dead eye, an answer I have known and longed for. I just want to hear him say it.

10

Twelve years he was mine. What are twelve years? But with every heartbeat we were *tizen fi libas*, like two buttocks in a pair of trousers. Cheek to cheek, my mouth to his ear, till you might have thought that he sprouted from my body, that I had borne him out of my hump.

For he was the comeliest of all the bastards that scurried around my courtyard. His face was unblighted by dullness and evil; his voice was ever fresh and young, his eye pure and unknowing, his crown without a hair. He was a moon child, sensible of his spirit hovering nearby when he turned to look with a searching, ever-longing smile, though he knew not what it was he longed for. And he was compassionate, quick to cry and easy to appease, and so thin and luminous.

Kan-ya-ma-kan, twenty-two illegitimate sons and daughters lived in my courtyard then, together with three or four women who came and went, and I never asked one of them for a night, or ran my fingers over her skin, for to me they were all like the bearded, foul-breathed *rulla* of the crooked lip when I remembered the lovely sloven, the golden lioness, Laila Sallach, who drew me into her with a moan when I was a blind but deadly arrow hunted in the illusion of her flesh. And the children, the twenty-two bastards, knew not that I was their father-by-law, who had purchased their pregnant mothers and blotted out their shame, and they called me names and ran after me, cursing and throwing stones, the most impudent of them chasing me around the courtyard with sharpened sticks, or stealing up to take the plug out of my barrel while I was inside it dreaming in bubbly bliss.

And before my Yazdi came to me, butter on honey, I endured their taunts in silence, and licked my wounds when they left, as I used to when my father pressed me against the wall with his paunch and flung his rubbery hand at my face, or as I did in the days of my youth, when a grieving father came to my cave, dragging a foolish, high-bellied girl, and stuck a bundle of moist notes into my hand, pleading, Take her to wife, and she will love you and bear you sons, and I asked no questions but replied, She is mine already.

And this continued even after there were six or seven women in my courtyard, and after four of them had left me, fled under cover of night, or in the light of day, and two divorced me according to the law of *khala*, and one dragged me by the hair to a judge in Juni to have the marriage annulled, in keeping with religious precepts, because, she said, everyone knows you are not a man among men. And the people of Andal made me the butt of their jokes and called me "Khilmi el Tartur," Khilmi Cap-and-Bells, and I, playing the fool, drank in their derision, knowing they were not to blame, for someone else was inscribing hatred in their flesh in order to dispatch great legions of pain into the world, but I fooled him according to the precepts of Darius, my patron and redeemer, and rent myself so his soldiers would stumble in, that we might breathe a little easier.

And I hid Yazdi from the women. With the cunning of the timid, I taught him to strip his trousers off in front of them so they would run away squealing and laughing, I taught him to drool from his nose and mouth whenever they wished to speak to him, and to shit in his pants at meals; in short, anything to distance him from others and bring him closer to me. And although we two still spoke together in the infant tongue, I sometimes dared to teach him a word of human speech, choosing a tender word, like "longing," or "caress," a word free of malice, proffered cautiously like a blind puppy for his amusement, one of the few words I could trust not to bite his uncertain hand.

But most of all, I trained him not to laugh. Because throughout my life I feared those who bare their teeth or groan for joy, or slap their bellies in readiness to strike. And therefore I took him with me to the enemy of my childhood and the friend of my old age, Shukri Ibn Labib, the beekeeper. Shukri Ibn Labib belonged to the *zawiya* of Sheikh Salakh Khamis, the dervish of Tarikah, who related the legends of Antar Ben Shadad to the people of the holy city of Jerusalem, and when Shukri returned from there, he vowed he would never smile again, just as Khassan el Basri, paragon of the Bakaaun sect of dervishes renowned for their weeping in dread of Judgment Day, forswore laughter for a full thirty years.

And at first the people of Andal said the cat blinked out of Shukri's eyes, that he had lost his wits among the whirling dervishes of the holy city, but by and by, they grew used to him and his contortions, and twenty-seven years after he returned to us, the cobwebs in the corners of his mouth are still intact, and he roams the streets, bearing his cadaverous horse's head so somberly and cautiously that even I—may ravens devour this blackened heart of mine—can scarcely hold back a smile, seeing him stifle his laughter by such means as carrying pins between his fingers in order to prick his flesh should the urge become too strong, or hearing the throaty breathing he practiced to divert the streams of stolen laughter into dry canals of grunts and groans.

And when Shukri tries to suppress his laughter, so strange and loathsome is the sound he makes that whenever mules are ailing or cows dying, the people of Andal ask whether they have given *Sot Shukri*, Shukri's call, or departed this life with a groan; and it was also said that Zeinat, Giafer's wife, miscarried seven times in a row, old Dahaisheh's spells being of no avail to her until she and her husband moved to another house far from Shukri's cave. And only then could Zeinat carry a child without being frightened into losing it by the piercing cries of the penitent Shukri.

Thus and so I carved in water, thus and so I quarried in the wind. We lived together in a nook of the cave, in the lee of the bower, in the cleft of the terebinth tree, gibbering in our language of birds and shadow-dancing with our fingers over the white rocks. Thus and so he grew between my hands, and the sign never faded from his face but revealed itself each time I looked for it, like a winking of light, like the bite of truth in his little being.

And gradually people left us alone, saying, This Khilmi wanted a son of his own, so he saddled a dog and called it a horse. But what did I care, when I had a babe like any other, sweet and naked, drooling and shitting exultantly, and drinking in the paltry wisdom learned by me through years of silence in the fields, or yoked to a plow, or scratching at hillocks of dung; and holding hands, we lay on our backs like upturned turtles, humming along with our dear ones on the transistor, lovers' songs and harvest songs, and the songs of thieves in the vineyards, and we writhed as if stung by ants with the *rababa* drumming in our ears, plucking the strings of sorrow out of our hearts with the melodious *kanun*, for what was there to say when the sun set just for us, and the sky was consumed like paper on fire, and there was only the honey of music in my heart, and his hand in mine, and it was good.

Kan-ya-ma-kan, Uri is here. He is the latest bastard to come to my courtyard in the dead of night, hidden in the swelling of my anguished heart, and abandoned at the cave door like the dead love child of an aging hope, and I know nothing about him.

Five days he lived with me inside the cave. Weaving his fancies of building a road to Andal and bringing us electricity and setting up a hospital here. And he would sit in Aish's café all day, to breathe in the atmosphere and feel the people—as he said—strewing bewilderment and doubt like Wednesday's child wherever he went, mixing in the conversations of old men and smiling at young girls, speaking openly of unmentionable things, saying that the occupation poisons the lives of both our peoples, or that they, the Israelis, subdued the memory of the continuing lie of our towns and villages, and that we must not abet them, and he spoke of other dangerous things, till people exchanged looks of rage and amazement and the only sound was the bubbling of their hookahs, and they were certain that he was a new kind of spy and that I was sheltering him.

Five days he was with me. At first we argued, then we fell silent, and I found I loved him. He was gentle, like the child who had been stolen from me, with his dwindling smile. And once I called him Yazdi, and he turned to me, his eyes aglow, and the living sign glowed within him, too.

And I began to tell my story. *Kan-ya-ma-kan.* A story within a story and a tale within a tale. The skein of pain rumbled in my belly, and out of it I plucked the threads. And I told him about Darius, my patron and redeemer, and about the fox traps he opened at night to free the frightened animals imprisoned there; and I told him about the locust plague and old Arissa, who used honey to paste sackfuls of locusts to her body and tried to fly above the trees; and I told him about Nuri, the gypsy of Khijaz, who drifted to Andal thirty years ago with a monkey on his shoulder, and the monkey died but Nuri stayed; and I told him about Naffi, who owned the big tobacco fields and diverted all the water from our meager spring to his property, and who was so miserly, people said, he feared to eat lest he shit; and I told him about Mamdukh el Zahrani, who tried to find oil in Andal, and in the end reduced the men to dust and sent me flying like an angel over the teeming village, over the caravan of hills forlornly headed for the horizon, and straight into the voluptuous bed of the lovely sloven, Laila Sallach, greediest of women, *tuta tuta khelset elkhaduta.*

Thus he grew between my hands. At first he tried to resist me. To argue. Like Yazdi, he claimed stories were not enough. That something must be done. But why it should be done by me I never understood. And he begged me to listen to him, and talked about duty, about setting up a bold leadership the Israelis would be forced to heed. Violence is no solution, he declared. But you will have to shake us out of our poisoned slumbers. Talk to us, he said, he yelled. Eventually someone will hear you.

He fought with me. His eyes grew round behind his thick-lensed glasses. And I beheld what was engraved upon his face. The grief that nibbled away at him. And he spoke of Yazdi, smoothing the thin, ruffled hair on his head; though he was not acquainted with my son, he felt a strange kinship with him, he said; he gazed ruefully at the hair caught between his fingers. It's no use, he said, twisting the hair, it's a lost cause, and he looked up to remind me that I had told him once that he would make a wonderful idiot, and then he let the hair drop with a faraway look: Anyone who fights is an idiot, and so is anyone who tries to change things, but that's how I am, Khilmi.

And after that he stopped fighting me. It's a strange game you're playing, he said wearily; and I smiled at him with love, and led him by the hand into the soft mists, into those places of seclusion where great deeds are done, and I told him more about our invisible village, the one we had ceased to visit many years ago, and I told him about the overripe fruit that hung from a branch of the terebinth tree while the guns saluted the betrothal of my sister Naima, and I twirled it like a coin in the maze of lines in the socket of my alabaster eye, and night after night we sat in the grape bower, or in the darkness of the cave, each in his own world, he in defeated silence, not knowing what to do, perhaps he would stay here forever, because he hadn't the strength to return to his own land, and I, in wonder and in secret, and *kan-ya-ma-kan*, there was or there was not, out of his grief and my compassion, out of my longing and the living sign in his flesh, the memory of the youthful Yazdi grew again within us, his smile and his voice, his breath smelling of sage, and the paraffin lamp rustled and danced, and in the curling smoke and the *kan-ya-ma-kan* we lurched into the clefts, into things that were not as they seemed, into the straits only secrets penetrate, not words recited or the serrated leaves of the *khashishat-el-nakhl*, or a crumpled photograph crudely clipped, or sunglasses that dull the living sign, or polite and tired army officers, or rows of stolen youths leaning against the wall before the eyes of their aged parents, or the unctuous gleam in the eyes of the mukhtar, or triple signatures on documents printed in a foreign tongue, or young men shining a flashlight in the face, only Yazdi, Uri, and I, and it is good.

11

It's evening, and the spotlights are going on over court number 3. The boys from the green ward are playing basketball out there, releasing their pent-up energy after a day of schoolwork, arts-and-crafts classes and workshops. The green-ward boys are next to Sigmund's cage, jests Professor Hillman, because the cage—always empty—is near the exit, and the green-ward boys leave us after only a few weeks' adaptation training, though we are experienced enough to know how trying and risky these few weeks can be for them. The approach of freedom brings difficulties.

Now they're out on the court having fun. Stamping like a herd of wild horses, only they don't kick up any dust because there is no dust at the institute, and there's no noise either, because the heavy windows muffle their shouting. I see the four attendants supervising the game from the sidelines. One of them, the stocky one, seems a little nervous. He keeps fidgeting with the cylinder in his pocket. He must be new around here. Needless to say, the ball keeps falling into his corner of the court.

I insert the third cassette.

Maybe now's the time to ask why you're telling these stories, Shosh, and to whom, because you must admit there's something a bit theatrical about the way you sit here talking to an imaginary audience, and don't pretend it's the blind narrator with the flashing magnetic eye you've been addressing for the past hour, when it was Abner all along.

Let me explain. It's quite simple really. Abner is the one who is telling the story, because he's so good at taking stock of things. And he and I know enough to keep a distance from each other, out of caution, not strangeness. Out of respect for each other's silences.

Abner can't possibly conceive of what I've been through. He loves, he demands my unwavering logic and cool lucidity. I know this, so I put on a good act. And I also know that someday, when he's forced out of his oceanic depths, mad with fear, I'm the one he'll soar to with all the might in his fins.

That's what happened when Chagai Strutzer committed suicide. Chagai was a young soldier in the Golani unit who'd been Abner's protégé in the Scout movement. During a reprisal operation in Lebanon, he killed a young boy who was hiding a terrorist in his room. A week later, when he came home to Nahalal on leave, Chagai killed himself. That's when Abner sprang across his grid of grandiloquent convictions and all the way to my room, where he begged me wordlessly to save him.

I'll talk to you, Abner, and you can either answer or vanish silently

119

behind the gray clouds of smoke wafting out of your pipe, throwing the whole room into turmoil.

I see you. I've studied you for years. There you are, curled up in the corner of the living room, staring blindly, listening deafly to friends who are not your friends, like the editors of the party paper you write for all too seldom, they say, or to the Knesset members with their PR people and all the intellectuals who have been trying for so long to recall you from your self-imposed political exile and put you in the vanguard of an exciting new movement, that's what they call it, yes, Avidan, it's true that nothing is more important than the education of our youth and the development of ideological reserves to which you have devoted yourself for the past fifteen years, but the roots are strong and vital, while the trunk—in case you haven't noticed, Avidan—the trunk is rotting and it needs you.

I'm going to talk about you, Abner. Don't be frightened: don't cast shadows into shafts of light. I see you with the people you love best, the youth you face from the platform or sit with cross-legged around a campfire in the open field; then you slump a little and curl your lip before you speak, reluctant to expose yourself to the clamorous audience, and where did you get that baritone sonority in a voice that is so often crushed to a whisper under the weight of words, wonderfully simple words about this country, about passing down the commitments of your own generation to your youthful listeners, who are mesmerized by the sight of the man of mystery, suffering untold anguish, no one knows how much you suffer as you embroider them into this lie, and they believe your platitudes, Abner, they believe you because you demand no more of them than you demand of yourself, a simplicity bordering on asceticism, a rejection of materialism, moral rectitude, severe self-censure, and also—here you allow yourself a strange, modest smile—the only luxury you indulge in, a certain blindness, or "heroic obtuseness," one might call it, in the face of that which cannot at present be changed.

I'm talking about you. Curled up in a chair with your legs crossed, with your haughty intellectual face, your thick glasses and your tight, egocentric mouth, you make me uneasy whenever you utter words like "solidarity" and "concerted effort" with so much conviction no one could doubt your sincerity. Sitting there with your sharp, assertive chin, as you pensively brush away a straggly forelock.

If you knew what I had in store for you, you'd be aghast. Definitions of any kind are anathema to you. You resist definition, you say, with the intensity of living, with your love for Leah and me; and today you would probably add: with drink. And you don't really know me. Ah, that hurts. Because we're such a tight-knit family, aren't we, we three, and Zussia too, of course, and now Uri; we're so close we don't have to speak at all, our thoughts circulate among us like silent melodies.

No, you don't know me. The similarity between us inhibits closeness. With Leah it's easier. You can argue with Leah and hate her. You can tease her and ridicule her: everything's out in the open. I often listen to her with Uri's ears these days, as she goes through her repertoire of pet peeves, her tirades against grammatical errors or the organizational flaws of the blood-bank campaign.

All the same, sometimes I feel fond of her. I can't help admiring her naïve enthusiasm when she's spouting benevolence or soliciting new recruits to her worthy causes, or the tenacity that yields to a kind of quiet disillusionment and hardens into despotism. There is something almost soothing in her compulsive rituals, the incessant prattle she scatters to the wind like chicken feed. In fact, she's rather predictable, and it's easy to find your way back to the truth from her lies. Now's my chance to contemplate her at leisure: the way she frets over you, Abner; her meanness toward Zussia; her well-intentioned organizing of readers for the blind, day trips for the elderly, and toy drives for children's hospitals, not to mention the campaign to help the family that was injured in a bomb explosion, or the couple whose home was burned down. Still, I can't help wishing she had a real friend, someone she was really close to. Then maybe she would be able to forget.

She's always saying, We're so much alike, darling, you're so levelheaded and rational, and you stand up for your rights just like I do; how hard it is to look after Abner without his noticing; do you think we would have survived if not for me? And then she starts in on her list of reproaches, that Abner never asked to be compensated for all the gas he used on party business, that he turned down the post of cultural attaché in London, and that he brought Zussia into our home, but she never mentions his drinking.

It amazes me that once I thought we were a perfectly ordinary family, and therefore perfectly happy. It was almost a handicap for someone like me, working in psychology. As a student I used to worry that I had no personal suffering to contribute to our class discussions. There were no upheavals in my history, our family history. No animal passions or towering rages. We were such a normal family. Only I never enjoyed the normal rights of an adolescent girl: the right to rebel a little or scream at you, or to complain the way my girl friends did that my parents were too strict, too critical. How could I argue with you about clothes or boys when you were always so enlightened about everything, so progressive. Everyone has a right to his own mistakes, darling, everyone has a right to his God-given *mishegas*, and we don't believe in coercion, we believe in setting an example, that was how you answered me, smiling tolerantly when I alluded to the conflicts I was feeling. Do as you like, Shosh, said Leah. When I was your age, I ran away from home and joined the Palmach, so don't expect me to stand here now and tell you to be home by ten.

And that's why you haven't asked any questions for the past three days, you don't want to intrude; it's enough for you to know that I said I want to stay with you until Uri and I clear things up between us, and I can't forgive you for that, especially not you, Abner, because underneath that paternal act of yours, you really like him, and I used to be amazed whenever I heard you talking to him, not like you talk to your colleagues, I mean talking or—more to the point—listening. And laughing, too. God, you actually laughed, with pleasure and relief, until you remembered to purse your lips in that obnoxious way.

I admit, you surprised me, you and Leah: you took him in with a wholeheartedness I'd never seen in you before. I knew he didn't stand a chance of passing one of your nonverbal examinations. That's why I was so eager to bring him home, I was hoping you'd disqualify him straightaway. Because I couldn't make up my mind; I wanted him, but I knew it wouldn't last; yet I was frightened, frightened of my need for him, my need for his gentle firmness and the still, small voice that leads him innocently out of himself and toward others. That's why I brought him to your doorstep and waited for you to decide, without a word, of course.

And against all the odds, he stood the test, whistling softly as he passed under your tightened reins, his hands in his pockets. You seemed relieved, but soon you set up new hurdles for him, made to order: He'll be a wonderful husband, dear, he's so kind and gentle and he has such a thirst for knowledge ("thirst for knowledge" had replaced "education" in the old criteria). And within a short time, a few weeks at most, you promoted him into the family.

Who would have believed it of you, Abner: you followed him approvingly, as though he were clearing a new propitiatory path for you. And maybe you were drawn to him with the same vague longings that mesmerized me, till I stopped believing in what he promised.

I remember how you used to wait for him to return from night school so we could all eat together, and how you listened patiently to those long-winded accounts about his classes, or his friends, or the new cabinet he and Zussia were planning to build in the bathroom; and you caught his excitement when he described the beautifully matching colors and the measurements of the cabinet from here to—whoops, sorry! And I glance at Leah, maliciously searching for the familiar flash of rage in her eyes when Uri toppled the glass, but I saw no rage, instead she said, That's okay, Uri, I'll pick up the pieces, it was an old glass anyway; and Leah was the one who helped him study for his grammar final whenever she could spare a moment; and you laughed till you cried when he told his jokes, even though he always ruined the punch line, and even though no one had ever told a joke around our house without impunity before, and you softened, you were utterly transformed by his presence, and Leah said to me with a giggle, You know it's wonderful, Shosh, we feel like young parents again, only this time we have two children, and we're more in love than ever, though we can't understand why.

You loved him intently, as though you were studying a rare animal or investigating a criminal whose cover was a little too pat. Let me give you a cruel description of the way you love: you never simply love, the person you love has to pass muster, to be on constant guard against stupidity, because as your mother will tell you, Shoshi, life with me is perpetual war, and I respect her for fighting back so well; but Uri tricked you, Abner, Uri with his gentle guilelessness destroyed the iron grid of your convictions, your unsuspected contempt for your fellow man.

No one would guess it, especially not Uri. He idolizes you, you know: he thinks you're a humanist, imagine! Forgive him, he isn't like the rest of us. He doesn't know how to see behind appearances yet. He has only just begun to learn the art these last few days. He wishes he could be a man of convictions like you. He wishes he could be quick to forgive. He wouldn't believe me if I told him the truth, that anyone who knows people the way you do and can describe them with such deadly precision in a taut little sonnet can neither love nor forgive. I don't know what you used to tell Uri when you and he were on civil-guard duty together, but he always came back in raptures about you, and I had to listen to the same stories over and over, to your pithy sayings and your brilliant predictions, only I wasn't impressed, because I knew you were falling apart; that on the other side of the picture he painted there was a terrifying darkness and a loathing for everyone and everything, my brave humanist, or maybe it was self-loathing, and terror of your power over people like Uri, and come to think of it, Abner, maybe it was your hollow empty words that sent Uri to Juni, to fight a terrible war.

The game is over. The green-ward boys are leaving the court, taking off their sweatshirts and swatting each other as they walk away, hugging their naked bodies that send up steam in the cool night breeze. Shadows form and vanish under their beautiful muscles. The attendants watch after them from a distance. They're keeping a low profile, as ordered by our benevolent Hillman, except for the new attendant, who doesn't notice that he's moved in dangerously close. But nothing happens: they go to the locker rooms. Did my indulgent interlocutor hear the invisible whip? Did he notice the sigh of relief from the frightened audience? Is he too blind to see that someone somewhere is marking a chart: Such and such a group played basketball for one hour. The blue-ward boys are being herded down to the locker rooms already. Someone's calling for attendants over the loudspeaker. Six of them will supervise the blue team.

I was talking about Uri. About how you waited for him to make his first wrong move and show his real face, but the more you took him in with your squinting eyes, the more clearly you saw what we all saw, what Katzman had seen the first time he met Uri, and what I saw when I threw myself at him, and you wanted Uri to be better than you are, so you could believe in a trusting, gentle fool like him, so you could hope to find forgiveness.

It was as if we'd been expecting him all along, like the last words of a story. Leah says laughingly, We really have gained a son, haven't we, and in her voice I hear that at last you have found the joy that children bring, because Uri is the son of your old age, and there's no mockery or jealousy in my voice now, I mean, some people just aren't cut out to be the children of their parents. Uri was never the child of his own parents, but he can bring Leah to her knees with a loving smile or a thoughtful gift. You and I, on the other hand, were always admonished to avoid the pitfall of small gratuities, though it's all right for me, Shosh, she would say, because I get such pleasure out of buying you gifts; or sometimes when Uri is in the kitchen washing the dishes on Friday night after dinner, singing off-key, while we three are joking around as we set up the board for our weekly Scrabble game, and Zussia snores in front of the television set, we suddenly hear Uri's ecstatic voice and our eyes light up, and we become a family.

And now, dear tape recorder, beloved diary, my father stealing by behind the little glass door, it is time to ask the obvious question:

Leah loved him, and Abner loved him, and even Zussia loved him, but what about me?

There's no need to answer that. Things will start to clear up now. The question is no longer relevant. The important thing is to find out whether Uri can provide a logical answer to what happened to me, but Uri is not the answer.

Nor is Katzman. He isn't what I thought he was—the person who could translate me into a foreign language. He was, at best, the steam that reveals the invisible ink spilled on the page long ago. You don't know him, Abner. You met him once, and said someone ought to tell that young man not to confuse sarcasm with wit. And I was sorry he hadn't been able to overcome his awkwardness when you met, because if he had, you would have realized how similar the two of you are. But Katzman was defeated. Defeat, he says, is the natural state of man, which is why nothing seems worth fighting over, and why your urge to struggle only brings a compassionate smile to his lips.

What an egoist he is. I detested him for that. You're a real egoist, I used to say in the tone we Avidans reserve for deserters, people who leave the country and are only out for themselves. But he's a different breed of egoist, Abner, he's a career officer, and he volunteered to serve in Juni and gave up his studies at the university and fought in the worst battle of the last war, and he doesn't have a home, he lives in a rented apartment the army provides; maybe he's an egoist in the way he keeps to himself and doesn't give out any personal information; and he doesn't believe in change, he's empty and unable to love because he doesn't want to open himself up to pain. You would call him a coward, but that wouldn't make him any less disturbing to you.

He wouldn't let me love him. When he told me that he'd never loved anyone, I didn't believe him at first. I should have understood, even then, that what attracted me to him so fiercely might eventually suck me in, use me up, and leave me scorched and him unsatisfied. He wouldn't let me love him. I humiliated myself in my attempts to tap a few drops of intimacy. But he turned us both into wrestlers and immersed us in bitterness, and I said, I don't understand why you're doing this to me, get out, get out of our lives, I begged, but he didn't believe me and he replied, It'll get easier for you once you stop pretending, once you understand that you can't expect more than you're willing to accept from me, and where we are, you and I, we can allow ourselves the grace of sincerity and self-forgiveness. Now do you understand, Abner? He was saying that I, too, am unable to love, that I can't even let myself feel desire, because pleasure frightens me as much as pain, and that I'll never know what it is to be human until I let myself go like an animal, and I bore it in silence, and clung to him because he was my lie, and all the while I kept laughing inside that here I was, having a love affair, but without any love, and in the end, even a stolen embrace turned out to be strife, so little wonder, Abner, that I brewed a draft of fury and remorse so potent it killed the boy.

No, Katzman isn't the answer. All that's left of him is a weak pang, like a wave of dissipated passion brushing the sand. And I also know that I'll go back to him one day. I'll go back and sleep with him again and again, without desire and without regret. Does that amaze you? Do you wonder which one of you I take after now? This is very important to me, Abner: have I managed to induce a barely visible quiver in your right nostril, do you know me now as I really am?

You're shocked. You sense the threat in what I say: Is this my Shosh? Is this my fair and luminous sonnet? Or perhaps only a bad dream, and where do I come into it, why does she torture me like this, forcing me to look again and again at her open wound.

But I don't care about your suffering anymore, Abner. I've always been conscious of it, however difficult it was to discern. Now you say you hid it from me as long as you could.

But I carried it within me for years before you broke down. Always, Abner, even that day long ago when you and Leah called me to your room, looking proud and secretive. I remember how tidy the room was, there was even a white cloth on the table that winter day, the day of my fifteenth birthday, and I remember the odorless narcissus in the vase, and the two of you giggling together, and then you said this year you would let me in on a little secret, and you'll never know how hard it was not to think of your suffering, Abner, how powerful the lies I invented to keep a step ahead of anything you and Leah might hurl my way with a proud and happy smile.

Listen to me now: I'm waking from a long sleep, and I have discovered that while I was out somebody used me as a battlefield; but who was fighting in me, tell me that. Help me, Abner.

Only you can help me. It's your forgiveness I want. No. Stop. I still don't know how to ask you for it. My pride holds me back. I have a long way to go before I can explain why—if you forgive me—you too will find comfort. I'm getting close to something, but it still has to be deciphered. Now press Record. Tell him a story. Something about Uri. He likes to hear about Uri. Tell him, Scheherazade.

Tell him about Uri, the boy who never ceases to amaze; he amazes us with the things he notices, and the things that hurt him, and the way he throws himself into such a variety of trivial things. Even the language he uses amazes us, the high-flown words that come out of his mouth, or the painful expressions that force their way out of him, like pus. You miss him. Go ahead and say so, stop being evasive.

Here's the story of young Uri and the pigeons he kept at boarding school. Naturally, that was the only job they could find for him there. They put him in charge of the pigeon coop, and Uri loved those twenty pigeons. Correction, I didn't hear this from Uri, I heard it from Katzman. Lovers often speak of the one they betray, to bring him closer and force him to share the burden of the lie. Katzman said Uri's classmates decided to roast a few pigeons at the end-of-the-year campfire. Uri's protests were in vain. Most of his pigeons were taken. He was inconsolable. He couldn't understand why anyone would do such a thing. A few weeks ago, for instance, one of the officers in Juni attacked him; they hate him there, not surprisingly. But the guy who beat him up told Katzman afterward that Uri didn't offer any resistance. That's so typical; after everything he's been through, he still can't understand why anyone would want to harm him.

But I wanted to talk about the pigeons, and I've changed the subject again, because I saw the little shadow of pain under Katzman's eyes when he said, "Go figure him out," sitting there naked and white. "He declared a hunger strike, only he didn't really declare it, see?"

No, I didn't see any more than you did. Because we two are so different from him. Uri whispered a hunger strike, he didn't declare it. He was instructed to by the still, small voice. And now you ask me why, which is just what I asked Katzman, and what Katzman asked Uri. "It was too personal," Uri explained illogically. For four days he fasted and drank only water, but no one noticed anything, till one day he fainted in the middle of gym class, so Katzman told me, and I suddenly felt a terrible urge to cry, as I do now.

I'm all right, Abner. I'm cool and collected. This woman may never write poems, but she will lead a sane and levelheaded life, that's what I overheard you telling Leah once. And now it's obvious that I will go on living a sane, levelheaded life. I will be very careful. I will turn Mordy's tragedy into a corrective experience, if I may borrow one of Hillman's pet terms, and I will be more in touch with myself. Amen.

And now I'll stop for a moment. I'll turn on the little desk lamp and go over to the window. The blues are out on court number 3. Pretty soon I'll hear faint noises from the dining rooms of both wards, green and blue. It's a cool September evening, and I close the heavy drapes behind me, leaving a crack for the moon to rise through, if it so desires.

A lovely, quiet moment. The internal dust storm is subsiding.

I want it to be beautiful. I want the lines to flow into each other; I want the lamp to embrace the round glass ashtray and create a sickle of light. Nothing but curves around here. Katzman said I'm developing an aesthetic neurosis, with a lot of aggression behind it. Of all people, he should have understood. He who spent his life listening to muffled hints and silent voices; because it isn't beauty I'm concerned about, but the things that happen in silence. The wonders of simultaneity. Invisible streams that change course when they hit the magnetic field of our thoughts. Forgotten information lurking patiently in wait. The gleam from Viktor Frankl's glasses has formed itself into the shining emblem of the institute on file number 3; that package wrapped in brown paper has been lying behind the bookshelf for the past two and a half months; and Uri and Katzman are both in Juni now. Did Uri understand the things I told him? Did he hear them? His eyes rolled up when I let out the venom that was trapped inside me for a year. He nodded his head right and left in mounting agony, and maybe I should have been more careful with him, maybe I should have given him a chance to recover, but his sheeplike calm was so infuriating I couldn't leave him alone. Did he grasp a single word of what I was saying to him, though?

His lips turned white, and he ran a trembling hand over his head and let it drop to comb his comical beard. How pitiful he looked, this man of mine, how badly I needed him then, but he just got up and ran away, forgetting to close the door, and I see him in my mind's eye, blind and stupefied, as the frost spreads inside.

12

My appetite is normally the best gauge, I think, and now I can eat again. But Khilmi isn't hungry. He pushes two hot pitas my way and watches me with a strange expression on his face. Najach was here a few minutes ago, but she ran off as soon as she saw me. I thought she was beginning to get used to me the last time I stayed here. Guess I'll have to start from scratch. Khilmi tastes the porridge she brought for him. He picks up a spoonful of soil, sprinkles it on the porridge, and stirs. He eats without relish, though. His mind is elsewhere. And I don't ask. He's already decided for both of us.

How pleasant this is. Now that I have my appetite back, my body is beginning to wake up. I know that everything is going to be okay.

It's got to be okay. From the village come sounds of women's voices and donkeys braying. The sun is bright and the sky is blue. This time last year the rainy season had already begun. And now it's like the middle of summer. Khilmi wants to prolong the silence. The transistor hums.

I try: "That's Fayruz singing, right?"

"Right."

He turns the volume up a little. Ah, Fayruz of Lebanon. How my grandfather Amram loved to hear you. He used to warble along as you sang.

Khilmi says, "It's only the tune I like. Do you hear the words she's singing?"

I listen. "*Zah'rat el-madaen*," she sings, "flower of towns," "*el jaras wal'awda fallatukra!*" I look up at Khilmi and smile. "Ring, O bells of return." Khilmi bows his head and listens. At the end of each phrase he raises his head and mouths the words: "I will not forget you, Palestine; sorrow surges through my heart. I am an eagle in your shadow. I am your flower, the rose."

He says, "The guilds of reciters admire her greatly. From her they learned to declaim like poets. That lovely voice, Uri, sent hundreds of boys to their deaths. When Abdel Nasser was President of Egypt, she sang to him: Ask for one *fedayee, ya* Nasser, and you will have thirty million *fedayeen*," and Khilmi switches off the transistor with an expert flick of his chin. Then he pushes his bowl away, still full of porridge. He leans back against the lemon tree.

"Uri?"

"Yes."

"I was thinking."

What is this sudden gaiety, this tingling of anticipation I feel? Is it his tone of voice, or the way he folded his hands, the way he looked off, the blue vein over his blind right eye swelling and throbbing? When Khilmi was a boy, there was a terrible explosion in Andal, in the menfolk's square, that killed all the men except for him. The shock waves sent him soaring over the village like a bird and he breathed the air of roses, the spirit of freedom. That's my favorite story. The first time I heard him say "the air of roses," I remembered Katzman telling me about his father and Ariosto's epic about the fool who went to the moon in search of the hero's lost mind, where he, too, breathed the starry air of roses. Khilmi says that, as he flew, everything he had ever seen was erased from his right eye, and the blind pupil fell back into his skull, or maybe it was his hump, where he can still put it to use. Why am I remembering all this now? I just feel happy, I don't know why.

I can't see Khilmi's face anymore. He tucks his head between his shoulders and the old beret hides his features. Only his hands move, as though scavenging for words on the ground. His hands are old and wrinkled, the color of dust, but his fingertips are soft and pink, like a baby's. He told me once that the first time I touched his hand, it made him shiver. He realized he'd been waiting for me to come. And that gave me a funny feeling, as if I, Uri Laniado, had no reality apart from the force that had brought me here to him, the will that willed me here from afar, from the distant future; last time I was here, I didn't like the feeling. It disturbed me, and I didn't understand it the way I do now. Shosh would probably say he's pulling colored scarves out of my ear as I stand here grinning. All I know is that if someone had told me a person like Khilmi existed I wouldn't have believed him. We don't really know much about the Arabs. We've buried them beneath our contempt.

"I have been thinking it over, Uri," he said. "Not today, no; perhaps the day my Yazdi was stolen. But things are more urgent now."

"Yes," I answered, though I wasn't exactly sure what he was

talking about. A strip of tin on the hillside was flashing in the sun and blinding me, but I didn't want to cover my eyes. I wanted to look at Khilmi.

"I am a very old man," he said. "Beyond my life, perhaps. Beyond shame and insolence, too. Far beyond."

I still didn't understand. He reached up, picked a couple of lemon leaves from the tree, and crushed them carefully. A low-flying crow cawed at us, and Khilmi gabbled at it familiarly, "*Kazab, kazab, kazab*" (Liar, liar, liar).

"And because of that, I am entitled to ask the world for what I want," he continued. "Even if I know that what I ask is impossible." I was becoming lost in these riddles. He sounded like a character in Ariosto's epic where wishes somehow come true. Or like Don Quixote triumphing over the windmill. But I couldn't tell Khilmi that.

"I have an idea," said Khilmi, rubbing his arm. The fresh scent of lemon burst into the air. I said I didn't understand what he was saying. He stopped rubbing himself and stared at me, amazed that I hadn't understood by now, just as he had when I asked him why he painted the red graffiti green. Suddenly I saw that his eyelid was twitching. He pushed back his beret and said, "Don't be angry, Uri. I will only ask them to withdraw by dawn from the territories you conquered in the war." And he looked away, rubbing so hard I was afraid he would hurt himself.

I approached a little closer, trying hard to hide a grin, and said in my most serious voice, "And what if they refuse?"

"I will kill you."

We both fell silent. He switched the transistor radio on with a nervous jerk of his chin, and Fayruz was back again. He switched it off. I was astounded. I wasn't afraid of what he wanted to do to me. On the contrary. It's sort of hard to explain, but I was almost glad. Shosh has always claimed that I'm "emotionally dyslexic," referring to my inappropriate responses. Could be.

I asked him casually if he had a weapon.

"Yes," he answered. "Yesterday I took one of Yazdi's pistols."

"And do you know how to use it, Khilmi?"

"Yes, in my youth I watched Sha'aban the hunter shooting."

I felt a little sorry for him. Before he mentioned the hunter I had a crazy feeling that he really was offering me a kind of solution. I was that eager to believe he had the answers. But Sha'aban was only a figment of his imagination. And so was the pistol. I felt terribly let down all of a sudden, as though we'd missed our chance. I didn't know what was happening.

"Maybe you would like to bring it to me?" asked Khilmi.

"Where did you hide it, Khilmi?" I asked him, the way you might ask a child about a buried treasure.

"It's in the *ta'aka*. Next to my mattress."

I got up slowly and walked into the cave, where it was cool and damp. I felt myself zip shut inside the moment I entered its shadowy realm. It was like saying goodbye to someone. And then I felt calmer, but also heavy with fatigue and emptiness. I rummaged through the niche beside his mattress. There were stinking socks in there rolled up with a *ba'aya*, and everything was very damp; I found a string of prayer beads I'd never seen, and wondered why I had to meet up with someone as weird as Khilmi and why I was always getting myself in trouble, but then I took it back, because I really do like the guy. I was in such suspense as I searched through his bundle that a gun was bound to materialize. And it did. I felt a shock as I touched the cool metal. Abner once said that every fiction has a core of absolute truth. Truth. I picked up the little black pistol, of a kind that Katzman has in his display of captured weapons.

I weighed it in my hand and thought of other things. Mostly I thought about disappointment, a disappointment that could make Shosh's kid feel so vulnerable he wanted to die. Or Katzman saying he's never disappointed because he never has expectations. And even Khilmi, who had always believed in nonviolent resistance, was losing faith now. And I started to feel sad and helpless. I believed in Khilmi, and I believed in Shosh and Katzman, too. I believed in everyone. Okay, that's enough, stop thinking about it. Let's get out of here.

I gave him the gun. He wouldn't look at me. There was a pungent smell of lemon in the air that shone like an aura around him. I noticed that smells and colors were extremely vivid all of a sudden. I sat down beside him. Slowly he ran his finger over the handle of the gun. I found to my surprise that I could see the tiny whorls of his wrinkled fingertips. Everything seemed big and distinct. Khilmi glanced at me obliquely. He never looks you in the eye, but casts his eye in the air, as it were. Sometimes, though, he stares at you like a flashing camera. Or a whiplash.

"I mean it, Uri," he said.

"You mean you're going to kill me? Me?"

He thought it ove., licking his dry lips with his pink tongue, and said, "I have no quarrel with you, Uri, but you are the one I have to kill. Forgive me." "But you know I—that people like me, we're your only chance of changing anything around here." "You are just an excuse, Uri." His voice trembled. "You are merely a mandrake plant for all the others." He squeezed his fingers, never letting go of the gun. "You are dangerous to me, Uri, because you keep the lie from growing."

"Isn't that a good thing? You said so before."

"I was wrong. Now I understand. The lie is using you, Uri. Your people are using you. You must not break the lie and you must not hinder it. It must grow big. There are three things that can't be hidden: love, pregnancy, and death. And to these I would add lying. To make sure that everyone will notice it, a lie must be allowed to grow. Until the eye cannot miss it. Now do you understand?"

The dazzling strip of tin on the hillside was blinding me, and my eyes filled with tears. But I gazed steadily at Khilmi. I felt my strength ebb fast and suddenly I knew it was all over. And then I had an idea, belatedly as usual: why didn't I just tie the donkey carcass to the jeep and drag it to the administration building? Surely Katzman would understand when he smelled the stench. Smells are something else that can't be hidden.

I said to Khilmi, "No one will take you seriously." I didn't want to say "your threat" or "ultimatum," because that would have complicated things even more. Then, with a glint in his eye, he said, "You will convince them, Uri, won't you?"

I didn't answer him. He was crazy. Did he think I was about to die for his ideas? But beyond my anger I sensed something else, a faint pecking Katzman once described, like someone breaking out of a shell. I shut my eyes and tried to block out the disturbing sound. But Khilmi asked again, so I answered, too loudly, "You'd better think of something else, Khilmi, because no one's going to listen to you."

Khilmi said, "I have thought about it, but there is no other way. Of course I do not wish you to die, heaven forbid." He peered at me to make sure I believed him. "You are like a son to me. I do not wish you to die, I only wish for my outcry to be heard in this village of sheep."

"By whom?"

"No matter, no matter. My people or yours." His lid trembled like a leaf and he said, "Perhaps I ask the impossible, but no matter.

139

Do not try to talk me out of it, Uri." He was silent for a moment, and then added, with a sly kind of smile, "Besides, you are in my hands now, and they will not soon abandon you."

"Ha," I laughed. "Plenty of people would be glad to see me gone." My voice sounded higher than usual to me. For a moment I really believed Khilmi's solution was the most logical one under these crazy circumstances. Then I came back to my senses. "It won't work, Khilmi. You can't do things like that. They'll think you're crazy. Even I'm beginning to think you're crazy. Come up with something a little more realistic, like a demand to meet with a journalist or an Israeli officer, or . . ." My voice trailed off so unconvincingly I shut my mouth.

And Khilmi said nothing. He looked exactly as he had earlier on when I told him about Yazdi: the same strain, and the blue vein throbbing on his eyelid. I wanted to shake him, I wanted him to hear me, but suddenly I understood and was afraid. He was watching me now. I was the one he was breaking down into splashes of color and points of memory. Uri Laniado, dissolved in the juices of *kan-ya-ma-kan*.

Damn me. For a moment I wanted to fight him and flee, but then I felt the tickling of an insidious joy inside, the excitement I had known while searching for the gun, and I wasn't afraid anymore, only nervous in a way that was new to me, and when Khilmi shuddered and said in quiet amazement, as though it had just dawned on him, "I am going to have to kill you, Uri," I realized he was right, that he really did have to do it, and that the same idea had been growing in me for a long time. It had brought me here this morning, in fact, just as it had brought me to Santa Anarella.

Katzman, I thought wearily, I'll have to tell Katzman about this. This is the kind of thing that interests him. He's a stalker of change. A hunter of malleable reality. How tiring it must be to be so perceptive. Never a moment's rest. Ah, all these words and ideas coming to me suddenly, and this feeling of sweetness: I'm beginning to understand: I was wandering around too blindly, or too wide-eyed, maybe. I saw only what I wanted to see. And that, too, is a facet of the art of lying. That's how I was able to love Shosh, and believe Katzman, and that's why I came to Juni with him. In fact, I was lying all the time without knowing it. But that's not the same as what's happening to me here with Khilmi. There everyone was lying to me, while here—how shall I put it—we share a lie, which changes it from a lie into a more tolerant kind of truth. Because a lie one person alone believes in is a cruel and deadly deception, while a *kan-ya-ma-kan* like mine and Khilmi's is full and vigorous, with many layers and a strong lemony fragrance and an earthy color, and the texture of Khilmi's cracked hands holding the gun, and it's so vivid I'm beginning to feel faded by comparison, which is rather pleasant, actually, and relaxing, too. You can rest and let it do the work for you.

And then Khilmi sighs sadly, and I am so startled I turn color. My short-lived happiness is over. What's happening to me? What's happening to you, Khilmi? I have to encourage you and help you, and tell you that we are the greatest *kan-ya-ma-kan* in Andal, and I'm not in the least bit angry with you for what you want to do to me. Not at all. This isn't anger. Maybe it's passing sadness. A pang. And I long to touch your hand again, but it might be too painful for you, so just remember that neither of us is to blame for what's about to happen, because we are—let's say—two slaves who are being forced to kill each other in the arena, like in *Spartacus*, and we shake hands lovingly before the inevitable battle, pitying the savage crowd that clamors for blood, but I won't hurt you, Khilmi. Not me.

Khilmi laid the gun down on the ground between us. I didn't have the strength to reach out. A column of ants crawled by, great big red ones, and they made their way up the gun. Khilmi's hand rested quietly at his side. Crumpled lemon leaves peeked out under the handle.

Then I said, "I have to go down to the car to get my field radio."

Khilmi gave me a long look. He seemed to be weakening and asked brokenly, "Why? Why are you going now?"

I said, "I have to tell somebody I'm in your hands."

"But why do we have to bring them into this?" he said.

I understood what he meant, in fact, but I was being stubborn. Because otherwise the whole thing would be pointless. "No, no," I said. "We have to tell them about your—ultimatum."

Khilmi looked up at me. "And will you come back afterward? Will you, Uri?"

"You have to trust me, Khilmi," I said. "You of all people."

Khilmi thought a moment, then shook his head.

"Come back soon," he said. "I will wait for you."

13

By noon Katzman was back in his office, upbraiding the mayor of Juni for his townspeople's crimes: a demonstration at the girls' school the week before, the stoning of an army patrol in the el Sa'adia neighborhood, and finally, the events of the previous night. The two youths killed when the soldiers stormed the house were from Juni, and there was a somber atmosphere in town. Katzman had a sensitive mechanism inside for gauging violence. Minutes after arriving in any strange city he could detect how much violence was latent there. Rome had been utterly unbearable for him in this regard, whereas in Santa Anarella, where the earthquake razed many houses to the ground and killed hundreds of people, he didn't feel the violent vibration at all. Today, though, on his way through the empty streets of Juni under curfew, Katzman felt the seismographic needle ready to jump out of his skin.

Katzman hated these scenes: the mayor belonged to the old generation of leaders in the territories. He was a heavyset man, blunted by pressures on every hand. He had no dignity left, and his voice sounded feeble and faraway. A month before, one of his daughters had been killed by a stray bullet during a demonstration at her school. This had unwittingly turned him into a hero in the eyes of the townspeople. His eyes sank lifelessly behind two swollen purple sacks of tears.

Katzman said, "Those boys hid out all day in Juni. We won't lift the curfew till we find out who sheltered them."

The mayor spread his hands in helpless supplication. "But you questioned their families all night long. Nobody sheltered them. They must have come from a neighboring village."

Katzman replied: "As for the families, you know the law as well as I do. The el Kadimi house will be demolished and the other family's house will be sealed up. It's too crowded around there to use heavy explosives." How enlightened and humane we are, reflected Katzman sardonically. Rationalizing with Uri was one thing, but when he was forced to mete out heavy punishment, the justness of his decision was no comfort.

The mayor spoke fast. His voice sounded so faint that Katzman had to lean over in order to hear him. He pleaded with Katzman to spare the houses. The loss of sons was a big enough blow to these families. "Have you no children?" he asked Katzman, and without waiting for an answer continued, "Can you not understand their heartache? These two boys were honor students, one of them was planning to study at the university in Oman. Now they are dead." Yes of course, he knew why they were dead, but the families had suffered enough already. "A family that suffers such a calamity loses the very cement that holds it together. I implore you, do not add to their grief."

His large weak face was quivering. Katzman knew the man had spoken of his own pain, to which they had never alluded in conversation. It was always the same exchange between them, in the same tone of voice. They were like two rooks facing each other across an empty chessboard, with only one move possible. They could never catch up with each other.

He despised such scenes. He hated everything to do with his position as governor of this dried-up town, veined with hostile alleyways, feigning mildness under a veneer of dust. This was the most disagreeable post he'd ever held in all his years of army service. The year before, he had planned to leave the army, in fact, and finish his master's degree in Arabic studies. He had painted himself a tempting picture of the pleasures of civilian life. The trouble was, he hadn't really been a civilian since the age of eighteen, except for a few brief interludes for his studies and vacations. Shosh had criticized him recently for being too damn scared to leave the army, and he answered her, without conviction, that the army framework, once you accept it, leaves you with plenty of freedom. But she claimed he was confusing freedom with anonymity, and she was right in guessing that freedom made him apprehensive. Katzman was loath to admit, even to himself, that it was Uri in his curious and carefree way who had introduced him to a distinctly civilian magic, a down-to-earth kind of freedom. But he had met Uri only after becoming stuck in his failure at Juni.

The mayor was staring at him, and Katzman realized that he was waiting for a reply. He answered him peremptorily in the negative. The old man wrung his hands. There was a big ring on his finger, set with a heavy black stone. Now he had to keep pushing it back down over his wizened knuckle. Katzman felt a passing sympathy for the man. "I'll have the curfew lifted for two hours this afternoon, so you can buy food," he added quickly. And much to his surprise, there was no pathetic gratitude in the mayor's eyes. Because the mayor was crying.

Katzman leaned back in his chair and studied his fingers. He heard the heavy, hollow sobs and didn't dare look up. He imagined himself on campus now, hanging out in the cafeteria or the university library, dressed in cool civilian clothes, or footloose in the city, watching the sea. For one deceptive moment, the possibility seemed tempting in the extreme. He should never have agreed to come here. To be exposed to the kind of violence the mayor was subjecting him to now. A year and two months ago the previous governor of Juni had retired from the army after a heart attack; someone at regional headquarters remembered the way Katzman had taken charge of the refugee convoy from Kalkilya after the war, and he was called in for an interview. At first he refused. Then he set conditions he was certain they would never accept. Then he was tempted. It was almost a relief to find out that his release from the army would have to be postponed for twelve months.

That was early in July of last year. Katzman had planned to take the month of August off for a trip to Europe and he decided to go through with it anyway. He spent the four weeks before his trip in a little office at the Judaea and Samaria command, learning the principles of military law and devoting much thought to the stamp he wished to put on his governorship in Juni.

Katzman had never held any clear-cut political views. Politics for him was merely a stage play without any bearing on real life. People involved in politics disgusted him, and he felt contempt for Shosh's father. Nevertheless, he did respect Moshe Dayan, his defense minister, and tended to agree with his views on the conquered territories. Dayan was more a military figure like himself than a politician. But there was something else, too. After his experience in Kalkilya during the war, Dayan had called him in for a briefing which very quickly and surprisingly had developed into an almost intimate conversation, by the end of which Katzman was in command of a camp in Nablus for refugees from Kalkilya. Katzman fancied he had managed to catch some of Dayan's more elusive characteristics and fit them into a definition that bore a great resemblance to himself.

He was grateful to Dayan for putting him in charge of the refugee camp. As he sat in a narrow office of the Judaea and Samaria command, the mellow feeling he had known in Nablus came back to him in flashes. He had been full of love and goodwill there, without the attendant feelings of self-betrayal and danger. The defense minister himself, he was sure, had been party to his assignment as governor of Juni.

Throughout those four weeks Katzman did what army personnel and Israeli civilians alike were normally prevented from doing—he carefully and honestly considered his attitudes toward the conquered territories. He didn't hate the Arabs he lived with side by side. He didn't love them either. He didn't want to go on occupying their territories, but an independent Palestinian state, fueled only by its hatred for Israel, was pretty frightening. Katzman found himself thinking in concepts that were familiar to him from the newspaper. This left him with a sense of banality, but it also roused his curiosity and led him to the depressing conclusion that there was no way out. The sense of absolute truth he remembered from Nablus made him kick out against his own self-declared defeatism: perhaps there was some way out after all. He would turn "his" city into a living experiment. The occupation would be humane. With the grace of sincerity and trust—here of all places.

Only after he arrived in Juni did he wake up. He detested the town from the moment he entered it in uniform. It was strange: before, during his preliminary visits, Juni hadn't seemed especially hostile. Katzman had brought with him three of his officers from the armored corps, plus Sheffer, whom he liked, to mediate between himself and the permanent administration staff. He eagerly assumed his duties like a tough glove protecting him from the inhabitants. All the promises he'd made to himself faded away the first time he stamped his name and new rank on an order to blow up a house. He wouldn't allow himself to remember the modest hopes he had cherished before his arrival in Juni. For not only did his exposure to the misery and injustice around him fail to elicit the feeling of goodness he longed for, it bored right through him. The townspeople of Juni barely recognized him. He rarely left the administration building. Even the local council members and the heads of villages he met with futilely once a week couldn't understand him. Sheffer, who knew him fairly well, felt he was persecuting himself, though he hadn't quite figured out why. Guilt and resentment had eroded Katzman, and he suddenly realized he was approaching a dangerous juncture. That Juni was telling him a story he had to heed. His conflicts were tearing him apart. He would work it out later when he got out of here, he rationalized. But there was a nagging fear that underlay his excuses, like a pea under a dozen mattresses, that maybe there is no justice, maybe there can never be. The concept of justice was probably insidious. He'd always felt that, only now he was condemned to take part in some cruel experiment designed to verify the hypothesis. He was governor of twenty-five thousand people who didn't want him there. And by his efforts to maintain the framework of their daily lives, by bringing in another bus line, repairing the bumpy roads, obtaining uniforms for the junior soccer league in town, or whatever, he had only managed to compound the injustice, and bind it even more tightly to the groundwork of reality.

And that was why, somewhat dizzily, full of conflict, and despising himself for doing so, he had asked Uri, the friend he met during his miserable trip to Europe, to join him in Juni. That was something else he would have to work out one day. When he got out of here.

The mayor blew his nose with a loud blast. His eyes were a network of little red veins. Katzman noticed with some surprise that his face had lost the expression of defeat. Crying had restored the mayor's dignity. Had even given him a certain advantage over Katzman, who was not inclined to cry. He asked permission to leave. No doubt he would have been surprised to learn how close he had come to Katzman's locus of sympathy. Katzman wanted to give a final word of warning, but just then a young second lieutenant walked in and whispered something in his ear. The mayor studied Katzman's hands, which were clenched all of a sudden. He waited trembling, as though his very life were in the grip of those strong dry fingers. Katzman said, "Something urgent has come up. Our meeting is over," and hurried out of the room, leaving the astonished mayor staring at the empty military governor's chair.

On his way down the stairs he ran into Sheffer, who already knew. Sheffer said, "That idiot had to go and make trouble." Katzman gloated secretly. Sheffer didn't like trouble. His life was a picture in sharp, clear colors. Katzman was one of the fuzzy, unpredictable elements in his life, and since he couldn't hate him, he had no choice but to tolerate the frustration and bewilderment or, alternatively, to feel mildly condescending.

"Who gave you the message?" asked Katzman. "The jackass himself," answered Sheffer. "He called in on the field radio he ripped off from Yuval this morning. Amos was on radio duty and took the message. Here it is." Sheffer rummaged through the pockets of his oversize trousers. He fished out one bandage, several service cards for an army vehicle, and some gas coupons; Katzman rasped irritably. With an astonished look on his face, Sheffer pulled out a key chain threaded through a bullet, a dogtag in a small khaki shield, a lottery ticket, and a hard brown wedge of old pita bread. Then he found what he had been looking for. He handed Katzman the crumpled note.

Katzman read. Instinctively, he glanced at his wristwatch. Sixteen hours until dawn tomorrow. He stared off into the distance. The situation was beginning to unfold certain dangers and possibilities, like a colorful bolt of cloth unfurled in the souk. Someone cleared his throat. The mayor was coming down the stairs. They moved aside to let him pass. He was trying to stand tall. His eyes were still red. They waited for his footsteps to die down the lower corridor.

Katzman said, "Get out there on the double. Take a squad from the stand-by company. Take the whole company, in fact. Seal the village off. I don't want any leaks. Do it quietly." How convenient military language was for such occasions. Sometimes Katzman felt it was his mother tongue, having lost his Polish and never mastered Hebrew.

Sheffer asked, "Should we break into the house?"

"Are you crazy?" Katzman's aesthetic sense of reality and its meanders had clearly been offended. Sheffer shrugged under his gaze. "Wasn't yesterday's raid enough for you?" asked Katzman somewhat ungratefully. Neither of them had mentioned it till now. The tradition of silence between them dated back to the Six-Day War.

They went down to the operations room and searched for Andal on the map, Sheffer's thick index finger running beside Katzman's talon. There it was. Katzman said, "Deploy your men at the foot of the eastern slope. The old guy lives up on the hill. Have you ever been there?"

"No."

"Hmm. Well, when you get there, you'll see for yourself. There's an old man named Khilmi who lives in a cave up the hill. An unpaved road runs down to the village—" Katzman quickly reconstructed Andal: the stony square with its dinosauric iron skeleton, the café built out of tins. In conclusion he said, "The hill overlooks the village. It's an eagle's nest." They smiled. The only written matter Sheffer cared for, outside of newspapers, was detective books, Alistair MacLean's in particular.

"How many people do you reckon are up there?"

Katzman shrugged. Uri's message had said, "Am being held hostage," and "being held" implied a number of people. Katzman suddenly recollected the old hunchback cackling as he danced around at the reception. It seemed he was a fairly isolated and unpopular figure. But you never know. And meanwhile, for the first time since he heard the news, Katzman realized that this was actually happening, and that he and Uri were very much involved in it. Inside him a little voice cried out, It's happened, at last!

But he was still bent on resisting the new intimation. "There could be several of them up there," he said. "We can't take any chances. Round up the villagers for interrogation. Take Yoni with you." Yoni was the administration's intelligence officer, and Katzman was counting on him to blunt Sheffer's zeal. Then he realized: "One of the kids who was killed last night was Khilmi's son." It amused him to follow Sheffer's surprise at his knowledgeability. "So there's a possibility that the house—the cave, that is—was used as an arms cache by the boys who were killed, or maybe their friends. It could very well be that they left for Juni directly from there. Be careful, Sheffer." Sheffer pouted. For a moment he looked like a defiant child. "Careful" was practically an insult to him. He asked, "When will you get there?" wondering why Katzman seemed in no hurry to rescue Uri.

Katzman reflected. It was hard work mastering his impulse to hurry off to Andal. But he knew he had to control himself. To let the whirlpool subside till he could see the bottom again. "I'll come later," he said. "You leave now."

And when Sheffer left, Katzman called him back: "No shooting and no attacking, Sheffer. I'm the one who gives the order to go in. Got that?"

"Got it," answered Sheffer, and left.

Katzman turned away from the map. He informed the operations officer on duty that the curfew in Andal would be lifted for two hours, beginning at 2 p.m., and then he went up to his office on the third floor. He sat at his desk and thought. He had to report on what was going on to the higher-ups. There was a fixed procedure for such things. Katzman reached for the phone, and thought better of it. In any case, he had already made up his mind to take charge of the situation himself. It was a private matter between himself and Uri, after all.

A quarter of an hour later, Katzman heard the squad leave. Their voices were usually soothing to him, but now they sounded loud and shrill. Something was about to happen. He lay down on his bed and let the vestiges of the past few days fly around him like feathers.

At first he thought it was excitement, but it was fear flowing through him, as though he were a hollow pipe. He quickly brought his knees up to his stomach to stop the flow. The decisive moment was fast approaching. And something was about to change irrevocably, like an unfertilized egg of failure dropping out with a ping to begin its journey toward the sperm of knowledge. Katzman's eyes were half open under his swollen lids. He waited. He had always been a stalker of change. In change he could find, for a blessed moment, the vivid meeting point between past and future that made a man unique and unrepeatable.

But it saddened him to glimpse his inevitable separation from Uri. He was never wrong about these things. He'd known since this morning that he had to send Uri away from Juni, and now it looked as though their parting would be crueler than he had imagined. As always, he was surprised to discover how vulnerable and defenseless he really was; although he claimed to have no real ties with anyone, he could still feel an occasional shock of loss.

14

"**T**ired, *ya* Uri?"

"No, no. Just thinking."

"Thinking about what?"

"Italy."

"What's Italy?"

"What's—? It's a country. In Europe."

"You were there?"

"Yes, and I'm here because of what happened to me there."

"What happened?"

"There was an earthquake."

" 'And it happened that the earth did quake—' "

"What?"

"In the Koran, there is a sura about an earthquake. What happened to you while you were there?"

"I don't feel like talking about it now."

"All right."

Between my hands he grew. I prepared the foods he liked best and breathed in the smell of him, like jasmine, while he cried *Ya ba, Ya ba*, tugging at my hair, and drumming on my hump, and I watched over him like a mother, the gentlest of mothers, and that is why in Andal I was known as Um Yazdi, Yazdi's mother.

And as he grew I saw I had not been wrong, he was a sign and a promise, and I set to teaching him all he would need to know, for it takes much wisdom to bide through life as an idiot, to blink away the old world and shape the passing new, and laugh at everything.

Kan-ya-ma-kan, he was twelve years old when war came. The comeliest bastard who ever toddled through my courtyard, tiptoeing sideways, warbling as he emerged from the shadows, more slender than the tendrils of the vine. A gentle child; a secret child. All mine. Mine.

Kan-ya-ma-kan. There was a war, and planes flew overhead. Yazdi stuck his fingers in his ears and ran screaming to me, to hide under my robe, his eyes hazy with fear. Then the soldiers arrived in their green uniforms, driving through the village, searching high and low, without a word to us. And at night the men would gather at Aish's café, shouting with fear and humiliation, and I was there among them, and Aish shouted with us, but when we paid him for the coffee and the hookah, he gave us change in small pink notes, and Naef's car had a new blue license plate from the Israelis which he was ashamed for anyone in the village to see, and Nuri el Nawar rode home from the holy city of Jerusalem astride a donkey laden with sacks of almonds, and instead of the samovars with cock-shaped stoppers, the silent music boxes, the red gum balls, or the fountain pens that reveal a naked woman when you turn them upside down, he brought us transistor radios with many different buttons, or perfumes with a scent like kerosene, or rare potions that turn into a semblance of soup the minute you pour boiling water over them, or soaps of every hue that smelled like fresh paint, or wonder-working drops against catarrh, or a green paste to cleanse dishes in place of sand, or beguiling toys like self-moving tanks, and dream dolls with golden hair that say Imma, which is what Israeli dolls call their mothers. When Nuri-monkey-face rolled into town on his sack-laden donkey, reading the pages of the Jerusalem newspaper, its headlines screaming red, I could guess what was written there.

"Uri?"

"What?"

"How old are you, Uri?"

"Twenty-eight almost."

"Yazdi was seventeen."

"I'm sorry I never knew him."

"He was a lovely child. He was an idiot."

"So you told me."

"Once Shukri Ibn Labib told me to take him to the doctor in Juni. I refused."

"Didn't you say I'd make a good idiot, too?"

"You are one already."

Kan-ya-ma-kan. There was or there was not. New colors and new sounds. And the flashing dark glasses worn by the officers, and their smooth language, its sounds gliding over us. And their coolness. Not hatred or fear, but coolness. No touching, no meeting of eyes. Even when they come to survey our fields or count the villagers, they think it unseemly to talk to us, except to say "Get out!" *"Rukh-min-hun!"* or *"Yalla etla!"* to the children swarming around them; and when they visit Aish's café and lean back to study the pretty pictures on the walls, our eyes meet over the copper tray in Aish's hands, and the shiny mouth of the hookah, and the tin walls painted green, but otherwise there is no meeting of eyes and no touching.

They are very careful, and we are afraid and suspicious of what they may be plotting against us in their audacity. Because why is it that they pay Aish for every cup of coffee they drink, and every baklava cake they eat at his café, what kind of occupation government is this which so far has not coveted our wives or put a single mukhtar or member of the wandering guilds to death, and why do they disdain us so much that they walk through Andal singly and unarmed, and why does their disdain bring us low and their cool contempt surround us like sticky webs, so that we wander among them as though stricken with falling sickness; and thus we gradually cease to argue with each other, we cease talking about *siasa*, politics, because we are afraid perhaps, but also because all this has passed beyond our understanding, for how is it that men of thirty years are suddenly as if grown old; and then slowly the soldiers leave us to ourselves and gather in the cities, Juni and Nablus and Hebron, and rarely do we notice them anymore, except when they ride by in their green jeeps or when we hear the rattle of their metal birds searching for prey in the night.

And what was happening to my Yazdi? I was no longer afraid. I remembered the days of the Turks and the days of the English, I had seen the Emir Abdullah and King Talal, and King Hussein, whose soldiers slaughtered us without mercy, and I knew what I must do. I stopped visiting Aish's café and kept away from the *maq'ad*, where the men gossip like girls, and I returned to my cave, now free of wives and bastards, and once again I plunged into the darkness of my divine pool, now rotting at the spokes; that which has no image cannot be touched by others. He who solves his dream need fear no disappointment. From Darius I learned this. And the land I envisaged can never be conquered, so come with me, Yazdi, let us draw back into the cloud of mystery and delight, back to the one who—Yazdi?

"Did you call me, Khilmi?"

"What? No, no."

Silence, and then:

"Uri?"

"Yes."

"When I told him about you, he broke into tears. He spoke to me in the infant tongue."

"So you said."

"I forget so quickly now. He hated you. He said I was collaborating with you."

"But he knew what you thought, didn't he?"

"He knew. But they made him into a counterfeit idiot. Uri?"

"What?"

"Did he suffer? Did he die suffering?"

"I— No. He didn't suffer at all. No."

He grew between my hands, but once when I peeked between them, I saw he was no longer there. Then I burrowed into myself, digging with my hands and feet, shouting his name, running like a bat through the maze of clefts, banging my head against the rocks, and the flickering of light I saw did not form the sign I remembered in his face.

And suddenly one night he returned, feverish and glassy-eyed, and began telling me that he had been to the *maq'ad*, that he had *lekhek azzalam*, come of age, and was therefore entitled to sit with the men and serve them coffee and rake the smoldering coals, and oh, the things they spoke of there, oh, the songs they sang, Yussuf

Makawi played his *rababa*, running down the string with a tallowy stick, and Samikh Hudhud—his head as hoary as his namesake, the hoopoe—took out a *darbeka* made of clay, and oh, *Ya ba*, an expectant hush fell over us, and out of the silence, out of the fever I felt here and here and here, came a thick thread of silence that stretched into a hum, and our wondrous Yussuf opened his mouth and sang.

And he sang of the prophets Noah and Mussa, and he sang of our beloved Job, whom Allah struck down time after time, yet still he would not curse Him and therefore we, too, should be long-suffering, and everyone clapped to the rhythm of his song, and I, too, *Ya ba*, clapped with them, and why did you never tell me those beautiful stories, who is this Allah of whom I never heard from your lips, *Ya ba*, and what is the *sumud*, this long-suffering which draws sighs of approval and grief, and why do you never sit with the men at the *maq'ad*, listening to the buttery tales told by your childhood friend Shukri Ibn Labib, about Antar who loved Abla, and about the twenty-eight stations of the moon, each the seat of wondrous deeds, and though I listened long, *Ya ba*, I never heard a word about Darius, your patron and redeemer, nor Sha'aban Ibn Sha'aban, nor Mamdukh el Zahrani, who searched for oil, nor did they mention you yourself, *Ya ba*, and I began to fear lest you, too, had never been, and hurried home to you, and praise be to Allah, here you are. You are angry now, *Ya ba*.

"Khilmi—"

"Yes?"

"I was accused of collaborating with you. Someone hit me because of it."

"Yes, I have also been beaten several times, mostly by the boys. Violence always breaks out first among the defeated."

"Yes, it's like that with us, too."

"You too are defeated."

"Let's not talk about us. Tell me more. Tell me about your loves."

"Darius loved me."

"Your patron and redeemer."

"And Laila Sallach, too, of course. You smile."

"How long did you live with Darius?"

"Seven years."

"Or a week, Khilmi? Or maybe a minute?"

"Why do you say that?"

"I was speaking to the people in the village. No one remembers him. Not even the graybeards. They told me they found you under a tree one night, and that you suddenly began to talk. They said you invented Darius."

"As I invented Yazdi?"

"Maybe."

"As I invented today and what tomorrow will bring?"

"I don't know."

"Who told you I invented everything?"

"The skinny old beekeeper."

"Ibn Labib? Don't believe a word of it. He is a dervish."

"He's known you since childhood. He knows everything about you."

"Memory lies. That is not how things happened. They happened very differently. Sit comfortably, Uri, and I will tell you."

Kan-ya-ma-kan. And throughout that time my father never mustered the courage to kill the hunter and the adulteress, for Sha'aban Ibn Sha'aban was the man, and the most beautiful women of the village were given to him with a wink, and my father explained to anyone who was willing to listen that Mother was not to blame for the eternal flame in her womb, and that he loved her all the same, and that he would take her back and love her when she was cured of her madness, and three months later Sha'aban Ibn Sha'aban sent her away, just as he always did when she became pregnant, and he packed his tent and animal trophies and his bottles of powdered hyena testicles for potency, and jars of raven blood and jackal claws, and headed for Mt. Lebanon, to kill the Syrian bear, and my mother returned home, shameless and high-bellied, to give birth to my sister Naima, or perhaps to myself, *kan-ya-ma-kan*, and my father bore his shame in his heart, and his body swelled with grief till his short legs could barely carry him, though he ate almost nothing, and his face sank into the gleaming folds of endless sorrow, and later, when there was no more room, his grief poured over into his right arm, which came to resemble an elephant's shank.

That was the arm he used to strike me when he pinned me against the wall. His face grew even rounder, and tears of rage would fill his eyes. It was only with me that he suffered such torment, because everyone else walked by him as though he were not there, they looked right through him and puffed cigarette smoke in his face, and Nimer, my elder brother, took over as head of the family while my father was still alive.

And though I was nearly grown by then, and could have avoided the arm and pinched his behind and run away, as did the younger ones when he assaulted them, instead I would shut my eyes when he approached, steering sideways through the door, and I let him come at me panting slyly, surprising me with a triumphant yelp, and I bit my lip as he pushed me against the wall, cuffing me and puffing and sweating, and I crouched motionless till he stood up, wax-white, recoiling from me as from a nightmare, and then waddled off.

Kan-ya-ma-kan, he was a whale that found its way to a rocky shore one evening, and struck it with one small fin, fending off the wind with the other, till at length he reached my terebinth tree, breathless and blinded with tears.

He did not see me lying there, tethered to the tree; my brother Nimer had brought me out earlier that day to hide me from the wedding party sent by the groom to Andal for my sister Naima. And now the betrothal paper had been signed in the village—I heard the women wailing for joy and smelled the meat roasting—and I could not understand why my father was not among the guests.

But he saw nothing, heard nothing, and smelled nothing. He was working hard at something I did not understand as yet: hanging a loop of rope from one of the branches of the terebinth tree. All I remember is this: he was no longer frightening. I knew he would not beat me anymore. And he was somehow a little less miserable, too. He saw me and was not startled. He was far away from me. He only said, Ha, it's you. And turned to the rope again, jumping and grunting with despair, trying to put his head through the loop, it seemed, or was he only playing?

Then he began to search for a rock to stand on, and he circled me, groping on the ground and stumbling, still trembling with rage, till at last he collapsed at my side, almost touching me, and cried out brokenly, Oh, Khilmi, Khilmi, I do not even know how to die.

And it was only then I understood, and a sharp blade ran through my bowels and I screamed. And there was a strange taste in my mouth, sweet as blood. And with the tip of my tongue I touched the soft airy substance, and there was suddenly a cunning in me that spread through my body and soul like rot through an apple, and a powerful malice was born in me, and blood burst in my eyes, painting visions: here was the elephant arm about to strike, and Nimer, leading me like a sheep to the terebinth tree, and I beheld strange sparks darting through the sockets of my eyes, the cleft-footed demons, my mother on hands and knees as she faced the karakul; and rifle bullets flashing through the thickets by the Jordan, and the king of beasts sliding into the silvery water, and the evil-hearted children, when they stuffed my mouth with live grasshoppers, and the vicious girls who would not let me near the well and overturned the bucket on my head and beat it with sticks.

That is when I opened my mouth and heard my voice speak for the first time. It said, Do not cry, *Ya ba*. And I ached because the words tugged at a prickly rope stretching from my mouth to my belly, which was so tightly coiled that to this day I have not reached its end. And my father looked up, wax-white, and said, You are speaking, child, you can speak, *ya walad*, and we did not know. And he laughed and looked at me again: We thought you were a cur.

He held out his healthy hand to me, and touched my chin with great gentleness, and gazed bewilderedly into my eyes. Then suddenly he pricked his ears and his lips parted, and a great peal of laughter cascaded out of the cavern of his mouth. And I felt a fine fear and a downy joy that made me light-headed, and there were hives stirring within me, fingers touching me everywhere, and like a dervish I was lifted up from here to there, not knowing what this pleasant torture meant, till suddenly I was cleft in two, and a strange cry broke forth from behind my knees, from under my arms, and a trembling giddiness took hold of me, and my father stopped shaking and stared at me in fear, but I did not tell him, even when my trembling subsided, that in his presence I had known the greatest miracle of my childhood, and for the first time in my life, I laughed.

And again I fell silent. The branches of the terebinth squeaked in the wind, and distant sounds of joy wafted across from the village. Never let them know that you can talk, my father said to me. Be cautious. And he, too, fell silent. From time to time he peered up at me in amazement, lying limply with his arms outspread, and I felt his remorse and the hesitation coiling in the darkness beyond him.

I could not leave him like that. His misery was sliding back to keep him alive; to kill him with slow cruelty. How could I let it hurt him like that after he had touched me so gently. After he had let himself laugh with me. Because it was this misery I had to fight, it was this which had put Sha'aban Ibn Sha'aban to death in his tent, on his bed, bloated and stinking from a liver ailment, while the hyenas skinned him alive. That is what had been killing us all for centuries, bowing us to the ground and crushing us till we called it kismet; and that is what turns men of thirty years into graybeards and keeps our youth from dreaming what people everywhere are entitled to dream. And therefore I crawled out through the darkness, stretching the rope tied to my leg till I was under the dangling loop, and then I brought my knees up to my arms and arched my hump.

I could see him upside down between my hands and feet, his round face turned to me in surprise. And the *rababa* bow began its dance of death across the taut dark strings of my hump. There was no hatred or evil in it, he simply had to die this way, just as Sha'aban Ibn Sha'aban had to die in a lion skin, just as Uri will die by my hand today.

He stepped closer, his shoes clicking against the stones, and set a hesitant foot upon my back, and I made my body rigid for him and my heart soft with the love that welled up in me suddenly and with the sorrow of parting so soon after we had met, and he grasped the trunk of the terebinth tree and leaned the full weight of his humiliation and despair upon me.

And suddenly—at first I thought it was the evening dew on the back of my neck until I realized it was his tears—I was jolted by his fall and left lying on my side, and by the light of the sickle moon I saw the image of the heavy fish floundering in silence, and the gleam went out of his eyes, till the immense body stiffened and relaxed, as if an unseen hand had finally let it go, and then he dangled in the breeze like an overripe fruit, and the stench filled the evening air.

I had forgotten that until this morning. Until Uri came and told me my son was dead. I was like a tent slashed by a knife. The flimsy fabric shrieked and the world flowed in. Under the terebinth tree I lay, swaddled and small, seeping into one faint point within me. Breathing life into it, panting wild with fear. I killed him. I—who am weak, who am tethered by my leg, who am mute—I killed him. For a moment there was darkness, black and thick. The hand that let my father go was waiting still, brushing against me with fingers of fog.

And then, *kan-ya-ma-kan*, the mournful fruit sailed through the night sky, colliding with the joyful sounds that came from the village and my last moment of loneliness here. A last spark of grace was kindled in me to light up my death and I fell upon it sobbing. I had to redeem myself. With both hands I pulled at the endless rope. A torrent of words flowed over my fingers, a pale light flickered within me, and out of the darksome clefts came Darius, the Greek hermit, my patron and redeemer. *Tuta tuta khelset elkhaduta.*

15

It was too hot and glary outside, so Khilmi and I have come into the cave and sprawled out on our mattresses with the gun between us. This isn't my normal fatigue anymore. It's different. Like being homesick for nowhere in particular. Even if I get out of here, I won't have any place to go. I can never go back to Shosh. I'll never be able to look Katzman in the eye again. I can't go on living in Tel Aviv, knowing that behind the veil just a stone's throw away a million human beings can see me with their eyes shut, in their dreams and in their lies, in my land of reveries, as Khilmi calls it.

Khilmi isn't much help either. He lies there curled around his iron core as if he's afraid I might pounce on him any minute and take it away. But I won't. Not me. For that I'd need a lot more hope and desperation. All I can do meanwhile is loll here like an invalid, too weak to care if I ever get better.

I can't create something out of nothing, the way Khilmi does. I only recognize emotions like hope and desperation when I'm deeply into them. For instance, I was ecstatically happy on those wild nights between Naples and Brindisi. There was a kind of justice there that swept me away. It's hard to explain. All I remember is the thrill I felt, like a missing plane that is suddenly met by the flashing beacons of home base. Death had come so close to life, almost touching it, and I breathed in the heavy air between them. That was a year ago. A year ago, my God! August '71. Shosh and I were supposed to be flying back to Israel after our two months in Europe. I wasn't ready to go home just yet, but Shosh couldn't wait. She had two unfinished cases at the institute. The treatment of the delinquent boys had been going well when we left on vacation, and she had scored a success. I, on the other hand, had nothing to go back to Israel for except my final exams at night school, and the hassle of looking for a temporary job; or maybe it was something else, I'm not sure. Maybe after two months alone with Shosh, I needed a little time on my own.

No, really, she was great. I mean, without Shosh's planning, we wouldn't have been able to do half the sightseeing we did. And without her confidence we would never have gotten anywhere. Still, there were times I caught an undertone of inexplicable rage in her voice. My slowness was beginning to exasperate her, and the way I stared at passing scenery from the train window, or the way I'd plant myself in front of a picture at a museum, while she had already photographed the entire exhibit with her eyes. It was so petty, I know, but sometimes I could hear the still, small voice saying, "You are alive now." This isn't a dress rehearsal anymore. This is it.

And maybe that's why I didn't feel like going home. And then, in Rome we heard the news about an earthquake in the south, and the Red Cross was calling for volunteers, so I jumped at the prospect and suggested to Shosh that we go to the south for a week before returning home. Shosh wouldn't hear of it. She thought I was trying to provoke her. She said her patients had been waiting for two months, and that they were more important to her than some anonymous village in southern Italy. It was the worst fight we ever had. Her anger was a little frightening. In a way, this was the coda to our fight about the guitarist at the train station. She berated me for my lack of ambition, for being a bum, and said it had taken her all this time to discover that I was extremely superficial, and she'd had to use a great deal of self-restraint to keep from telling me so. We were standing—I remember it exactly—on the lawn of the Piazza Vittorio Emanuele beside the white statues covered with red graffiti. Shosh was seething, and I waited silently for a chance to get a word in edgewise. Before you start worrying about some stupid village, she screamed, why don't you learn how to worry about yourself; she said my charm had faded for her, and worst of all, she didn't believe in me anymore, she couldn't believe in that vaunted do-goodism, maybe I was only a do-gooder because I didn't have the guts to hurt anyone. "There's no such animal, Uri," she said. "Not as far as I'm concerned." And she turned and walked away.

That's how we parted. She went back to the hotel, and I wandered around downtown Rome, with no money in my pocket (she had the wallet as usual), unable to remember the name of our hotel. I did consider running after her, but decided against it. When I looked up I saw a big hospital across the street, and suddenly I knew what to do.

At the reception desk of the hospital I was nabbed by a young doctor who didn't understand a word I was saying. He rushed me through the corridors and into his truck, and away we drove. I don't speak Italian and his English was terrible, but the whole way he kept trying to explain that I had arrived just in time, and I answered, Yes yes, though I didn't know how right he was, and he said something about supplies and medicine, and I understood that we were on our way to the airport to load equipment. But I wasn't really listening to him. I was too overwrought, trying to figure out what Shosh had meant. She had never spoken to me that way before. We arrived at the airport. Someone peeked into my knapsack and stuck a tag on it. It was evening by then and I wanted to get this over with and go back to the hotel. A tall man with high shoulders and a blond mustache asked me to come with him. I felt a little like a lost piece of luggage. He wore a Red Cross band around his arm and walked very fast. I didn't, and he kept turning around and yelling at me in Italian, but I couldn't catch up no matter how fast I walked. Then we arrived at an airport minibus with some people who must have been waiting for me, because the moment I got in, we took off across the landing strip. I looked around. Everyone seemed pretty jittery, glancing at their watches all the time and up at the sky. The man with the mustache was our driver, too, and he kept frowning at me in the mirror. Maybe because I didn't seem involved enough, or because I wasn't wearing a watch. (Some people find that annoying.) It was a stifling, hot evening, and I was hungry and depressed. The people around me, the Red Cross people and the altruistic types who'd volunteered to save their fellow man, didn't look especially friendly. Eventually we came to a landing strip where all the mosquitoes of Rome swarmed over us. I told myself I would be back at the hotel in an hour. Why was there such venom in her voice when she called me a do-gooder? Suddenly everybody woke up. A heavy plane approached from the distance. A big bulky thing, a C-130, I think it was, but I'm not good at airplanes. There was a red cross painted on its side. The landing lights went on, and people started waving at it from the ground. Some of them wore Red Cross bands on their arms, and the crosses were crossing each other.

I was thinking I shouldn't be so lethargic when there were victims in the south who needed every bit of my strength. I vowed to try my hardest. And then the plane landed and turned its tail and slowly opened up. The tall guy with the mustache shouted orders and everyone started running. And so did I. A wave of intense heat scorched my face. For some reason the plane didn't shut its engines down. I was swept along with everyone else through the hot air and the deafening roar of the engines, till we reached a small landing platform and boarded the plane, and everyone shouted as if they were having the time of their lives. I looked around for the supply crates we were supposed to unload. It was dark inside but I could see the people buckled to their seats. They beckoned to us cheerfully and shouted things we couldn't hear over the noise. Suddenly it seemed to get even darker. I heard a propeller screaming in my ear, and before I knew it, someone pushed me down on the canvas bench; a moment later the plane took off for the south.

Sure, now I can laugh, but at the time it was really scary. I writhed and screamed under the safety belt. Everyone started to stare at me, so I stopped screaming. I curled up miserably, and I think I fell asleep. Sometimes I do under stress. I woke up with an incomprehensible feeling of relief. The plane shuddered all over. I looked around. Most of the people were Americans, some of them really old, though there were also one or two student types and a couple of girls. Three lamps gave off a pale light. I unbuckled my safety belt and stood up on the seat. Through the porthole I could see nothing but darkness. The plane was flying into the night. Over the sea, perhaps, through open space. I was suddenly happy, something in me piped defiantly: I made it. I've escaped. I'm going to meet new people. Something is about to change.

When I sat down again, I smiled at the guy sitting next to me. He smiled back. Someone opened up a can of beer and passed it around. For the first time in my life, I think, I liked the taste of beer. Someone asked my name, and a moment later someone else shouted, "Hey, Uri." I was starting to feel better. The flight lasted two and a half hours. It turned out that most of the people already knew each other. They had a sick-joke contest, and I laughed so hard I almost cried, though I didn't always understand the English or the humor. The older guys started reminiscing about other places, about a plague in the Sudan, an earthquake in Turkey, a mine disaster in Rhodesia, typhoons in South America, floods in Romania, refugee camps in Vietnam, and famine in Nigeria; there was a priest with us who had served at the Albert Schweitzer hospital in Gabon, and one of the girls had been with Mother Teresa in India for three years. (In Calcutta, I believe.) When they heard I was from Israel, they all said, "Hey yeah, Abie Nathan!" and opened up another can of beer to drink his health and mine. It was a flying party of world-catastrophe alumni, and I was there among them, laughing my head off, still unaware that the tickling in my stomach was happiness trying to break out.

Kan-ya-ma-kan, we took off from Rome on a sultry evening, and by the time we reached the makeshift terminal somewhere in the south, the second phase of devastation had already set in; that's what the experts explained to me. Rains flooded the region, and the wind raged. I'd left Rome in my jeans and high-school T-shirt. At the airport someone threw me a blanket so I wouldn't freeze to death. Everywhere there were people struggling with massive tents, or running around in all directions, bowed against the wind and calling to each other. I shivered with cold and excitement. I didn't know exactly where I was yet, but I knew this was where I belonged.

I couldn't account for what was happening to me. It was still a few days before my meeting with Katzman, before he told me that truth is more than an equation that matches words with reality, that truth is a natural force. That's what he called it: a strong, vital force that requires nurturing and protection, though like any other force in nature, it's utterly despotic, and can split a man down the middle in its haste to be translated into action. At the time I suspected it was this force rather than the Italian doctor from the hospital in Rome that had sent me flying there. And now it's obvious to me that that's what sent me here, Khilmi, to your cave. To the blue hollow of your eyelid. To this pile of jars and pots.

There in the south, the refugees slept in the flooded fields and stole each other's rations. They tossed the pills that were handed out to them over their shoulders, yelled like maniacs in Italian, and copulated all over the place. We stopped noticing after a while.

Volunteers from around the world were digging in the ruins, bringing up bodies and dismembered corpses. Before long I stopped staring and vomiting. Twice a day we dug a mass grave and covered it as quickly as possible. At night the dogs drove us crazy with their chewing. I behaved with a crudeness that astonished me, but at times I was extremely emotional and felt a strong urge to cry. Truly. Truth and love were the only legal currency in this stricken zone. You could sense it as soon as you neared the area. Because people were themselves again.

A strong centrifugal force was at work impelling us there. It had a strange effect on me: it stirred up a residue I was barely aware of. A Scotsman I met named Wilkins said he knew the feeling very well, but in his case the residue sank down again between disasters so that he could go back to functioning normally, to being as obtuse as necessary, that is. But with me I guess a delicate inner balance had been upset and my glands secreted a sweetness that flooded through me. Later Shosh told me she regarded this as my first experience of love, though she added derisively (she hated everything to do with Santa Anarella), "But a first self-love, that's a new one."

Listen, Khilmi, this is a great story. It was in Santa Anarella that I met Katzman. He'd lost his evacuation squad and was dragging himself up one of the eerily silent alleys like a wounded cat. When he saw I was an Israeli, from the writing on my T-shirt, I guess, he said Shalom and walked on, but then stopped and turned around. He was a little shorter than I, and very skinny. A week's beard blurred the contours of his narrow white face, and his eyes were so wide-set you couldn't quite look into both of them at once. He was staggering because he hadn't slept for several nights, and before we had exchanged a single sentence I thought to myself, He'll always be a stranger. A stranger at home. A stranger with women. I guess it was his walk that made me think that, because he seemed so detached from everything. He was thirty-seven at the time, and very old.

I invited him to join our squad. There were four of us—two Englishmen, Wilkins, and myself. Our job that day was to clear the ruins at the cathedral. Katzman said it was all the same to him. He joined us, worked like a maniac, and didn't say a word all day long. I thought he must be suffering and I didn't want to intrude, so I kept my distance.

That evening, after the others had turned in, he and I sat by the fire together. Behind us, in the fields, there were hundreds of survivors, and I could almost hear the earth sighing in its sleep. Katzman nodded at the writing on my T-shirt, and we both smiled.

"Reality," he said out of the blue, "is something very fragile. As fragile as an eggshell." Then I told him the story of how I'd gotten there from Rome.

In the same slow, guarded way he said, as though testing me to see if I understood, "Everything is fragile. Brittle. I don't just mean material things. I mean beliefs, too. Values. You have no idea how easily they break." I didn't understand why he was saying this now, but I kept quiet. Usually when a person starts talking like that, it means he's getting at something.

And then, unasked, he told me the story of the pit.

Kan-ya-ma-kan, fi kadim elzaman, etc. etc., in far-off Poland on the continent of Europe, lived Katzman's grandfather, a wealthy timber merchant, and when the war broke out, Katzman's father collected as much money as he could and gave it to a certain peasant woman in return for hiding his family in a pit under her abandoned barn. Katzman was six years old at the time, Khilmi, and he and his parents lived in the underground pit for many long months. They bathed twice in all that time and stank very badly, but eventually they just got used to it. Katzman's mother had played violin in the Warsaw Symphony Orchestra, and when the war broke out, she was committed to a mental hospital because of depression. His father taught Italian and Spanish literature at the University of Prague, and also in Berlin and a few other places I can't remember now, and Katzman hardly knew him, because he was always away on lecture tours. When war broke out he was working on a book—and Katzman sat up, took a deep breath, and said, "Get this, a book about the moral parallels between *Orlando Furioso* and *Don Quixote*. Not bad, eh?"

I said I'd heard of *Don Quixote*, but not the other one.

Katzman studied his fingers, and then the sky, which was black and blue. He said, "You want to hear a strange story?"

He didn't have to tell me I was one of the first people ever to hear it. I knew by the way his shoulders stiffened.

When Katzman's mother was taken to the hospital, he had gone to live with his aunt. One night while he was sleeping, his father walked in, bundled him up, and drove away with him. He woke up in the car and saw that his mother was there, too. This was the first time Katzman had seen her since she went to the hospital. She gave no sign of recognizing him. They spent the first few nights on the estates along the road. His father's friends had organized an escape route. A week later they were in the backwoods, where they met the peasant woman. Friends had promised to keep an eye on the pit, but none did. Katzman spoke quietly. He pulled the blanket up around him, and his face gleamed white as paper in the frozen air. Katzman's father had lost the manuscript of his book during the escape, and he set about reconstructing it from memory as fast as he could. Lacking pen and paper to write with, he had to repeat the main ideas out loud. Katzman was only six when they went into hiding. The new proximity to his father was even more terrifying than his stranger mother, who lay curled on the blanket beside him, muttering to herself and rocking to and fro as if in prayer. He was alone between two strangers.

Katzman scratched a line in the dirt and traced it with his finger. "My father used to pace for hours on end," said Katzman. "I remember his brisk little steps. Mother lay here, see? My place was over here. He drove me nuts, pacing back and forth like that. His hair was white, and it would float up every time he turned on his heel. There wasn't much light down there, and sometimes when I looked at him through half-closed eyes, all I could see was the glow of his hair. He never spoke to my mother. I don't think they'd really lived together since before the war."

Suddenly Katzman smiled broadly. "And eventually," he said, his voice alert, "Father realized that there was no way he could remember everything. His memory just wasn't good enough. So he decided to use me. To use the clean slate of my childish mind. How about that?"

At the time I didn't understand the menace behind his smile and his changed tone of voice. I just sat there, stunned. "He wrote me, or in me, maybe, he wrote everything he could remember. All day long I parroted words I didn't even understand. And I was hungry for new material to imprint on my mind and keep it busy. Father loaded me with information. At first he would lose his temper whenever I forgot something. I was afraid of him. But it got easier eventually. He became less aggressive, and I tried harder. It was more than just an arrangement, it was a kind of hope we shared. A kind of trick we were playing on the whole lousy world."

Katzman reached out from the blanket and raked the coals with a stick. The smoke made our eyes tear. He glanced at me sharply. Go on, I said voicelessly, go on—

"I know now that our being together must have been as awkward for him as it was for me. He didn't know how to act around children. And I didn't make it easy for him either. I wouldn't talk because I didn't want to betray my secrets to a stranger. But as I said, eventually it got easier. Once, he sang me a nursery rhyme. He sang it quietly, looking back to see if my mother heard him. He was a little shy, I think." Katzman paused. This was my last chance to get away. To excuse myself and go to sleep. I knew it, but I stayed just the same. Katzman went on: "His face relaxed the more he unburdened his memory. He also stopped his damn pacing. We had a corner called 'the library,' where we went to recite. And that's where he taught me how to read and write: we would scratch letters in the dirt and I would read. Sometimes the pit filled up with words. He made up a little game for me, hopping over the letters. That was good exercise, too. But the main thing was Ariosto's epic." Katzman chuckled. "At an age when most children meet Snow White and Little Red Riding Hood, I was swallowing monsters like Geronimo de Mondragon, about whom you have no doubt heard."

I said I hadn't.

"No, of course not, I might have guessed," said Katzman solemnly. "Oh well, in times like these one can't be choosy about companions." I could only stare at him dumbfounded. Then I realized he was joking. But I was in no mood for joking.

He said, "I knew a lot more about the Saracen war against the French than I knew about the war in Poland, because the former was the occasion of Ruggiero's meeting with Bradamante. Do you read me, over and out?"

It was a good question. He was impossible to understand. I never knew if he was mocking me or stinging himself. I suspected that he was completely nuts. His voice and face seemed frozen. All around, people were shrieking hysterically in the phantasmagoric landscape. I managed to nod my head. Go on, man, I whispered. I'm with you.

He went on. Gradually a bond formed between him and his father. They would quiz each other on the minutiae of the knights' tales or the magical feats of their creator, Ariosto. They conversed in lines of poetry which Katzman's father had translated into Polish from the Italian. They retired to a world where the language was Ariostic, where names and images that had at first been unintelligible gradually took on meaning and life, because thanks to them, he knew his father loved him.

Katzman wasn't looking at me anymore. His voice was barely audible. There are times, Khilmi, when it doesn't matter whether something's true or not. I believed Katzman with the beads of sweat behind my knees and with my clenched fists.

They created a world for themselves, *kan-ya-ma-kan*. Their companions were the brave Ruggiero and the gullible Astolfo, weaver of heavenly magic, who flew to the moon to retrieve Orlando's mind. You hear that, Khilmi? I must know the whole thing by heart, I've made Katzman tell it to me so many times.

But I didn't yet know that someday he and I would also share a private language. I asked, "Did you ever study the poem? I mean after you got out of there."

"No, I never did. The bulk of Father's treatise compared it to *Don Quixote*. I can't even stand that anymore."

Again he laughed nervously. I noticed that his upper lip was paralyzed. This, too, was a result of the pit: a cold had damaged the nerve. "It was there that I learned what a secret is. My father ordered me to keep a secret a day. I wasn't even allowed to tell it to him. He was smart. He knew that if we kept it secret, the reality of our lives would make a little more sense. He wanted to protect my sanity."

"Did you make up the secrets yourself?"

"Every day. I still remember them, too." He laughed and gave a kind of gasp. "I haven't changed much when it comes to that. A secret creates a kind of tension. A muscle tone of consciousness. I enjoy that."

"How long did you live like that?"

"For years. My mother was dying slowly, spitting blood and clawing herself to death. There was nothing we could do for her. We were very frightened. The two of us would sleep curled up together. Then one morning, I don't even know how long it was after we went into hiding, we found her dead. Just like that. It was a great relief. Not because her presence was so oppressive, but because I realized that the peasant woman wasn't the only power who knew we were in the pit. You understand?"

He sighed and stretched. The coals hissed quietly. Every once in a while the wind lifted a red curl of flame. A plane whirred by.

Out in the fields, someone was whistling to himself. We were attacked by swarms of midges. There was a sudden gust of hot air.

"I've told this story to only one other person," said Katzman. "Of course, I've told the gist of it to certain people, when I wanted to make an impression. But like this, the way I'm telling you tonight, the only other person I told it to was my adopted father on the kibbutz. He was very dear to me. He's dead now. So is my father. He died right after the war."

"And the book?" I asked. "Was it ever written?"

"No. Eventually my father went a little crazy, too. He started destroying his own creation. I didn't quite know what was going on, but I sensed that the facts were taking on a different interpretation. That the details were becoming confused. One kind of madness was as good as another. It took me years to figure out what he was doing. Like the way he let Don Quixote defeat the windmills, and made that fool Astolfo the hero of *Orlando Furioso*. It was his private resistance movement, you see."

"Not really."

"He believed that we deceive ourselves, that it's easier for us to think we're tilting at windmills of injustice, evil, and tyranny, which is only a convenient lie, one of the threadbare lies of our system of morality. By tilting at windmills, mankind teaches children who the enemy is. And mankind is only too happy to send out its Don Quixotes to be killed." Katzman blew into his fists and said slowly, as though deciphering the muddled letters on the ground, "If I understand correctly, what he meant was that the enemy is within ourselves. You see?"

"Sort of."

"What he meant was that the really insidious windmills are justice, reason, and progressive politics. Any moral system we take pride in." He was speaking into his fist now and I could barely hear him. "Those are the windmills Don Quixote and Astolfo should be tilting at. I don't envy them, Uri. They're the loneliest people in the world. Everyone is against them. Because you and I, all of us are windmills."

Then there was a heavy pause. I closed my eyes and waited for what he said to sink in. But Katzman had to spoil it. "Some weird childhood, heh?" He yawned. "They ought to put me on that radio program, *My Father's House*, and call it *My Father's Pit* instead." And he laughed harshly.

But I didn't laugh with him. After all the terrible things he had told me, he was cracking jokes to cover up. He had touched me and recoiled. Behind his cool, quiet voice and cautious movements, he seemed to be pleading with me, and I didn't know why. I didn't understand most of what he said that night, but that didn't bother me. Later, when he talked about the fragile eggshell again, I felt as if I was about to break out of mine. When he talked about the love between him and his father, it made me happy, because I myself was awakening to a new love for the world and for myself. Toward dawn we fell asleep wrapped in army blankets. The next morning we avoided each other's eyes. It was a little strange, but that was clearly how it had to be. During our lunch break I went off by myself, and on the only piece of paper I could find, a page of the New Testament I had picked up in the ruins of the cathedral, I wrote a few words to Shosh: "There is an indivisible nucleus in each of us, a nucleus of love." When I saw what I had written on the page, I knew it was exactly what I had wanted to say. In fact, it had such a tyrannical ring of truth to it, and such a wild desire to be translated into action, that it reverberated all the way to Shosh, and sent her flying in a gyre, *tuta tuta*, but not yet *khelset elkhaduta*.

16

The jeep pulled up beside two command cars, and the crazy dogs stopped barking. They drew back panting, eyeing each other uncertainly. Katzman got out of the jeep and looked around. The villagers were all assembled, it seemed, a tense and silent crowd. The old ones dozed against their canes on wicker chairs, evaporating out of the folds of their wrinkled skin. Children with shaven skulls goggled at him. Sheffer, sweaty and red in the face, approached with broad strides. The sun was directly in Katzman's eyes now, and ne had to shade them as he searched for the hill.

Sheffer grunted an angry greeting: "This is some hole, Katzman."

Katzman smiled sweetly. "For you, Sheffer, nothing but the best."

He nodded at the villagers flocking by the roadside like birds. "I see they know already."

Sheffer scanned them with a lethal glance. "They know. Nobody went out to the fields today. Gotta hand it to Laniado, he sure knows how to keep them entertained. Let's go."

As they walked past the army vehicles, Katzman caught sight of the Carmel sedan Uri had stolen from him that morning, parked haphazardly in the middle of the path with the windows down. It had all the earmarks of dereliction that tragedy leaves on familiar things.

Sheffer lowered his voice: "He radioed again."

Katzman stopped expectantly.

"About an hour ago. Said we'd better not take any chances. They're armed up there and completely insane. He repeated his—his"—Sheffer searched for the word—"his ultimatum. Thinks he's a real big shot. He's been making us puke for three months with his bleeding-heart philosophy, and now the son of a bitch is going to get us killed, too, and—"

A tap on the shoulder from Katzman silenced Sheffer like an electric shock. He took a deep breath and dutifully communicated the rest of the message: "He was angry that you weren't here yet." Katzman walked on. A group of schoolchildren in striped uniforms beset them, sniggering conspiratorially. Katzman was nervous and Sheffer knew it. He swerved around and shouted at the children, who only giggled in response. The strip of tin on the slope of the hill sent shimmering ripples their way. Katzman took a pair of sunglasses out of his shirt pocket and put them on.

They walked toward the makeshift tent of camouflage nets. Soldiers setting up pup tents watched them approach. Katzman spotted a water carrier and a camp stove. A soldier stood pissing against a low stone wall. Katzman rolled back the camouflage net and saw the rest of the soldiers reclining in the dappled shade. They were half asleep and chewing gum while green flies idled blithely on their lips. Katzman grudgingly admired their soldierly acclimation: only three hours here and they had been ground into the dust of the place. At his feet lay a long-legged soldier with a hat over his eyes and his chin protruding. Katzman kicked him lightly in the ribs and the soldier grumbled. He kicked him a second time, and when the soldier found Katzman standing over him, he slowly rose to his feet.

Katzman waited till he was up. "Now sit down," he ordered, malevolently pleasant. "Everyone sit down." He motioned Sheffer to sit beside him, and slumped against the slender marble column the net was tied to. "Now tell me what's going on."

The soldiers grumbled, straining the dust between their fingers. Sheffer fidgeted angrily. Beads of sweat covered his big red face.

"We were supposed to break in as soon as we got here this morning," said one of the men. "Now it's too late."

Another soldier, the one Katzman had kicked awake, muttered, "This is a job for a special outfit, not guys like us who—" Katzman interrupted and asked Sheffer if the necessary inquiries had been made in the village. Sheffer spoke coolly, taking care not to betray his impatience. "We questioned some of them, but we don't have enough Arabic speakers here. The intelligence officer is with the mukhtar right now. Oh yeah, the guy who owns the café saw Laniado running up the path to the cave at six o'clock this morning. He says he seemed frightened and confused. He also claims that old guy Khilmi is crazy as a loon."

"Did he say anything about weapons?" asked Katzman.

"No. He doubts the old man knows how to use a gun. For your information, most of the people around here think Khilmi's dead. He hasn't been seen in months." Again he fell silent, and then recalled, "Oh, there's a little girl, the one he calls his grand-daughter—she brings him food every morning."

"Has she been interrogated yet?"

"She's mute. What can I tell you, Katzman, the whole thing seems pretty weird to me. Like his family, for instance, they claim—"

Someone cleared his throat outside, and Sheffer rolled back the netting. The mukhtar entered the tent and began performing salaams, till he caught sight of Katzman and stopped abruptly, clearly mortified to be standing over him. The district intelligence officer entered after him. Katzman invited them both to sit down. The mukhtar, shiny with perspiration, burst into a troubled speech. Katzman silenced him, and glanced inquiringly at the intelligence officer, who shook his head. No, he had learned nothing new from the mukhtar. "Who's up there with the old man?" Katzman asked in broken Arabic.

The mukhtar spread his hands despairingly. He knew nothing about Khilmi's visitors, except for the child, Najach, who brought him his food out of pity. Katzman wasn't listening. He was staring in amazement at the streams of sweat flowing down either side of the mukhtar's nose. Something must be wrong with the man's sweat glands. The intelligence officer said, "Whoever they are, they're not from Andal. The mukhtar has a list, and so have we. They check out."

Katzman wrinkled his nose. If a terrorist ring had come across Uri by chance that morning, then the situation was a lot more dangerous than he had supposed. "Has anyone taken a look at the footprints on the path?"

"I sent someone up to the bend," said Sheffer. "There isn't any fire cover after that. In any case, the footprints start at the bend."

"Maybe they got here a few days ago and covered their tracks."

The intelligence officer spoke: "I left orders with operations in

Juni to ask regional command about sending a tracker out here." He looked at his watch. "He should have been here by now."

Not a muscle twitched in Katzman's face, and this, too, required a minimal effort of consciousness. Sheffer picked it up. A tiny seed of suspicion sprouted within him. Slyly he asked, "What does the general have to say about all this?"

"The general," replied Katzman, "sends his love."

The only sound in the tent was the buzzing of flies. It was sweltering hot. Sheffer picked up two stones and banged them together. His suspicion was confirmed. For some reason Katzman had chosen not to report the event to his superiors. Sheffer was puzzled. This was a severe departure from army rules. Was Katzman trying to get Laniado out of the mess quietly to save his skin? It didn't make sense, considering how many witnesses there were. Sheffer rankled with resentment. Why in the hell was Katzman hiding behind those dark glasses, here in the shade of the camouflage net? "So what do we do now, sir?" asked Sheffer, and Katzman registered the defiant tone but did not react. He dismissed the mukhtar with a warning that he would be held responsible for the maintenance of order. His first task was to disperse the crowd.

The mukhtar walked away. Katzman turned to Sheffer and said with a malicious smile, "We do nothing. We wait." He had been running his finger around the smooth marble column behind his back and was suddenly struck by the strangeness of the sensation. He stood up to look at the column. It seemed to be a pedestal for a statue. With an incomprehensible sense of urgency, Katzman spread the holes in the netting and peeped through. Above him stood a little angel, and Katzman stared at it in amazement. The statue's face was cracked and riddled with holes, but the wings were perfect, floating high above the khaki camouflage nets and the whole dusty village. Katzman touched the wings and felt sad.

"Fine," said Sheffer savagely. "When you decide—"

Katzman veered around like a snake striking. There was something reptilian about his face. "When I decide, Major, I'll let you know." Again he caressed the statue, without pleasure this time.

A soldier came in under the net carrying a carton of soft drinks. Sheffer popped the caps with his teeth, evoking cries of weary wonder. Katzman took a warm, nauseating gulp. He read the label in Arabic: *7-Up*. Business was booming in the village. A yellow-haired captain with a boyish face peeked in. He nodded at Katzman and called the men out. They groaned and tore themselves away.

As soon as they were gone Katzman said, before Sheffer had a chance to open his mouth, "Forget it." And with that, their recent flare-up—though not Sheffer's baffled indignation—was extinguished, and they sat down to discuss strategies.

Sheffer had spent almost his entire army service under Katzman's command. He had been in Katzman's company in the armored corps, and later, during the Six-Day War, had fought with him in the Sinai. Their tank had been hit. Katzman was hurled out but somehow managed to crawl back almost immediately to help Sheffer. Sheffer never forgot it. He had been lying beside the dislocated tank turret, with help at hand, but paralyzed with fatigue. He had never in his life felt so helpless. Inside, below, a fire had broken out and he could smell the stench of burning flesh. And Katzman was on his way, slow-moving and ashen-faced, reaching groggily through the flames to pull him out. His eyes were so lifeless, Sheffer thought a corpse had come to rescue him. He himself had a rash sort of courage that spreads through the body like flames, but he knew deep down that it was not very different from fear. Katzman, on the other hand, was truly amazing. Danger seemed to make him relax. He had said once, after a chase, that danger gave him a kind of pleasure. Sheffer didn't understand what he meant, and Katzman could never have explained that in fact it made him feel warm and protected, like a baby.

Then they had been separated. Sheffer rotted away in the hospital while Katzman was transferred to the central sector, where he took part in the conquest of Kalkilya, and where, surprisingly, he was put in charge of the new refugee camp that sprang up in Nablus after the war. By the time Sheffer was released from the hospital, Katzman was an instructor at the armored corps training camp. He had Sheffer transferred to the camp, and later, when he was offered the position in Juni, proposed that Sheffer join him there as well. He trusted the grouchy bearlike major with all his heart. Sheffer was his intermediary with the men, translating his often obscure intents into the language of orders. And yesterday, in the house where the terrorists hid, Sheffer had rescued him from certain death.

"I still want to send a tracker up the path," said Katzman. "Just a few meters beyond the bend."

Sheffer scratched his chest good-naturedly. "I'm kind of worried about sending a soldier up there." He hesitated a moment and asked, "What the hell's going on, Katzman? Aren't you reporting this further up?"

"At this stage, no."

"You have to."

"I have to do as I see fit. At this stage, Sheffer, I'm not reporting it."

"It's because of Laniado, isn't it?"

The tiny spasm crossing Katzman's face was not lost on Sheffer. Katzman answered with restraint: "No. It's because I want to settle things ourselves. There'll be time for reports later on."

"You're making a big mistake, Katzman. This isn't some cut-and-dried assignment, you know. We may be up against a real terrorist ring here. They think before they act. Not like those crackpots yesterday. Katzman, you've got to—"

"No."

Sheffer stared at him dumbfounded.

Katzman said, "Okay then, send a man up the path. I just don't believe there'll be any—um—" He paused. What right have you to play games, he asked himself. Not everyone is as warped as you. Especially not Uri. Still, he was willing to bet his life that he was right. "I just don't believe there'll be any problems," he continued. "For the man you send, I mean." As soon as the words were out, he was surer than ever of the strange idea which had flashed dimly through his mind earlier when he touched the angel.

"What—what's that supposed to mean, Katzman?!" Sheffer was nearing his boiling point, which was low in any case.

Katzman glanced up casually. "Chances are there's nobody up there but Laniado and the old man."

Sheffer searched his face for a hint of a smile. Finally he gave up. "What do you mean, nobody? Laniado himself—" and he groped in his oversize pockets for the crumpled note. "Listen, Katzman, it says here—"

Suddenly there was a glint of enthusiasm in Katzman's eyes. "Tell me, Sheffer, didn't you anticipate something like this?"

"Something like what?" Sheffer finally found the note, waved it, and stuck it back into his pocket. He took out a pack of cigarettes and cooled down with fire and smoke.

"Something like this happening here." Katzman checked himself. He laced his fingertips together. Doing so always gave him a little thrill, like matching the parts of a jigsaw puzzle. His skin seemed to stretch back across his cheekbones. The hollows sank deeper.

Sheffer made himself obtuse. "I don't understand you, sir." He wasn't stupid, but sometimes Katzman was really impossible to comprehend, not to say maddening; they were at it again, the same old game of cautious sniping; the wicked speed of Katzman's thoughts and the sweetness of his smile against the obtuseness of Sheffer's face, and his disturbing way of calling him "sir."

Katzman thought: Like an animal prowling in the dark. The natural instincts of a million people, their desires thwarted and held in check. Indestructible living matter. Rage mounting, and tiny, obstinate drops of futility trickling out slowly to form stalactites. He felt these venous phenomena throbbing in the thick of thought. In every thwarted desire there lurks a threat. In every bow of submission there is enough latent energy to stand tall. Katzman gauged this inwardly. In the arteries of enforced moderation, poison had begun to froth. For a moment, on the tattered screen of his brain he saw projected pictures of their ironic straw hats. Humiliation entitles man to save and store the necessary energy for maintaining a hollow pride. Katzman winced.

You have to be as crazy as Uri to step out of your life and view it from the outside, to rub your eyes and wonder how such a thing had happened. How we had all been turned into hostages. He had no wish to open his eyes and see Sheffer fidgeting impatiently before him. Like a sphinx, he thought. A mythological beast at the gates to the city, the gates to us all, devouring those who cannot solve the riddle. He had never actually believed there was a solution to the riddle, but now it occurred to him that if Uri had done what he suspected, then Uri had found it.

"Something like this was bound to happen sooner or later," he said. "It's a matter of statistics. One in a million was bound to fight back, don't you think?"

189

"Fight back?" Sheffer laughed uncertainly. "What are you talking about, Katzman? There's a terrorist ring up there. They're bargaining for a hostage—what do you mean, fight back?"

"You're right, I was only thinking—" he said, gesticulating incoherently. And inwardly he thought, Uri and the old man are fighting back. I know it. They're fighting back against me. They're talking absolute values. Either the army withdraws from all the territories, or else—Uri dies. They're demanding justice. Justice pure and absolute.

He recalled his conversation with Uri in Santa Anarella. He had believed what he said at the time, that true justice is like a hormone secreted by the brain. But of course, Katzman had defenses against the sway of words, defenses Uri lacked. Which is why Katzman was such an expert dissembler, while Uri remained the ludicrous amateur he was, infuriating in his clumsiness.

The sense of loss he had been overwhelmed by in Juni that morning came back to him. Because of the little angel, perhaps. For the first time, Katzman considered Uri a possible threat to himself. The tension they had both been under since Uri came to Juni was gathering a sudden and painful momentum. Katzman felt sad: he had hoped to find a friend in Uri—for the first time in his life—or at least what others call "friend" so easily. There was no rational reason for the instinctive affection they had felt for each other in Italy. Uri was hopelessly different from him, or perhaps that was just it. Uri is the only person I allow to feel responsible for me, he thought. Yet there's no way he can possibly protect me. And now I'm losing him. The sour irony made him scowl; for once he had almost decided to fight for something that really mattered.

Sheffer stubbed his cigarette out. Katzman opened his eyes and tried to focus, only half there. Sheffer stood over him, tall and heavy.

"You can go rest in the operations tent. They'll be finished in there pretty soon." And he ducked under the net and walked away.

Katzman rested his eyes. He sank down.

It was hard to determine exactly when his clandestine relationship with Shosh had begun, long before she blurted out the painful words that shocked them both. Katzman had had affairs like this before, and he no longer even wondered why women seemed drawn to him against their will, in sad resignation, as it were. He had always gone through women at a feverish rate, to assuage the loneliness inside him, which he envisioned as a big empty tent flapping in the evening breeze. He was quick to fall in love in his loveless way. Women fascinated him: in addition to the women who washed up on his shores, Katzman would love and abandon several others each day, unbeknownst to them. Army girls walking by, girls on the bus, women in shops. In each he found something to love. Even the ugly ones possessed something worthy of his affection, his compassion, the dripping kindness that suddenly filled him. But he always awakened as soon as they emerged out of his vaguely cannibalistic reveries, and then he would regretfully bid farewell to the girlish ankle, the magnificent ivory neck. Over a luscious pair of lips he would slowly discern the big nose, the heavy cheeks or vacuous eyes, like the ill-favored relations of a lovely bride. Since he couldn't very well spend a lifetime in love with a pearly ear or a naughty mole, Katzman proclaimed himself a hopeless romantic. This was a convenient excuse for his brief and loveless affairs.

Still, the women came to him. Experience had taught Katzman to sense the first encounter long before the woman did. For a few days of intense passion he made no move at all. He played an almost joyless waiting game till the cool knowledge of it penetrated the woman's consciousness, too. And then, in amazement, unstirred by his conquest, he would follow the throbbing and trembling and batting of her wings, these short-lived struggles merely landmarks in a spiral that led to him, staring at her with his strange eyes, all compassionate. Most women came to him this way, joyless, terrified, and hollow. For him the process was only a clumsy variation on the theme of the mighty spark.

And that was why it had taken him by surprise. He'd trained himself to give women a kind of lit.nus test in his mind: would this one be right for him? Would she surrender? And with Shosh, he had been so careful. He had refrained from the clever words and the intense looks that usually paved his way with women, making them forget his appearance. He was proud of having protected her from his instinctive cunning. Uri was his friend, and Shosh, too, was just a friend, Uri's wife. He loved Uri, and he liked Shosh as much as he could. When he realized what was happening between them, it was a devastating blow. Again he saw, with depressing clarity, how pathetic and hopeless he was, and he despised himself more than ever.

He was eager to find fault with her: her solicitude for Uri, and the way she cultivated his tastes and educated him, outraged Katzman. He guessed how it would end. Once, as a child, he had watched a mouse having a litter. The mother licked the afterbirth and devoured it hungrily, and then she began to lick her baby with fierce concentration. Katzman guessed.

When Uri made him a member of the household, Shosh had been engrossed in her work with four delinquents at Professor Hillman's institute. Two of her cases had been concluded successfully and she was still struggling with the other two. Sometimes he heard their voices coming out of her room, as she transcribed the tapes of their sessions. And then Uri and Katzman would stop talking and listen to the husky voices, and Katzman's seismographic needle would start to quiver.

There, the path led to Shosh. To her provocative methods and the senseless evil piled up on her desk which had so fascinated him: drugs and drug dealers and petty thieves and sadistic bullies, all under the age of sixteen. Shosh was flattered by his interest. She eagerly answered the questions he fired at her, and even showed him photographs: the boy who threw acid in his sister's face looks like a bristling tomcat here in the picture that was taken when he first arrived. But here curiosity is stealing into that tense little face. Do you see it? Katzman held the picture to the light, and turned it sideways. Shosh asked, What exactly do you expect to find there? And Katzman, looking thoughtful, troubled perhaps by the dangerous glint of the artist at work or the overly impassioned scientist in her eyes, said, "I'm looking for you, for your reflection in the pupil of his eye." "Me? I'm merely a tool, and not a very important one at that. You won't find me there." Then maybe I'll find him in you, he mused, tyranny translated into senseless and compulsive violence. And Shosh told him about the challenge, the careful groping for a way in. How good it is to talk to you, she said, surprised. Uri is against what I'm doing. That was a dangerous thing to say, thought Katzman, look out. But Shosh was already talking about her breakthroughs with the boys, and there was a new ardor to her words. Katzman imagined her delicate lashes fluttering with pleasure whenever her hunches proved true. The joy of the hunter. "That's when the change comes, and one reality is forged out of another," she said. "And I'm there to describe and record it. I find that very exciting." He knew then how similar they were. A decision had to be made, but he didn't have the strength.

Shosh hadn't guessed yet. She would have been shocked if anyone had hinted about such a possibility to her. A betrayal, and the betrayal of Uri in particular, would have been like extracting the cement that held her body and mind together. Katzman was Uri's friend, that's all. Annoying sometimes with his indolence and cynicism, his tough-guy pose, when he was just a child, really. A lost and lonely child. Help him; make him feel less lonely, facilitate his spontaneous friendship with Uri. They're so happy together. And he's so bright, so intelligent, so interested, so appreciative of what she was accomplishing by the sweat of her brow.

Little by little she told him how she worked on them until she found the nucleus Uri had so aptly described, the nucleus of love that exists in every human being; and though it was sometimes very remote, it left feeble tracks on the emotions that led inexorably to what she called the first experience of love, love for one's mother, or an older brother, a teacher or a movie star, or even a puppy. One delinquent had eventually confessed his love for the anonymous girl whose picture he had seen as a child on a box of chocolates. He had lavished his longings on her.

And then she would attack this nucleus and blow it up from the size of a pea to the size of the globe, charting its oceans of loneliness, its frozen continents at the poles, and its hidden, lush-green valleys; and then she would map out the patient's feelings and color them in, showing him where there were underground tunnels connecting distant lakes, and where entire continents of feeling had sunk into the abyss, and where innocent-looking mountains might suddenly turn into volcanoes. And she would lead him down his own pathways and make him see that all his hatred converged at a certain latitude, and that he had poured rivers of hurt into a single sea of tormented memory.

All this was done openly, she wished to stress. With total sincerity. And she never proceeded further unless the patient himself showed an interest in travel. But why wouldn't he, when she flooded him with pleasant memories and cradled him with forgotten images, with the names the world had called him when he was still at peace with it? And she would infect him gently, but she never used the word "love."

She recorded every word and analyzed it, looking for significant clues. A tremor of curiosity, a shudder of distaste, a hesitant stammer. His hand was like a sensitive magnet, casually scratching his wispy hair; it seemed to draw out the iron filings in her own depths, too. Fragmented images began to fuse, light as a feather, heavier than lead. These, too, she had to note, of course. She had to know herself very well. Her psyche was her working tool.

Katzman wanted to know what satisfaction it gave her. Surprised, she answered, "Why, the knowledge that I'm helping, that's all, there's no greater satisfaction. They hand me a juvenile delinquent, someone who is alienated from himself and from society, and I return him as a useful member of society and a more sensitive human being." Katzman guesses: intellectual satisfaction, too: a kind of human crossword puzzle? Shosh: "That's a dig, isn't it? Actually, I agree with you, though I don't like your tone. Yes. Intellectual satisfaction, too. It's a tremendous challenge, Katzy." Katzman: "And when you find that nucleus—of love, or whatever—is that very exciting?" Shosh: "Well, it's definitely interesting."

She didn't tell him about the sweet anguish running down her spine as she neared the solution, but he was with her in the house so much he perceived what was going on. These were happy days for her. She was more and more attuned to the stirrings of her body, as she sniffed the air, in search, in longing. Her head was a display of fireworks. Even the language she used to summarize her sessions revealed the innermost workings of her psyche. Katzman observed her closely as she neared the solution of the case before Mordy's. She began to share the experience so freely it startled him. The only thing she withheld from him was the boy's name, and that for ethical reasons.

Katzman was completely caught up in the strange adventure: he could see the boy's hostility quite manifestly being absorbed into Shosh, the coolness of it summoning her out of the darkness where she lurked. Then came a phase of mutual groping. Trial and error. The crudeness Shosh was exposed to. Near-fear trickled through to Katzman: there was so much hatred in the boy. Careful now, said Shosh, we're getting closer. Look, his teeth are clenched to protect a memory. That's a sure sign. Notice his choice of words here. Katzman looked at her. She was calculating her moves with a cunning he had never noticed in her before. Almost insidiously. And yet her intentions were good. What we need, she remarked, is a Trojan horse combined with the Stanislavsky method. Strategy and empathy. The "feeling-memory" his anguish stirs in me. The approaching quaver of love. Katzman noticed that she was unconsciously aping the boy's mannerisms. His walk. She was shutting herself off as though waiting for an explosion. Katzman was alarmed. She and the boy, and he, too, in his way, were involved together now, and danger sprayed their nerves like lubricating oil. Again and again she ran the tape back. Why did he say that? Why did he use these words here, the ones he usually reserves for destructive experiences? She tapped the table with the tip of her pen, mumbling to herself like a sniper in ambush: Come on. Come on. Don't be afraid.

And suddenly, with a swat of her leonine paw, everything was shattered. Though it might have taken several weeks, in Katzman's eyes the final stage was swift. A moment more the victim writhed and then was still. Limp. Her expert clutches tore him into sections to be charted, marked, defined. The boy touched himself inside and found love. He could love. Around a hidden nucleus, like Saturn's rings, were tender, dormant memories, no longer actively dangerous. She showed them to him. This is where you were happy.

Try to remember. Try to feel it again. This person liked you. He was your friend, though you didn't realize it at the time. This woman in the picture is nursing her baby. She wants the baby to be happy. Close your eyes and feel good. Take your time. There's no hurry now.

But Uri was not a part of this. He was busy with night school, and he closed himself off from her attempts to share what she was experiencing. And when the three of them would talk, late into the night, Shosh's words to Katzman were charged with other meanings, still blind; text and subtext. Currents of conflict flowing between the faceless characters that inhabited them. Worried undertones: what was it?

But they were already in collusion. All that remained now was the slow, painful accomplishment of their doom, of that which was catching them and searing them inside. Maybe the pain would go away. Maybe they could cool the fire with the soft breath of coition and the writhing of their bodies.

Only with her it was different. Stolen water was cloyingly sweet. The rapid permutations of the triangle exhausted him. He was spending every minute of his time with either Shosh or Uri, or both of them together. And learning just how treacherous he could be, as he juggled with meanings, always parrying some wise guy behind the one he was talking to.

Lies accumulated. He discovered that in his own way he was still playing his father's game of keeping secrets. He had a childish urge to take the fun to extremes. To find out how far he could go. He was disappointed to find out that people were so easily fooled. He began weaving little lies into the reports he sent the military governor; he caught the mayor of Juni up in a tangle of seemingly logical contradictions; he learned to exploit the smallest interstices between words when speaking with his soldiers. He became elusive, immured in the heavy anguish he pretended to see as a subtle, private joke.

Uri was the one who suffered most from Katzman's elusiveness. He spent many hours in his company, learning about his new job and trying to slip a little content through Katzman's restrictions. He didn't yet know what Katzman had contrived in bringing him to Juni. As Katzman expressed it once to Shosh: Uri has this excuse-me-for-living quality that would make him superfluous anywhere, but in Juni, he's reached the limit.

Katzman was drifting away. He would make promises to himself and earnest decisions, knowing all along that he wouldn't be able to abide by them. There was a frozen, tyrannical magic luring him in between the two rows of her pearly teeth.

He was getting lost. He had believed he was immune to such a danger. That the cat would always fall on its feet. But this time he seemed to have fallen on top of the cat, and hurt himself in the process. It was in Shosh that he found his image now, as if a caricature of his seed had germinated and bloomed within her, mocking him with monstrous flowers. That's how fast the change took place. Where had her malice been before he hovered around her with shadowy wings?

She had been an eager pupil. At first she wrote him love letters. Tortured, passionate letters she stuck in his hand as soon as Uri left the room. Her latent sensuality was suddenly revealed. Even her official reports for the institute were warm and vivid.

But she soon found out that Katzman wasn't pleased with her words of love and passion. Perhaps it was her explicitness that grated on his innate animal cautiousness. And then she understood: it was her love that frightened, that offended him.

He was very much afraid. He struggled against her with all his might, but couldn't leave her alone. He comforted himself with the cheap rationalization that this was as low as he could get. That here, at the core of the lie of his life, in the heart of untruth, he had finally reached the bottom of his vileness. From here on, the only way was up.

But Shosh left him no choice. She swept him away. And like a jaded pro, he couldn't help marveling at her quick initiation into the rules of the sinister game. Sometimes he felt like a craftsman teaching a more talented apprentice. They vied with each other in viciousness. They devised a sly language of signals and insinuations to use when they talked in Uri's presence.

Katzman did this out of loathing, out of a spiteful urge to defeat, not Uri, but Shosh. Shosh did it with a strange zest she had discovered in herself. It was like a wild race through new mazes. One day she came up with an idea that turned his stomach: if she kissed Uri's nose when they said good night, that would be an invitation, a signal to Katzman that she would be waiting for him the following day when Uri was in Juni. It was so simple and so devious, Katzman knew she had bested him. In any case, she needn't have gone to such lengths. Uri was always urging Katzman to visit Shosh "for an occasional square meal and a good night's sleep in a civilian bed," when he stayed in Juni overnight to supervise the roadblocks. Katzman knew this wasn't how Shosh wanted him. She wanted to love him. His defenses were nothing in her eyes but a kind of subterfuge: fear of the love she could give him, or of what it might do to him. She didn't understand why he wasn't exploiting his natural bent for secrecy, the complex masks he wore in public, and why he wouldn't dive with her into their secret. She was still discovering the milk teeth of malice and duplicity. He knew what awaited her, and wouldn't let her inside.

And so, she touched him only where he let her: his quick wit, his razorlike cynicism. His bitterness. She began to develop these traits in herself as a defense against him. This was how they lost their unborn love. All they had left was a hungry passion and a sense of waste. Even when they made love they had to wrestle with their falseness and despair, and with the smile of the lamb.

There were footsteps outside. Sheffer stuck his head in under the camouflage net. "Lunch, Katzman. Come on." Katzman sighed and got up. He waited for Sheffer to walk away, and then, shyly, spread a hole in the net with his fingers. There was mildew on the little angel's face. It looked like a very old little angel. Like the stone remnant of a passion which had vanished long ago. Katzman wanted to say something to it. Then he shrugged his shoulders. Another time, perhaps.

17

It's stifling hot in this room. I wish I could take off my clothes and plunge into the cool shade, unencumbered by names and feelings and this loathsome tape I'm winding around myself. Now that I've used up the last three cassettes with words and silence, I'll have to record over the first one. It will be interesting to see which words defy erasure and survive. Are some words, like "kill" or "love," more potent than others?

I don't know the answers yet, but I'm not going to let hereditary curses permeate the fermenting matter of my psyche. That may work in literature, but a case like this has to be approached with the astuteness of a great detective. He will expose the imposture that took place in a certain sealed room, and then he will bend down to remove a muddy rust-eaten object, scrape it with his pocketknife and say, Here, madame, is the clue you have been searching for. It was inside you all along. Mordy. Now I will speak of him.

Here are the three cardboard files with the shiny star of the Hillman Institute above the name Mordy. For weeks now I have been caught up in this ritual torture: every free moment I have, after hours, too. I pore over the summaries, looking for something behind the subterfuge of words, trying to work my way back from his death to the crucial moment when I was in the very act but didn't know it yet.

The first file doesn't interest me anymore: no surprises there. Mordy barely opens his mouth. Doesn't respond or answer my questions. Shows no interest whatsoever in the intricate wooden blocks and simple puzzles, or even the colorful paints I set before him on the table. He looks tough, with his arms hanging stiffly at his sides; unprepossessing as he tallies up his teeth with his tongue, blinking sluggishly.

He doesn't arouse any desire in me to help him, or much antagonism either, for that matter. The first typewritten pages of the file contain his case history. Hillman told me he had never come across anyone with such a severely impaired will before; life force, I corrected him. Mordy was a real test of Viktor Frankl's theories, and the patience of his previous therapists at the institute. He might have starved to death if they hadn't forced him to eat. If they hadn't filled his schedule in with squares of activity, he would have lain in bed all day, staring at the walls. He began the career that landed him in the institute as a decoy for a gang of criminals. Once, says the report, he slid down from the roof of a twelve-story building to open the door for them.

Mordy didn't know the meaning of fear, any more than he knew the meaning of love, hope, or hate. He was a *tabula rasa*. He didn't know who his parents were and never expressed emotion. The most detailed section of his record is the list of homes and institutions he was sent to in alarmingly quick succession. The usual reason they gave for transferring him was "incompatibility," with an occasional "crowded conditions."

None of these places had left any mark on Mordy. He presented a limp challenge to people's noble intentions. "I simply couldn't make contact with him," wrote one foster mother from Tel Aviv, in a moving summary of her stay with her. "No signs of violence," wrote the police officer who examined the body in the kitchen of the blue ward. "No apparent link between the psychotherapeutic treatment received by the deceased and his suicide." Can I prove there was a link?

He sat here in this office, on the other side of the table, meekly answering the surprising questions I tossed around him like rings, and writhing in his chair when I scolded him. He never saw beyond the dark veil that covered his eyes, and I never approached him closer than this table. That's what the second file is about. There ought to be a big question mark on the folder instead of a star. And the second half of the file ought to float up quizzically with all the questions in it. I can't really say he was hostile, because I always sensed a raw desire in him to help me, to set my mind at rest. Had he known how to, he would undoubtedly have cooked up some accommodating answers. But he wasn't able to lie.

He would sit before me, this fifteen-year-old with his small head, the stringy brown hair that fell across his bleary eyes, and his tongue, the only clue to the misery in him, darting out between his teeth to moisten his lips. As I noted in file 3: Who needs a pen for self-expression with a tongue like that? But Mordy used it to say only the clearest, truest things, like yes and no; I don't understand; I don't know; I don't remember; you're angry with me.

How could anyone be angry with him? You felt sorry for him, but compassion, like anger, requires some sort of feedback. And Mordy set up a slippery surface I couldn't walk across; there were no familiar footrests between us.

All my efforts were thwarted. Everything I had learned and successfully put into practice with the patients before him. No, he isn't suspicious. He doesn't test me. But he shows no interest in the exciting games I set before him either, not even in the magazines with pictures of pretty girls and soccer players. He never remembers to say goodbye when the attendant comes to take him at the end of the session. Nor does he seem to recognize me when he returns the following day. The only clue I had came from Anichka, of all people. Anichka, the lively little dietitian of the blue ward, casually mentioned that Mordy was addicted to chocolate. She complained that he devoured candy bars but would barely touch her nutritious food. And the next day she sent me the medicinal supplies, noting in the little pad tied to her belt: "6 bars bittswt choc. S. Avidan-Laniado for therapy, sign here here and here"; and she sneaked in an extra bar, "For you, Shoshkeleh." At this point success seemed assured, or at least the kind of breakthrough I had achieved with the previous three cases. Even before the session began, I could hardly wait to write about the delight in his eyes as he reached for the dark squares (the wrapper folded back just a little, the torn silver foil offering an enticing glimpse of chocolate). And he fell into my trap: To get it, all you have to do is talk. Talk more—and you get more. And pairs of opposites, like punishment and reward, give and take, stimulus and response, jiggle in the belly of my ballpoint pen. I grow hopeful again; sometimes even a square of chocolate can serve as a foothold.

It's hot. Really unbearable. And I'm starting to turn numb. Itchy. My body is whispering, Come away. It's dangerous in here. Poetic justice is very painful. Come away. But if I get up, if I stretch my legs and walk around the room, it won't be to escape. I'm the one who condemned myself to stay here like a sitting duck, waiting for the tap-tap-tapping of old Mother Truth, who has been searching for me so long, and I will listen to the prayerlike whispers inside myself, because maybe now's the time for a confrontation, here—no, here —hiding behind two fat books on the treatment of delinquents, is a small brown package with a pair of shorts and a shirt inside, his clothes.

Put it on the table. Get used to it. Now tell me what went wrong with the chocolate. Go on. Tell me how he devoured vast quantities of bittersweetness, and about the look on his face as he stuffed it into his mouth, and his dirty fingers, and the sticky stains he left on the table! But that's all that happened during our sessions. He wouldn't talk. He didn't know how to. No, he doesn't remember Naomi, his counselor at Ofakim; he doesn't remember Mrs. Nardy from Ashkelon, or Tirza from Tel Aviv. He can't explain what "friend" means. What is this baby in the picture doing to his mother? Eating her? He doesn't know. You're angry with me.

But he doesn't know how to ask for more. He doesn't reach out across the table. Only if I actually drop the chocolate in his palm will he put it in his mouth and eat it. Otherwise, he doesn't complain. He doesn't even look at the tempting squares. Only his tongue will take the bait.

These sessions are painful. I munch too much of the chocolate myself. Anichka expresses mild astonishment: Oh dear, my supplies won't hold out, she jokes, and you'll break out in pimples, Shoshkeleh. And Mordy and I, on our respective sides of the table, watch each other munch. We have to try something else. Like what? Hillman suggests an honorable retreat, but I refuse, too irately. Not yet. He hasn't even been with me three months. Katzman says what I hear whispering inside me, that I'll never give up. That I'll fight to his last drop of blood.

And Abner sweeps in from the other side of my doubts with bemused interest. He, who never listens, sharpens his wits for the story of Mordy. "This boy wants to retreat from the world," he says, trapped in his literary perspective. "It's a case of 'heroic obtuseness' pure and simple, and to tell the truth, I don't see why we should harass a person who has risen to such a level of self-containment. In the Middle Ages they would have made him a saint: Saint Mordy."

And what about Uri? Uri didn't have a relevant response to offer. He would become evasive whenever I wanted to talk about Mordy. As if he sensed what was about to happen. The only time he broke his stubborn silence was when he said to me, It takes a lot of guts to do what you're doing with those boys. But in Uri's language "guts" doesn't have its usual connotation. I tried to lead him through the maze of my deliberations, but he would always withdraw. I don't understand anything about psychology, he would say, and I would angrily accuse him of putting on an act, of not being supportive when I needed him; he was silent, as usual at such times, and I knew that his silence showed forbearance; and his eyes were clear, even as mine were blurred in the heat of attack; and he didn't believe me.

Uri never shows his anger when we fight. He folds it in against himself like a sharp blade. He sinks into depression. It's as if I have nothing to do with the fight, it's all going on inside him. If he wins, he makes up with me; if he loses, he admits his mistake. There's no point dragging it out, because whatever I might say to him or what he might say in reply is already contained inside him, and I feel stifled by the clarity of his impassive eyes. It isn't fair, you know, I try to explain as sweetly as I can. We have to talk our problems out, to verbalize our disagreements, and most important— to be completely open with each other; though luckily he doesn't hear this claptrap, because he's out of earshot by then. All the ingredients have gone in, and all that remains is to wait for the cake he bakes in the fire of inner feeling and absolute truth. This is Uri's trial by fire.

And spite comes into it. Little poisonous remarks. Uri suffers: I bring out a vindictiveness he never suspected in himself. He agonizes over it, gets scared and aggressive when he hears the things I make him say. He relaxes only when Katzman's around, becoming more patient with me. He seems to need Katzman as a mediator. It's a kind of dance: we're three warriors bearing three human shields. Simultaneity can be dizzyingly manifold: we are each both a means and an end. A poison and a balm.

Uri more than any of us: as he walks out blindly to the precipice of truth, he turns into a dangerous enemy, but also into a miserable victim. His serene innocence makes me furious and jealous in turn. He's ridiculous, he's pathetic, as he misses the point between me and Katzman; and his failure to stop us is destroying our lives. He never asks the right questions, so his anger misses the unforgivable target of my transgression. Could such a tangle of feelings be called love?

Here's the point, then. The point of the matter. Whom am I threatening? Myself, I guess. I hesitate as I leaf through the file. But you have nothing to worry about. The files have been thoroughly examined by the police. They read every word, and asked you to explain what they didn't understand. Hillman himself went over them and came up with nothing. Naturally. At most he noted in the margins once or twice: "Too impressionistic" or "This is a scientific

207

document, not a poem, if you please." Otherwise he found no fault with me. Because in file 3, in the heart of the lie, there are no signs of violence. No blanks. Except that the summaries in this last file were intended as a cover-up, a fraud, not a disclosure, and they were concocted at home after work, Yes, I lost myself in a thrilling creative endeavor, as I invented a different Mordy, a lively, cooperative Mordy, and led him down the paths I knew so well, through all the phases of therapy, attributing him with a little initial hostility ("Why the sudden regression?!" Hillman queried), and expertly abating his mistrust. "Today Mordy smiled for the first time." How marvelous. For hours on end I lean over the file, putting in my corrections. Words can change when you write them down. Not like spoken words, but like living creatures hovering around you, worthy opponents for a writer. The struggle is fierce, but how sweet the victory when it comes.

Before I face Uri and Katzman again, I am careful to wipe away the cinders from my eyes and orient myself to the world. How can I meet with poor disintegrating Mordy tomorrow when I have just left the living boy, rubbing up against my curiosity, peeling off layer upon layer of himself in the warmth that I emit?

Are you listening, Abner? Are you here again? By trying to be an expert on love, I became a technician of its mechanisms in myself, in everyone; an expert on "passion," "lust," "love," all those tyrannical words that poets use. But I know the pretty names we give emotions are like the names that sailors give approaching typhoons in the vain hope of appeasing them, of making them easier to understand. I learned this long ago, Abner, when I began to hear the riddles whispering inside me, and listened to the warnings blow through the cracks in your talk about marriage as the key to lasting happiness, or the sanctity of sex, perhaps the only word I ever heard you utter with genuine awe, your eyes smiling mystically at Leah, as you caressed her sagging cheeks and traced an invisible line with your finger, like the embroidered thread in the lining of your double quilt.

And all the while I felt a slow stirring, the nectar of anticipation and the honey of longing deep inside, and I burrowed into the heavy, humid earth of memory to search for a name to call it, trying out a new and secret name for myself as well, in my diary, in my loose-leaf notebook, on my school desk covered with cracks, because Shosh will not do anymore, Shosh is too much like me, like home, and that, amazingly enough, was when I came across the poems of a certain Aviv Raz, who named the names, who kneaded me into words—no, not words—but shattered syllables, swollen letters that sank into me with a cold flame.

Enough. I don't want to go into that again. The worst sort of tyranny is self-imposed. You say, You're being defensive, Shosh, you're only rationalizing. Maybe so, Abner, maybe so. But there isn't any one explanation I can accept wholeheartedly. Look at it like this: Mordy never had any love. That's why it's impossible to reach him. With the other boys you found something to hold on to, but here you feel it's hopeless. Try to touch him with whatever it takes. Someone else inside me quietly remarks, It isn't fair. He's so dead. He'll never know what love is. Help him. And there are other whispers that explain nothing.

I tell you this, Abner, and ask forgiveness. Not face to face, that would be too overt, but maybe in the poems I'll write someday, if I ever have the guts, in Uri's sense of the word. Not that I would spell it out for you. We don't talk much, you and I. And what we say to each other is usually unimportant. Our repeated protestations of candor constitute an effective camouflage for prolonged and quiet deception, and the two of us, Abner, are like disciplined actors in a play fretfully composed by Leah; we never say what we're supposed to because the glassy atmosphere of home will not tolerate an explosion of feelings, and that's why we tread softly as a family, why there's no tooth-baring hatred, and why there's no love.

Listen to me, stop being evasive. I'm going to tell you everything, and though I know you much prefer the shadow realm, tonight I will shine a neon light into every niche and corner, and into the darkness behind the books on the shelf, because I, too, have become a connoisseur of shadows, Abner, after all the silences and quiet mistakes, and like an artist I know their different hues: the shadow Katzman cast upon me is different from Uri's shadow, or the shadow between the two of us, Abner, it's time I said it, a shadow that emerges out of the darkness, out of the silence; and now that I've told you this, I may dare to speak to you for the first time about that night, almost four years ago, when you burst into my room and asked me to listen to something you had just written, but I didn't listen, all I heard was the deafening noise the paper made as it trembled in your hand.

I was holding a pen in my hand, I recall, over the open textbook before me. I must have been studying for a criminology exam. Don't be angry that I remember all the petty details. I hadn't understood yet why your intrusion horrified me so. Maybe it was the injured look on your face, or because you had never burst into my room like that before. You hardly ever came to my room, in fact. The room was a mess, my clothes were lying around everywhere. I hadn't seen you for two days: you had disappeared after Chagai's funeral, and Leah and I came home alone from Nahalal. It's so difficult to talk about it. Your face was stubbly, twitching with cruelty and pain, and you gave off a strong smell of perspiration, you who never sweat; I remember how I tried to stave it off, suggesting coffee or a shower, and you pushed me out of the way, cleared your throat, and began to read aloud. More than anything I feared—silly me—that you had come to ask forgiveness, that it was a kind of confession, and only then I understood, and the words erupted inside me, words like a cruel lesson, like a scream of fear mounting in me, and you slumped down and said, What right did I have to poison him with ideas like "purity of weapons" or "combat morality," what right did I have to plant these explosives reality was bound to detonate in his young body? How many other youths have I planted with mines of good intentions, ignoring the world I was sending them into? And their doom was locked inside them like a post-hypnotic suggestion.

No! No! I scream silently. You mustn't, you can't, I beg you, please don't show anyone what you've written. And I decoct a few cool drops of logic somehow, frosty with anxiety, that pass for serenity; I restrained you firmly and led you through the traps, deaf to your real voice, which pleaded with us both not to abandon you, wounded and gaping, while my mouth created words for you, bereft of poetic justice and containing only dead logic, that it's wrong to stop wanting to teach the young to love their fellow man and to pursue peace, and you, Abner, argued your clever Shosh, who always knows what to say and how to say it, you are no ordinary man, you are almost a symbol to so many, and you must continue your work as an educator, you must look for a better answer in yourself than the one that failed, and I added in a wordless whisper, if not for them, then for me, for your selfish daughter, who will not, cannot let you stray out of your darkness ever again.

Your selfish daughter knew that fear would make her fight to your last drop of blood, and keep her from doing what she had to do—to save you from the lie, to hear it from your own lips, to teach you to give it your name, and when she pushed you back into it she could still say sweetly—in spite?—that conflict and ambiguity prepare a person for life, enabling him to choose, and even to lie a little, and that, too, is important, and so, Abner, there are a few more things I want to say to you tonight, some nice and some not so nice, like about the fish, for instance, about a strange thought I had concerning you and Leah, but just now, when I feel so light-hearted all of a sudden, let me tell you that it isn't forgiveness I want from you but a kind of approval. A wink of complicity between spies in enemy territory. That's what I need to give me strength. And when you understand this, you'll finally realize what happened to me, that by throwing myself at the boy I invented, I was abandoning the one who sat before me, staring at me from behind a veil with a pair of eyes sewn on, tallying up his teeth with his tongue.

That's how I abandoned him, I guess. That's how I dumped him into the hands of Shosh, that sly invader, plucking expertly at his hiddenmost chords, speaking out to him from behind the words, from out of the shadows of thoughtful smiles and indolent sighs. I sometimes encountered her on the glass-top table, when I wasn't careful. The feverish face of this unfamiliar woman frightened me. So willful, like passion itself. And I fled her and ran to my new friend, the one who lives in the privacy of my room between the tip of my pen and the page. She's so glamorous, she shatters into a thousand colors. Even Mordy gaped at her in amazement, allowing her to lead him back to the self he had lost. Who is she? Why do I cling to her? You'd think she was the focus of the case; that this whole campaign of lies is being carried out in order to reach an understanding of her—not Mordy.

Like you, Abner, I have learned to pick the pockets of life. To steal from those around me. From Zussia I took hesitation; from Anichka, a smile. From Leah, her infantile steeliness, but not without the steel. Even from you I've filched something, can you guess what? And I put your phrases together: yours, Katzman's, old Hillman's, threading beads on an inky string, and so, from next to nothing, I create a new Shosh, very much like me, yet not like me at all.

There's one woman in the room, and another in the glass. So many personalities in a single person. One of them will always give you shelter, help you lie, see you over the border.

And here in the room I throw hints out to Mordy. Long, troubled glances, my hand resting on his shoulder. It wasn't seduction: I want to stress this—it wasn't seduction. It was a suggestion: maybe there's another ancient road we can take? Who will tie up this clump of roots?

But Mordy ignores my suggestions. He isn't trained to decipher them, any more than I am trained to give them. He is ignorant of signs that everyone else can recognize. Stop. I have a question. At this stage, were you at all conscious of what you were plotting? Of what you were about to do? No. All I saw was my ultimate goal. Which was? I was trying . . . that is, I wanted to awaken him to love. To a first experience of it. In the final analysis, I acted out of good intentions.

Of course. Go on.

Once again: love was only a means. Mordy was the end. Maybe I should have realized that people love with different intensities. Some people can love to death. How could I have guessed that's what love would do to him? Therefore I plead: I was not conscious of what I was doing. Lies can very quickly assume the mien of reality. As soon as your attention strays, they trap you and there's nothing you can do.

And maybe, knowing there was no way out of the tunnel, I suddenly realized I had to try something wild. That that was my one hope of communicating with him. Only with his frozen body, with his living tongue, would he ever learn the secrets.

I searched for this wild something, to use in my work, I mean. And I lost and found myself between the faked summaries of our sessions and in the fabricated interviews, running on tiredly without the power to brake, banging into the cool walls of my fears, of my consciousness of what I was doing in the name of science, in the name of altruism, till I fell, like Alice, into a world of cruelty and isolation, of twilight turning to darkness, of savage beasts that lunged out at me from behind the trees as I steered myself with a bestial roar into the hole that gaped open, worshipping it desperately in case it was the name that had been branded in me by the fall, the name which had found this of all ways to make itself known.

18

There seems to be more movement down in the village now. Clouds of dust rise up from the main road to Andal, and I hear that sputtering of transmitters. When I stand on the rock I see them pitching tents below, and there's a water carrier, too, and tall, quivering antennas, all in my honor.

What's going on? It's like a bad dream. I don't want to die here. The whole thing started as a hoax. Partly childish protest and partly foolhardiness, with a little desperation thrown in. You look away for one minute and you find you've been surrounded. I go back to the lemon tree. Khilmi is watching me closely. But it's not the same Khilmi anymore. He's hard, wound up like a spring. Humming along

with the orchestra in his high-pitched voice as he prepares coffee
for the two of us, stirring the brown beans with an old tin spoon,
the gun on his lap.

"Uri?"

"What?"

"A lot of soldiers there?"

"Not so many."

"Go and talk to them again. Maybe they didn't understand."

"They're just not taking you seriously, Khilmi. Or me either."

He gives me a long look, nodding to a slow rhythm. Now I see
that his eyes, both of them, are very red. As if he's been crying.

"But what should I have done, Uri?"

"You should have asked for something a little more reasonable,
like newspaper reporters, or the general in command of the—"

"I do not want newspaper reporters, I don't know how to read."
Now he's really angry. He trembles all over, and the cracks in his
face crisscross each other in spasms. "I want the occupying army
out of here. I want to forget you. I thought you of all people understood that." I suddenly see him as he must have been long ago, at
the beginning of the century—a suffering child, cramped up in his
hump, breaking everyone down into dots and splashes, and if they
had let him stay hidden there, he would have died happy, only
events are forcing him to go back to where he doesn't stand a chance.
And the worst of it is, I haven't decided yet with whom I should go.
That's how I am. I always wait for something to decide for me. And
Khilmi stirs the coffee nervously with one hand in the *mahmaseh*,
and gropes under his robe with the other. He takes out the *mendil*,
his filthy wrinkled kerchief. What's happening to him? I can't bear
to see him in such pain. Now he spreads the stained yellow cloth,
and his fingers dance over a little box that may have once held snuff
and now contains razor blades and old papers. "Look, Uri, the

identification card your people gave me. The *huwiya*. This blue paper is worth more than I am. And I have kept it here in the *mendil*, next to my heart, these past five years. If one of your soldiers catches me without the *huwiya*, he will take me to the prison. Once Shukri Ibn Labib went to the Holy City without his *huwiya*, and a woman soldier shamed him in front of the crowd in the street. And then she took him to the police station. As someone in Juni once said, there are no men left among us, only papers. Watch what I am going to do now, Uri, and do not reach out to stop me."

He holds his identification card to the small flame of the primus under the *finjan*, and the blue cover starts to crinkle and gives off a smell of burning rubber. I am transfixed. Khilmi sits before me, erect and frightened, trying to seem indifferent. The way he did when I discovered he'd painted over the graffiti. I shouldn't have let him burn it like that, though it doesn't really make much difference anymore. It's just that after my three months in the West Bank, what he's doing now scares me to death, because there's no turning back; the *huwiya* is a kind of receipt the Arabs get to prove their existence. To prove they're real. But it's more than that, it's a paper-thin line between our military laws and regulations and a kick in the balls. Not that it matters to Khilmi. What does he care? He's beyond all that. He carefully pours the roasted beans into the mortar and begins to grind.

"Bring me a little water from the bucket, will you, Uri?"

"Okay."

I go to fetch it. The water is murky. Najach brings it to him from the well in the village every two or three days. She isn't strong enough to carry more than one bucket.

"Help me pour it into the *finjan*, Uri. There—watch out for the fire."

I sit down and put my head in my hands, unable to decide whether to laugh or cry. I don't know myself. Don't know what I want. Here I am, almost twenty-eight years old, and what do I know about life? I have no experience, no wisdom. And whenever I try to concentrate, to think clearly and forget that I'm just playing a role in the *kan-ya-ma-kan*, the only thing I believe in is Santa Anarella. The lucid truth I experienced there. And I tune myself to that sweetness, as Khilmi tunes himself to the living sign in Yazdi's face, and I must never forget that sweetness, even for a moment. I must recall what I learned, and out of the fragments of memory reconstruct the Katzman I knew, the strange man who's letting me die alone here, who won't bother to come from Juni and save me from myself.

I mean, he owes me so much, he said so himself once, and he hurt me so badly, I don't see how we'll ever get over it. We're falling to pieces.

Oh, Katzman, Katzman. I've known him for only a year and already he's reflected in my every cell and every thought. Sure he's provoking, and dangerous, too, and most pathetic, I do feel sorry for people like him. Anything can hurt him. He has no defenses.

Only one year. He, too, arrived in Italy at the end of his trip through Europe. He had wanted to do some traveling before he started working in Juni. He was wandering around feeling bored and full of poison, to use his words, but he forced himself to stay to the end because he didn't want to admit he wasn't having a good time (that's how Katzman is). And while he was in Lugano, Switzerland, he heard about the earthquake and left for Santa Anarella at once, with a sigh of relief.

When he told me about that sigh of relief, I told him about the joy I'd felt, like a burst of creativity, as soon as I arrived in the south. He worked like a maniac on my crew, throwing himself into danger with a strange self-contempt, and I couldn't understand what drove him like that. We were in the Promised Land, after all, he had said so himself once, laughing. "Because there's no God here." It was a peculiar thing for someone like Katzman to say. Why was he talking about God when he wasn't religious, or anti-religious either, for that matter? It had nothing to do with religion, he explained, but with a kind of private faith: "When things look grim, here in the ruins, with the mass graves and all, I don't feel deluded, you see?"

I didn't really. Not till long after we left Italy did I begin to figure him out. To know that Katzman had to leave an invisible print wherever he went, the way some people hang a picture of their family in their hotel room to take away the strangeness. This print of Katzman's wasn't something tangible, it was a kind of atmosphere. Or mood. He had to destroy the illusion he called "faith." His Promised Land was swept clean of promises or expectations of friendship. I felt this most cruelly in Juni. You and I aren't friends here, he let me know from the start. And once he said, When something good happens, it isn't natural. Disappointment is natural, but anyone who knows the game will never be disappointed.

That's the Promised Land where he feels good. So good, in fact, that it's dangerous, because he forgets to play the game. I remember the way he galloped around the canteen with that filthy kid on his back, laughing to high heaven.

I think that was what made me suspicious. He seemed so pleased with the barbarism of the Santa Anarella refugees that he had me fooled for a while. He had a store of disgusting jokes, and even made fun of the dead sometimes. But then, a few nights after I understood about the nucleus of love in us all, I began to think maybe Katzman was fighting that nucleus of love in himself. I hate to sound like Shosh, but I think it's true. I wouldn't call him a good man, that wouldn't be the right way to describe someone like Katzman, but he does have a kind of anguish in him, a childish struggle, maybe a fear of letting that part of him reveal itself. Well, maybe that's a little exaggerated.

Anyway, I remember one evening, a little after the daily burials, we were watching two Italians fight over a retarded girl who stood off from the crowd, giggling. The scene made me sick, but I was mesmerized by the expression on Katzman's face. He was almost smiling. His eyes, which were usually half dead, suddenly lit up. I remember the way his jaws clamped shut like the gills of a dangerous fish. Suddenly he noticed that I was watching him and his face froze. He was angry with me. He walked away. It was a few days before he thawed enough to approach the subject. That's when he told me about the "lower depths," where he longs to be. "Those men who were fighting over the girl had helped us bury their dead only a few minutes before. You'd think that after touching the lower depths with their own fingers they would try to find a way to transcend the experience. But what did they do? They fought like animals over a retarded girl. They were nowhere near the lower depths. How low must we go, Uri?"

Suddenly I understood: there was no need to be upset by all the twisted things he said; what he was really looking for was hope. How simple and how surprising it was. A little hope, though he'd never admit it.

"Uri!"

"Huh? What?"

"The water is boiling, do you not hear?"

"I—I was dreaming."

I carefully turn the primus off, burning my fingers as usual. Khilmi shakes the ground coffee beans into the *finjan*, together with a leaf or two of some plant that caught on his hand and fell in. Oh well, *maalesh*. The pot is filthy anyway. Now I hear the ancient rustling sound I like so much, the sound of Khilmi slowly stirring with a dry twig, as though he were playing a musical instrument.

"It is Thursday today, Uri."

"So?"

"You have forgotten. Soon, after sunset, Um Kultum will sing for us on Cairo radio. We can listen to her all night long."

Hip-hip-hooray. "Okay. If you want."

"Once a month, on Thursday nights, there is a program of Um Kultum's music on the radio. Everyone listens, *min elmukhit ila elkhalij*, from the ocean to the Arab Gulf." And he smiles a weird smile and sings to me softly as he sways, *"Rajauni einek li'ayam illi rakhu; allamuni el'ayam illi fattet*. Your eyes take me back to bygone days, reminding me of time past. Beautiful, is it not?"

"Yes, Khilmi, it's beautiful, I'm just not in the mood."

"Are you afraid?"

"Yes."

"But why, Uri? We will be happy. We will be very happy. Trust me, Uri."

And he pours our coffee into a pair of tin tumblers, making sure we get an equal share of the thick froth, and we sip slowly. That is, I do, while he watches me with a curious, worried expression. But I don't care. The sun has reached the horizon, and the green inscription on the wall, behind Khilmi's back, is flashing gaily—traitor, traitor. Overhead the birds fly in a lovely arrowhead formation, crying softly. The end of another day. Something to drink, a little conversation, a little silence, and then you say, Bye now, see you around, and you go your way.

Katzman returned to Israel a week before I did, because his vacation was over and he was expected in Juni. On his last night in Santa Anarella he was nervously talkative. He told me he had been married once for a few months to a woman he didn't love. "A marriage of curiosity," he called it. "I want you to know I've had a lot of women," he said. It wasn't a boast, he just wanted to give me this clue about himself. "I can't understand why it keeps happening," he said. "I'm such an ugly bastard; no, don't try to reassure me, dummy, I've been living with it for forty years. I don't know, I never show I'm interested. Women just seem to want to save me. Some of them have told me so outright. They fuss over me and try to help. They can be married, or old enough to be my mother or sweet young things. It isn't love they offer, that's what drives me crazy. It's forgiveness. They're always so eager to forgive me. For what, I'd like to know. Or else they offer serenity, a balance in my life. That's what they call it. Women have an overly developed sense of symmetry. Take my word for it, Uri."

Then he asked me about me, about my experience with women before Shosh. I was open with him. I told him I'd never really had a girlfriend before Shosh. I also told him that for a year and a half during my army service I corresponded with a girl I'd never met. She wrote me a letter saying she saw me hitchhiking and found my name and address on a discarded envelope. That's how it began. She said she had a boyfriend, but he didn't mind her corresponding with me. I fell in love with her, I told Katzman, but of course I couldn't ask her to leave her boyfriend. All the guys in my company knew about her. They cheered and hooted whenever I got a letter, or whenever I went to mail one at the army post office, but I didn't care.

A year and a half later I found out by chance that in reality Ruthy, the girl of my dreams, was two guys from my company who had been writing to me, using the mailing address of one of them. And everyone was in on the joke except for me. The worst part was that I went on loving her. It was totally irrational. Even when I got out of the army, I couldn't help comparing girls I met to Ruthy, my first love. I was a little wary of involvements after that. It took me four years to get over it, with Shosh's help.

We talked a lot that night. Katzman's laugh sounded different, much freer than usual. We both knew we'd stay in touch. It was strange, but I felt kind of responsible for him. He was the one who set me on the right track, I think, but that night, I had the feeling a little something of me would stick with him. Which is why I'm here now. A led to B, and B will lead to my death. And there's no logical connection between them. I understood very little of what Katzman said in Santa Anarella; it was only nine months later, in Juni, that it burst inside me and began to scream. He was talking about justice that night. He'd thought a lot about it, because he knew that his new post in Juni would force him to commit many injustices. Justice isn't a social, ethical convention, it's more like a hormone secreted at varying levels of intensity. Something a sensitive brain produces as a response to injustice, the way it does in response to sexual stimuli. When he said this, it was as though he were kneading the dough of my life in his hands. It was almost dawn by then, and I knew he was just beginning to open up. That throughout our two weeks together he had been testing me. In careful preparation.

"Goodness and honesty," he said. "Doing the right thing, the just thing, is the most sophisticated form of protest I can think of. But only the very strong, or—maybe—the very desperate can protest that way. It's a double-edged sword, Uri. You have to handle it with care." I remember how the smoking embers rustled, and we wrapped our blankets tighter. Katzman talked about people who are drawn to disaster, like the ones I had come on the plane with. "It's a compulsion with them," he said. "Like the compulsion an artist has to paint. An urge to put things right. A deep, true sense of symmetry. Like art, Uri."

And I also remember his monotonous voice, and his face, so pale, transfixed in the darkness like a distant neon light. I asked him how he planned to go about the job in Juni, and he said he wished he knew. Slowly, as if trying to clarify something to himself, he said, "Anyone who looks for absolute justice today is only fooling himself, paying lip service to a cowardly evasion of commitment. Because with the world as complicated as it is, and people as complicated and contradictory as they are, the concept of justice has lost some of the meaning it used to have.

"Which is why anyone who believes in absolute justice is powerless to act," he said. "Absolute justice is an invention of weaklings, good only for philosophy, which is why justice has to be a private and subjective feeling, as I said before: a hormone secreted by my brain." His long face fairly gleamed in the darkness when he leaned over and told me that the underdog always wins in the end.

And then I saw the weirdest sunrise I've ever seen in my life: a soft, penitent light broke out in the far corner of the sky, like big, luminous drops that spread through the air, trying to connect and become a sunny day. We watched the sky in silence. There was a strange battle in progress. For ten minutes somebody up there was mixing the colors, trying out different patterns of light and darkness. In the end we won. For the first time that night we looked at each other without shyness. We smiled.

And now, what now, one year later, and the circle is closing in on me slowly but surely. This coffee has a strange taste. Drink your coffee, Khilmi, why aren't you drinking? Here I sit drinking it on a nearly empty stomach, drinking to stay awake, to regain control of the situation, because soon the sun will set and a long difficult night will commence; oh, let everything be over already so I can go back to Shosh and learn to live with her somehow, maybe it isn't her fault, and maybe it isn't Katzman's fault either, maybe it isn't anybody's fault, except mine. And I'm through with war. I'm no good at war, but then I suddenly leaped up and howled at Khilmi, that demon in a black beret, wagging his neck like a crafty turtle, because this is my last chance to get out of here alive, to jump him before I have time to regret it, but no, he hops aside on his bandy legs and grabs the gun, God he's quick, he's already standing over me, and all I can see are his skinny legs sticking out of his sneakers, and I look up at this stranger panting as he aims the gun at me with shaking hands; oh, don't let him fire a stray bullet. Shoot me, shoot me, I scream in Hebrew. Let's see you kill me, I don't have the strength to wait out the night, and I'm scared, Khilmi, I'm scared, and I lie on my back at his feet like a child, crying tearlessly, with a weak, strange-sounding voice, and I watch as once again somebody up there mixes the paints in the sky for a new work of art.

Khilmi, oh, Khilmi. He doesn't shoot. He doesn't kick me. He stands over me, tensely pointing the gun at my head, moving his lips and mumbling as the blue vein throbs like crazy, and it looks as if he's reciting a prayer or incantation as he sits me back down and ties the ropes that tore when I took my foolish leap *kan-ya-ma-kan*; like an enormous spider he weaves around me again, repairing the damaged web, and I make no attempt to say anything or do anything, I curl up where I fell. The coffee tasted strange, a little sour, maybe I should try to sleep awhile. Maybe I should try to think about myself and what happened. We each have a key, she said. Where did I lose mine? Never mind. Go to sleep.

In Juni I had many keys. And there were many locks there, too. Katzman started me off with a hell of a job, fitting keys to locks, and the Italian sweetness flowed through me again. For a while, I felt good. I had plans. Everything had to change. There's an occupation government, that's what people say unthinkingly. It's like a story you hear so many times you can't tell whether it's true anymore. And before I came to Juni, it was just a phrase for me, too: an occupation government. But there were barricades, and body searches for men and women, and midnight interrogations and administrative arrests and house arrests and demonstrators scattered with force, with tear gas, and houses blown up at night, and house-to-house searches, and no friendship. As though both sides were forced to expose their darker aspects. The trouble is there are always justifications. There are always arguments either way: the Arabs held a demonstration, so we used force to scatter them. Someone threw a grenade, so we imposed a curfew on the neighborhood and carried out house-to-house searches, and when there are house-to-house searches, things get a little rough, a TV set is smashed up as pajama-clad children watch in silence, and naked couples tremble in their beds. So we're right and they're right, we're a pretty enlightened occupation, as Katzman always says to me, and if we're so virtuous, I don't understand everything that's been happening here for the past five years.

The local inhabitants would come to me, to my office in the administration building, to file their complaints, glancing around anxiously, and it took them a while to understand that they wouldn't be harmed for talking to me, and that they could rely on me to move heaven and earth to get army compensation for a merchant whose car was hit by one of our jeeps tearing through the streets in hot pursuit, but they soon found out how ineffectual I was, that I could only holler and eat myself up, because no one in the military administration took me seriously, since, as Katzman explained my first week in Juni, friends are friends, but we all have a job to do around here, so during work hours we go by the book, no special treatment. If my claims were justified, he would see to them. Otherwise he wouldn't. And I agreed, because it sounded reasonable enough, and only much later did I realize he'd brought me out to Juni as a kind of alibi, or maybe even to punish me for some unknown crime.

So I marched into his office and said, Look here, Katzman, I saw the bruises on the boy's stomach with my own eyes, and I seriously doubt that it was an admonition that put them there, and he answered me, One of Akhmad Gibril's cells has been active here for months now, and unless we find it, you can be sure it'll find us, and that will be very bad for us, and worse still for the inhabitants, people who live in glass houses shouldn't throw stones at IDF patrols, and he was right, and they were right, and I felt I was going to explode, and so in a moment of terrible despair, in a moment of angry compromise with everything, I decided to hell with it, from now on I will listen only to the lucid voice of that hormone in my brain that tells me a great injustice has been committed against these people, and I don't care that they were the ones who started it with their own aggression and their continuing hatred for us, I don't give a damn how enlightened our occupation is, or that there's very little overt violence, both sides have valid claims, so from now on I will move blindly on, because you have to be a little blind sometimes to get anything done, and then I knew what I wanted, I knew myself again.

In Juni I learned how the wheels of injustice turn. When you do someone an injustice, you become trapped in the movement of the wheel; you forfeit a part of yourself to injustice and thereafter you are its representative wherever you go, and though it may not show, you're crippled for life. This is why I decided to go to war, alone, with all my might.

And this is why I tagged along with every search party on every arrest, and spent nights on end at the roadblocks, even wangling permission from Katzman to be present at the interrogations of minors and sending a girl soldier in to the interrogations of female minors. I had never been so stubborn before. I didn't care about anything: not the hostile soldiers around me, not the beating Sheffer gave me once, not even Katzman's jibe that I went around like a positive electron, blindly unloading my charge in all directions. The important thing was to try to change something. Minor successes like an old man's amazement when I got his son, a diabetic, released from prison; or a merchant I procured a license for to reopen his shop; or a visitor's permit for a cousin from Jordan; or the countermanding of an order to destroy a herd of infected goats, putting them in quarantine for a month instead. Everything like this wears down the wheels of injustice, but it leaves many scars. Still, I felt good, because I was fighting.

Maybe that's why I lost Shosh. I was so involved with myself that we drew apart. When I went to work in Juni, she was immersed in the treatment of her fourth juvenile delinquent, about whom I knew nothing until three days ago. She stopped talking to me about her patients. All I knew was that after a long stretch with no results, he suddenly started making progress and just as suddenly relapsed. She rarely mentioned him at home, which was fine with me, since I was opposed to those modern methods they use at the institute, but of course I said nothing to Shosh. I had no right to.

Idiot. Numskull. Cap-and-Bells. Uri el Tartur. I used to lecture her and Katzman about my plans, telling them about my newfound joy, my lucid sense of truth. They would watch me in silence, with a kind of sadness in their eyes. I didn't know her boy had died of love. How did she hide it from me? I should have listened more carefully to the cracking sounds her face made. She went into a fever of improvement. She painted our bedroom a dazzling white I didn't like, though I said nothing, and she spent a fortune on new clothes and all sorts of household gadgets; even Leah asked, "Whatever has possessed our Shosh?" She talked about aesthetics all the time, about color and movement, but I didn't understand her, I didn't realize I had become like a grain of sand in her eye, that she wanted pure beauty.

She always seemed to be somewhere else. Far away from us. When I spoke about Juni, about the sense of truth and the good feeling it gave me, she got up and left, saying, "Excuse me, but I've had an awful day, and tomorrow's going to be even worse. Good night, Uri; Katzy, I'll probably see you when you come next week." I—I was almost hurt that she went off like that, but then she suddenly stopped by the bedroom door, smiled at me like the old Shosh, slowly walked over, and, right in front of Katzman, kissed me on the nose.

19

Wisely, prudently, like fine embroidery, the unseen threads are
fast entwining; no need to pluck them out of my belly, out of the
hollow of my eye; all living matter dissolves into strands of memory
and ripples of longing, like the grape bower and Um Kultum hanging
from my neck, and the rays of the weary red sun unraveling across
the blue, and Uri, out of weakness and fear and the sleep-inducing
sakran leaves I ground into his coffee, and the unburnt shreds of
my *huwiya*, and the green inscription blooming on the wall, and the
humming antennas that rise up from Andal, what are these but matter
crushed by the gravity of anguish till it is thin and flimsy, there and
not there, *kan-ya-ma-kan*, and Uri and I will sniff it greedily like

a dream potion, and walk through it, clinging and burning, into the clefts where the rose air of freedom blows and time cannot be measured with clocks, because it is the time of the heart, and the dark road ahead will be lighted for us by the beacon of Uri's countenance, this open wound, the bite of truth in his meager flesh, and who can stop us now.

But slyly, with timid cunning, Yazdi was taken from me and from himself. I will not let Uri be taken from me, too. Whosoever is bitten by a snake fears the tail. And therefore I have put him to sleep, and while he slumbers, I will dissolve all remorse in the darkness beyond him, and use the hour before dawn to do what he has begged me to in silence since the morning, and he will be the most fortunate of men, struck down in a dream, and it is good.

I will show him the way. How he fought with me. In the rocky soil of this old carcass he wished to bury the seeds of his thoughts. The innocent child. All night long he spoke: We must strive against war and hatred, if only upon this narrow battlefield, a battlefield for one. Together, he vowed, we will turn back the wheels of injustice. He held forth like my idiot Yazdi, only he said the opposite, his eyes filling up his glasses as he rubbed his stubbly chin. Again and again I told him it was senseless. That if we pit ourselves against the wheel, it will mow us down and roll on. That his vision would only grease this wheel, and you, roared my heart, you and Yazdi are both accomplices to injustice, which cannot be fought the way you say, Uri, nor in the ways set forth by the wandering guilds, for when you touch it, it corrupts you; so I say, Run, Uri, grab the whip that lashes your face, and get thee out of thy country, like a blind man trapped in sunbeams, unto the land that I will choose for you, and leave this wheel to roll recklessly on until its spokes break through to the anguish inside it and it crashes down the final slope, running over itself and its drivers.

Follow me now, moon child, most comely of my bastard children, you who are so good that when you touch a sore you heal it, let your head droop against your chest, and stare not with fearstruck eyes, have faith in me, Uri: I will teach you to tread lightly and never touch the ground, to walk on dough and leave no tracks, till at last you see, till at last you stop striving, entwining like the unseen thread of my embroidery, for you are made of musings, my son.

Come, my child, be Uri or Yazdi, I care not who you are, who I am, so long as we feel love throbbing between us like a young bird; so long as your eyes dream with mine and a weary smile breaks forth from your lips, where a fine thread of spittle sparkles in the sunset like the web of an old memory, the strongest fabric to be found in the crack between earth and sky, but why speak when Um Kultum is singing songs of love and songs of the grape harvest, plucking threads of sorrow from our hearts with the thrumming of the *kanun*, and the sun is setting just for us, Uri, the sky is crumpling overhead like paper catching flame, your hand in mine, and it is good.

Kan-ya-ma-kan, fi kadim elzaman, usalef elaasar walawan, a whole nation cannot walk through these clefts, so no one listens to me, not even here in my village of sheep. That is why no one listens to you in your country, in the flexed muscle of an army where you live. Nor can three pass through together, Uri. This road is for one man alone, with perhaps a friend at his side. For deeds of truth are done by one, or rarely perhaps by two. But when there are three, one of them lies and casts a blind eye at the third. And we three tread lightly through the clefts, Uri, because one is dead already, and the second is about to die, and the third may never have been born at all, but formed himself out of a figment.

I have decided, Uri, I will not hearken to the fear and mercy screaming inside me, I will not look into your panic-ridden eyes;

as the saying goes, if you want to go carousing, why count your cups, so I will pour you out into myself like a dose of medicine.

Kan-ya-ma-kan, Uri, *kan-ya-ma-kan*—he no longer listened to me and my story, he refused to go down to the wadi with me, to burn *awarwad* leaves and count our heartbeats, and cast finger shadows on the rock: now a hare, now a hound, now a pigeon flying, and he quit me when I rose from my barrel dripping water and refused to bring my robe, but sat under the lemon tree, my lavaliere at his ear, listening, no, not to our beloved singing songs of honey and butter, but to the cold, broken words of the speakers of news, as he stared dimly ahead, mouthing their transistor phrases the way he used to echo mine in the tales he loved so well. He was like the steel-voiced muezzin the people of Juni installed in their minaret when the Jews gave them electricity; I heard this from Nuri el Nawar, who said that Abu Amaad no longer had to climb the tower five times a day to call the faithful to prayer, because the scarecrow muezzin did it better, and it never lost its voice in the middle of the *Alfaatekha*, like Abu Amaad. But then, Nuri may have been lying.

And Yazdi would gaze after me with empty eyes, and pretend to embrace me before he disappeared for days on end, returning to me in a raging fever, smelling of scorched flesh instead of sage. And once as we supped together and peace descended upon us both, he said to me, "*Ya ba*, how skillfully you prepare the bulgur wheat," and I was filled with a strange longing and tried to regale him with a favorite tale I used to tell on days when we had to content ourselves with onions and pita bread, a story of the gloomy feasts of Sha'aban Ibn Sha'aban, but he suddenly burst out of his shell, screaming, How long, *Ya ba*, how long will you go on dreaming thus, and his trembling hand overturned the plate, and the bulgur scattered at his feet. Don't you see, *Ya ba*, that we have been beaten by strangers who rob us of the very air we breathe and who plunder the beauty of our countryside with their eyes, the ripening fields and the olive trees, and do to us now what you and I would do when we lay on our backs in the wadi like upturned turtles, dreaming of the village empty of everything, and now they are sucking out our very life and will and pride, to them we are no more than a kind of pest, mere shells of men, and I tell you, *Ya ba*, yesterday at the roadblock in Juni, as people left at dawn to work at the homes of the Jews and in the building sites and hospitals and factories and restaurants and fields and orange groves and in the city streets and public parks and in the kibbutzim and gas stations and grocery stores and sewing shops and slaughterhouses and ports, do you hear, *Ya ba*, yesterday at dawn, as the people filed out of the bus driven by an Israeli Arab, that's what they call themselves, those dogs, the slaves of cats, who have learned to hate a rat, who cut us dead, crying *Yalla etla*, never looking into our eyes when they hand us our change in little pink notes, you hear me, *Ya ba*, yesterday at the Juni roadblock the Israeli soldiers stepped on the bus and ordered the men off so they could check the *huwiya* of each, and there was one, Saif a-din A-sha'abi, he was an old man like you, *Ya ba*, a venerable old father of countless sons, the issue of his loins, and he had not been out of Juni since the occupation, and no one knew why he boarded the · bus that morning with all the laborers. And when the young officer turned and growled at him, *Ya'ala enzil*, Saif a-din said in a loud clear voice that was heard by the Israeli-Arab driver and the soldiers and the officer and by our sisters in the bus as well, and by all the men who had stepped off, "I, Mr. Officer, *khadrat eldabet*, I will not stir from here, because you ordered the men off the bus, but there are no men here, sir, only empty shells, not like the men of my day, who were men of flesh and blood, these men are made of paper bound in blue, and as he spoke, he grabbed the officer's gun and aimed it at his own head, and before anyone could stop him, he shot himself and died. And you, *Ya ba*, speak shamelessly of the rose air of freedom you breathed as you glided over Andal like a bird, when all the while you were a slave among slaves, calling the man who raped your mother Father, and in my eyes, *Ya ba*, the deed performed by Saif a-din A-sha'abi is far nobler than all your stories of Sha'aban Ibn Sha'aban, of whom no one in the village has ever heard.

He grew between my hands, and flowed out between my fingers. At night he would slip away from the pallet at my side and join the boys and the men, and return with the scorching smell upon his breath, not the smell of the cigarettes he learned to smoke, that he lit before my eyes from the butt of the last one, and I never knew or wished to know, but once Shukri Ibn Labib, the enemy of my youth and friend of my old age, came dragging his bag of bones up the hill and sat with me under the lemon tree, sipping coffee, and he heaved a sigh to the four winds of heaven and said, It is no good, *ya* Khilmi.

A beekeeper is Shukri, and his honey is sweeter even than honey from Hebron. His hands look like punctured dough from the stings, and his fingers swell and bleed from the pins he sticks in them in order to keep from laughing. He has only three years left to stifle laughter, he says, before attaining the ascetic rung of Khassan el Basri, who never laughed once in thirty years. "These are restive days. The boys I teach in the *kutab* have thrown off the rule of my rod. If you could but see them, Khilmi: they are hatred in the flesh. All have been infected." And he shakes his horsy head, running his hands over his sunken cheeks, and says with a penetrating glance, "Your Yazdi is among them. He follows them and does their bidding. And as you know, whosoever follows the owl ends in ruin."

Shukri spoke with a weariness I had never known in him before, not with anger or with scorn. I gazed at his face, at his hands, reflecting how old he had grown. I still remembered him as a laughing child with catlike eyes, stuffing grasshoppers into my mouth, but then, when he returned from the *zawiya* of Sheikh Salakh Khamis, everyone mocked him, and only I rejoiced with him. And now we are both very old.

And he told me everything I did not want to know. That Araf, the oil merchant's son, was wounded in a demonstration in Hebron, his skull cracked by a club, his wits gone ever since. And a young girl, thirteen years old, from the girls' school in Juni, was arrested and questioned all night long by Israeli men who would not allow her mother to be present in the room with her. And that houses have been blown up in Nablus and Jericho, and pastures and wheat fields have been commandeered—which means stolen and paid for—and families have been separated, with some members exiled over the river and others forbidden to leave their homes.

So he spoke, till I could bear it no longer, and I raised my voice, for soon he, too, would spout words about pride and vengeance. You see, I explained to him, all this may come to a hasty end one day, for the Jews are not a stupid race and they have probably realized by now that the conqueror is also the conquered, and that injustice has teeth in its tail; and Shukri replied that truly the Israelis may come to harm as well, but ours is the graver harm, because, as they say, whosoever receives the blows does not compare with him that counts them, and so we two old ones argued with each other, leaning back against the lemon tree, and I screamed that the Jews cannot long withstand our patience, which moves mountains, and that if we listen to reason and protect ourselves from the electricity they bring, the medicines they give us, the vegetables they sell in our markets, and the money they offer us in return for the confiscated lands and for a glass of *kahwe* at Aish's, if we protect ourselves from all their fair-mindedness wrapped in rules and regulations, those poisoned webs they weave around us, more deadly than naked hatred, but just then Shukri gasped and raised his hand to heaven, saying I had become like unto a broken jar with the wind blowing through the cracks, and that what they say about me in the village is true, that I no longer hear what my own mouth utters: they have all been stolen, young and old, while I dream of a war like fine embroidery. a war like the shadows of dancing fingers on the rocks, and though he would never commit an act of violence himself, because it is not in his nature, he could only scorn my cowardice and my stupidity, and I whispered to him, Take my son Yazdi, for instance, but he suddenly neighed like an angry horse and screamed that Yazdi is not my son anymore, for they are all sons of hatred and war, and they are lost to us, and we are alone, *ya* Khilmi, alone.

Kan-ya-ma-kan, daylight sank into me like a cinder glowing through the night in the winding clefts, in the belly of the hill upon my back. Look through the fading light, Uri, for when darkness hangs like heavy drops in my branches and spreads over the horrors of my dreams, and the severed hand on Yazdi's shoulder in the jagged photograph, and all the burdens in this old gourd make it droop so heavily against my chest, it almost breaks the thread of my neck, and when, *ya* Uri, the painted silken map is unfurled to the four corners of the earth, and a hand walks on its fingers, groping after me in the gloaming, then, once again, with new vigor I assail that last glimmer of grace, the remembrance of a day which has sunk into my hill and ruddled the shreds of my memory, raising a youthful blush on the cheeks of my dead ones, and I fan the cinder, sobbing with all my heat and rage, and I spit like a cat and groan like a rutting bull, till my strength gives out and the pouring sweat drips into my eyes, and out of my belly a new day breaks forth, my son, my offspring, may he shine upon me, and upon the grape bower, upon my village of sheep, and upon this rough-drawn country, and it is good.

Look through the dusk, *ya* Uri, strain your eyes a little more, before the blossoms of the *sakran* drift into the yellow glow and light your dreams. And be not afraid: the *sakran* gives only pleasure. And if we had all the time in the world, I would take some flour now and knead it into dough, grind *sakran* leaves in, wrap my handkerchief around it, and put it on your brow, so you would know the taste of a truly peaceful dream.

Let me lull you to sleep. I cannot sing you a cradle song, for my voice is harsher than a braying donkey's. I can hum along, though, with our loved ones hanging from my neck. But now old Mother Um Kultum is singing, and if I hum along with her, I will surely cry, so let me lull you to sleep with a story as in childhood days gone by.

Lie here in your swaddling flesh, child of the moon, a moment ago you trembled with a passing fear and tried to leap at me and grab the shining toy I took from the turd that was dropped by the iron horse in front of my cave yesterday, where once, I recall, anguish dropped tender babes, or frightened mothers, their bellies swollen with sin, and now they drop these iron toys here, and even you turned to iron when you tried to cut loose the fetters of love I girded around you, so sleep and rest, let me cover you with gossamer quilts, with the silken map unfurled as always to the four corners of the earth, where a likeness of you is dimly visible, and soon the cloth will touch you and the images will kiss each other and you will know no more pain.

Lie still. I will cover you. I will tell you *kan-ya-ma-kan*. It is difficult to remember now, the old appear in the faces of the newborn, and in the end everyone looks alike. Perhaps not in appearance, perhaps not in words so much as in a kind of painful thread that binds them, men, women, and children, except for the one who was cast out of the tumult, who looked out for himself, and now, Uri, I am trying to remember the face of that woman among women, Laila Sallach, whose boldest, most penetrating lover I was, you see—I cannot remember.

What is happening to me, Uri? I say the words as I have always said them, but their savor is gone. No more do they pour out boiling hot upon my fingers. Is it a sign? Listen, wake up.

For she was the lovely sloven, the sauciest woman who ever roamed the winding paths of Andal, taking shape out of the dreams of men, caking on their lids at night, coming to life in fleeting visions they discharged while in their arms they held the mustached monster they called "my wife." No, no, Uri, this is not what I meant to tell you, this phantom was not Laila Sallach, though perhaps—oh no, how could it be, such a woman must have lived here, and she loved me, you know, I was the lustiest of lovers whose fancy gave her form, and she was a brazen woman with the eyes of a cat, and God sent her a fiery little angel to ignite her womb, and all the trees in the forest were not enough to feed the conflagration burning inside her, and men would throw themselves at her feet, begging to be consumed in her flames, to be melted like candles, till they were cool waxy casings with a blackened wick, indifferent to women forevermore—do you hear me, Uri, do you believe me—and then Shukri Ibn Labib told me this, too, was a lie, that there never was such a woman in our village. "The only woman resembling her was your own mad mother, ya Khilmi, who wallowed in the mire till she disappeared one day and never returned," but the things he said did not pain me, for I explained that there was a woman named

239

Laila Sallach, there must have been, for hope is gone unless such a wanton jet of passion erupted out of these arid sands, and some say, Uri, that it was her lust that brought Sha'aban Ibn Sha'aban to his death, and not an ailment of the liver, that it was not the hyenas who tore him apart while he was still alive, for many a man was devoured alive in her service, ravaged by the fangs of passion, as happened to my father, Shafik Abu Sha'aban, inflated by grief, stuffed in death like a massive fish, like a doleful overripened fruit, and it is fear, Uri, fear and fervor cutting loose the cords of memory and the threads attached to the old gourd, that makes me spit out my folly like watermelon seeds, and it turns in my belly like a ball of prickly rope, like splinters of colored glass, and perhaps this is a sign that I have returned for the fifth or sixth time to my mute childhood, and before me lies the tortuous road; where will I find the strength to follow it once again, to kill my father and bring myself forth, to conceive my children and my days, and now, rest, my son, out of this fever come the cool breezes; I will draw strength from them to hew out a few more words and tell you a story.

Kan-ya-ma-kan, one day two soldiers in a little gray autotruck drove into our village of sheep and climbed my hill and asked if I was Khilmi and if I had a son named Yazdi and politely ordered me to come with them. I did not remove my robe or wind a *kaffiyeh* around my head, but rose and walked between them like a corpse, and for the first time ever, I left Andal, where I was born, and rode in a car, and they took me to the city of Juni, about which I had heard only in the stories of Nuri el Nawar and Shukri Ibn Labib, but I saw nothing, because fear blinded my one eye, and Yazdi-Yazdi, sang the wheels of the car, my son-my son, drummed the boots of the soldiers on the road, and all around I was touched by their scorching breath, but there was no smell of sage in it, and the soldiers led my empty shell to the administration building in Juni and escorted me to a big hall, where there were numerous other human shells, old like me, and younger, too, men and women, disaster lying heavy on their lids.

Then, at a signal from one of the soldiers, boys and girls filed into the room like tired ants. Their faces were empty and confused, and my Yazdi was among them. I felt joy welling up in me: he was alive. They had not killed him. Last in line, he stumbled into the room, smaller than the rest, falling behind with his halting walk and leaning with them against the wall. And I flew up and whirled around him, flapping like a wounded bird, and I dropped like a stone when I saw that his features were there, and the movements of his hand, and the fine thread of spittle in the corner of his mouth, but I could not recognize him anymore, for he had lost the living sign upon his countenance, and how could I know he was Yazdi, and his smell was the smell of hatred, and beyond the compassion that touched me for him in his endless loneliness I felt a new revulsion in me, like a cat that pushes its kitten away when it bears the smell of strangers.

Then a weary ashen-faced older officer came into the hall. Two and a half years ago this was, and his words to us still choke me. "These boys and girls were trapped by the army while plotting against public law and safety." The man spoke of explosives, and about a newspaper of some sort, but I no longer listened. Yazdi's head was tucked between his shoulders, and his lean legs wobbled under his trousers. "Any other conquering army," said the older officer, "would execute them posthaste, but we are no ordinary occupation army." He paused in his speech and looked at us. I thought, They are already dead, all of them. Shukri was right: this hatred has plundered them all. They are already like animal hides turned into trophies of hatred. Suddenly one of the youths groaned and fell down. His mother and father tried to hurry to his side, but a soldier holding a gun stopped them. Two soldiers came and carried him out, to the other room. I watched the parents of this youth. They stood like their own living gravestones, covered with a fine layer of frost, though it was exceedingly hot. The weary officer wiped the sweat from his brow with a handkerchief. The movements of his hand were small and sure. Then he folded his handkerchief four times and put it in his shirt pocket. We watched him in alarm.

Yazdi leaned against the wall, seemingly asleep. The officer said, "This is your first and last warning. We are turning your children over to you now, because it is your duty to raise them. We won't do it for you. You will not have a second chance. Now take them."

And we left for Andal on the bus. I felt like an exploding oven, but on my face I wore a mask. We were silent all the way home. What could I say to him? I had killed my other children with folly when they were weaned. Only him did I spare, and he had done this to me. And on the way I had my first glimpse of the army camps, and the soldiers and the barricades, and the soldier women, and the tanks by the roadside, and the big yellow signs. In the seat before us sat one of the youths who had been released, talking to his father. The words streamed out of his mouth, fluent and hollow. Vengeance, he said. It is our duty to rebel. And he spoke of armed resistance and of acts that are symbols, and I listened to him, and Yazdi listened, too; the father of the youth was silent. He merely stood up and walked away from his son, who was no longer his son. And the boy said, We have suffered enough humiliation, and the *sumud*, the phase of passive resistance, which is nothing but cowardice, is over and done with, and I agreed in my heart, and he said that there are secret associations and plans, and arms from over the river, and trained fighters passing through the roadblocks in secret and absorbed into our midst; he spoke, and Yazdi's lips moved as though echoing his words. Tyranny will be met by force, the iron fist will be crushed by a leaden one. A light went on in Yazdi's eyes. A white and leprous light. Two and a half years ago he was lost to me. So wisely, prudently, with timid cunning now.

20

At seven o'clock that evening, the soldiers greased their guns and loaded their magazines. Katzman sat at a rickety table in the little command tent, watching Sheffer and the intelligence officer trying to pin a slippery roll of cardboard—the plan of the "cave hill"—to the tent flap. From the nearby café, Arab music wafted hot and heavy through the air. Flies frazzled by the heat of the day continued to buzz after dark, hanging in clusters from the tent flaps, the table, and the ammunition belts in the corner. A notebook lay open before Katzman, and he was trying to write something on the page, but the silence outside threw his thoughts into turmoil. The men hadn't said a word in almost an hour as they listlessly went about their preparations. Katzman knew what their silence meant.

Sheffer approached, surprised to see Katzman's notebook, and even more surprised to see that Katzman was trying to hide something written there with his hand. He smiled. "So, writing a poem, Katzman?"

"No. I'm writing a will. Yours, incidentally. Go call the men."

"Sir!"

Katzman smiled. He carefully folded the page, which was blank except for the date and a single sentence. It was a kind of letter, addressed to Uri, which he would give him as soon as they were out of here. A letter of explanation, or vindication perhaps. "I need to tell you why I asked you to come out to Juni with me": this was the harvest of an hour's writing. Out of everything that had come between them, this, he felt, was what most urgently required an explanation. But how would he put it in writing?

The men trudged in, sighing as they sat on the ground and cursing without rancor. Katzman stood before them, his back to the plan. He waited for silence and began to speak. As usual he was laconic, tediously to the point. His voice and face were expressionless. He had nothing new to tell them. The ultimatum was set for dawn, i.e., approximately 0430; there had been two messages from Laniado so far: "our only source of information about what's going on up there; we don't know for certain how many of them there are—okay, now Sheffer will explain the topography."

Sheffer stood up, ostentatiously removed a silver pen from his shirt pocket, and pulled it out till it resembled a long antenna. The soldiers chuckled. Sheffer had a weakness for such gadgets. He pointed the silvery antenna at the bottom of the plan. "There's only one way up," he said. "The path is steep, and there's gravel for the first few meters, so you'll have to be careful. The stone wall starts here and gets lower the closer you come. The last two men in line will lie down on it. The whole yard can be taken from there. Is that clear?"

The soldiers nodded.

"Good. The rest of you, file up to the entrance. Here we might try a little deployment. Our intelligence officer thinks there may be"—Sheffer threw the young, dark-haired intelligence officer a cold, suspicious look—"some kind of bush or tree growing out of the cave wall which might give us a way to get up. For everyone's sake, I hope you're right about that, Yoni."

Yoni explained from his seat: "This tree or bush, or whatever, is just a possibility worth keeping in mind. It's not a sure thing by any means. The little mute, the old man's granddaughter, drew some pictures of the terrain. Here, in the middle of the wall, she drew something that looks like green foliage. It's the same in all the pictures."

"Just remember this," grumbled Sheffer, who was not exactly thrilled to be embarking on an operation based on the drawings of a mute girl and Katzman's harebrained ideas. He tried to continue: "If there is a bush, then Nathan, Ezra, and Gaby will climb it and lie down—hell, Katzman!"

Sheffer couldn't go through with it. He had been charged with the presentation of a plan which to his mind didn't stand a chance. He gave Katzman a piercing look and pouted defiantly. Katzman sprang to his feet and ordered Sheffer to sit down. The men followed this exchange attentively.

"Questions," said Katzman.

These burst like steam from an engine. Doubt, bewilderment, and anger blew out his way. It was impossible to hear a word in all the clamor. Katzman silenced them with a raised hand. "It's clear that a plan like this will fail. If they leave one scout out on the path, he'll be able to snipe at us like ducks in a shooting gallery." Katzman paused and brought his fingertips together. The soldiers saw the skin stretch back over his cheekbones, making the hollows look deeper than ever. "But this plan is only an alternative to the main strategy, which involves me alone, with the rest of you covering. It's based on the assumption that we're all wrong. That the only one up there with Laniado is the old man."

He waited for this latest storm to die down. The tent was too narrow to contain the steam of excitement. "Don't ask me about it, because you won't get an answer," said Katzman. "I looked at the same facts you have, and added a few you don't have, and that's what I figure I'm going up the path to talk to the old man and get Laniado out of there. There won't be any shooting. The rest of you will follow me as a precautionary measure, that's all."

A long-limbed soldier in filthy work clothes, the one Katzman had found sleeping under the camouflage net, raised his hand. Katzman listened wearily. "Sir, something stinks here," he said. "This isn't just a normal hostage strike."

"I don't want to hear anything about hostage strikes," said Katzman roughly. "What's going on up there is a private struggle between—um—the old man and Uri. The ultimatum business is merely a pretext. Is that clear?" He felt extremely unconvincing.

The long-limbed soldier continued in the same indifferent tone, somewhat provokingly. "In my opinion, and I'm not the only one, sir, you ought to think twice about this, maybe talk it over with somebody. Wait for the trackers Yoni sent for to get here. You can't just climb the hill and—"

Katzman stopped him short with a poisonous white stare. "The old man is holding Laniado up there all by himself. He's insane and he's over seventy. I'm practically convinced that he doesn't have a weapon. And if he does have one, he doesn't know how to use it."

The soldier nodded, slowly deferential, as Katzman spoke, but the moment Katzman stopped speaking, he continued, "What do you mean the old man is holding him all by himself? Laniado said specifically that there were several of them up there and that if we force our way in they might kill him!" The soldiers murmured assent. A red-haired soldier added quietly, "And let's say the old guy's crazy, from the stories we've heard, he sounds like a pretty stubborn character who knows what he wants. I've been in the territories a long time now, sir, and I've never heard of anything quite like this. I don't believe you have either."

Sheffer waited, well pleased, for the waves of hostility to swallow Katzman before offering his own small ripple of grace: "And if he doesn't have a weapon, how do you account for Laniado's cooperating with him? Look, sir, you know how much I like Laniado, but he's not a complete dolt, and if he didn't take the old man out right away, it must mean he's being threatened with something, no?" Sheffer looked around, bubbling over with his own cleverness.

Katzman listened. He knew he couldn't explain what was going on up there. It was too complex. He couldn't even articulate it to himself very clearly, but he sensed that he was on the right track, that there was only one explanation for what was happening. He watched the obstreperous men before him, but no longer heard their voices. He knew they were worried. They hadn't slept since yesterday morning, and the dangerous raid on the house in Juni had frayed their nerves. Just as they were due to go on leave that morning, they had been urgently summoned here. But it wasn't lack of sleep that troubled them. They were deeply bewildered. There had been a breach in the rules of the game. For some reason, this Khilmi impressed them as a man who could shape reality any way he liked. Katzman decided that his most urgent task was to destroy this mystical impression. "Yoni," he said, "stand up and tell the men about

Khilmi. Everything we found out about him in the village today."

The intelligence officer stood up, dark and balding, his face sharp and very determined. "We're talking about an old man," he said. "Seventy—maybe seventy-five. He has no friends in the village, apart from another old guy who's also a little loony. We talked to him, too, but couldn't get anything out of him. Khilmi has no family in the village. The little girl isn't really his granddaughter. His son wasn't really—"

A curly head with thick glasses peered in.

"Yes, Amos?"

"Sir. He radioed. Come quick."

Katzman hurried away to the signal operator's tent. The lights on the panel flickered red and green like the eyes of deep-water fish.

"Amos to Laniado."

There was static and then Uri's voice broke through. Katzman sensed Uri's exhaustion almost immediately.

"Laniado here. Where's Katzman, Amos?"

Katzman took the receiver from Amos and pressed the butterfly-shaped switch. "Katzman speaking. Listen, Uri—"

"Listen here, Katzman." Uri sounded utterly hollow. "He's going to kill me. He's gone completely nuts in the past few hours."

"Is he standing near you?"

"Yes. He doesn't stop talking to himself. He has the gun aimed at me all the time."

"And doesn't he care—" Katzman paused. The gun. His eyes met Amos's. "Doesn't he care that you're talking to us?"

"He doesn't care about anything, he's got one thing on his mind. At dawn he's going to kill me. For my own good, you understand. Nothing else matters to him. I suggested to him— Katzman?"

"I hear you. Listen, I'm planning to go up there and talk to him."

"That's exactly what I proposed to him before. Wait a minute."

There was a moment's silence. Amos doodled on the page before him. Uri returned, sounding relieved if somewhat surprised. "He agreed. Hey, he remembers you from our visit to the village that time."

Katzman was astounded. "He agreed? You mean, just like that? Without—"

Uri said impatiently, "Yes, you don't understand, it doesn't make any difference to him whether you're here or not. He just wants to kill me, now do you understand?"

Katzman noted a new tone in Uri's voice. It sounded something like contempt. He asked, "When should I come up?"

Uri consulted with Khilmi, leaving the switch open. Katzman could hear the old man's cackly voice. He also heard a radio in the background. An idea flickered through Katzman's mind. This music could be very convenient when the backup force arrived. Uri asked a question and the old man answered. There was no tension in his voice, Katzman noticed, as if he was completely oblivious to what was going on. This would make Katzman's task much easier, though it also made the old man's reactions entirely unpredictable.

"At midnight," said Uri. Katzman and Amos glanced at their watches. Another four hours.

"Couldn't it be a little sooner—" A prolonged and quiet ring, like the purring of a contented cat, cut off Katzman's question. Uri had signed off. Maybe Khilmi had told him to. Katzman left Amos and returned to the command tent, careful to conceal his great relief.

"The kid was raised by the old man, then he joined El Fatah with some of the other local *shabab*, and yesterday in Juni he was killed." Katzman stooped as he entered. It was oppressive inside. His seismographic needle quivered. The intelligence officer was saying, "And that's all we know about him. We had only a couple of hours to interrogate the people, and couldn't get any more translators from the Judaea and Samaria command." He looked at Katzman accusingly.

Katzman turned to the small group of soldiers. Now he understood his mistake: he had tried to make them less afraid of Khilmi but had achieved just the opposite. The old man's connection with the boy who was killed last night in Juni had turned him into a nemesis with a terrible, ancient power.

The long-limbed soldier broke the silence: "He's a weird old man. But frankly, he doesn't sound that crazy to me."

The soldier with the red hair added, "Sir, it's beginning to look less and less like a normal offensive. This isn't something you can fix up by charging in and firing a few shots, which seems to be what we're getting into, despite what you said before." The soldiers nodded and grumbled, looking away from Katzman.

Katzman answered slowly: "I spoke to Laniado. It's just as I thought, only the old man's up there with him. And he's agreed for me to come alone, at midnight. Questions?"

Sheffer stood bolt upright. "As simple as that?" And Katzman replied with growing anger: "Not as simple as that, because the old man does have a gun; otherwise, it's pretty simple." But the simplicity which he had been ignoring since he'd left the signal operator's tent began to trouble him as well.

Sheffer was agitated. "It's a trap, Katzman. They're laying an ambush for you up there. You're a higher card than Laniado; listen to me, Katzman—"

Katzman approached him and said loudly, "I heard you, Major. Now go with the men and impose a little curfew on the village until 0600 hours tomorrow. Dismissed." The soldiers stood up, amazed at the rapid turn of events. Katzman and Sheffer still bristled as they faced each other. Katzman said slowly, "We will treat this like a civilian matter, because that's exactly what it is. There's nothing military about it, and I don't want to hear anything more about that idiotic ultimatum, not from you, and not from anyone else. This is between me and Laniado. Is that clear, Sheffer?"

Sheffer nodded, clenching his great jaws to keep from blurting out certain words. "Now set the curfew," added Katzman. "I want a quiet curfew. No loudspeakers. Go around house to house. I don't want them to notice anything up there." Sheffer nodded silently. He turned to leave. Katzman grabbed his shoulder. "And tell the guy at the café to turn up the volume on his radio."

"What? Turn it higher?"

"Maximum volume. It might help you when you start up the gravel. You see, Sheffer, I'm still considering every possibility."

"That music will drive us insane long before we get there." Sheffer ducked out to the sound of crickets chirping and antennas humming. Katzman hurried back to the table. What he wanted to write to Uri had weighed on him throughout the briefing like an overfull bladder. He had to articulate it clearly before they met. He was certain that he would be better able to understand himself when he saw what came out on paper. That he would be better able to tolerate himself.

But when he sat down before the almost blank page, his spirits fell again. For a few minutes he chewed the end of the pen, doodled on the cracked table, and drummed his mouth. Then he decided to make an outline, as he always did before writing his reports. In the margin he printed, in tiny letters: Kalkilya; the convoys; Dayan; Nablus.

He adjusted the big field lamp on the table and attacked. "It all started in Kalkilya. We razed the city in a single day. We went on shelling long after there wasn't a house left standing." He stopped and read. Not bad, but he hadn't described how he felt each time a building on the other side of his tank gun crumbled down. He was already being dishonest. Katzman was furious: even a letter like this could not escape contamination. He continued: "By nightfall the shooting stopped and the inhabitants started to leave town, several thousand of them, taking everything they had, loading it on their donkeys or on their backs and setting off." Again he recalled the endless caravan sleepwalking out of the ruined town. He wanted to write about the way their brightly colored clothes and belongings contrasted with what was happening and with the expressions on their faces. Katzman felt he was missing the point. He added: "The old and the wounded were left to die. I found one very sick child who'd been forgotten in the exodus, and I chased after the caravan in my jeep and found his parents." It was ridiculous to mention this here. Was he trying to exonerate himself before Uri? But a big eraser mark would be out of keeping with such a sincere letter. Katzman wanted to tell Uri how he and a few of his fellow officers had tried to stop the dismal procession from leaving town, shouting at the inhabitants in Arabic that no good would come from wandering off to some other refugee camp; that if they stayed they would not be harmed. The people stared blankly at the officers. There was no expression on their faces, not even hatred, as they trudged ahead. It was an incongruous scene: a conquering army running after the people and imploring them to stay, out of pity, or maybe compunction. The caravan moved on. Katzman didn't write this down. He was aware of having deviated from his original intention. Perhaps he would start somewhere else.

One evening, after the three of them had showered and eaten supper, Shosh suggested a game of Scrabble. It was a pleasant evening. Uri had finished his last exam that day, and Shosh had triumphed over another delinquent. Only Katzman was feeling tense, because of the proposal he was about to make, which he didn't know yet how to put to Uri. They set up the Scrabble board on the carpet, brought out a tray of sunflower seeds and cookies, picked their tiles, and fell silent. Katzman recalled: he had thought out his moves, had waited till he had all the letters he needed, and then said casually to Uri, "Why don't you come work with me in Juni, now that you've finished night school," adding hastily, "It's just an idea, but hey, why not?" And on the board he spelled out the word "timely."

Shosh pressed the tiles closer on the board. Her gestures were irritable and efficient, reminding him of the way she washed herself after the act of love. Uri was still looking at him with a perplexed smile. Shosh's lips were thin and pale. She understood exactly what Katzman's offer meant, and she planned to fight back.

"I don't understand. What do you mean?" said Uri finally. Shosh slammed a V down above the I in "timely," and four tiles after it.

" 'Victim,' " read Uri. "Sixteen points for Shosh. Now it's my turn. Quiet, everyone. Let me think."

Katzman stared down at the wooden tiles, avoiding Shosh's furious eyes. He had figured that was how she would react. She, too, needed Uri there to ground her. Katzman spoke quietly: "We used to talk about it in Santa Anarella, Uri. You said everyone has to fight on his own private battlefront. Neither of us has done much since then. I'm in Juni to fight on my own private battlefront and I want you out there with me. What do you think?" Shosh studied him with an amazement she made no attempt to hide. In her eyes he saw that she thought he was lying. He wasn't so sure himself what it was he wanted. It was true, he did want Uri in Juni, but that wasn't his only reason for asking him to come. What was it, then? In Shosh's eyes, Katzman read the only possible answer, which surprised him: in this charade of lies, with each of them fighting on his own narrow battlefront, a certain advantage came to the one who had Uri nearby.

The field lamp flickered. Katzman kicked it, and the light seemed to steady itself on the page. Somehow it was easier for him to express his feelings with wooden tiles. Words on a page seemed to scatter and lose their meaning.

Katzman wrote: "Someone high up must have regretted the order to shell Kalkilya. The minister of defense himself was utterly shocked when he visited the town. He wanted to speak personally to each of the commanders who had taken part in the bombardment, but something unusual happened while I was talking to him, something—"

Something what? Cruel. And perplexing. Like a gaping wound. Katzman wrote: "A little weird."

The man with the patch over his eye, with the doll face and the hollow voice, asked Katzman why he'd gone on shelling so long. Katzman was startled by the lack of recrimination in Dayan's voice. He was merely curious, deeply so. Katzman was weary of war, of the aura of death that enveloped everything; of the painful sobriety that followed the euphoria of destruction. He spat out the truth, like a seed stuck in his throat. Throughout the violent shelling, he said, he had been trying to assuage the pain inside him, the pain that was still inside him now. The defense minister asked Katzman what he meant. Katzman said, "This war. All the destruction. The killing. I couldn't stand it anymore." He hadn't expected what he said to be understood, because it was only a raw and self-inflicted wound. But something trickled through to the man. Katzman shook himself and wrote on the page before him: "Dayan interrogated me about the shelling with the greatest interest. I told him it gave me relief, because it was an act of protest."

There, thought Katzman, now it's coming.

"It's your turn," Shosh had said angrily.

Uri was looking at his letters. It seemed to be difficult for him to concentrate on the game as he tried to make sense of Katzman's proposal. He was searching for a flicker of a smile in Katzman's face but couldn't find it. All he saw was tension, gloom.

"Will you play already," rasped Shosh.

Uri woke up with a start and promptly set his tiles down on the board. A happy smile lit his face, bringing pain both to Shosh and to Katzman. "Hey look, I have an eight-letter word, very timely indeed!" He played his tiles down from the final Y of Katzman's "timely": "Yearning," he said. "That's twenty-eight points for the word and fifty for the bonus. Whoopee!"

Katzman rubbed his chin and hummed. He had pressed every button. By mentioning Italy earlier on, he had stirred Uri's memories till they were practically visible. Katzman said, "I sure am getting lousy letters today." In fact, the tiles he picked were exceptionally good ones, only he, like Shosh, had already noticed what was transpiring on the board. He scanned it, crossing the words in his mind like a rickety bridge. For a moment he was sorry they weren't playing cards instead. King. Queen. Jack. Or better yet, queen, jack, and joker. "Bridge," he spelled around the G in "yearning." "Thirty points."

Shosh looked over her rack with a poker face. Then she played her tiles around the T in "victim." "Subtle," she whispered. "Twelve points."

"More subtle than any beast of the field," said Katzman.

Uri asked, "How long would you want me there for?"

"For as long as you like. No longer than nine months, though, because that's all the time I have left to serve there, but you could come, say, for half a year. On a trial basis at first, and if you like it, you could stay on. By the way, you wouldn't have to wear a uniform. I have a thoroughly civilian position in mind for you in Juni. Something right up your alley, dealing with the local population, looking after the—"

"The idea only came to you now, of course," muttered Shosh.

Uri spread his hands out between them. He began to grasp that Katzman was serious. "I don't understand, Katzman, why do you need me there?"

To look after me, thought Katzman, to connect me with the sweetness I've lost. "It's hell out there, Uri, you know that. You have to blow up the homes of innocent people, you have to arrest children and tyrannize people who don't want you there. I had big plans before I took over the job. Just three and a half months ago I thought I could change the world." He looked into Uri's face imploringly. "I haven't been able to implement a single one of my plans. I admit, it gets complicated. There are so many sides to consider, and so many voices you have to listen to, and I cheat, Uri, I play the game they expect me to play." Inwardly he thought, Which is why I need a prompter in the wings, someone to whisper my lines to me, the lines I've forgotten.

Shosh said dourly, "I don't see what Uri could do there." She didn't look up as she chose her new tiles from the pile, turning each one over as though it might be hiding some loathsome crawly thing.

"He could assist the Arab population. He could be their official military representative, or something like that."

"Does such a position exist?" asked Uri.

"No, but we'll invent one. That was one of my ideas before I took the job. The army approved it. Look, I brought some armored corps officers with me to Juni and that was just as irregular. They'll agree, I know it. We can drive home together every day."

The word "home" startled Shosh. She blushed. "That's preposterous!" she said. "That's utterly preposterous, Katzman! I don't understand you. Think what you're proposing."

The arrogant minister suddenly split open before Katzman's eyes. He began to interrogate him: What kind of pain was it that had driven Katzman to use cruelty as a protest against cruelty; and what kind of relief did it bring? Did he feel purged in some way, or had he plunged even deeper into anguish? Dayan's one eye shone brightly as he spoke, riveting Katzman so he couldn't sink back against the cushions of torpor. He seemed sure Katzman understood exactly what was being said. Katzman wrote on the page before him: "But I just kept saying the same thing over and over. That I had fired my guns in protest. There was no pleasure in it, no revenge, no hatred for the inhabitants. Only pity for them, and for us, too. And that's why I fired like that. But Dayan seemed to be waiting for a different answer. Or maybe I hadn't explained myself well enough. I never went into it all the way with you either." Maybe I'm finally doing it now, he thought.

Even through his veil of fatigue, Katzman could not help admiring the man who questioned him so unrelentingly. Dayan was like a trapped wolf scurrying around his cage. His whole life had been a nervous repetition of this behavior. In his youth, defying death on the battlefield, he had never known what was impelling him. In later years he liked to publicize his adulteries, and he brazenly broke the law by robbing graves; and still something was missing—the answer to the question which had poisoned his life and mocked his intelligence. Then he shot up to the summit in politics, as he had in military life. He got richer and greedier, too; but eventually his bitterness drove him out to the booby-trapped jungles of Vietnam; yet he never found out what Katzman had just understood in a moment's empathy: that the cage that held Dayan prisoner was infinitely elastic. It was infinitely elastic because it had no walls, no roof, and no floor. A man could spend the rest of his life there without ever touching the limits. Now suddenly Katzman recognized that his overzealous shelling of the town had been a means of urgently testing the confines of his own cage. A yearning to touch the iron bars. Stop. Come back to yourself. The search is over. It felt as if a powerful hand had grabbed Katzman and set him on his feet. He had just one request, he told Dayan. The man listened, a vein throbbing in his neck. He was clearly impressed with the controlled violence in Katzman. Katzman wrote in his letter: "I told him that the refugees from Kalkilya were drifting into Nablus and someone had to look after them. It was June, and the weather was pretty hot, flies, diseases, etc., and no one had the patience to deal with the population. He asked me why I was volunteering for the job, when it clearly meant trouble. And all I could say was that I had to do it, I simply had to. I had no better explanation to offer him. But you, Uri, I want you to know about it now, it's important that you know. You see, I wanted to touch"—he searched for the right word—"the system; no, not the system, but its worst results, its worst expressions of injustice and suffering. Suffering I myself had brought on others. To torture myself"—he scrawled—"to know myself." Again he stopped. He had to say it right. This was the heart of the matter. If he could explain his feelings in Nablus and Kalkilya, maybe he wouldn't have to tell Uri, with so much awkward emotion, why he'd needed him in Juni.

"It's your turn, Uri," said Shosh. "Make up your mind."

"Final." He played his tiles down to the L in "timely." "That's sixteen points."

"Final for all of us, I'd say," muttered Shosh, looking daggers at Katzman.

"I'll have to give it some thought," said Uri. "It's a little scary. And I have no experience with that kind of thing."

"What are you talking about? You have plenty of experience," answered Katzman.

Katzman puzzled over these simple tiles that could reveal such intricate secrets. He had lost his delight in Uri's friendship. All he had left was the stubborn need to stick close to him. Maybe he needed him for his salvation. Or maybe it was something else, something very wicked. And Shosh, too, had caught the infectious double sadness. He looked at the battlefield of her face.

"Why are you both looking at me like that?" she said.

"What do you say to Katzman's proposal?" Uri asked Shosh.

"You'll do what you like, no matter what I say."

"You don't sound too pleased," said Uri.

All of a sudden she smacked the board. "Hey!" cried Uri, staring from her face to the board. He tried to reassemble the words, his beautiful fingers fumbling over dangerous combinations, fatal truths, silent laments. His fingers know already, thought Katzman and Shosh, and slowly Uri drew them back across the board, in shock, in pain, until they rested on his lap like the dead. There was silence again.

Katzman wrote feverishly. The words poured out of his pen. Oh, please, don't let anyone come in now and interrupt me. "And that's when something stirred in me. The same thing you experienced in Italy, that's what I felt in Nablus. Italy was only a pale imitation. Nablus was the place where I felt that flow of benevolence for the first time. In Santa Anarella you talked to me about your newfound happiness. For me it wasn't happiness. It was more like passion. And it tormented me as only passion can. You've already heard the story—about how in a matter of days I succeeded in organizing the biggest refugee camp in Nablus. I didn't sleep for over a week, I was so excited, so alive. I brought them food and medicine, and I selected a group of potential leaders out of the fear-drugged masses. I persuaded the people of Nablus to help them, too, especially the better-off, educated Christians there, and I felt so wonderful—"

Suddenly the heavy air burst over Katzman's head. Someone in the café nearby had turned the radio up full blast. A singer wailed a cloying melody. Katzman stuck his fingers in his ears and allowed the tumult in his head to die down.

Then he attacked once more: "I haven't felt that way since. The reason I accepted the position in Juni was that I was hoping to find myself again. In Italy I found you, and you, without knowing it, gave me hope." Why am I writing this to him? "But when I arrived in Juni, everything went wrong. It's a matter of chemistry, Uri, hope sours fast. Even iron rusts, and dreams are such paltry things."

He paused. He was surprised to read what he'd written on the page. It wasn't at all what he'd wished to say. Why had he poured out this confession? He forced himself to forget that anyone else would ever read the words. Blinking with effort he wrote: "So I brought you out here to contaminate you. To beat you, to watch you break, and make you admit your mistake, and the lie you live. Stop smiling like that, Uri, I—"

Sheffer peeked in, shouting to make himself heard above the din. "A full curfew, Katzman!" Katzman, startled, shook himself. Sheffer stared at his anguished face. Something was happening to Katzman. Better keep an eye on him. Yesterday, in the house in Juni, he'd made a mistake that almost cost his life.

"Supper's ready, Katzman."

"I'm coming."

A moment more. The noxious words slinked round the Scrabble board. The three of them beheld the world in a drop of water. Letters condensed. Concepts melted and writhed in agony. And Katzman and Shosh knew in a flash that nothing would ever be the same again. Katzman stared frozenly at Shosh. He had followed her split. Here was her boy-man, whom she wasn't sure she wanted or deserved. And here was the pale-faced stranger, rotting inside, sapping her strength, her inner being—

Katzman gazed at the page before him. He started to read and winced with distaste. Then he hesitated, and scored his first victory in a very long time. He didn't tear up the paper. He folded it four times and wrote *Uri* on it. Sticking it in his back pocket, he found a piece of cardboard there. He took it out and stared at it uncomprehendingly: it was an orange tag with the Red Cross insignia and the airport stamp. He crumpled it and put it back in his pocket. Then he turned off the lamp and left the tent.

21

It's night. The clock expresses it a little more finically, but that doesn't matter anymore. Because I'm in a different time zone now, with quality time even Opus can't rival. You have to work yourself into a special state to be admitted, and they allow only one person in at a time, but how I wish I could sneak Uri and Katzman through with me.

And I wish I knew what they were up to. Did the burned-out match heads slowly meet to strike a flame of truth? Will we ever be as we were before we landed on this merry-go-round? And which of my selves will I choose to believe? Will I ever know who is speaking when I say "I"?

How much longer before I can bite myself and feel who I am? I killed someone in order to find out; only suddenly, as I revolved in the gyre, I saw how frenetic my movements were, as if they were all that was left of me, and by the time I woke up and summoned myself back to my body and my face and my personal history, before some dirty villain had the chance to pull a picture of the ground out from under my feet—by that time, Mordy was dead.

"Mordy was dead." There is so much meaning in the shadow that falls between the words. And now let me tell you about a new shadow, about a wonderful weaver of shadows, Abner the poet.

Abner is a poet, that's one of the "necessary absurdities" he revels in. His newspaper articles, his messages to his Scout troops, his public speeches, they're all studded with gleaming lights. Measured words that radiate assurance, leaving no room for doubt or time for regret. Too much is lost between the folds of meaning, he explained, in the twilight of tired ideas. And now, Shosh, we wordsmiths are charged with bringing new significance to old saws like "pioneering spirit" and "setting an example" and "cherished values," and I will go on tearing at the hair that fell out long ago, trying to make everyone see the terrible wrong we've done, the chasms that have opened up in our society, the devil knows how, and the corruption of the leaders of this shtetl where we raised a herd of digital youth, but I will not let them sit here lamenting, I will kick their butts out into the world to repair and transform it with never-ending faith.

Abner writes poems. For sixteen years he has been hiding behind his pen name, and only a few people know the secret, like us and his publisher. And now Katzman, too. Yes, Abner writes poems. Limpid sonnets of fixed meter and rhyme: a thousand tongues tickle the words, he wrote once, lines torn by rage, crushed by despair. Dark, wild words, meaningless syllables. And Leah says she can't make head or tail of them. How could I have been so blind? On my fifteenth birthday they finally let me in on the secret, my gift on reaching maturity. But I should have guessed sooner, the way I used to follow him around. He would always emerge from his room in disarray, extinguishing the sparks in his eyes with the heels of his hands, stretching sensually, his big body suddenly alive. And it never dawned on me that all those articles and speeches and worthy deeds of his were not enough to pinch the color back into his haggard cheeks.

Take it easy. You're sparking up again. Ten years have gone by since then. And you've been through far more astonishing things than the discovery that set you on the wild and frightening course of reconstructing yourself as you ought to be, reinforcing the frayed seams, filling in the loopholes to keep the lie from showing, and the quiet buzz of amazement you hear inside you moves you to its rhythm—what happened, how did it happen—but the voice on the loudspeaker barked, Nothing happened, go on, go on, and your new and treacherous humor helps you span the dark spaces between the asteroids of lonesome truth that sail you through a galaxy, white with lies, where parents kill their children with the smiling disclosure that they are not the people they pretended to be, which means that you, too, are no longer who you thought you were, that you are an exile, so stitch up your seams with the thread of movement, learn to laugh when it hurts, to shudder instead of crying, to set mine fields of generosity and encouragement around a center of flickering fear, and hurl yourself on the merry-go-round of activity to explain the smoke that pours out of you, blackening your face, giving people cause to say, Look at her go, she's a dynamo, that daughter of Avidan's; come on, take it easy, take it easy now, Shosh, hold the brown paper package in your hand, and look at this from a more humorous and storylike perspective, because, you see, this, too, is a modern art of the lie, where one thing always stands for something else and one person is always the tool of another, and nothing is in and of itself, so that my passion for Katzman could be diverted to Uri, and my desire for Uri was cruelly translated into my language with Mordy, deciphered by his fluttering tongue, which reminds me of a beautiful sonnet Abner wrote about Judas Iscariot, who kissed Jesus to signal the priests that he was the one they were to crucify, and I have also learned the many uses of a kiss . . . Oh, damn the compromises of simultaneity that slyly offer us an honorable retreat and expose the lines of least resistance where we need never suffer, never really be. How frightening this momentary pause. There, I dared, I did it. Now I'm being punished: my life is flowing into me from everywhere at once.

What is the machine recording now? The rustling of paper, tearing sounds. What does Viktor Frankl see? He sees a pair of shorts on the table, and Spider-Man leaping out of a stained T-shirt in the pursuit of justice, a helmet gleaming red and green over his steely face. Was that a flicker of recognition, Mr. Frankl? You do remember Spider-Man, don't you, and the way I peeled the T-shirt off Mordy's boyish body as I dived down on the glorious carpet with him into the shadows between two squares on his activity chart, throughout that week of madness, opening up with a groan like a tunnel before a train, knowing there was no excuse for what I was doing, unless it was longing, and in the back of my mind I remember what Abner says, that to believe in God you have to leap beyond reality, because there are no logical way stations between the world and faith, and here, in my cozy office, I learned that to believe in reality requires the same kind of leap, and that man, like God, is a desert island of conventions, and there's no way back from the big lie, and I felt my body turn into a huge antenna, trembling with fear and searching frantically for the borders that melt at a touch. And so I hovered between Katzman and Uri, an enormous butterfly who will never write poems, crossing over to the boy who waited for me on the other side of the table with his eyes shut, and out of the sparks I saw under the pressure of Zussia's thumbs, I drew new pictures on the clean slate of Mordy's body, and in amazement I watched the letters turning legible, the hills and dales of him identified, his highs and lows, and Mordy needed me the way he needed chocolate, staring blankly till a short, wild sob testified that his body had become a pillar of fire consuming us both, and if I had stopped to observe, I might have noticed that something was happening inside him, but I didn't notice anything, not till it came home to me cruelly one week later when I met him for our regular session but didn't get up to put my hand on his frightened shoulder, or peel Spider-Man away, cultivating a whispered, prayerful scream in the space he was drilling inside me, but instead said, Now, Mordy, we'll continue where we left off yesterday, can you complete this lovely puzzle here? And I was too frightened to look in his eyes, and later, after a terrible hour of silence, I walked him to the door and turned him over to the attendant, as I did each time for the next four sessions, wiping out all that had happened on the carpet, and he never asked, he wasn't the kind of boy who would ask for more, though his face dropped and his tongue floundered like a fish on the rocks, battering against his teeth, and when I arrived at the institute the next morning, the doctor had already pronounced him dead by asphyxiation, mentioning that there were no signs of violence, which means there was no suspicion of murder.

Smell that smell. The faint perspiration. Thick with moss, the secret moss of longing. A boy's T-shirt, nothing more. And you did like him in a way. At times, when he was riveted to you and you turned into a pinpoint of pleasure, and you knew it was through him that you touched the steely core of your lie, so don't be ashamed,

Shosh, you're beyond that now. As Katzman said, Where we are, Shosh, we can allow ourselves the grace of sincerity and self-forgiveness, so get up and do what you've been wanting to do for a long time now, ever since an unknown person tossed this package into your office, and as no one is here and no one is expected, take off your choking turtleneck and put on this mossy little T-shirt; oh, please, don't raise your eyebrow, Mr. Frankl, this is as good a way as any to get to know someone from the inside, especially when that person is deceased and only his shell remains; don't look so alarmed, I'll take it off soon, this is only a ghastly little game I'm playing, and I'm the one who will suffer, because you have to let go when you suffer, otherwise the suffering that is filed away and tape-recorded and discussed at staff meetings (two sugars, please) becomes a wicked travesty, and if it's hard for you to look at me, just close your eyes.

Fine. That's easier for me, too. I was talking about Abner, about Abner who used a pen name. This they shyly revealed to me in the little ceremony they prepared for my coming of age. Zussia had gone off to one of his quixotic meetings, and they shut themselves up in Abner's room till Leah came out and called me in, and the two of them giggled. You're such a big girl now, we can trust you, and I looked around and saw that the room was very tidy, on the round side table there was a white cloth and a vase of white narcissus. Nu, Lealeh, tell her, said Abner, and she said, Now, Abner, I'm not going to take your chestnuts out of the fire, ha ha ha. Come here, our bright, perceptive daughter, don't be angry that we've kept this little secret from you. You see—how shall I say it— Just say it, Abner, and if you can't, I'll say it for you, as I always do, ha ha ha; you see, Shosh, you have three illegitimate stepbrothers, oh dear, she looks so pale; we were just kidding, darling, how could you believe such a thing of your father, not real children, Shosh, it's these books on the table, they're your father's; he wrote them, that is.

Now concentrate on what you felt: press down the wings you sprouted so suddenly they tore you to shreds. And name the feelings one by one: humiliation, hostility, and the pain of isolation. Something was lost forever, yet here was this fabulous bastard. But, but, but, you sputter, we, we studied one of these poems in school, and I bought this book at the bookshop; I remember once you even asked me why I keep it at my bedside, and how—

And don't forget the new pride, that sparkle in his eyes, and Leah smiling with pleasure. Darling Shosh, you have no idea how hard it was to keep this secret from you, how much we wanted to share it with you, but there were several reasons why we decided it would be better to wait. Mainly because we were afraid someone would point out the discrepancy between Abner the poet and the Abner we know, which is nonsense; the reason Abner chose to be anonymous in the first place was that the poems are so personal, as you no doubt have noticed yourself, and I can't tell you how happy we were that you loved the poems, though I daresay he might have used more elegant syntax, Bialik did, Shlonsky and Pen did, but that isn't important now, what a relief, you can't imagine, darling, it was so hard keeping you in the dark about even such a small thing, and how good it is that there won't be a single secret between us from now on; why are you smiling at me like that, Abner, I'm merely enjoying the surprise on her face, and I suggest we go out and celebrate somewhere, what do you think, Shoshik?

And Shoshik stands there, gazing at the strange, beloved name on the covers of the slender books, as though these verses she knew by heart and had copied into her secret notebook were floating inside her now, stirring up the dust, seeking a way out, an immediate exit, because they had to go. Quickly!

How could I have been so blind. He always said that the meaningful things in life can be expressed only through poetry. That the events of life, the facts per se, are not important, but only that which we know how to describe, the pulsation of experience they give rise to, the poetic justice that decrees their transient reality. Not to mention all the poetry books he used to buy, or his special attentiveness to the budding poets in the youth movement, and of course his closeness with young Chagai Strutzer; then there were his vehement debates with Leah about teaching poetry in the schools, and his curiosity when he questioned me about the poetry book I came home with, never dreaming that he was the author, and now he tells me these poems were inspired here, in our very own home, in the silence lurking behind his pipe, behind his eyes and his gray woolen vest.

Don't stop now. Go on. It will hurt, but you've got to go on. Tell us about the fish. About the first poem. Don't press your knuckles to your eyes that way. His gestures are imprinted in you, like a melody. Shosh takes after me, says Leah, sounding strangely harsh, which is how she lures Abner with a vicious smile into the gilded cage of backhanded admiration, killing him with categories, and Abner, she explains with a patient nod, has such a special magic that we forgive him, though luckily there's somebody else behind the scenes to run the show, I mean it, and I can't bear that "I mean it" of hers anymore, but why are you talking about her now, Shosh, when the tape is almost full, forget her; but before I do I have to solve a simple dilemma, Abner wanted Leah to trap him, though you wouldn't think she was the type to kindle the passions of a man like him, because all his life he had trapped himself, and even in the heart of the lie, in the sonnets he wrote, he denied himself the grace of sincerity and self-forgiveness, and didn't give the lie his name, and he roped himself to Leah, and sewed up his passion with

270

wire threads, and I saw the dewy-eyed women gazing at him, and Leah, smiling mysteriously, said, Did you see how she was staring at you, did you notice that high-school girl lusting for you all night; and he would answer, No, I didn't notice, why didn't you tell me sooner, and they would laugh fondly, and he would run his finger lovingly over her prematurely wrinkled face, and I know he wasn't lying then, any more than he was when he said, "The crucial need for a new Zionist ideal," or when he made himself believe in it. But at night, in my bed, as I run my finger over the lines of his poems, all I can find is disintegration, a curse blowing in the shadows, all the loose wires. And there I come to know the stranger, hounded through an empty kingdom.

What was that—a knock at the door—maybe I didn't hear right. I'm sure I didn't hear right. Who could it be? I could check: in this room we trap reality, we have documents and recordings, everything is neat and orderly, let us rewind the tape and listen. And now another knock; this time it seems to be coming from the door, but I'll erase it and listen to its faint echo on the tape instead, and what do I discover, that I have been very careless, that for a long time —all evening?—I haven't said a single word, at most I have been mentally aping the tape, silently engraving my thoughts on the slate of my mind, and now here, in the depths of this silence, a weak knock has been registered on the tape, which means that someone is standing outside. And right after the drumroll on the door comes the familiar voice—it couldn't be—murmuring, "Shosh? Shoshik?" And I am filled with joy and sadness, and I turn in my chair, calling, "Come in," and when the door opens I see Abner, and standing timidly behind him, like a giant shadow, Zussia.

22

It looks like the end, because he and I are like a pair of bloated nightbirds with spooky bloodshot eyes, and because Khilmi is totally insane now, sobbing and shaking and telling me stories I don't understand, revealing things I never knew about myself, things that never happened, and because his pungent odor is orbiting us, fast and suffocating, like some secret weapon he's launched against me, and because I keep falling asleep every minute, I don't know why, waking up in a panic with Khilmi there, chirping along with the radio and giggling to himself, and I can't hear anything, because down in the village someone has gone mad and turned on Um Kultum full blast, though I can't understand why Katzman hasn't shut it off, he hates that music, and because, because because because, like a geometric proof, Khilmi has won this battle of nerves, the twittering tyrant bending over me every minute to see how I am, calling me Yazdi and my son, my son, with so much love I'd rather be Yazdi than Uri.

But who was Uri, anyway. Just a figment of other people's imaginations, only sometimes, when the figments touched, they struck a spark of life in him, though it was still impossible to know who Uri was or where his loyalties lay, or why he did what he did, and now Uri is just an empty head, a bundle of fatigue, a receptacle for other people's lies and Khilmi's madness, to him I'm Yazdi, and Darius, too, his patron and redeemer, and even that hunter character, and soon he'll probably lead me down to the Jordan in the moonlight.

He's so restless. I can barely follow his jaunts around the yard. He lights the primus and brings a *jarra* of water from the cave with those dancing movements and a sickly joy, his hand on the gun.

And he comes and stands beside me, and the muscles of his face contract, and by the light of the primus I can see that his eye is red and white, and then with an awful grimace he says there's one story he hasn't told me yet, the story of Laila Sallach and the silken map; and meanwhile, he gropes for something in his robe, it has a hundred secret pockets, and in each there is a surprise, and now he seems to be searching for the story of Laila Sallach, but instead, he takes out a little tin box, and when he opens the lid, an almondy smell fills the air, and overcomes the other smells; yes, the smell is familiar to me, I remember it from my last visit here, and now I realize he's getting ready to shave, but his ceremoniousness is troubling.

There's cyanide powder in that tin, and Khilmi rubs it over his face, and I get a crazy idea that he's going to swallow it, which is not his plan at all, he really does intend to shave with the powder,

273

as all the old men around here do. Carefully he spreads the poison around his lips, then gropes in his robe again, with the gun in his other hand—it seems to have become an extension of his body— and now he's found what he was looking for, a folded piece of cardboard which he spreads very carefully, and in it finds a thread, a thread not for sewing but for shaving. I watch in fascination, curled up on the ground; I can't get up. I see him put the gun on his lap and dip the thread in the water boiling on the primus, and then he stretches the thread and runs it over his cheeks and chin. How amazing!

"Uri?"

"What? I can't hear you, yell!"

"Are you tired yet?"

"No. You asked me already."

"Sleep. Sleep. It will be better."

"No."

"Perhaps you could ask your friend to come?"

"What do you want him for?"

"So you will be less afraid."

"We've already asked him to come, haven't we?"

"Have we? I don't remember. I don't remember anything."

What's going on? He's probably set a trap for Katzman. And I'm the bait. Anyone might think I was taking revenge. But "anyone" is unaware how little strength I have left. Not enough to take revenge, and not enough to forgive either. Only enough to sleep and not to be. To wake up a week from now and find out everything's all right. So I cover my ears to stop that awful din, and curl up as tightly as I can, and no more Uri. *Khallas.*

I could forgive him everything except the donkey. It wasn't so important, but that's what opened my eyes in the end. I mean, big deal—a dead donkey. Some kid threw a stone at a jeep patrol in the el Sa'adia neighborhood, and a reserve soldier was hit in the head, so the soldiers fired at the kid, who got away, but the shots killed a donkey.

Kan-ya-ma-kan, a beautiful donkey, with a big white belly and sturdy gray legs. I never saw such a beautiful donkey before. I knew that donkey inside out. It had been lying in the lane for three days before I found out Katzman ordered the villagers not to remove it until they turned in the kid who threw the stone.

And three representatives of the neighborhood came to see me, three old men in warm woolen suits with the *kaffiyeh* and *akal* wound solemnly around their heads, and they asked me to do something. Fine, so we drove down in my jeep, and even from a distance the stench was so bad I almost threw up, but I controlled myself. And there in the lane lay the donkey, bloated but still beautiful and proud, his gray legs in the air, and his neck stretched back, looking straight at me with one oozing eye.

And around me stood the villagers, all talking at once, asking me to do something, right away, and the women held their babies up to me, shrieking so loudly I couldn't hear anything. And I couldn't breathe because of the stench, so I put a handkerchief over my nose and said, Okay, get it out of here. And I didn't care that I'd given my word to Katzman that I would never do anything without his permission, because he broke his promises, too, so I gasped, Get that donkey out of here, and whatever happens, I'll take responsibility.

Suddenly there was silence. Then a few of them started to grin with embarrassment, averting their eyes, and people in the back mumbled questions, and I stood there, not knowing what was going on, till one of the three old men stuttered, "*Khawaja* does not understand, he has to ask the colonel's permission to remove the donkey, and if the colonel grants it, then we will do as *Khawaja* says."

They waited anxiously for my reply. The brown women with amulets on their brows, and the beautiful wild children, and beyond them, the donkey with his oozing eye, looking straight at me, and the first thought that crossed my mind was that I had to get back to my jeep and they could all choke. But then I remembered that they weren't the ones I was fighting, and I breathed in the stench and the rage and got in my jeep, looking at them, at this colorful, bewildered crowd, and at the brown houses facing the lane, and I made a decision.

And so began the donkey days.

Who would have believed it of me, this person curled up with his cheek on the ground like a sun-dried insect, sniffing the weeds? I had more strength in the old days, a week ago, a million years ago, *kan-ya-ma-kan*, as I zoomed back and forth between the little lane and the government building, screeching past the obstructed water well and the traffic platform of Abu Marwan, the policeman, running over cartons of potatoes in front of the stores, the terror of geese and chickens and boys carrying tea trays on their heads, and I was drawn like a green fly to the scene, and I switched off the motor and looked.

The air was heavy with the stench, and at first I just sat there covering my nose with bits of soap on a handkerchief. The donkey had burst open, and its coiling intestines poured out into the dust. Birds circled patiently in the sky, and I watched and waited for them to descend, and went right on watching after they did.

Day after day. The neighborhood folks grew used to me and no longer crowded around my jeep or asked me questions, because they realized I wasn't going to answer them. But they also grew used to the donkey. The women walked right past it with babies in their arms, sometimes covering the babies' noses with a corner of their *kaffiyeh*, and sometimes not, and the children played stickball up and down the lane, their shouts blotting out the stench somehow, and I watched, I had decided not to make a move until I understood. I stopped discussing the subject with Katzman, because he wouldn't listen, and because I didn't feel like talking to him about other things either. I didn't go home for a number of days, and didn't even call Shosh to let her know. It was a kind of obsession. I had to see that donkey. Once, just before sunset, a man in an undershirt walked over with a sack and began to winnow flour right in front of the donkey, flour for baking pita bread. Then an old woman led her husband out to sit beside the man, and a few minutes later they were joined by three more old men. One was smoking a hookah, and I could almost hear the water bubble in the pipe. Fine white flour flew in the evening breeze and landed gently on the donkey carcass. Another old man rolled himself a cigarette. He sealed it with a slow movement of his tongue. Two little schoolgirls wearing uniforms skipped gaily past the donkey. I started the jeep and took off, oblivious to everything. I burst into the government building. Where's Katzman? I hollered down the hall. Where are you, you fucking bastard, and why'd you bring me out here? What the fuck do you think you're doing?

Even now I feel a ripple of rage. Even now, when it's not important anymore, when we're all dead, in fact. I barged into his room without knocking and stood before him, red-faced, perspiring, and trembling with rage, Get that donkey out of there, Katzman, get it out of there!

Katzman got up and walked over to me, his shoulders raised as though he thought I was about to bash into him or something, and said, The donkey stays. One of my men was wounded in that lane, and two months ago something similar happened there, and if they

277

refuse to turn in the culprit, when we're sure they know who it was, let them choke.

I forced myself to speak quietly, though I couldn't stand him or the humiliation anymore, and I said deliberately, There will be no more collective punishment, your idol Dayan was the one who gave that order. Then I begged him to take the donkey away, I was asking this of him as a personal favor, me, Uri, and I would never ask for anything again.

Katzman started walking around the room and talking, and I knew it was hopeless, because his argument had a certain logic to it, which is always the problem, and he spoke about the carrot and the stick and about give-and-take, and I just kept saying inwardly, The stench, the stench, but Katzman sensed I was diving into myself to escape him, so he just kept talking and talking, and nearly succeeded.

Then with a last desperate effort I managed to conjure up the stench in my nostrils, and I was saved, and I suddenly shouted, Katzman—I screamed it like a curse—that's out-and-out harassment; it's not enough that they have to see us around them all the time and listen to us and work for us and earn our money and obey our laws, now they have to smell us, too, with every breath they take, and let me tell you, Katzman, that stench has an unconditional truth of its own, more powerful than justice or reason.

And Katzman stood before me, turning pale, and said, "The donkey stays, and you get out of here, get out." He screamed it with terrible hurt in his voice. "Get out of my sight, you hear me!"

I turned around and walked out to the parking lot, feeling nothing, not even humiliation, and I waited quietly for the first car to Tel Aviv, and all the way there I kept telling myself rationally and maturely that we're through, that I'm leaving Katzman and Juni and going back to Shosh, and I was so glad to find her waiting for me at home, I wanted to take her in my arms, to beg her forgiveness if I'd hurt her over the past year, but she put her hand out to stop me and told me to come to her study because there was something she wanted to say, it was time we had a frank and open talk, and we went to her study, and I waited for her to start talking, because I was eager to get it over with so we could begin to live our life the way we used to want to, and she crossed her legs, and her fingers trembled when she said, Listen, Uri, there are a few things you ought to know, and *tuta tuta khelset elkhaduta.*

23

Katzman stepped out of the tent and looked up at the moon, then down at his watch. Eleven o'clock. The bivouac was utterly dark, but loud music penetrated every cranny, and there was no refuge in the night, no intimacy. Soldiers lay dozing under the camouflage nets with their army blankets wrapped around them, and their coats over their heads to muffle the music. Katzman walked slowly through the little camp with his hands in his pockets.

There was, however, a fine thread of light coming from the command tent. Katzman ambled over and peered in. Sheffer was there, sitting at the table with his back to the opening, flipping a matchbox. The lamplight was dim, but Sheffer didn't seem to care. With a flick of his thumb he shot the matchbox up off the table, trying to make it fall on its side. Sheffer was a pro at this.

Katzman studied the broad back, the smooth motionless neck, the crack of buttocks showing over his trousers. On the table lay a dog-eared paperback. Alistair MacLean, no doubt. Katzman watched the matchbox bounce rhythmically over Sheffer's shoulder. There was something gloomy about Sheffer and his matchbox. Sheffer was like some stubborn animal trainer working with a hopelessly stupid creature. It always fell back on the table.

Katzman let go of the tent flap and walked away. For some reason he felt as if he'd just peeked in on a very private scene. Sheffer, he reflected, did far more dangerous things than the characters he admired in books. He was the kind of man who was doomed to live beyond his dream. Maybe we're all in the same situation here, thought Katzman, and that's why we have nothing to aspire to. Katzman got into the jeep and leaned his head against the rail. He longed for bed. For dreamless sleep. Quietly he said, as if rehearsing his lines, We have accepted your demands, Khilmi. I am happy to inform you that a few hours ago our soldiers began their orderly withdrawal from all major cities in the territories.

And he chuckled tiredly. He tried to imagine the withdrawal. Thousands of unloosed cords, convoys of civilians and army personnel. Then his thoughts ran in the opposite direction: Arabs laying down their work tools and returning to their villages. And the feeling of relief. Getting out. Separating at long last. Though it was impossible to say how many more generations of misbegotten children would be born to them and to us.

With his forehead on the rail and his eyes puffy and irritated, Katzman tried to duck the resounding wail of the Oriental orchestra and the womanly voice of Suher, the Cairo radio announcer. He imagined consciousness as a kind of sponge that can absorb the most voluminous fictions and intricate lies, and then wring them out again as fresh truth. There were so many incongruities in his life, and so little reason or truth to be found in the world, and yet people went on glibly using terms like reason and truth as if they knew what they were talking about.

It was hot in the jeep, but outside there were swarms of mosquitoes lying in wait. The glove compartment was open, and Katzman rummaged around in it for cigarettes and matches. He lit himself a cigarette, inhaled, coughed, and spat. He hadn't had a cigarette in several months and the smoke burned his lungs. But at least it will keep the mosquitoes away, he thought, puffing determinedly, holding the cigarette with unaccustomed fingers.

A pale ring of light illumined him. He and Uri had spoken once about the frailty of life. About how one touch of reality was enough to topple the most solid-seeming structures, like the sturdy houses that collapsed in Santa Anarella, or the armored tanks that were shattered in the war. Or his marriage, based—so he had believed—on love. Or words like "idealism" and "faith." Katzman puffed a few elliptical smoke rings. With the flashing of the match he'd lit just now, he had been struck by the deep realization that this impossible night, as he sat here before the cave of the crazy old Arab who was holding Uri hostage, and all the similar things that had happened to him in his life, like his most secret desires, his unspoken fears, his peccadilloes with married women, his father's voice imprinting Ariosto's epic on his brain—everything that seemed like a pale dream, barely kissing reality, had proven, with the passage of time, to be highly resistant to the vicissitudes of human affairs. And they would never leave him, not even after the vivid shells of his life dried up and fell away. He would always know how to find these things inside, to touch them secretly, longingly, in times of trouble, and through them he would reach his own abiding truth.

Then joy, light as a minnow, silvered in him suddenly. How clear it was: these were his assets, his only wealth. He even stopped hearing the intrusive music that desecrated the night. His thoughts became a comforting murmur. Everything around him murmured: the village homes, the haunting presence of the past riding the bumpy hills, even the danger stretching out above, at Khilmi's cave.

You'd better be careful, he thought. You'd better protect these assets. He remembered Uri's story about Ruthy, his imaginary girl-friend, and his irrational feelings of guilt for pushing too hard against the walls of reality and destroying her. To Katzman she seemed like one of those prehistoric cave drawings that crumble to dust the moment they're exposed to fresh air and the lamps of scientists.

He stretched and touched the tarpaulin on the metal rail of the jeep, flinging his cigarette away. He sat up with the sudden reali-zation that tonight would bring him closer than ever to his heart's desire, the cool touch of a single symmetrical line: tonight Uri would tell him that he knew about him and Shosh, that he'd known all along and had chosen to say nothing, just as he'd said nothing about his four-day hunger strike in high school.

Or perhaps he had found out three days ago from Shosh. Katzman recalled Uri's outbursts then. The tension. That farce about the donkey. There had been moments when Katzman suspected Uri of using the dead donkey as an excuse for waging a battle of nerves. And Katzman's own reactions were not directly related to the subject of their quarrel either. Did he know?

Katzman felt very tense. The ever-gnawing hunger for a moment of truth, of complete honesty regardless of the consequences, evinced itself: that final moment when you were punished for your sins, when you were made to suffer the pain you deserved; but at the same time, everything inside him—his abilities, his training, his in-stincts—cried out: Truth is only the last resort; the poison pellet you take when the last bunker falls and you find your escape routes blocked. Did he know?

Katzman coldly followed the hunt in progress: the false trails he left had begun to converge. He watched in fascination: he realized now that in this, too, he had left his personal signature. He stubbed his cigarette out and hastily lit another. Uri knew. There was no doubt that he knew. Katzman leaned against the windshield and stared out at the small ring of light, glowing like a vision. Every devious change he'd engineered in his life preserved a residue of him, with his own genetic code. So, even his lies could give him away. Katzman laughed soundlessly. He had always tried to evade the truth he believed in so superstitiously, negotiating it with lies and a cunning silence. And this was why he was so secretive in love, concealing from himself everything that was dear to him, in order to protect it from his own malevolent consciousness.

Like Uri, for instance.

Now a sense of impending loss erupted from his stomach into his throat. He had failed again. He had, as usual, made a mess of things. Bitter streams wore channels through his hinterland and, finding each other suddenly, surged through him. It was the same old failure embracing him comfortingly; here's where you belong, as you've always known. There's no need to pretend, your other failures are all here patiently waiting, the loveless life you try to live in your quasi-scientific way, as a diverting sequence of natural misunderstandings, not bothering to fight for anything because there isn't enough reality in you to struggle for, and all you needed was some crazy mixed-up Uri to show you how much you lie even to yourself, the one person you thought you would never lie to; there must have been something about Uri's lively, chipped-tooth smile that showed up your own pretentiousness and despair. A cool jet shot through Katzman. He vaguely remembered something Shosh had once quoted to him after her meeting with the family of one of her delinquents. It must have been the opening line in a book Katzman had read, too: Happy families are all alike; every unhappy family is unhappy in its own way. The same could be said about success and failure. For him success had been an empty shell, something that made you a stranger to yourself. And people always used the same trite words to describe their successes. But failure was always personal somehow. It was intimate and had to be deciphered in one's own private language. Katzman joined his fingertips together. He had made several discoveries about himself since morning. This whole exhausting day seemed to him like a series of riddles leading up to a final solution.

Someone approached the jeep. Katzman switched on the headlights and trapped a lumbering animal between them. Sheffer walked up and, in typical Israeli fashion, leaned over the jeep with his hands on the roof and his forehead on his hands. Katzman could smell the pungent army mosquito repellent on Sheffer.

"I've made up my mind," said Sheffer. "I'm going up there with you."

Katzman laughed. He'd been expecting this since the briefing. "There's no need. I'll be okay on my own."

"It's a trap, Katzman. Laniado said what he said with a knife at his throat. You're being rash. You're being foolhardy, Katzman."

Katzman remembered the night before, an age ago. He'd rushed headlong into the darkened house and the kid had nearly shot him. What hurled him into the fire? What was driving him up the hill now? He said, "I won't be in any danger up there, Sheffer." At least, he thought, not from Khilmi. "And I'll have one gun in my belt and another in my shoulder holster, just like in the movies; you'll be going up right after me, and everything'll be dandy. Let's not talk about it anymore, all right?"

Sheffer said nothing. Then he poured his rancor out on the Arabs, the village, the goddamn music, and the mosquitoes that hadn't bothered to read the label on the bottle of repellent. Katzman listened with amusement. Sheffer's arguments were easy enough to contest, but he always spouted them with enviable conviction. Now he described what he would do if he met up with Khilmi. Sheffer wasn't a sadist, but his character allowed him to be an enemy, which, in these regions, was a valuable trait.

Katzman teased: "Forget the old man. What would you do to Laniado?"

Sheffer ran a beefy tongue over his lips. "They're the worst, these Commie types and bleeding-heart liberal kids playing conscientious games under our feet; they're damn lucky to have us around, to get them out of trouble in the end."

Katzman said, "Go on, Uri's no Commie." He remembered Uri's telling him once that he had been brought up to hate Arabs and his father had even made up a prayer for their extermination. Uri admitted that he could still remember the appeal of those hate slogans. The prayer was positively intoxicating when chanted to a driving rhythm. He was ashamed of that.

Sheffer said, "Those guys ought to have their balls cut off."

And with spectacular timing, the air around them suddenly resounded and poor Aish, in pajamas and red tarboosh, appeared before them at the entrance to his café, stamping his feet and waving his arms at the heavy darkness, screaming, Enough! Enough! The noise was driving him crazy, and he couldn't stand it anymore, let the soldiers kill him if they wanted, at least he'd get a little quiet, and muttering furiously, he turned around and disappeared in the café, closing the rickety door behind him, and blessed silence reigned.

Katzman and Sheffer burst out laughing.

"Listen here, Katzman—" Sheffer tried to exploit Katzman's jocular mood.

"Enough, I said." Katzman stubbed his cigarette on the fender and got out of the jeep. They walked to the command tent together and got their holsters and revolver bullets. Several soldiers drifted over to watch. Sheffer tightened the gun belt to fit Katzman's slender proportions. He stuck two bandages into his pocket. Then he helped him load the magazines and hid the small gun in his shoulder holster. They worked quickly and in silence. The soldiers were silent, too.

Then they coordinated watches. It was ten minutes to midnight. Katzman said, "At midnight I go in. You start moving and take positions like we agreed. You shoot only if shots are fired. Otherwise, you wait for my orders. But there won't be any shooting. Got that, Sheffer?"

Sheffer said yes.

"Good," said Katzman. "Then walk me out a little."

The soldiers divided as they passed, and the two of them walked around the tent. Katzman paused for a minute beside the camouflage net. But there was no point in going in again to touch the angel. The feeling had gone. They stopped to piss behind the abandoned Carmel. Steam rose from the ground.

Katzman said, "I'm quitting the army."

Sheffer was silent.

Katzman felt a little hurt. Sheffer's silence could mean only one thing. He, too, thought Katzman should get out of this game. Even the army, his way of life, had proved a failure.

"As soon as this business is over, I'm terminating my contract and getting out for good."

At long last Sheffer offered a feeble response: "You shouldn't make a decision like that under pressure, Katzman. Decide when you get back."

"No. I've made up my mind." And he felt relieved.

Sheffer passed Katzman a cigarette. They buttoned their flies. Katzman remembered: "Hey, it's my birthday today." And Sheffer was disconcerted by this intimate disclosure thrown at him like an unknown baby. "Happy birthday," he blurted out at last, feeling reprieved.

There was probably more to say, but there was no need to say it. Katzman tossed the still-burning butt on the ground. Sheffer stubbed it out. Something passed between them as he did. "I'm out of here," said Katzman, and walked away.

Sheffer watched him stumble off. He waited till Katzman had disappeared in the darkness, and stood there a little while longer, listening to the sound of Katzman's footsteps on the gravel path. Then he went back to the bivouac and found his men waiting in the command tent.

24

And now, my Uri, we come to the end of the route that was graven in us, like a brand on the back of a bull, when you arrived at my cave many days ago, and I only regret that I knew you so little, that I never knew your father or your grandfather or whether you loved a woman or suffered pain in love, but perhaps it is better so, perhaps a certain measure of strangeness is needed to perform a deed such as ours, just as I will need love aplenty to lead you through the clefts of the blind fear that sets my thighs and forearms trembling.

So let us not spoil it, and let us not speak of this moment or this gun, and while you lie there on your back beside the low stone wall, and I, with a soft, smooth-shaven face, rub myself with crushed lemon leaves, I will tell you one last story, voicelessly and word-lessly, about the things that were or might have been, because I see that fear is overcoming even the sleep I brought you with *sakran* leaves, and now let me dull its sting and dip you from head to toe in the solace of my stories as we face this sliver of a moon.

Kan-ya-ma-kan, the portly man with a shining countenance and hair as white as jasmine found me tethered to the terebinth tree in the wadi, while a doleful overripe fruit gave off its stench above me, and I, sprawling on my side where my father had kicked me before his soul departed, listened in terror as the guns went off and the clapper tongues of the womenfolk celebrated the betrothal of my sister Naima, and the baying dogs went mad with the smell of roasting meat, and I heard his footsteps behind me and writhed with dread on the ground till at last he came near, this round-faced man with a knife gleaming in his hand, and my eyes closed with relief when the rope loosened and I heard it snap, and his fingers lingered over the sores on my neck and shoulders, and I opened my terrified eyes again, because the warmth of his touch spreading quickly over me was too bitter for one so used to pain, and then I saw his grieving face before me and his wrath-red eyes, and he groaned and gnashed his teeth as he rolled the rope over my body, and I saw the shaven crown of his head, and I was impatient to escape his hand, but I heard him say, My child, my child, why do they do this to you, and he touched my brow with both hands, and I was borne away on a great wave of gentleness that fused the colorful splinters of glass inside me, and a river of honey flowed over my wounds and flooded my heart, and I was sweet as the water kept in jars for the "night of nights," when the gates of heaven open.

Seven years I was with him. Or was it seven heartbeats? Who can tell? Shukri Ibn Labib says no such man existed in these hills, that he is a figment of my heart. And I say, He did in truth exist.

How could it be otherwise; for what hope remains unless his goodness and love flowed through these arid sands; it matters not that I alone beheld him, I do not know, perhaps he was a hermit Greek who went into the desert, retiring from the world to keep alive his love of man. Or a mad saint, who opened hunters' traps by night, releasing fox and marten, rat and rabbit, gladly suffering their bites and scratches because his war was not with them, and swabbing their wounds with ointments made of herbs, his only companions, before he sent them on their way.

And perhaps he ended his days as the opulent man I heard of once from Nuri el Nawar, the one who during the first great war used all his wealth to buy an airship, then gathered a clan of gypsies, some friends of Nuri's among them, to sail over bloody battlegrounds and fire-scorched fields, and wherever they landed, the gypsies brought delight to soldiers and townspeople alike, with a dancing bear in a frock, or a nanny goat wedded to an ape, or they would tell fortunes and use their pay to buy fuel for the airship's belly and roam on, because that is their life, and in truth, I know not who my Darius was, because he never spoke of himself, his only care being me, and he drew my torments out into soft, melodious words, prayerful words, and dipped me in a tub of kerosene first, and then a tub of alcohol, to rid my body of its curses and its stench, and he whispered in my ear, as he slipped the boiled beans between my toes to banish the mildew blisters there, Fear not the one who would kill the body, for he cannot kill the soul, and I understood nothing, but yielded to his gentle voice and warm touch.

And, oh, the silences between us. And the sorrow in his eyes when he saw he failed to heal me with a touch or give me a new skin with the breath of his nostrils. How he whispered in the darkness, asking me, when he thought I was asleep, to go out into the world of men and teach them love, to fight with all my strength and wisdom against the hand walking round us on its fingertips, and, oh, the love that was born in me.

Seven heartbeats. Between his palms I grew into a human being, from him I learned all there was to learn, and throughout my life I have repeated what I learned that shining moment when he touched me at the foot of the terebinth tree and made me the freest of men, and though I no longer remember his voice or the shape of his mouth and lips, everything he said was engraved upon my soul, letter for letter, and I read it over to myself the way a falling stone reads its fall.

Kan-ya-ma-kan, but not until my Yazdi was born did I understand the words, and like him I secluded myself from others so their hatred would not make sport of me, and I could not fight anymore, so I hid in caves and the clefts of trees, and roamed the wadis, sleeping in empty kennels, but they pursued me everywhere, for even in my dreams I saw the boys rubbing me with sugar and tying me to the hives of Labib, the father of Shukri, and the girls stealing out by night to prick me with their needles, and my older brothers I heard laughing—Khilmi is a perfect idiot with one ear made of dough and the other of mud—and I heard my mother screaming, Get-him-out-of-the-kitchen-his-stench-will-spoil-the-soup, and felt the swollen hand of my-father-who-was-not-my-father rebounding over my face.

I could not escape them, and I was too weak, Yazdi my son, to flee very far from this village of sheep. But one night, *kan-ya-ma-kan*, as from my hiding place I beheld the bonfire of some Bedouin shepherds far away, and saw the flames set the hems of their *abayas* swaying and fluttering in the air, I suddenly knew what to do. It was so simple: smoke is lighter than air, and so it rises, and hot steam rises from the kettle, and so does everything that melts in thought or reflection, once it is free, and I kept this to myself.

And in those days, Uri, they told a story in the village about an old woman—Arissa was her name—who during the days of the locust plague filled up her sacks with locusts and tore their wings off one by one, till, mad with hunger, she locked herself in her house, rubbed herself with honey, and pasted the transparent wings all over her body, and then, naked and luminous, she climbed a tree, spread her arms, and flew away.

Kan-ya-ma-kan, was it so, or was it only a story? I hadn't enough locusts, nor could I find it in my heart to hunt for birds, so I trapped the smoke curling up from the fire and the steam from the kettle in earthen jars and beakers, goatskin bags, plugged with a cork, and stored them in the back of my cave, and in stealth I sent them the subtlest wisps of my reflections, but the bastards growing in my yard would walk in on tiptoe and poke holes in the jars, or unplug the corks and unravel the goatskins, and I would shout at them and fill my vessels again with flying fuel, and I slept beside the jars by night and set my meal table beside them by day, guarding them with vigilance, heeding their rustling of life, till at last I knew the hour had come, that I had all I needed to fly away, and I went down to the village and borrowed a large handbarrow from Nuri, the gypsy, and loaded it with everything I would need, and many ropes besides, and I never looked back or bade farewell to my courtyard, my pool, and my lemon tree, or my wives and children, either, for Yazdi and Najach had not been born yet, and at twilight, my sleeping-waking son, I went down the side path to the terebinth tree in the wadi, tied the sealed earthen jars to my legs, and held the small beakers under my arms and the copper *ibrik*, and I tied the big goatskin, swollen with choice flying fuel, to my behind, and I crept up the tree, pulling myself onto the branches, never pausing to rest or catch my breath, till at last I perched on the highest limb and saw before me the narrow ravine and the smoke rising from the village houses and the countryside, and I closed my eyes, telling myself that only thus would I know what Darius had revealed to me with a touch of his fleshy hand under this tree, and then I spread my arms and flew away shrieking, but a moment later my bones shattered with the beakers and the jars, and the goatskin, swollen with flying fuel, let off a terrible blast.

Kan-ya-ma-kan, not till Yazdi was born did I understand the words of Darius, my patron and redeemer, when in the living sign upon his face I beheld the way, and the sign was the beaconing light by which I led you, my son, and taught you to seclude yourself and to love, to be good and stay hidden always. And I gave birth to you anew each day, innocent child who knew no wrong, in order to fight the evil hand that walks on fingertips, and though my words and intentions are confused, you have come back to me now, you have come forth like wondrous lichen out of a soft figment, and once again I will lead you by lantern light.

Are you sleeping, Uri? Do you hear me? Distant footsteps draw near. Perhaps it is the bitter man approaching, your friend, the man without love. The moment he took the path I heard him, only his footsteps sound very strange and lost. Do not sleep, my Uri, here he comes. He needs only a few moments to climb this winding path and enter my courtyard, and then we will speak. And meanwhile, look at me, at this old onion with Yazdi's gun in my hands, crouching at the cave door, in case your friend tries to fool us and steal you away from me. I do not like his walk. Listen. Do we have enough time left? Do you want to hear?

I will tell you; this is how it happened:

Kan-ya-ma-kan, fi kadim elzaman, once upon a time, many years ago, over fifty years ago, on a morning fresh as jasmine, a certain Mamdukh el Zahrani arrived in Andal. He was the only one among us in our village of sheep who ever went to seek knowledge as far away as Amman, and even other continents, and he returned one fine day in a long red car, wearing green spectacles to protect his eyes from the harsh glare of the sun, and told the men and boys to gather in the square the following morning, and an hour before dawn Darius woke me from my sleep and gave me rosewater he prepared himself for drinking on feast days, and he dressed me in a new white robe and led me from his hut in the wadi up through the fox trails, till we arrived at bald Issa's hill that overlooked the square, and his eyes were glowing all the way there, and his hand gripped my shoulder like a vise, and he muttered to himself, calling me the shepherd, the shepherd, and gazing at me with pride and misgiving.

We climbed the hill, and Darius led me to a large rock and ordered me to wait for him there, not to come out from behind the rock, but to lie there and wait for a sign. And I did not understand what sign he meant, and why he was touching my brow and kissing my head with his fingertips, and why he reeked of the sorrow of parting, when he only planned to leave me for a few minutes, and Darius did not answer my questions but suddenly turned, and I saw his white robe, embroidered at the hem, flowing out behind him like a tent as he skipped over the rocks until he reached the square below and disappeared in the crowd.

And waiting in the square was Mamdukh el Zahrani; ah, never will I forget the sight of him: his red tie shimmering at his Adam's apple and his yellow shoes shining at his feet, and standing behind him there were four callow youths white of face and white of hair, who gazed at him with their hands folded over their chests. I peeked out from my hiding place behind the rock and saw him raise a hand to silence the crowd, and I pricked my ears and listened to the wonders Mamdukh el Zahrani revealed in the village square that morning, fresh as jasmine, more than fifty years ago.

He spoke of the cities he knew, of paved roads, of the electric creature that runs through wires, and of dead pictures that come alive in what is called the cinema, and he spoke of the sea, and of a device that tames the rivers called—a spigot; and he spoke of buildings taller than any tree, and of roads with a thousand cars, and his voice rolled out to them, he waved his hands excitedly, till at length he realized they had not understood, because they could not grasp the stuff of dreams and had never burrowed into the hills or heard the intimate speech of babes in their cradles, or listened to secret spasms behind the wall, and they did not understand that he was only a magician of words, inventing a lovelier world for all of them, and shame made them angry and powerful.

And poor Mamdukh el Zahrani saw how different he was from them and could not imagine anyone understanding him or loving him with his red tie and the broad sweep of his hand that meant the world, and so he decided enough of words, and stuck two fingers in his mouth, and a sharp whistle pierced the air, and far away I spied a kind of smoking *rulla* galloping up the road to Juni, an iron monster, with long bony paws, and riding on its hump, the bravest of his kind, half man half devil, with a big round head, unnaturally red, and behind the exploding *rulla* came a little yellow autotruck loaded with swollen sacks of gray powder, and at a signal from Mamdukh, the *rulla* fell silent, and the driver alighted and took off his head, and a murmur of fear went through the crowd, and only the cleverest saw it was the man's red helmet, made of steel, and the yellow autotruck drove around in a grand circle and came to a halt in front of Mamdukh, like a small and dangerous animal sprawling at its trainer's feet.

Then Mamdukh spoke to the men and boys of Andal about the wealth that would be theirs if they left the onion and tobacco fields behind and came to do men's work for him, drilling and quarrying the belly of the earth and squirting out its black blood, called oil, and he snapped his fingers, and the autotruck driver hastened near, bearing a red leather-bound scroll, and out of it Mamdukh snatched a kind of silken map, which the four white youths unfurled, and Mamdukh explained to the throng forgathered that this map held a precious secret which a certain German who had sojourned in Andal once with a hunting party had prepared many years ago, and according to the measurements and sights he had taken then, there was a black sea of bubbling oil halfway between bald Issa's hill and the hill of noseless Ishmael, and anyone who reached it would find the wealth of a sultan, and Mamdukh spoke smoothly and the four dainty youths without faces unfurled the map, walking in opposite directions as though bewitched, because the map spread endlessly, and a few moments later the four youths stood, one beyond the crowd, one beyond the monster *rulla*, and two beyond the hills, but the map continued to unfurl in their soft hands, and a shadow fell across the crowd as the map flew above them, and the four youths separated farther and farther, climbing over hill and dale, and through the silken map with its red arrows and shining stars, I could see Mamdukh el Zahrani smiling as he spoke, and much to my bewilderment I realized I, too, was under the sheer silk, yet I could see above it and watch the youths vanish to the four winds of heaven, and like mildew spreading, there appeared on it a silhouette of the iron monster, and as it touched the iron monster in the square, *kan-ya-ma-kan*, my eyes grew wide with wonder, for I discovered the complete picture of my village of sheep on the buoyant silk, the well and the caves where the Bedouin live, and the terebinth tree in the wadi, and the onion and tobacco fields, and I rubbed my eyes, but the apparition was still there, only now I saw the painted figure of Mamdukh more clearly, and the shaven crown of my patron and redeemer, and everyone I ever knew: my brother Nimer and my sister Naima and my sister Widad, and old Naef, and Shukri Ibn Labib as a small boy and also as a very old man, and even Nuri, the gypsy, who had not yet arrived in the village with a monkey on his shoulder, and I looked up and saw above me the silken canopy fluttering in a friendly sign that I had nothing to fear from it, that it was floating down gently, and I saw my own figure drawn upon it, and the story coiled inside me like a prickly rope, my birth, and all that came before my birth, my mother as she faced the karakul, and the wind sweeping up the portrait of a lion in the sand, and the severed hand resting on the shoulder of my son, and the overripe fruit, and the frightened child of anguish at the door of my cave, and the gun I now hold in my hand, and the sheer silk almost touched my head and carried me away, when suddenly someone in the crowd flicked the burning butt of a cigarette, and I thought it was Darius, because I saw his likeness in that flash and the whole valley suddenly arched and floated through the air with the cigarette butt, and the menfolk's square glimmered with precious light, and nothing remained of the fifty-eight men and boys, and the yellow autotruck with the sacks of gray powder, or of Mamdukh el Zahrani and his shimmering red tie, or of Darius, my patron and redeemer, not even a piece of cloth or a chipped tooth, only the iron machine remained, its charred paws raised to heaven, and I beheld this from a bird's-eye view after a violent hand grabbed me by the hump and hurled me out of my hiding place behind the rock high above the two dusty carob trees in the square, high above the brown hills, and the narrow wadi and the desert, and high above my village of sheep, gurgling below and rustling when the silky map floated down and touched it, melting at its touch, and painting its lanes as they might have looked at the mournful feasts of my Sha'aban, and high above the great, wise people, the people who knew courage and love and mercy and desire, I glided by enjoying the sights, my eye so keen I could see a crack in the terebinth tree, and the iron filings of my dreams at the bottom of the barrel, and thus I learnt the wisdom of flying for a full seventy-seven years, blessedly suckling the rose air of freedom, and below me, the women of the village ran silently through the lanes, still trying to understand the calamity which had befallen their husbands and sons, and they raised their eyes and beheld me, the little hunchback, God's angel, his organ stiff with fear and pleasure, folding invisible wings inside his hump, where they would remain forever, and he floated gently over their outstretched palms, over their aprons spread toward him in silence, sailing over the village streets like a quiet old bird, and passing unharmed through the mud roof into the warm bed of the lovely sloven Laila Sallach, most lustful of women, who groaned, *kan-ya-ma-kan*, when the blade went into her, faster and bolder then any she had ever known.

Tuta tuta khelset elkhaduta.

25

"We were worried," explains Abner, entering the room. "It's Leah, she was worried," Zussia divulges, and one whiff tells me they're both in their cups. You've been drinking, I remark in Mother's voice, amazed to hear how harsh I sound.

They stand before me like shamefaced children, and in the dim light I can see a slight resemblance between them, not in their features or gestures really, but in the cord that stretches painfully between them. Now they stare at me in amazement, Abner curling his lip, Zussia bashing his fists together. I don't care. I haven't got the strength to pretend anymore. Not with them. By now, we can allow ourselves the grace of sincerity and self-forgiveness.

They look me over silently. My appearance, my wild hair. They've never seen me so disheveled before. The expression on my face is baffling to them, and they recoil from mighty Spider-Man about to leap. Zussia catches sight of my discarded blouse, and lifts it gently, setting it on the table like flowers on a grave.

The little lamp distorts their shadows. First they're two sinuous bulls, then a pair of eggplants on the wall. And I can smell the brandy vapors.

Abner staggers over to the other side of the table and sits down. What's wrong, Shoshik, he hiccups tiredly, and when I don't reply, he raises an inquiring hand and says, Uri disappeared, and now you're hiding something from us. You and I have never had any secrets from each other, you always told us everything, please say something, Shosh.

I'll say it. If I don't say it now, the suffering I've inflicted on myself will have been in vain. I'll say it.

"All right, Abner. I'll tell you. It's time I told you. It's about the boy, my patient."

"The one who died? Who committed suicide? What's his name?"

"His name was Mordy."

"But that was ages ago, almost a year, wasn't it?"

"Three months. Zussia, why don't you pull up that chair and sit down."

"Three months? And I was sure a year had gone by."

"I didn't tell you the whole story. Sit down, will you, Zussia."

"What do you mean?"

"I killed him."

"Don't talk like that. Zussia! Will you sit down already!"

He sits up straight. His eyes flicker, then die. Now I can watch the old routine: Abner running away.

" 'I killed him,' " he parrots shrilly, sketching a smile of amusement on his lips. "Bang!" he shoots me with his fingers. "Just like that. So plain and simple. Well, let me tell you, Shosh, the old stylistics don't always work." And he walks over to the window and peers through the curtains. Then he takes out his pipe and a box of matches, rubs two together, and strikes a little flame. "Maybe—foo!" he says, blowing out the match. "People have forgotten the art of conversation. At best they exchange bits of relevant data. Abbreviation, that's the key word of the digital set. In fact, all they ever do is abbreviate and manipulate, only they've relinquished one of our basic rights in the process, the right to describe the—"

"I killed him, Father."

He's trapped. The harpoon hits him in the back and rivets him to the window. Now he gasps, drawn to me, the hunter who brought him down, not with the words "I killed him," but with the word I haven't used in so many years; and now, laid low, he slides a chair over with his foot and sinks down on it. His face is pale, with unhealthy blotches of color on his right cheek, on the tip of his nose, and on his limp neck where he neglected to shave the silvery stubble.

"You're not listening, Abner. You never listen."

I was twelve the first time. Riding on the bus one day, there was an old man sitting in front of me, smelly and unshaven, with bulging shopping baskets grouped around him, and in the basket that was leaning against my foot I saw a fish wrapped in newspaper, and my straying eyes took in the letters printed there, though I still hadn't made sense of them, and I was filled with a strange longing, smoldering darkly, as if I'd always sensed that it would find me, and I looked at the scaly, bloodstained newspaper and knew from the first stanza that I would never be the same again, that a great promise or cruel threat lay at my feet, and I leaned down for a closer look at the fragmented words that growled in warning, the savage letters rearing up and trembling under the strain, and I could feel the whip of the anonymous tamer, the cruel spell he cast on me, and beneath the soiled, translucent paper, I suddenly saw that the fish was still twitching, its eye bulging with effort, and I leaned still closer to the briny smell of it wrapped in seaweed, its quivery life writhing into the poem, and there on the bus, on a bright Tel Aviv afternoon, the key to poetry turned in me, and the poem—though I didn't know it yet—was his.

"Why do you say so?"

"He died because of me. I—um—I used a method he couldn't take, you understand?"

"You're torturing yourself, and you're torturing us, too; according to your line of reasoning, all of us are murderers." Now he storms out of his confusion, and Zussia, by the window, turns his slow, sad bull face toward him. "In matters like these, Shoshik, you mustn't be too clever; you mustn't delve too deeply, you have to put on blinders, because otherwise, all of us are murderers, don't you see, all of us are accursed."

"Maybe you're right, but not in this particular case. My connection with Mordy's death is absolutely clear—to me, at any rate." Abner covers his mouth with his hand and reflects. He is a little frightened. My calmness worries him. Zussia also walks over and sits down. He takes a pencil out of his pencil case and draws a rhombus with a tail on the brown paper. I notice that the tape recorder is still on. Zussia doodles a fine line from the kite to the ground, where he tries to draw a little boy, only this difficult task requires the cooperation of the hand that grips the back of his chair to hold the paper down, but when this, too, is not enough, he is forced to enlist his big pink tongue, thrust resolutely between his teeth.

"Well, supposing you're right," says Abner. "Just supposing. Do the police know about it? No! And they carried out a full investigation, after I used my connections to have that impudent young officer replaced. They cleared you completely, and still you blame yourself?"

"I killed him."

Zussia is deep in his drawing. He has now doodled a little sausage with four nails stuck into it—a boy running and waving his arms— and a bigger sausage—the mother or father of the little sausage— watching anxiously from afar.

"Are these his clothes?"

"Yes. That's one thing your police don't know about."

"That's still not proof. And frankly, it's none of my business what you wear." Suddenly he slams his hand down on the glass-top table, making Zussia jump from his chair, and decapitating the cucumber in top hat that has just appeared on the brown paper. "We can't root out the evil in us, Shoshik," he whispers. "We can only try to minimize the wrong we do our fellow man, to be more charitable, more loving, oh, who knows—" And here, without warning, he lets out a guffaw that ends up a cross between a gasp and a cough, and Zussia and I watch him with alarm.

Abner shakes his head. He sets his pipe down in the glass ashtray, takes a blue tissue from the small box on the table near me, and soundlessly wipes his nose.

"Water, Father?"

"No. I'm all right. I'm all right." His voice sounds funny through his fingers. "I'm all right. Excuse me. Something I said made me laugh all of a sudden. You're old enough and smart enough to know when I'm lying. I'm not so charitable or loving myself. Knowing that is sometimes hard to admit, as I'm sure you yourself know. You find out one day at the age of forty or forty-five, during a routine checkup. And you're not even too upset when you hear the results. But that's how it is. I just don't know how to love. I love your mother, of course, and you, of course, but 'love,' Shosh—" and again he wipes his nose, saying as he does so that I still haven't explained anything yet.

"Well, the boy fell in love with me."

"But that's marvelous, isn't it? As I recall, it was love you were working with. I'm just kidding, of course."

"You see, I made him fall in love with me, but then I was so frightened I cut him off. And that was too much for him."

"He was very young; seventeen, you said?"

"Barely fifteen. I was his first love, and it was a great shock to him."

"And what did Uri say about it?"

"Uri didn't know."

"I see."

And there is silence again. At least we don't have to say everything out loud.

"You've changed lately. There's an air of anxiety about you, I've noticed. A kind of bitterness. You're always somewhere else—"

I don't believe him. He's the one who's always somewhere else. He rarely notices anyone, in fact.

"—but I didn't dare interfere. You're such a private person, you want to solve your own problems. I've always envied your serenity, Shoshik, I used to say to Leah, Shosh is—"

"I know what you used to say. It's almost an insult."

"An insult? But I rely on you so much. And I needn't remind you what I owe to your sound judgment. It's not an insult, Shoshik."

I know he doesn't mean it as an insult. I know that he needs me like a cool polestar to navigate by when he loses his way. And none of this would have happened if we had simply been open with each other, if he hadn't hurled me into the secret of his poetry. Because all the time he and Leah were talking to me, I watched their lips move but didn't hear their voices, trying desperately to rescue the survivors, to repair the damage, to start rebuilding right away, training myself to smile serenely, to be ever on my guard, but who will show me how to drain the anguish festering inside me, how to get rid of this corruption I let in by mistake, and before me stand Abner and Leah, looking so aghast that I will never be able to ask their help again, because they have no idea what they've done to me, and I see them flinch when I cut a secret passage through to the invisible tunnel inside me which rips open along its basted seams at the sound of the deep, hoarse wail coming out of me, which is not my voice at all but a bellowing bull caught in a labyrinth, or a baby screaming its final scream in me, and everything is swept into the tunnel, all the things I imagined were mine, ours: the words, the quiet smiles, the Saturday outings, his affectionate finger on her wrinkled cheek, and his quiet love for both of us, the love and hope that animate the articles he writes and youth-movement speeches he makes, and, of course, the cheerful banter that never betrayed his bitter strength, and the bedtime stories and birthday presents under the pillow, and supper in the cozy kitchen; but they all vanish in the darkness, blown away by the raging wind that tears me apart, and the only thing that's left of me is the will to go on screaming, with all my fear, though I can only rasp like a wounded snake, hissing curses too vile to utter, shocking Abner and Leah, and for many hours after, I tremble and press my clenched fists to the defiant mouth that won't stop spouting venom till the cistern runs dry and the scream pierces through Abner's room, but I refuse to leave, and there are holes in Leah and Abner, too, and Leah cries and carries on, and Abner walks around me as if I were a dangerous pit he fears he will fall into, together with all who are dear to me, and so it continues till I am nothing but a heap of phrases on the ground, to be put to bed and covered with a blanket, and the windows are left open to let out the typhoon, and we watch over the childish face at last becalmed, and recognize our features in it, our signature, and in the morning be very quiet, don't mention anything, your egg is ready, darling Shosh, and in comes darling Shosh, hoarse and shamefaced, tempted to burst into liberating tears of remorse, I'm sorry, Mother and Father, for what happened yesterday, I don't know what came over me. Never mind, girl, you don't have to explain, we saw that something pained you, or frightened you, something you may not understand yourself, these things are often too subtle to understand, but we want you to know that we're with you all the way, to help you, there's no point in talking about it; and I must say they kept their word, and several weeks went by before Leah blurted out, apropos of something else, that even in the worst of times one mustn't be an animal, and I knew I was not forgiven.

I was thrown into the violent whirlpool yet again when Abner came into my room and in a broken voice read me something that sounded like a cross between an elegy and a treatise, with the same wild diction and deadening despair that blew through all his sonnets and the hypnotic meter of a pendulum clock, and I couldn't believe my ears. We're tearing them apart, whispered Abner, we can't go on tearing sensitive young people apart; we can't inspire them with lofty ideals and then order them to kill, even for a just cause, and I tried to shut myself off, to quell the storms raging inside me. You mustn't, I begged, you mustn't say that, but Abner said he couldn't go on, that he knew we had no choice, that the fighting had been forced on us, and so had the hump that's been on our backs since the June war, but still, how is it possible, he bellowed, his mouth like an ugly sore, how is it possible for a whole nation, an enlightened nation, by all accounts, to train itself to perform such a complicated operation and live in a moral vacuum; and after Chagai, how can I go on educating youth to love and respect their fellow man, and to question everything, those values that are the basis of culture and morality, when, far from equipping them for life, I may only be—sabotaging them, throwing them into the whirlpool of conflict; no, it isn't idealism, it's a curse, because anyone who chooses to live by the old saws dies of confusion, stricken from the society that has learned to play such a masterly game of heroic obtuseness, and I, Shosh, am as guilty as anyone, I helped them lie and gave them comforting words, instead of spitting my opinion of them in their faces, because I didn't know what was going on myself, and someone had to die before I woke up and saw how I condemned the sensitive to death, while the others used me as a kind of fig leaf for their lies; but what's it all about, this world we live in, this country, the dream that was, it's as if some tormented Russian playwright cast us, of all people, in the role of conquerors and murderers, and how many future generations will bear the stigma; and the gun in Act One of our historic pageant about, say, the pioneering period a hundred years ago is now shooting at us, and we hear the curtain going down, but no applause.

Not a rustling; more like a scratching and a scurrying outside in the bushes and a strange, muffled sound. Abner crosses his lips with his finger, and Zussia hops up from his chair with silent, surprising ease: they're a team suddenly. They spread out along the curtained window, groping for the handle. There: we heard him again, close to the window. And then a sharp knock on the pane. Someone's there. Someone's been spying on me all evening. I look at Abner. He is on guard. Playing the panther. Now he pulls the curtain, Zussia yanks the window open, and a grotesque scream is heard, and I'm sure it's the unknown person who put the package with Mordy's clothes in my office, the one who came even closer to truth than the impudent young police officer, and smeared that truth crudely over the blue-ward bathroom wall, the truth that will eventually be found out, but I don't care, maybe it will be a relief, and outside a battle of titans is in progress, with terrible screaming and an inexplicably violent fluttering, and Zussia groans, curses in Russian, one foot here, the other foot out the window in the bushes, and he's back a moment later, holding something to his chest, laughing hilariously as he sets down the jumble of horror and flying feathers, one abusive goose.

Now all three of us laugh as we stand around poor neurotic Sigmund, Sigmund, whose spotted bill is open as he pants at us with a foolish threatening expression, forced by some compulsive vengefulness to throw back his neck in moments of danger and preen his ruffled tailfeathers.

I introduce everyone around. Abner bows, Zussia rubs his brow. Sigmund gives a short honk. Zussia, with no consideration for the goose's feelings, reports that in Russia they eat birds just like him, only bigger, with red legs.

Sigmund, like a nobleman fallen from his high estate, waddles over to the bookshelf and reviews his difficult position in the room. He cranes his neck to follow our movements. Abner sits down again. Zussia is still fussing over the window, which refuses to shut. Abner asks if—how to put it—Uri's sudden decision to work in Juni has anything to do with—um—the case.

It has something to do with it.

"But you said he didn't know about it?"

"It's too complicated to explain. I've been withdrawn lately. And Katzman influenced him and—"

"Katzman? That's a familiar name."

"Sure it's familiar. Uri's told you about him at least ten thousand times. Don't you remember anything people tell you, Abner?"

"Ah, you know me. It's lucky for me that Leah comes to my rescue in such situations."

His eyes fall on the brown paper wrapping under his hand; he picks it up and studies the two sausages and the kite drawn there.

"So Katzman is a friend of Uri's?"

"Uri's and mine. He's the military governor of Juni. He's the—"

"Ah yes, of course, I met him once at our house. Very thin, pale. I remember. He kept making sarcastic remarks he thought were amusing. Yes, Katzman." He mulls the name Katzman, Katzman, over to himself, his pencil poised above Zussia's creation, as though concentrating on how to improve it, but I can read more than his face, I see how he dives inward to the pale, troubling light that went on at the mention of Katzman's name. There is information there that has to be deciphered, and he plunges down, turns over a big stone and looks under it, at the black seaweed and scuttling creatures of the depths; I can see his forehead wrinkling under the water. He puts the stone back exactly where he found it, so that no one will know it has been moved. Now he fins his way up to confirm one last conjecture, inquiring obliquely, "You used to mention him fairly often, didn't you?"

"That's right."

"You were pretty enthusiastic about him, as I recall."

"Right."

"I see."

Of course he sees. He knows everything. The bad and the loathsome in every possible permutation of reality is always comprehensible to him. He's been trained to ambush it, self-righteous fish of the dark that he is. Now with a hum he draws a thin Latin mustache on the mother sausage. Then he adds a saucy sombrero and a pair of round glasses. I despise him so much for a moment, and am seized with terrible self-pity, with longing for Uri, for his duck walk, his pretty brown toes protuding from his sandals; for his shirttails always sticking out of his pants. And his smile, and his chipped front tooth, and, "Oh, Abner," I suddenly groan, "everything is so unreal."

He, too, sighs. His wounded, wilting mouth glows red as he scratches his neck with the hand that holds his pipe. "You know what I think of reality." He smiles. "Let's take this room, for instance, what's real about it?" He indicates all of us with his hand— Zussia still struggling with the recalcitrant window, Spider-Man flying off Mordy's shirt, and the goose eyeing us with contempt from his perch. "Don't talk to me about reality."

Zussia prevails over the window and joins us again. "Real, shmeal," he grumbles. "Let's go home, Leah will worry." Abner and I watch him intently. The silence is suddenly as thick as smoke. The moment has come to ask.

"Zussia," I say, "you never told me—"

"On our way over, Zussia was remembering how he used to give you a ride to school on his bike—" How eager Abner seems to crush the sprout I planted in this conversation, and Zussia beams, blushing to his earlobes, his Adam's apple bobbing as he starts to talk, to recount with simple excitement how I used to sit on the back of his bike, hiding under his big raincoat, my skinny legs sticking out like two tails, and the three of us laugh, and Zussia screws his mouth to his nose again, pleased to have given us a moment's pleasure, blowing on his palms, hiking up his trousers, and Abner doesn't make it easy for him, doesn't take the scepter of embarrassing attention away, but sits there, pipe in hand, gazing at him with seeming appreciation, skewering him thus until he's enjoyed Zussia's punishment to the full—or maybe he wants to punish me now for trying to cross the border—and comes to Zussia's rescue with the outstretched hand of an experienced host. "And what else were you remembering, Zussia? That Shoshik told you she preferred to play with boys because girls are made of secrets?" A ripple of laughter washes over him. "Leah recorded it in her album of your wise little sayings. She thought that was very poetic for a five-year-old. Ah, Shosh, you used to make such cute mistakes."

"I still do." I bite my lip.

Now a cork pops, and gulping and gurgling, Zussia wipes his lips and passes the bottle to Abner. Abner takes a long sip with his eyes shut. I never realized how much he enjoys drinking. He holds out his hand. "Have some. It's good. No? Really? Too bad. You don't know what you're missing." And he returns the bottle to Zussia.

"It's nice here," he says. "I've never been here before."

"Yes."

"And it's nice to talk like this."

"Right, we haven't talked for a long time."

"Well, you know, we're both cold fish."

"If you say so."

Silence. He looks around the room. Starts to say something, changes his mind, and smiles at me. "You're so grown-up, Shosh. Sometimes I hardly feel any age gap between us."

"Abner—"

"Yes?"

"Never mind."

"If you say so."

"Nu? Coming?"

"Just a minute, Zussia."

Just a minute. I don't need much. Let me rest my forehead on the cold glass tabletop and purr softly, feeling your joy, Zussia, because now just as I used to, when I was a child, I ask you to soothe my tense and weary body, and Abner smiles, and Zussia giggles, nice, nice, a little to the left, Zussia, and I smell a faint odor of perfume, and a faint odor of brandy, and in the darkened room his hands move nobly, like the ears of a great elephant, sliding down to the water, down my neck, sculpting my body, pressing, caressing, and in his own compassionate way, repairing me like a broken doll, a naughty doll, and I internalize his dark heat, the silence prolonged over so many years, trying to learn wisdom and suffering from him, and with my eye open I watch my open eye in the glass and transmit the time-lapse pictures of my healing. Something inside me is sealing up. I can leave now, I guess, and keep busy and forget, and have my successes and break my vows and lie like an expert; oh, you get used to it, you learn how to kill and leave no clues, to love and leave no stain, to do wrong without suffering too much. Like courtly life in the Middle Ages. And in my open eye in the glass there is no fear or guilt anymore, it watches me with a lucid, practical concern, and how can I explain the single tear that suddenly falls on the cool, thick glass and blurs my reflection?

We can go now, Abner. Where are the tissues, Zussia? Here. Good. Everything's okay. Just go out to the hall a minute, and I'll change my clothes. Go on, get out. Don't worry. Nu?!

All alone. And for one last lonely moment I strangle the burning urge to run away; to fool those waiting for me outside and run out through the big window, over the fields and roads and army bases, over shame and regret and evil, to Uri. Wherever he may be. No-Such-Animal-Uri is a healer, and if I touch him, all my bad blood will be expelled.

Off comes Spider-Man, and I put on my vest—just a minute out there! I'm hurrying!—and I brush my hair before the portrait of Viktor Frankl, who hasn't recovered from this evening yet, and I roll Mordy's clothes up and wrap them in the brown paper, which will one day be worth millions because of Zussia's immortal doodles there, and carefully I stuff the parcel behind two books on the shelf and put them back in place. No one will notice anything.

A moment more to look around and arrange the files. To unplug the poor tape recorder. To stack the cassettes and wipe my tears from the glass. Now I can smooth my tartan skirt with two stiff thumbs. I'm out of here.

Hey, says Abner after I lock up, what about the goose?

Let him search for meaning, I answer.

And down the long, winding corridor we go, the three of us lulled by the soft tune coming over the hidden speakers, only before the turn, before the front gate and Yankl the watchman's booth come into view, Zussia suddenly stops me, laughs, and asks me to close my eyes, and when I obey, offering up my little-girl face, he presses his thumbs against my lids, and the yellow sparks fly.

26

"Stop. Stop."

Katzman stopped where he stood. Waiting. The old man came toward him from the courtyard on wobbly legs, holding a gun in both hands. By the light of the moon Katzman saw the large writing on the hillside, and smiled, remembering the pictures drawn by the little mute girl.

"Wait there. Don't move."

Tart rings of the old man's lemon smell encompassed Katzman, and then the old man himself approached: surprisingly small, humming to himself excitedly in a high thin voice as he circled Katzman, watching him and nodding like a hen examining a strange but harmless piece of sculpture. Katzman stood erect, wondering about the way the old man was holding the gun: had he been watching Westerns all his life? Maybe we're all born knowing how to hold a gun.

The busy humming behind his back did not cease for a moment, not even when Katzman felt the sprightly hand shaking his ammunition belt and removing his gun. Then he heard a distant clang, as the gun hit the hillside and rolled down the path.

"Now please come in. *Tfadal.*"

Katzman trod with care, trying to observe as many details as possible. He bumped into a small stool and was startled. Khilmi's voice prodded his back. Now he stopped humming and began a feverish debate with himself. It was hot. Katzman was perspiring from his swift climb up the path, and the sweat stung his face, but he was afraid to reach out and wipe it away. Where was Uri?

"This way. Here."

Katzman turned to the grape bower. Dry tendrils brushed against his forehead. Now he noticed a big barrel, and the heap on the ground that tried to sit up as he approached.

"Katzman?"

"Uri?"

"*Yalla, rukh,* keep going."

What was wrong with Uri? His voice sounded strange and lifeless. Khilmi walked around Katzman and leaned down to help Uri to his feet. Uri groaned, his legs barely able to support him. Katzman watched them stagger together, holding each other up. He could have jumped Khilmi from behind. But he didn't. He walked obediently behind him. As he did so, he tested himself: he couldn't yet feel the blessed fog that usually descended in moments of danger. Or maybe there was a danger here he was untrained to defend himself against. The sliver of a moon was shining on his face again, which meant they were out of the bower.

"Climb over the fence."

"Where?"

"Over there. *Yalla etla*."

He's planned the whole thing out. Katzman tries to help Uri, but Uri seems to ignore him. Over the low fence they go and down to a wide rock shelf. Below, in the village, Katzman sees red dots floating in the darkness, the eyes of a deep-water fish. He and Uri have not yet looked into each other's eyes.

"Now sit down, both of you."

Katzman glances questioningly at Uri. Uri collapses with fatigue. With resignation. From his movements Katzman sees the extent of Khilmi's power over him. He sits down beside Uri on the warm rock. Khilmi stands over them, on the fence, wobbling in his sneakers.

And all is still.

Katzman is suddenly aware of the dull hot night enveloping him and weighing down his hands and lids. Perhaps this is the worst punishment Khilmi could have devised, reflects Katzman wearily. Bringing Uri and me together like this, and making us sit here in stifling silence. And now I'm frightened; for the first time since Uri ran away from Juni this morning, I'm frightened. Why doesn't Khilmi say something? One word. One curse. It's like being in a trap within a trap. Uri's silence within Khilmi's silence.

Katzman glances furtively around and guesses the inclination of the slope. He presses his arm against his chest and feels the coolness of the metal. If the old man decided to shoot him now, it would be all over. For the past few moments Katzman's confidence has been on the wane. Someone inside seems to have outwitted him.

He realizes he has to make an effort and start acting in accordance with what he planned below. Without turning his head away from the devil-in-a-robe wobbling on the fence before him, Katzman says in Hebrew, no question mark inflecting his voice, "Just-the-old-man-here."

His eyes are riveted to Khilmi, who doesn't respond, but listens with interest, nodding to the sound of Katzman's voice. Yes, but Uri is silent, too. Katzman hears his heavy, uneven breathing, and only that. He tries again.

"Just-the-old-man-here-yes."

And Uri wheezes out the words with evident strain: "Just the old man."

Now it's Katzman's turn to gamble, to dictate the terms in a harsh-sounding, inappropriate voice: "You lied."

"So did you."

Katzman is shattered. From the village below comes the humming of antennas. In a minute or two, the soldiers will start up the path. A distant plane rumbles in the sky. Katzman looks up. The stars are being crushed between vast blocks of darkness. And again, carefully: "Does-he-know-how-to-shoot."

Khilmi coughs. His gun barrel traces a small arc on Katzman's body, sending out arc-shaped ripples of fear. And yet—Khilmi lets him talk. Why does Khilmi's generosity make him feel so hollow and contemptible, so insignificant with regard to what's taking place here between Uri and Khilmi? Katzman steals a sideways glance. Uri is still sitting in the same position, hunched over, his arms hugging his legs and his chin resting on his knees. Staring ahead.

"Don't be afraid, Katzman. He won't shoot you. It's me he wants."

"Does-he-know-Hebrew."

Uri smiles weakly. "He understands everything we're saying. It's only the language he doesn't understand."

Katzman shakes his head uncomprehendingly. Now he begins to notice Khilmi's peculiar stench over the smell of lemon. He remembers Uri telling him something about it. A mosquito lands on the back of his hand, and Katzman lets it sting him. As an alternative to pinching himself. He licks his upper lip and tastes the moist, salt skin. It would be bright out tonight if not for the heat moving in like heavy fog. Katzman shifts his position, crushed by the silence between them. Even here, on this rock shelf where we sit like the last three people on earth, those two have made a pact between them.

"Uri, I've come to help you; you asked me to, Uri—"

"Help me what, against whom?" Uri's thoughts barely crystallize into words in the silent darkness.

"I'm here to get you out alive."

"I'm not sure I want to get out." Uri laughs weakly. "I don't know anything anymore, Katzman; everything I used to know is dead."

Did Katzman hear her voice in his? Or was it a random echo? And yet what is that evanescent glow, creating and dissolving itself each minute out of the darkness between them? A dance of shadows weaving by in the hush of night. Is Uri scoffing at him with his silences, his innuendoes? The mosquito bite starts to itch in ever-widening circles on the back of Katzman's hand. Sweat collects on his eyebrows.

"I'm beyond all that now, Katzman, beyond you, too. You wouldn't understand."

I would understand, I would. Katzman wants to plead with Uri to take him. Not to leave him behind here all alone with himself; with his knowing, conniving self, even now just waiting for the right moment to jump Khilmi.

Uri quietly explains, his voice also white and dreary now: "You yourself explained it to me, Katzman. It's only anguish, calling me louder than the other voices. Like a craving. Like a passion. For a woman, let's say. Yes."

He really is mocking me, thinks Katzman. He's using words I put in her mouth that she passed on to him. You can't trust the words he says anymore, you have to look beyond them. The same keys now open another door.

Down in the village, the cocking of a gun can be heard. They're probably setting off now. Dogs bark, and a jackal answers from over the hill. Or is it a hyena? A thought flares up and plummets down again like a smoking firecracker in Katzman's mind, scorching all fear in its trail: Maybe this really is an ambush. But different from the one I anticipated. Instead of terrorists, it's the two of them. And if I decide to attack Khilmi, I'm not so sure I'll be able to count on Uri. I don't know. I don't know.

"You." He turns to Khilmi angrily, in his best university Arabic. "You should have demanded something simpler, *khaga basita*, this way you make it very difficult for us—" and even as he speaks, he realizes how silly he sounds; how unworthy it is to address Khilmi thus, in the pitiful words of a rational negotiation.

Khilmi shakes himself. Again he raises the drowsing gun barrel. "What did you say?"

Katzman softens his voice: "Your demand isn't rational. *Mush maakula*. We're willing to hear you out, to give you something maybe, but not—um—"

And he stops, defeated. He can't even try a small imperative lie here now in front of Uri. Khilmi flicks on his transistor. Languid sounds spill out into the thickening night, winding like honey around anything still sharp and bright and piercing. Uri breaks in, strangely gentle and sad: "It's pointless, Katzman." Katzman is glad to hear the gentleness in Uri's voice, till suddenly he realizes it was intended for Khilmi. Uri was speaking Arabic.

Now he continues in Arabic: "You've got to understand, Katzman. It's pointless to try to convince him. All his life he's run away from us. From people like us. And he never fought back. He thinks those who fight wind up the slaves of what they were fighting. Because in order to fight you have to have some points of similarity, you understand."

Khilmi smiles at Uri in confirmation, and Katzman blenches at the animal love that lights up his one mad eye. Katzman turns his fear into anger. "You accuse me of lying, right? Of being the representative of a nation of liars. But he's a liar, too—" he says, nodding at Khilmi. "And so are the others who live here. Listen, it takes two to carry a big lie," and he flashes Uri a frightened look, but Uri doesn't seem to catch the slur. "And I have no respect for them, you hear, I have no respect for the million or million and a half who live quiescently under a regime they don't want." The words spill out with hatred, with a strange pain. But that's not why he's suffering now. This, too, is a sham. Another stream of self-hatred has frozen into the wrong words. "Okay, maybe there's an incident now and then: a few fear-crazed boys set a bomb off and run away. Or shoot at a school. They're beneath contempt." His body hums. Acutely painful sensations shoot up inside him. Will he ever be desperate enough to admit the truth and win Uri's forgiveness? The wretched gambler in him is still trying to win a smile from Uri as he adds, "They'll never breathe the rose air of Ariosto." And he laughs beseechingly.

Uri answers, sailing the light, airy words out of his mouth: "She killed that kid, you know."

Katzman veers around. "What kid?"

"That kid of hers. Mordy. We used to hear his voice on the tape, remember?"

Katzman nods weakly. That's what it was, then. Uri mutters, "He killed himself because of her, and she didn't tell anyone what really happened. She had sex with him. A fifteen-year-old kid. And half retarded." Uri spoke on without pain or rancor. Katzman wasn't listening anymore. The news Uri had planted in him made him gasp. He felt himself freeze around the dead fetus that had been thrust at him, and only now did he surmise the depth of her secret, her lie, her suffering.

Uri says, "She said she learned a lot of things over the past few months: that you can go on living, even after something like that. She said the enzymes of the mind are amazingly strong, strong enough to decompose anything." And he moves over till he is sitting cross-legged in front of Katzman. His glasses shine. Khilmi seems to be drowning in the darkness now, except for the occasional gleam of his gun and his flowery robe shining in the moonbeams; and his voice drones on, embroidering stories for himself with threads of melody.

Uri watched Katzman and spoke through him: "When I ran away from you this week, I found her at home. She told me everything. That kid, it was his first experience of love." He gave a short laugh and licked his chipped front tooth. Katzman was only a fading vision.

Khilmi spoke from his perch on the fence. Like a cool breeze, his words broke loose from the feverish leaven of hallucinations, wafting down to the two at his feet: "We should have kept silent," he said. "We should have drawn into ourselves. Each person to his house and village in silence, to wait."

"And then?" asked Katzman slackly, puffing his question Uri's way like a fading smoke ring.

"Then," said Khilmi, "you would be struck with terror. Perhaps

322

you would resort to violence. Think of it: a million people never touching you at all. Silence growing. Mass hunger strikes. Voluntary curfews. In the beginning you may shoot us, but we will kick a hole through our killers. And you are not made of very hard stuff." Again he forged the words into a wild stammer.

"And then," said Uri, "I asked her how she could have hidden such a thing from me for so long. And she said—you know what she said?"

Katzman shook his head no. He knew.

"That there was more, there were other things she'd kept hidden from me. And that kid wasn't the only one she'd been fooling around with. There were others. You hear, the wife I trusted. That kid, and there were others. Who is this woman I've lived with so long, Katzman, how could I have been so blind?"

Katzman bows his head, waiting in pain for Uri to deliver the final blow. But Uri takes his time. Torturing him. And in the grief-filled silence Katzman suddenly realizes something—lies are like magnetic filings of the truth that wear it down and hide until they bear a perfect resemblance to it, and then they forget what holds the filings together.

"But it can never be," says Khilmi suddenly, his small body hardening. "These are only the vain imaginings of an old onion. And therefore I have decided—" and again his voice rises to a peep. Katzman is dizzy. It's like fencing on two fronts. Rashly he begs, "No, no, Uri, don't think that, really—" and Uri slowly looks up and smiles that smile at him. Katzman is petrified, because Uri's features are still there, and the smile lines are drawn across his face, but it isn't the smile of the lamb anymore, it's a grimacing mask of evil, a grim curse Uri hurls at him, too weak to say the words.

And he continues to smile like a cruel death-shell, and Katzman can't tear his eyes away from this face he himself has created with his heaviest sin, and he struggles inwardly to rouse the sense of duty that brought him here in the first place, and to refract the malicious glare of the glassy jester's smile, and all he has to do is to jump Uri and knock him down, and roll off the rock shelf with him and hide in the shadows till Sheffer and his men surround the courtyard, because by now he has seen there is no other way to break out of the trap, this nightmare he is caught in, but how can he jump Uri, how can he touch him with his wolfish smile when the doors have slammed shut and his keys have been flung in his face, and the fearful night suddenly clings to him, and prickly pears of darkness grow inside it, only at this moment Katzman hears a faint sound coming from the path and sees that Khilmi has also heard, and now he has to do something fast, though there seems to be no point, and he hugs his shoulders, his fingers slowly groping for the leather belt and the buckle till they feel the naked butt under his arm, and quickly, quickly, because Khilmi suddenly stiffens and his gun barrel fills with life and trembles over Uri from afar, painting ephemeral pictures there, magic spells and fairy tales, and his muttering grows urgent, more insistent and frantic, and quickly now, lean over, loosen the gun from the holster, but he moves so slowly, hypnotized by the frozen slash on Uri's face, that he doesn't see Khilmi aiming his gun at Uri's heart with his eyes shut; and that is why he doesn't hear the piercing wail through Khilmi's head, something untranslatable in the infant tongue, a private throbbing, awkwardly echoing a prayer: Please, not Yazdi again, and with great suffering Khilmi presses the trigger and shoots Katzman.

Katzman manages to lunge aside. Then, out of his remotest depths, out of some forgotten abyss, he fishes out a soft smile of surprise. A kind of promise to Uri. He gazes in wonder at the palm of his hand, still fluttering inside his shirt like a heart bursting out of its rib cage or, perhaps, knocking on it. Then he falls slowly down, painlessly, obliviously, hitting his head against the rock, his eyes gazing at Uri with dead love.

And then the strange commotion outside the courtyard. Flares explode the blocks of darkness in the sky. Uri looks up. His glasses are fogged over. He takes them off with a slow, airy movement and wipes them on his shirt-sleeve. He puts them back on his nose. His hand hesitates. One last moment of hope. Maybe it was only a bad dream. But with his glasses on he sees the soldier striking Khilmi on the back of the head with the butt of his Uzi, and knocking the gun out of his hand. And he sees Sheffer hopping over the fence and landing beside him, staring at Katzman in stony amazement, and then at Uri, and slowly, firmly shaking his head.

Now all the transmitters in the courtyard and up the path are screaming metallically, and there are frantic footsteps and orders shouted. Several soldiers surround Khilmi, stand him on his feet, and lead him quickly off somewhere; two others help Uri, without a word, and he staggers off between them. As they make their way down the path, someone runs up carrying a folded stretcher, and far away, in the city of Jerusalem, a helicopter takes off and the pilot traces the little squares on the military map with his finger, searching for Andal.

May 9, 1982

David Grossman
The Yellow Wind £4.99

'*The western media have scarcely done justice to Israel. It requires a book as dignified and moving as this to correct the bias*'
JONATHAN KEATES, THE INDEPENDENT

'*The Yellow Wind* is a novelist's work of non-fiction, with all the virtues and defects of the genre ... Grossman does this by laying out his sketches with strong simplicity, with a rage barely suppressed and sometimes with the acid irony of Orwell' SUNDAY TIMES

'Grossman writes well because he writes in anger. He has a life-or-death stake in what he calls "the situation" ... Now we can have some idea of who is throwing the stones – and of who is being hit by them'
LITERARY REVIEW

'David Grossman, an acclaimed novelist who is fluent in Arabic, had recorded his talks with Palestinians and Jews in the Occupied Territories. The result is both moving and harrowing' ECONOMIST

'A book that deserves to stand beside Orwell's *Shooting an Elephant* as a reflection of what oppression does to those who oppress'
MICHAEL IGNATIEFF, OBSERVER

'Beautifully written' LONDON REVIEW OF BOOKS

David Grossman
See Under: Love £6.99

'Wickedly readable. It crackles with sparks of artistic invention. It tells its multiple tales of memory and suffering and degradation and courage with a Dostoyevskian compulsiveness . . . In a few nearly mythic books, such as Faulkner's *Sound and the Fury*, Günter Grass's *Tin Drum*, Gabriel García Márquez's *One Hundred Years of Solitude*, large visions of history get told in innovative ways. *See Under: Love* may be a worthy successor to this small but awesome cannon'
EDMUND WHITE, THE NEW YORK TIMES BOOK REVIEW

'David Grossman makes something dazzling and imaginative in engaging head-on with the worst horrors of the twentieth century . . . This novel is so innovative, yet at the same time so readable . . . It is a tour de force of pure storytelling . . . I consider it a triumph' ROBERT NYE, THE GUARDIAN

'This is unquestionably a novel of enduring power and fierce intelligence. It makes embarrassing any comparison with the lacy domesticities which now pre-empt so much of English fiction'
GEORGE STEINER, THE SUNDAY TIMES

'A stunningly ambitious literary style – part fairy tale, part stream of consciousness, part 'encyclopedia' . . . disturbing, thought-provoking, sometimes even funny but not, at its heart, depressing'
ROBERT LUSTIG, OBSERVER

'He deploys a humanistic, virtuoso imagination in an attempt to comprehend the Holocaust and take something positive away from it . . . For the foremost quality of this book, see under: brave'
JOSEPH O'NEILL, THE SUNDAY CORRESPONDENT

'A brave and moving attempt by an outstandingly talented writer to redefine love, having looked the Facts of Death full in the face'
CLIVE SINCLAIR, THE INDEPENDENT

All Pan books are available at your local bookshop or newsagent, or can be ordered direct from the publisher. Indicate the number of copies required and fill in the form below.

Send to: **CS Department, Pan Books Ltd., P.O. Box 40, Basingstoke, Hants. RG21 2YT.**

or phone: 0256 469551 (Ansaphone), quoting title, author and Credit Card number.

Please enclose a remittance* to the value of the cover price plus: 60p for the first book plus 30p per copy for each additional book ordered to a maximum charge of £2.40 to cover postage and packing.

*Payment may be made in sterling by UK personal cheque, postal order, sterling draft or international money order, made payable to Pan Books Ltd.

Alternatively by Barclaycard/Access:

Card No.

Signature:

Applicable only in the UK and Republic of Ireland.

While every effort is made to keep prices low, it is sometimes necessary to increase prices at short notice. Pan Books reserve the right to show on covers and charge new retail prices which may differ from those advertised in the text or elsewhere.

NAME AND ADDRESS IN BLOCK LETTERS PLEASE:

....

Name

Address